OUT OF THE EMBERS

MESQUITE SPRINGS, BOOK 1

OUT OF THE EMBERS

AMANDA CABOT

THORNDIKE PRESS
A part of Gale, a Cengage Company

LIBRARY OF CONGRESS CIP DATA ON FILE.
CATALOGUING IN PUBLICATION FOR THIS BOOK
IS AVAILABLE FROM THE LIBRARY OF CONGRESS

ISBN-13: 978-1-4328-7873-3 (hardcover alk. paper)

Published in 2020 by arrangement with Revell Books, a division of Baker Publishing Group

Printed in Mexico
Print Number: 01   Print Year: 2020

For Bonnie McKee,
whose love of history and dedication
to its preservation are truly inspiring.

MESQUITE SPRINGS, TX

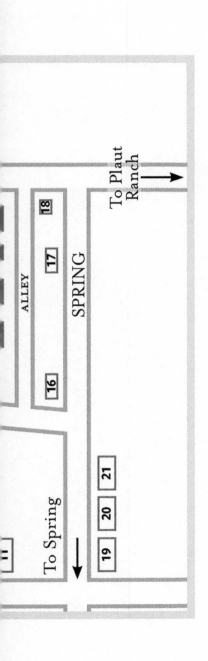

1 – Cemetery
2 – Park
3 – Widow Lockhart's House
4 – Downeys' House
5 – School
6 – Parsonage
7 – Church
8 – Mayor's Office and House
9 – Sam Plaut's Law Office
10 – Dressmaker's Shop
11 – Saloon

12 – Mercantile
13 – Polly's Place and Evelyn's Home
14 – Post Office
15 – Sheriff's Office and House
16 – Taylors' House
17 – Boardinghouse
18 – Doc Dawson's Office and House
19 – Smiths' House
20 – Blacksmith Shop
21 – Livery

CHAPTER ONE

Friday, December 21, 1855

Someone was watching. Though a shiver of dread made its way down her spine, Evelyn Radcliffe kept a smile fixed on her face. No matter how her skin prickled and how every instinct told her to flick the reins and urge the horse to race forward, she wouldn't do anything to worry the child who sat beside her.

She took a deep breath, then exhaled gradually, trying to slow her pulse, reminding herself that this was not the first time she'd sensed the Watcher. The feeling would diminish when she reached the outskirts of Gilmorton, and by the time she was an hour away, it would have disappeared. It always did. The only thing that made today different was that she was not alone. Today she had a child to protect.

Evelyn took another breath, forcing herself to think about something — anything —

other than the danger she'd sensed. It was a beautiful day and an unusually warm one for so close to Christmas. The sun was shining, bringing a genuine smile to her face as she gazed at the now dormant cotton fields that brought so much wealth to this part of Texas. White gold, she'd heard some call it.

"What's wrong?"

Evelyn turned toward the girl who looked enough like her to be her sister. Polly's hair was silver blonde rather than Evelyn's golden and her eyes were a lighter shade of blue, but she had the same oval face and a nose whose tip flared ever so slightly, just as Evelyn's did. Besides the difference in their ages, Evelyn's skin was unmarred, while a prominent strawberry red birthmark on her left cheek destroyed Polly's hopes of beauty.

"Nothing's wrong." Evelyn wished the child weren't so sensitive. "I'm just anxious to get home." Logansville was three hours away, far enough that the Watcher had never followed her. But Polly didn't need to know about the Watcher. Evelyn tickled the girl's nose. "You know Hilda can't be trusted to heat stew without scorching it."

The distraction appeared to have worked, for Polly giggled. "She's a bad cook. Buster spit out the oatmeal she gave him 'cuz it had lumps. Big lumps."

10

Lumpy oatmeal was a better topic than the fear that engulfed Evelyn almost every time she came to Gilmorton. Mrs. Folger had told her she needed to confront her fears. That was one of the reasons she insisted Evelyn be the one to make these trips. But Mrs. Folger didn't know that even ten years later, Evelyn could not bear to look at the building she'd once called home and that she detoured to avoid that block of Main Street. Mrs. Folger scoffed at the idea that someone was watching, calling it nonsense, but Evelyn knew better. Someone *was* watching, and it terrified her.

The tension that had coiled inside Evelyn began to release as the town disappeared from view. She wouldn't have come to Gilmorton if she had had a choice, but unless she was willing to be gone for more than a day each time she made a delivery, there were no other outlets for the lace the children made. The owner of the mercantile gave her a fair price for their handicrafts. Today there'd even been enough money left over after she'd bought provisions that Evelyn had been able to purchase a piece of candy for each child. That would make Christmas morning special.

"When you're a little older, I'll teach you how to make oatmeal."

Evelyn laid a hand on Polly's shoulder, wanting contact with the child who'd become so dear to her in the month since she'd arrived at the orphanage. Arrived? She'd been deposited on the front step as if she were no more important than the piles of clothing some parishioners left when their children had outgrown them. Like worn dresses and overalls, Polly had been discarded.

Unaware of the turns Evelyn's thoughts had taken, Polly grinned. "I know how. I watched you. You gotta stir, stir, stir."

"That's right. You're a smart girl."

"My daddy said that too. He said I was the smartest girl in the whole county and that I was worth more than a thousand bales of cotton."

Polly's smile turned upside down, reminding Evelyn of the story she'd told about her father being put in a box in the ground. Evelyn was all too familiar with those boxes, but she'd been fortunate enough to have her parents with her for thirteen years before the night when everything changed. Polly was only six, or so she said.

Think about Polly, Evelyn told herself, not the night when it had rained hard enough to muffle her screams from passersby. The sheriff had told her he'd arrested and hanged the man responsible. He'd assured her she had no reason to fear, and yet she did. Ten years wasn't long enough to erase the memories, particularly when she could feel someone watching her.

"I miss my daddy." Tears welled in Polly's eyes. "I want him to come back."

"I know you do."

Despite her nod, tears began to trickle down Polly's cheeks. "Buster said some girls get new daddies. He said people come looking for good little girls." She looked up at Evelyn, pleading in her eyes. "I've been good, haven't I?"

"You've been very good," Evelyn reassured her. But that wouldn't be enough. Three couples had come to the orphanage since Polly's arrival, and all three had been unwilling to adopt a child with such a prominent birthmark.

"It's Satan's mark," one woman had announced. When she'd heard that, Evelyn had been tempted to gouge the woman's cheek and give her her own mark.

"I want a new daddy." Polly was nothing if not persistent. Persistent and stubborn. No matter how many times Evelyn and Mrs. Folger asked, she refused to tell them her last name. "I can't," she insisted. "I can't."

Evelyn made a show of looking in every

direction. "I don't see any daddies here. Maybe if we sing, someone will hear us."

As Polly's eyes brightened, Evelyn smiled. Singing would be a good distraction for both of them. And so they sang song after song. Neither of them could carry a tune, but that didn't bother them or Reginald. Evelyn imagined the gelding twitching his ears in time to their singing, and her spirits rose with each mile they traveled. Polly was once again cheerful, there was no rain in sight, and it would be another month before she had to return to Gilmorton — three reasons to give thanks.

Her smile was as bright as Polly's until she saw it. It was only the slightest of limps, and yet Evelyn knew something was wrong. Unwilling to take any chances, she stopped the wagon and climbed out. A quick look at Reginald's front right leg confirmed her fears.

"What's wrong?" Polly asked for the second time since they'd left Gilmorton.

"Reginald's lost a shoe."

Peering over the side of the wagon, Polly grinned. "I'll find it."

Evelyn shook her head. "You need to stay in the wagon." Though the sun was past its zenith, the day was still warm enough that snakes could be out, and ever-curious Polly

14

might reach for one. Evelyn glanced at Reginald's hoof one last time. There was no choice. She wouldn't risk permanent injury by having him pull the wagon all the way to Logansville.

"We're going back to Gilmorton." As much as she wished otherwise, it was closer.

"Okay." Polly watched wide-eyed as Evelyn unhooked the wagon. "What are you doing?"

"We need to leave the wagon here." Even though it meant that anyone coming by could steal the contents, she had to take the chance. "Reginald can't pull it until he gets a new shoe."

Evelyn lifted Polly out of the wagon and placed her on the horse's back. "Hold on to the harness."

Normally agreeable Polly turned petulant. "I wanna walk with you."

Evelyn wouldn't argue. "All right, but when you get tired, Reginald will be glad to carry you." The horse was exceptionally good with children, which was fortunate, given the number who called the orphanage home.

"This is fun!" Polly exclaimed as she began to skip down the road. It was no longer fun by the time they reached Gilmorton. Polly was tired and fussy. To make mat-

15

ters worse, the blacksmith was in the middle of shoeing another horse and told Evelyn it would be at least half an hour before he could see to Reginald.

"Whoever shoed this horse the last time deserves to be shot," the blacksmith said when he was finally able to inspect the gelding's hoof. "He didn't know what he was doin'."

Evelyn tried not to sigh. Mrs. Folger had wanted to give Buster a chance, claiming he had an aptitude for caring for horses, but it appeared that the matron had been mistaken. "Did he do any permanent damage?"

"Nah." The blacksmith scraped a rough edge off the hoof. "Just be sure to bring Reginald here next time he needs a shoe. He may be gettin' on in years, but he's a fine piece of horseflesh."

Evelyn and Polly rode the fine piece of horseflesh back to the wagon. Fortunately, the contents were all there. Unfortunately, the delays meant that they'd be very late arriving home. In all likelihood, everyone would be asleep, even Mrs. Folger. The matron wouldn't be pleased, but at least Evelyn hadn't lost the supplies she'd purchased today.

Darkness had fallen long before they reached Logansville, and Polly — worn out by the walking as well as the excitement of the day — slept on the bench next to Evelyn. Though she stirred occasionally, each time she did, she drifted back to sleep. This time, however, she sat up, rubbed her eyes, and pinched her nose.

"What's that smell?"

Evelyn sniffed. "It's smoke." She squinted, looking for the source of the odor, but saw nothing.

"Phew! I don't like that."

"I don't either, but we're almost home." Though it was late, someone must be burning trash. "It won't smell as bad once we're indoors."

Evelyn had already decided to let Polly sleep with her tonight rather than risk waking the other girls. That prospect, along with the promise that she could help stir the oatmeal tomorrow morning, had buoyed Polly's spirits when the only supper Evelyn could offer her had been the cheese and bread she'd purchased while waiting for the blacksmith. Though Gilmorton had a restaurant, that was one place Evelyn would not enter no matter how hungry she might be. When they reached the orphanage, she would warm some milk for Polly.

They were almost there. Within half an hour, Evelyn would have Reginald in his stall and Polly in her bed. The horse tossed his head, perhaps disturbed by the smoke that had intensified.

As they rounded the final bend in the road, the cause of the smoke was all too clear. The light from the almost full moon revealed the ashes and rubble that were all that was left of the building that had been Evelyn's home for the past ten years. She stared at the blackened foundation, trying to make sense of something that made no sense. Well aware of the danger fire posed to a frame structure, Mrs. Folger was vigilant about safety. Yet, despite her caution, something had happened. The orphanage was gone.

So were its inhabitants. There should be close to two dozen children swarming around, yet Evelyn saw nothing more than a few men. Though her heart was pounding so violently that she feared it would break through her chest at the realization that she'd lost her home, she clung to the hope that Mrs. Folger and the children had escaped and had been taken in by some of the town's residents. If not . . .

The possibility was too horrible to consider. Her mother had told her not to borrow trouble, and Evelyn wouldn't. Instead, she'd ask the men what had happened.

Surely everyone had been saved. But though she tried to convince herself that she would be reunited with the matron and the other orphans, in her heart she knew that was one prayer that would not be answered.

Evelyn bit the inside of her cheek, determined not to let Polly see her fears. But she failed, for the child began to tremble.

"What happened to the 'nage?" Though Polly's diction was far better than one would have expected from the shabby clothing she'd worn when she was abandoned, whoever had taught her hadn't included "orphanage" in her vocabulary.

Evelyn wrapped her arms around Polly and willed her voice to remain steady as she said, "It's gone." And, if what she feared was true, so were Mrs. Folger and the children who had been her family.

As she descended the small hill and approached the front drive, Evelyn saw that the men were wandering around the yard, their casual attitude belying the gravity of the situation.

"Ain't no one left," one called to the others, his voice carrying clearly through the still night air. "Smoke musta got 'em."

No. Oh, dear God, no. It couldn't be true, and yet it was. Once again, she had lost everyone she loved, everyone except the girl who clung to her, her own fear palpable. Once again, it was night. Once again, she was powerless to change anything, but at least this time it had been an accident.

Evelyn shuddered and said a silent prayer that Polly wouldn't realize the extent of the tragedy. Somehow, she would protect her. Somehow, she would help her recover from all that they had lost in this terrible accident.

"Can't figger it out," another man chimed in. "Who woulda wanted to do 'em in? No mistakin' them kerosene cans, though. Somebody set the fire."

Evelyn gasped, feeling as though she'd been bludgeoned, and for a second everything turned black. The fire wasn't an accident. Someone had deliberately destroyed the orphanage, planning to kill everyone inside. Including her.

Where is she? The memory of the voice that still haunted Evelyn's dreams echoed through her brain, shattering the fragile peace Mrs. Folger's assurances had created. Tonight proved that she wasn't safe, not even here. Someone wanted to kill the last of the Radcliffes.

Why? That was the question no one had been able to answer ten years ago, the question that had kept Evelyn from leaving the

20

sanctuary the orphanage had promised. Now that promise was shattered.

She closed her eyes as fear and sorrow threatened to overwhelm her. The life she had built was gone, destroyed along with the building that had been her refuge and the people who had become her family. *Oh, God, what should I do?*

The response was immediate. *Leave.*

It was the only answer. She could do nothing for Mrs. Folger and the others, but she could — and she would — do everything in her power to give Polly a safe future. The question was where they should go. Evelyn stared at the stars for a second, then nodded. Gilmorton, the one place she would not consider, was east. Resolutely, she headed west.

"What happened?" Polly asked again, her voice far calmer than Evelyn would have expected. Either the child was too young to understand the magnitude of what had happened, or she'd experienced so much tragedy in her life that she was numb.

"We need a new home." For the first time, Evelyn gave thanks that Polly had formed no strong attachments to anyone other than her. That would make her transition to a new life easier. While grief had wrapped its tendrils around Evelyn's heart, squeezing so tightly that she had trouble breathing, Polly seemed to be recovering from her initial shock.

"Okay." Though the child tightened her grip on Evelyn's arm, her trembling had stopped. "Where are we going?"

"It'll be a surprise." At this point, Evelyn had no idea where she and Polly would find their next home. All she knew was that it had to be far from here, far from whoever had set the fire, far from the Watcher.

Polly was silent for a moment before she said, "It's okay, Evelyn. You'll be my mama, and you'll find me a new daddy."

CHAPTER TWO

In three days and two hours, it would be Christmas. In three days and one hour, Mesquite Springs's stone church would be crowded with people eager to celebrate the birth that had taken place in a stable probably only a fraction of the size of this one. Wyatt Clark knew he should be filled with anticipation by the approach of what his mother had once called the season of miracles. Instead, he frowned as the rank odor assailing his nostrils left no doubt that Emerald had contracted thrush.

It shouldn't have happened. The stable was clean and dry; she'd never been left out in muddy conditions; none of the other horses had developed the ailment. Yet Emerald, the mare who was carrying what he hoped would be the Circle C's finest foal, had a bad case of thrush on her left hind hoof.

The only cause Wyatt could imagine was

the shape of her hooves. He'd heard that horses with long, narrow hooves were more susceptible to the disease than others. That was why he'd bred Emerald with a stallion whose hooves were a little broader than normal. Though not everyone agreed, Wyatt believed that characteristics from the sire and the dam blended in foals.

"Sorry, girl," he said as he scraped away the spongy part of the hoof, then reached for a bottle of iodine. "I know you don't like the smell of this, but you need it."

"There you are."

Wyatt looked up in surprise. It was unusual for his mother to come to the stable this late.

The woman whose dark brown hair and eyes were so like his frowned. "I might have known," she said, her accent more pronounced than usual, a reminder that Ma, like many of the residents of the Hill Country, had been born in Germany.

"You ought to be asleep," Ma continued, "but no — you're out here with the horses." The horses had been her husband's dream, not hers.

Honor thy father and thy mother. It was good advice, but sometimes it took more than the reminder of that commandment to keep Wyatt's angry retorts from escaping.

24

He'd spent over a decade turning the Circle C's stable from a fledgling enterprise into one whose fame stretched far beyond the Hill Country, and yet his mother still begrudged the time he spent with the horses.

Wyatt bit the tip of his tongue before he said as mildly as he could, "A lot hinges on Emerald. Right now she can hardly walk because of the thrush." He placed the horse's hoof back on the ground and patted her side.

"Oh." Ma's tone gentled. "I didn't realize what was happening. I'm sorry, son. I know you do your best." Though she kept her distance, lest the mare consider her an intruder and lash out, Ma managed a smile for her son. "It's just that I worry about you. It's time you settle down." Her smile broadened. "You need a wife and children of your own. There's more to life than raising horses."

Wyatt bit his tongue again as he considered his response to what had become a regular refrain. Ma didn't want a new bonnet for Christmas. She wanted the assurance that there'd be a new generation of Clarks.

He watched Emerald take a tentative step on her cleaned and disinfected hoof before he turned back to his mother. "What you said may be true, but right now horses pay the bills around here."

Wyatt didn't want to think about the first year after Pa had been killed. If he hadn't taken the two most promising yearlings to Fort Worth for the big sale and encountered men who spent more on horses than slaves, the Circle C would now belong to someone else. Fortunately, the yearlings had brought enough money to get them through that horrible year when Ma had . . . Wyatt shook himself mentally. He wouldn't think about that. Not tonight. Not ever again.

Ma straightened her shoulders and gave him the look he remembered from his childhood, the one that both he and his sister quickly learned meant that they were supposed to obey. "I'd rather have a grandbaby than a new bonnet."

It wasn't the first time he'd heard that, and Wyatt knew it wouldn't be the last. Still, he wouldn't tell Ma that the mere thought of a wife and children scared him more than anything else on Earth. What if he married and had children and a bandit or a snake or a lightning bolt killed him? Who would protect them then?

He couldn't — he wouldn't — put those he loved in the position his family had been in when the Comanche killed Pa. No, sir-ree. Marriage was not for him.

"She's dead."

Rufus Bauman looked up from the board he'd been sanding. Though her words were solemn, his wife did not appear distressed. "What are you talking about? Who's dead?"

Winnie fisted her hands on her hips, her expression saying he ought to know. "That girl. The one you thought could replace Rose."

Rufus tried not to sigh. Though he loved his wife dearly, there were times when her dislike for the girl tested his patience. This was one of them.

He laid the sandpaper aside and looked directly at Winnie. "I wasn't trying to replace Rose." No one could do that. He hadn't even been trying to right a horrible wrong. No one could do that, either. When he'd suggested adoption, he'd wanted to give the girl a home and maybe — just maybe — bring some joy back to his own home.

It wasn't natural for parents to lose all their children, but he and Winnie had. While he'd mourned both Rose and Isaac and the tragic circumstances of their deaths, his pain had begun to lessen. Winnie's had not.

She'd clutched it to her like a shawl, declaring only another woman could understand. That was one of the reasons Rufus had broached the subject of adoption all those years ago. He'd thought his wife would enjoy having another female in the house, but she'd been adamant in her refusal. And now giving Winnie female companionship was no longer a possibility. The girl was dead.

"How do you know she's dead?"

"Jeb Perkins told me. It seems somebody set fire to the orphanage in Logansville last night. Everybody died."

The anguish that had lodged deep inside Rufus threatened his breathing. Not an accident but a deliberate killing, just like the last time. And just like the last time, he hadn't been able to stop it.

Basil Marlow watched the man enter the room that was now his office. He'd thought Bart foolish when he refused to conduct business in what had once been their father's office, instead ordering a separate building constructed far enough from the main house that none of the daily noise would bother him. Tonight Basil applauded his brother's foresight. The isolation and cloak of darkness ensured that this meeting would remain secret.

He narrowed his eyes slightly as the man closed the door behind him. Though the spring in the messenger's step told Basil everything he needed to know, he still posed the question. "Is everything taken care of?"

"Yes, sir. Just the way you ordered." The man straightened his shoulders with pride over his accomplishment, perhaps hoping for an extra reward. He would get it. "It weren't hard to track down the gal once that old slave let slip that she weren't dead."

Rising from behind the massive desk, Basil struggled not to frown at the thought of the woman who'd betrayed him. He'd believed every slave knew the penalty for anything less than total loyalty, but at least one hadn't. The one that Miriam had insisted on bringing as part of her dowry when she'd married his brother had told Basil the girl died while he was gone. She'd even shown him the grave, but she'd been lying.

Somehow, she'd snuck off the plantation and left the girl at an orphanage.

The stupid woman thought he'd never learn what she'd done, but he had. One of the other slaves who'd sought to curry favor had told him.

"Did you take care of her?"

"Yes, sir. She won't be talkin' no more."

The messenger mimicked a knife slicing across his throat.

"Good work. What about the girl herself?"

"She won't be talkin' no more, neither. The fire took care of that. I done just what you tole me. Ain't nobody coulda lived through that fire." The messenger practically strutted as he took another step toward Basil. "I hung around long enough to make sure nobody was alive."

"Excellent." Though it had taken longer than he would have liked, most of the loose ends were tied up. His brother had stolen the woman Basil loved, but he was dead, and so was his spawn. Basil might not have Miriam, but he had everything else. The plantation, the horses, and all that money. Vengeance was even sweeter than he'd dreamt.

"This deserves a celebration." As the messenger grinned in anticipation, Basil turned to the cabinet behind him and withdrew a bottle of whiskey and two glasses.

The man's eyes widened in surprise when he saw the label. *Enjoy it,* Basil urged him silently as he filled the glasses. This was the first and last time he would taste such fine whiskey.

As the man raised his glass, Basil reached into his desk drawer, pulled out a pistol,

and fired. The last of the loose ends was
gone.

31

CHAPTER THREE

Friday, January 4, 1856

"Do you ever think about leaving the ranch?"

Wyatt kept his eyes focused on the horse he was currying while he formulated a response. It wasn't like his sister to ask idle questions, and the fact that she'd waited until they were back in the stable to pose it told him there was more to the question than idle curiosity.

He shrugged and raised his gaze to meet Dorothy's. "Sure, I do. Every time Ma scorches the beans. If the town still had a decent restaurant, I'd figure out a way to eat all my meals there."

Dorothy fisted her hands on her hips and glared at him. "That's not what I meant. Do you ever think about living somewhere else?"

Every day, but Wyatt wouldn't tell her that. "I guess most people dream about a different life." Those dreams had sustained him through the difficult years, and even now, though he doubted they'd come true, he clung to them. On days when the wind blew from the wrong direction and both the horses and Ma were cranky, he dreamt of a life with no responsibilities, a life where no one and nothing depended on him. He'd wander the country, seeing the sights Pa had told him about, taking odd jobs when he needed a bit of money, but never staying anywhere long enough to put down roots.

That was the life Wyatt envisioned — a life of freedom, not one with a wife and children — at least for a while. But he couldn't tell Dorothy, who'd always seemed far younger than he though only four years separated them, how he longed to escape.

"What about you? You've seemed restless lately." And that worried Wyatt more than Emerald's thrush had. Though he might dream of another life, there was no possibility of leaving the Circle C until he was certain his mother and sister no longer needed him.

Ma hadn't had a spell in months, and until recently, Dorothy had caused him no worries. Now . . . Wyatt had no idea what he'd do if it turned out that Dorothy had inherited Ma's temperament. Though she wasn't as thin as their mother, everyone said that otherwise she was the spitting image of Ma twenty-five years ago.

"I hate the ranch!" Dorothy spat the words, her vehemence making the mare she was grooming flinch.

Wyatt stared at his sister, shocked by the fact that she not only looked like their mother, she suddenly sounded like her. "What brought this on? You've never said that before."

"What good would it have done?" Dorothy tossed the currycomb onto the floor, then sank to the ground beside it, drawing her legs beneath her as she'd done when they'd been children.

"What good would it have done?" she repeated as Wyatt abandoned the horse he'd been brushing and lowered himself to the spot next to her. "Where would I go? What would I do? I'm as tied to this ranch as you are, maybe even more." Tears filled her eyes, but Wyatt had no idea whether they were tears of sorrow or anger. "Everyone tells me I ought to get married, but I don't want to do that."

Wyatt slung his arm around her shoulders and drew her closer to him. In those first dark days after their father's death, they'd sat like this, trying to convince each other that their world hadn't been shattered. At the time, Wyatt had done his best to comfort Dorothy, telling her he'd always take care of her. It seemed he'd failed, for he hadn't realized how unhappy she was.

"I think you're lonely," he said. "It's only natural that you miss Laura." Her best friend had gone East last fall to attend a finishing school in Charleston. Though Laura had planned to come home for Christmas, her parents had decided to join her there, claiming that would be their long-delayed wedding trip. While the decision made sense for them, it had left Dorothy without her only confidante.

Wyatt kicked himself mentally for not realizing how Laura's absence might have affected his sister.

"It's not just Laura," Dorothy insisted. "It's everything. I'm tired of my life. I want a change, and don't tell me that I need a beau." Her eyes sparked with anger. "Ma does that often enough."

"I know." Wyatt gave his sister a conspiratorial smile. "When she told me she'd rather have a grandbaby than a new bonnet for Christmas, I was tempted to say that Mrs. Steiner didn't have any babies for sale."

As he'd hoped, Dorothy chuckled. "Ma thinks marriage is the answer for both of us,

35

but she's wrong. I want to do something else. Don't you?"

Wyatt nodded. "I want to travel." As much as he loved Ma and Dorothy, as much as he enjoyed the horses, he wanted time by himself, time to see the parts of the country Pa had crossed when he'd come to Texas, time to discover whether he was meant to do more than raise horses. Some would call it sowing wild oats. Wyatt called it tasting freedom.

Dorothy leaned her head against his shoulder, seeming to find solace in his closeness. For a long moment, she said nothing. Then she raised her head. "Just promise me one thing, Wyatt. Promise when you leave, you'll take me with you."

That was an easy enough promise to make. "You know I can't leave. Who would care for Ma?"

Dorothy's lips pursed in an expression so much like their mother's that Wyatt caught his breath. "She can take care of herself. She's stronger than you think."

Dorothy was wrong. Ma wasn't strong. He doubted she'd ever been. "You know what happened when Pa was killed."

"That was more than ten years ago."

"But it could happen again." Ma wasn't used to depending on herself. When he'd

didn't understand why Evelyn hadn't yet found her a new daddy. She'd stared at each man she'd seen as they'd passed through towns, sighing loudly when none met her criteria — whatever they might be — and grumbling when Evelyn refused to stop so she could look for other men.

Evelyn had given no explanations for their lengthy journey and her seeming inability to find them a new home. It had been all she could do to continue the pretense that everything was normal. Nothing was normal.

Each time they'd enter a town, the smell of smoke from a chimney would make her cringe, and the image of the smoldering ruins of the orphanage would sear her brain. Each time she prepared a meal from the food she'd bought that day in Gilmorton, she'd remember the meals she'd served to Buster and the others. Each time she saw a woman in a black bonnet, she pictured Mrs. Folger donning hers, and waves of grief would wash over her, threatening to drown her with their intensity.

The crime was unspeakable. So was her part in it. The knowledge that, though she hadn't lit the fire, she was still responsible filled Evelyn with an overwhelming sense of guilt. Her friends, her companions, the closest thing she had to a family were gone, all because she had shared a home with them.

Why had the sheriff been so certain he'd arrested the man who'd murdered her parents when it was clear that he was still alive? What turned a man into a monster, someone so evil that he would kill two dozen innocent children simply so that the last of the Radcliffes would be gone? And why had he waited so long to act again?

Evelyn had no answers, only the overpowering need to keep herself and Polly safe by fleeing. With each mile that took them further from Logansville, she felt a bit more secure, but she still had the urge to continue. Until today.

Today was different. Today she'd awakened free from the fears that had weighed on her. The sorrow remained — she doubted it would ever disappear — but the overwhelming fear had dissipated. Evelyn hadn't been able to identify the reason for the change. All she knew was that for the first time since she'd seen the rubble of her last home, she was at peace. What a wonderful feeling.

Polly hadn't been happy with the hasty breakfast she had served, but Evelyn had felt an urge to be on the road again. Though the child refused to be distracted by songs, stories, or any of the other ploys that had worked previously, Evelyn found herself entranced by the countryside.

As the morning fog burned off, it revealed a mountain rising above the plains. The terrain had changed gradually over the past few days, the rolling hills becoming higher, but this was the first time Evelyn had seen anything that could be called a mountain. She stared at it, catching her breath at the sense of homecoming that washed over her. Inexplicable and yet undeniable. Mama would have called it the still, small voice of God telling her she'd reached her journey's end.

Yesterday Evelyn had marveled as she'd driven through what seemed like a green tunnel. Though she'd seen hundreds of live oak trees, there had been none like these, their branches creating a canopy that practically blocked the sunlight. Even Polly, who'd been complaining about every bump in the road, had fallen silent as they'd driven beneath them. The tree-lined road had been magnificent; this was breathtaking.

Sunlight glinted off the limestone cliffs, dazzling Evelyn with the sight of what appeared to be a fortress rising above the tree-clad slopes. There was no fortress; she knew that. The cliffs had been made by God, not man. And yet the rocks that had been sculpted by wind and rain seemed to be forming a protective wall. For the first time since they'd left Logansville, she was safe.

Though she had no idea what the future would bring and how she would make a living for herself and Polly, she no longer felt burdened by those worries. At least for the moment, she was filled with confidence.

"Now! I wanna stop now!" The reddening of Polly's face told Evelyn a tantrum was imminent.

"We'll stop in the next town." Surely they were far enough from Logansville that the Watcher would not find them. After the fire, he had no reason to continue his search, for as far as anyone knew, Evelyn Radcliffe had perished with the others. And even if someone were searching, he would not be looking for a woman and her little sister.

Perhaps she was being overly cautious, but until today Evelyn had been unable to dismiss the fear that she was still in danger. That was why she'd decided to change her name and why she'd spent the past two weeks telling Polly that if anyone asked, they were sisters. She wouldn't claim to be Polly's mother — that pretense would be harder to carry off — but they looked enough alike to convince strangers that they were related. Even now, though the feeling of safety had overcome the worries that had been her constant companions, she would take no chances. The charade that she was Evelyn Radner, accompanying her sister on a journey to visit family in western Texas, would continue.

Polly poked Evelyn's ribs. "Make Reginald go faster." It was a familiar refrain.

"You know that's bad for him."

As the horse's ears twitched, Evelyn studied the sky. Though it had been clear with only a few cumulus clouds an hour ago, now the small, puffy white clouds had been replaced by a single huge one the color of charcoal, and the sky had turned an ominous hue. As the cloud obscured the sun, the temperature plummeted, leaving Evelyn shivering from more than the chill. She hated storms. Oh, how she hated storms.

"I want that cloud to go away."

So did she. "Let's sing. Maybe that'll chase it away." It wouldn't, of course, but perhaps singing would distract Polly while Evelyn searched for shelter.

"I don't wanna sing."

Though she'd suggested it, Evelyn was as reluctant as Polly. Singing wouldn't stop the storm. The dark cloud was moving quickly now, accompanied by the distant rumble of thunder. Thunderstorms weren't supposed to happen in January, but there was no mistaking that sound or the fear it brought with it.

Please, God, let the storm pass by. Evelyn's prayer was still winging its way to heaven when a loud thunderclap caused Polly to shriek and Reginald to shy. A second later, the sky opened, sending torrents of cold rain earthward. Faster than she'd thought it possible, Evelyn and Polly were soaked to the skin.

Not again. Please, God, not again.

Polly wrapped her arms around Evelyn's waist and buried her head in her lap. "I'm scared."

So was Evelyn. The thunder and lightning were all too familiar. Memories of the worst day of her life pelted her brain with more power than the rain. *Stop!* she cried silently. *It's not happening again.*

It had been night then, not midafternoon. She'd been indoors that day, not outside in a wagon. But the fear was the same, overwhelming her with its intensity. She'd cowered under her bed then, covering her ears as she tried to block out the horrible screams. There were no screams now, only Polly's whimpers.

44

Evelyn had been a child then; she was grown now. It wasn't the same. She was no longer powerless, but despite her brave thoughts, she was terrified.

She tightened her grip on Polly. No matter what happened, she could not let fear reign. She hadn't been able to save her parents, but she could save Polly. She *would* save Polly.

Tugging on the reins, Evelyn stopped the wagon, then climbed out. "C'mon, Polly," she said as she extended her hands to the child.

"Where are we going?" Polly demanded. "I don't like this."

Evelyn didn't like it, either. "We're going under the wagon." Though they were both sopping wet, at least the wagon would protect them from the worst of the storm, and the shelter might lessen her fear. "We'll be safe there."

"Are you sure?"

Evelyn wasn't certain of anything other than that she couldn't let Polly be frightened. "Yes," she said. Surely God hadn't brought them this far to let them die.

CHAPTER FOUR

"You're just the man I wanted to see."

Wyatt stopped midstride as he left the blacksmith. So far, it had been a good afternoon. He'd managed to convince himself that Dorothy's outburst was caused by nothing more than loneliness, and he was pleased with the outcome of his conversation with Caleb. Now all he wanted was to get home and check on the horses, but it seemed there was one more thing to do. For some reason, the man who spent his life protecting Mesquite Springs wanted to talk to him.

"What's up, Sheriff?"

Fletcher Engel wrinkled his nose. "How many times have I told you to call me Fletcher?"

"More than one . . . Fletcher." It still seemed strange to address him that way. The sheriff was old enough to be Wyatt's father, and while he lacked Wyatt's height, his muscular build and stern demeanor coupled with a firm sense of justice had garnered the respect of the town's citizens.

"Is there a problem?" Fletcher's expression was more serious than usual.

The sheriff glanced in both directions, frowning when he saw two of Mesquite Springs's biggest gossips approaching. "Not necessarily. Let's go into the Taylor house," he said, referring to the empty building at the corner of Spring and River. "I heard there'd been some damage there. This'll give me a chance to look around, and it'll make sure folks don't overhear what I'm going to tell you."

For a second, Wyatt wondered if there was something about the new year that made people a little crazy. That would explain Dorothy's outburst and the sheriff's unexpected request. "You're not normally mysterious," Wyatt said as mildly as he could.

"This isn't a normal situation." The sheriff waited until they were inside the house with the door closed behind them before he spoke. "Ken told me he's planning to retire."

"Ken McBride?"

"He's the only Ken I know of in town." Fletcher continued his explanation as they walked through the rooms. Fortunately,

47

other than a broken window, the damage appeared minimal.

"It came as a surprise to me. I thought Ken would stay on at least another ten years, but he claims he's lost heart ever since his wife died. He's not going to run for reelection in June."

The news was a surprise to Wyatt as well, but he had no idea why the sheriff was telling him and why he was shrouding their discussion in such secrecy. "I can't imagine Mesquite Springs with a different mayor."

Fletcher chuckled. "That's because he's been mayor for longer than you've been alive." He stopped and faced Wyatt. "Ken's been a good mayor — no doubt about it — but he's right. It's time for a change."

"Why are you telling me about this, and why the secrecy?"

Though he leaned against one wall, apparently relaxed, Fletcher's brown eyes radiated intensity. "Because I think you should announce your candidacy before anyone else. The first to declare has an advantage."

Wyatt stared at the man he'd known his whole life, dumbfounded by his suggestion. "You think I should run for mayor?"

"I just said that, didn't I? You're a good man, Wyatt. You'd be a good mayor."

"No." The idea was preposterous. It was

bad enough that he had to worry about Ma and Dorothy and the horses, but a whole town? There was definitely something in the air turning normally reasonable people crazy.

"I can see this came as a surprise. It did to me too, but don't be hasty. Think about it."

Wyatt frowned. There was nothing to think about. He was still frowning five minutes later as he left Mesquite Springs. Run for mayor? Take on more responsibility? Even if Caleb proved to be as much help as he expected, Wyatt had no desire to be the mayor. Whatever his future held, it did not include being mayor.

What a ridiculous idea! It was almost as ridiculous as Ma's suggestion that he marry and produce grandchildren for her to spoil or Dorothy's eagerness to go with Wyatt whenever he managed to leave Mesquite Springs. None of that was going to happen. Suddenly raising horses for the rest of his life didn't seem so bad. At least they didn't pester a man with crazy ideas. Wyatt would be glad to be back with them, but first he had to get there.

He frowned as he stared at the sky. There was no ignoring either the sudden drop in temperature or the ominous black cloud that hovered overhead. If this were summer, he'd welcome the cooler air and rain. But this was the middle of winter, not July or August, and the last thing Wyatt needed was a cold rain, maybe even snow.

The cloud was scudding across the sky, telling him he'd be lucky to reach the ranch before the storm broke.

"C'mon, Thunder," he said as he bent over his gelding's neck, hoping to outrun the storm. "We've gotta get home."

As if on cue, a bolt of lightning split the sky, followed immediately by a loud clap of thunder. Only seconds later, the sky opened, sending torrents of almost freezing rain earthbound. A thunderstorm in January? Another oddity in a distinctly odd day.

"Not a good time to be outside, is it, boy?" Wyatt kept his voice calm, knowing that was the best way to stop Thunder from spooking. The horse would react to his tone. "It's a good thing I didn't bring Dorothy with me, isn't it?" While Thunder wouldn't understand the words, he would absorb the reassurance with which Wyatt infused them.

Wyatt's decision meant that not only was his sister safe, but he could also travel more quickly on horseback than if he'd brought the wagon. Right now, though, speed was secondary to safety.

Since there was no longer any question of outrunning the storm, he slowed Thunder's pace, unwilling to push the gelding on muddy roads. He wouldn't risk Thunder injuring himself, but he wouldn't deny that he was anxious to reach the ranch and Emerald. Mares, particularly this close to foaling, tended to become agitated by lightning.

Wyatt leaned forward, grateful that his hat kept the worst of the rain off his head and neck. As it was, the rain appeared to be a solid sheet of water, falling so hard that he could barely see through it. It was only Thunder's nickering that told him the horse had spotted something he hadn't. Wyatt squinted, looking for whatever had alerted the horse. There it was. A horse and wagon. While the wagon appeared to be empty, perhaps abandoned because of the storm, the horse was stationary.

Almost without volition, Wyatt assessed the horse. Good conformation, some Appaloosa blood, just over fourteen hands, start of a swayback. This was no Circle C quarter horse, but it was also not an old plow horse. Wyatt brushed those thoughts aside. The question was, where was the driver?

Motion underneath the wagon told him that the driver must have sought shelter from the storm. A wise move.

He reined in Thunder, slid from his back, squatted down to peer under the wagon, and blinked in surprise. Instead of the grizzled man he'd expected, the wagon sheltered two people, a woman and a child. Huddled together for warmth, they stared at him, and for the second time in less than a minute, Wyatt found himself surprised. While the child's eyes were filled with curiosity, the woman's were wide with fear.

Fear of the storm, fear of him, fear of both? He had no idea. All he knew was that this woman was terrified, and that puzzled him. Though the storm had been violent, surely she had endured worse. And while Wyatt knew he was sometimes fierce, surely there was nothing in his demeanor today to frighten her.

"Can I help you?" he asked, keeping his voice as even as if he were approaching a frightened foal. "The storm seems to be passing."

Mercifully, the rain was lessening. Unfortunately, it was too late to save the woman and child from being drenched. Their sunbonnets had been no protection from the rain, and the cotton shawls they wore would be of little good now that they were soaked.

Wyatt studied them as best he could, given the shadows that the wagon cast on them. The wisps of hair plastered to their foreheads told him both were blondes, although the woman's hair seemed to be more golden than the girl's. Both had blue eyes. Both were more than passably attractive, despite their bedraggled state. Both had — Wyatt's thoughts were derailed when the child shifted, revealing a strawberry birthmark on her left cheek.

She was a stranger; they were both strangers, and yet Wyatt knew he'd seen a mark like that before. A memory teased the edges of his brain but remained elusive. He could wonder about that later; what mattered now was helping these ladies who seemed unwilling to utter a word.

"Do you have a place to stay tonight?" Whatever belongings they had stashed in the back of the wagon must be as wet as they were. "You're less than half an hour from Mesquite Springs, but the town doesn't have a hotel, and I know for a fact that the boardinghouse is full."

Still no response, although the woman's eyes narrowed slightly, as if she were assessing his honesty and perhaps his integrity. Fortunately, the stark terror that had startled him had begun to recede.

"You're welcome to stay with me tonight," he offered. When she recoiled and tightened her grip on the girl, Wyatt realized his mistake. "My mother and sister will be glad for the company," he added, trying to allay her fears at the same time that he tried to assure himself that his impulsive invitation had not been a mistake.

While the woman remained silent, the girl leaned forward and stared at him. "Are you gonna be my daddy?"

Evelyn felt her cheeks flush, and in that instant, the fear that had paralyzed her vanished. The poor man! The storm had brought back memories that refused to fade, and she'd stared at him as if he were an ogre. In truth, he was only trying to be a good Samaritan, but then he'd been blindsided by Polly's question. Evelyn crawled from under the wagon and rose to her feet, determined to make amends.

"I'm sorry, sir. I hope you can excuse my sister." The word came easily, perhaps because she'd repeated it so often. "We've been traveling for a while, and when she's tired, I never know what will pop out of her mouth." Evelyn gave thanks that her own voice sounded steady and that her legs, which had been trembling while the thunder boomed, did not quaver. She was fine, and Polly would be too.

As if to contradict her, Polly shook her head as she emerged from the wagon's shelter. "You promised me a new daddy." Though her voice was firm, she gripped Evelyn's hand.

"Not now, Polly." This wasn't the time to remind the child that she'd made no such promise. "This nice man just wants to help us."

Mrs. Folger would claim that he had ulterior motives. Evelyn was certain of that, but her instincts told her the stranger meant no harm. He was a nice man. Even with the rain dripping from his clothing and a stray drop making its way down his nose, he was also one of the most attractive men Evelyn had met. His dark brown hair and chocolate brown eyes were appealing, but it was his smile that reassured her. There was something so genuine about it that Evelyn was able to dismiss her worries. He was not the Watcher.

And then there was his voice, much deeper than the one that still figured in her dreams. He was not the man who'd searched for her. But what convinced her more than anything that he was a nice man was the fact that he had not flinched at the sight of Polly's birthmark. He'd seen it — Evelyn knew that — but he had not recoiled.

As the stranger smiled again, the feeling of safety and homecoming that had washed over her this morning when she'd seen the mountain increased.

"I hope you'll accept my offer." The smile that accompanied his words continued to warm Evelyn almost as much as the sun might have. "The ranch is only a few minutes from here, and we have plenty of room. I assure you, you and your sister will be welcome."

She could trust him. She *would* trust him. Evelyn nodded. "Thank you, sir. We could use a place to dry off." She knew without even looking that their few articles of clothing and the blankets they'd used for warmth each night were soaked. "Come, Polly. It's time to get back in the wagon."

As Evelyn reached down to lift the child, Polly shook off her grip and scampered the few yards to the man. "I want him to help me."

Evelyn said a silent prayer that there would be no more references to daddies, and there weren't. Polly simply grasped the man's hand and looked up at him with such longing in her expression that Evelyn doubted anyone other than a curmudgeon could refuse. The stranger did not.

His smile turned self-deprecating. "Ma told me to never refuse a lady's request," he said as he deposited Polly on the bench. He turned back to Evelyn, his smile now rueful. "Of course, Ma'd have my hide if she knew I hadn't introduced myself. I'm Wyatt Clark of the Circle C."

"A pleasure to meet you, Mr. Clark." The commonplace words had never felt so true. "I'm Evelyn Rad . . . ner." Evelyn hoped that Mr. Clark hadn't noticed her hesitation. This was the first time she'd had to say the name she'd chosen, and it hadn't come out smoothly.

There was no choice, though. As unlikely as it was that anyone was still searching for her, Evelyn couldn't risk anyone tracing her. Her own safety was no longer her primary concern. Now she had a child to protect. An innocent child. What would happen to Polly if Evelyn were killed? There was no point in worrying about that now. They were safe, at least for today.

"You've already met Polly." The illusion of warmth that his smile had created had faded, and Evelyn shivered.

Wyatt Clark might not be the Watcher, but he saw the shiver and reacted immediately. "I have a blanket in my saddlebags. Why don't you let me drive your wagon? I'll tie Thunder to the back, and you and Polly can wrap up in the blanket."

"Are you certain?" The freezing rain seemed to have permeated Evelyn's bones, leaving her feeling colder than she could ever remember. Even though she told herself it was her responsibility to drive Reginald, she wasn't sure her hands could hold the reins steady.

"I wouldn't offer if I weren't certain. One thing you'll learn about me is that I say exactly what I mean."

He was acting as if this were the beginning of a long acquaintance. If she settled in the next town as she'd promised Polly they would, she and Wyatt Clark would almost be neighbors. The thought reassured Evelyn as much as his words did. "Then I accept gratefully. Thank you, Mr. Clark."

He helped her climb in the wagon, then spoke again, his reply surprising her. "How about calling me Wyatt?"

It was unconventional, to say the least, for people who'd just met to graduate to first names, and yet it would solve one problem. Being called "Evelyn" was much easier than remembering to answer to "Miss Radner."

"Certainly. I'm Evelyn."

■ ■ ■ ■

"What do you raise on your ranch, Mr. Clark . . . er, Wyatt?"

He couldn't help smiling. There was something endearing about the flush of embarrassment that colored Evelyn's cheeks as she fumbled his name. Perhaps he'd been presumptuous in asking her to use his first name, but he was so used to being on a familiar basis with Dorothy's friends that the formal address seemed wrong.

"There doesn't seem to be any cotton in this part of Texas, so I'm guessing it's cattle."

As she tipped her head to one side, he noticed that the tip of her nose flared a bit. Wyatt suspected Evelyn might consider that a flaw, but he thought the minor imperfection made her seem more human . . . more approachable.

Whoa! What was getting into him? She was a woman he'd befriended. By tomorrow morning, she'd be gone to wherever it was she was headed, and he'd never see her again. There was no reason to be thinking about anything beyond giving her a warm, dry place to spend the night.

Bringing himself back to reality, Wyatt

shook his head. "I raise quarter horses."

"Those are the ones everyone races, aren't they?"

Wyatt shrugged. Raising racehorses had been his father's dream, but he'd tried to expand beyond that. "Most of the men who buy my horses race them," he admitted, "but I've started to sell to the Rangers too. Quarter horses have great agility as well as speed. That makes them good mounts for men who have to change direction quickly or go into tight places."

Evelyn nodded as if she agreed.

Though the little girl had said nothing since Wyatt had placed her in the wagon, she appeared to have been listening intently to the conversation. "Is Reginald a race-horse?"

At least she wasn't asking about daddies. That had been downright embarrassing. Though Wyatt knew it was impossible, when he'd heard her question, he'd wondered if somehow she had met Ma.

The look Polly gave the gelding pulling the wagon told Wyatt this was Reginald. Although he appeared to have good blood-lines, he was most definitely not a racehorse. Wyatt hated the idea of disappointing a child, then realized he did not have to. Since Polly had directed her question at Evelyn,

he could let her respond.

Evelyn, it seemed, was up to the challenge. She smiled at the child and gave her head a short shake. "I'm afraid not."

"Then what is he?"

"Our horse."

When Polly nodded, apparently satisfied by the answer, Wyatt blinked in surprise. Who knew it was so easy to placate a child?

This time Polly looked at him. "Can I ride one of your horses?"

Evelyn's expression told him he'd have to answer this time. Though the thought of a girl as small as Polly atop one of his prize horses was almost ludicrous, Wyatt knew better than to dash her hopes.

"Why don't we wait until you meet them?" he suggested. "You can see what you think about riding one then." In all likelihood, their skittishness around strangers would convince her that it was not a good idea.

Once again, she seemed mollified. "Okay, Mr. Wyatt." Polly snuggled closer to Evelyn, then looked up at her. "I like him, Evelyn. He's a nice man."

"Yes, he is."

The simple, unexpected, and yet heartfelt words warmed Wyatt. He'd been called many things, but this was the first time anyone had described him as a nice man. It

61

felt good. Amazingly good.

He settled back on the seat and focused his attention on the road. Though Reginald had adapted easily to a different driver, Wyatt couldn't afford to be complacent, not with passengers in the wagon. His gaze strayed to the woman on the other end of the bench. Even though she looked as bedraggled as the cat Dorothy had dropped into a bucket of water when she was a child, something about Evelyn intrigued him more than anyone he'd met.

There had been the initial terror, which he still did not understand, but that had faded. Now she was wary. Wyatt had no trouble understanding that. A woman traveling alone needed to be wary. Despite that, he sensed an underlying strength.

When she'd emerged from beneath the wagon, her posture had been dignified, as if she were accustomed to being in charge. Wyatt liked that. It was so different from the ladies in Mesquite Springs who fluttered their eyelashes and blushed when they spoke to him. It was almost as if they believed men were a different species of animal.

Evelyn did not simper or blush or flutter her lashes. When she spoke, she seemed straightforward, and yet he couldn't dismiss

62

the feeling that she was hiding something. There'd been no furtiveness in her expression, but he knew he hadn't been mistaken in thinking that she'd stumbled over her name.

There was more to Miss Evelyn Radner than she wanted the world to see. The question was, what was behind the pretty mask, and why did she feel the need to hide?

CHAPTER FIVE

"We're almost there," Wyatt said as he turned onto what was obviously a private road.

Evelyn nodded, grateful that this phase of her journey was coming to an end. Fortunately, the sun had emerged from the clouds as quickly as it had disappeared, and though her clothing was still sopping, the combination of the sun and the blanket had stopped her shivering. Still, it would be good to be inside and have a chance to dry her clothes.

Polly was dozing, which Evelyn hadn't expected, given the girl's excitement over the appearance of the man she thought should be her new father. As Evelyn had wrapped the blanket around her, Polly had whispered so loudly that Wyatt must have heard, "He's the daddy I want."

Perhaps that was the reason he'd been so quiet. After all, what could a man say when a child he'd just met made such a declara-

tion? Whatever the reason for his silence, it had proven to be more comfortable than Evelyn would have thought possible. There was something relaxing, almost reassuring, about Wyatt, and that was a surprise.

Other than the shopkeepers with whom she did business, Evelyn had had little contact with grown men. Mrs. Folger had insisted that boys leave the orphanage when they turned sixteen, although girls were permitted to stay two years longer if they proved useful. And, while most women her age had married, Evelyn had had no suitors, for not only had Mrs. Folger forbidden unmarried men to visit the orphanage, but she'd never missed an opportunity to warn Evelyn about the perils of marrying the wrong man. Evelyn reminded herself of those admonitions every time she'd gone to Gilmorton, but — though she couldn't explain why — they did not seem to apply to Wyatt.

She smiled as the wagon crested a small hill, revealing a house and outbuildings nestled in the valley below. More horses than she could count grazed in the paddocks; two cows appeared to be chewing their cud; and a flock of chickens scratched in the dirt. Other than the number of horses and the fact that it appeared to have both a

stable and a barn, it was a pastoral scene that could have been repeated almost anywhere in the Hill Country, but what caught Evelyn's eye was the main house.

While not as large as the plantation homes she'd seen near Logansville, it was both spacious and attractive. As she gazed at the two-story white frame building with dark green shutters and a wide front porch boasting three rocking chairs, her smile broadened. This was not simply a house. It was a home.

The sound of the wagon's wheels must have alerted her, because a taller-than-average, thin woman appeared on the porch before Wyatt had had a chance to rein in Reginald.

"What on earth happened?" The woman's resemblance to Wyatt left no doubt that she was his mother.

Her slight accent that made the *w* sound like a *v* did not surprise Evelyn, for she knew that the Hill Country had a large number of German immigrants. What did surprise her was the wariness she saw in Mrs. Clark's eyes as her gaze moved rapidly from Evelyn to Polly before landing on Wyatt. Though Wyatt had claimed that his mother and sister would welcome them, Mrs. Clark appeared almost afraid of Eve-

lyn and Polly.

Apparently unconcerned by his mother's agitation, Wyatt calmly set the brake, lifted Polly out of the wagon, and helped Evelyn onto the ground. "These ladies were caught in a storm. I told them you'd give them a warm, dry place to spend the night. They have no one else."

While it was nothing more than the truth, Evelyn wondered how he'd known that. She might have regretted Wyatt's revealing their sorry state, but she could not regret the effect it had on Mrs. Clark. Her expression softened, and the wariness left her eyes. She closed the distance between them in a few quick strides.

"Oh, you poor dears." Mrs. Clark wrapped one arm around Evelyn's waist and drew her to her side, then laid her other hand on Polly's head as if to comfort her. "Come inside. We'll get you some dry clothes." She turned toward the house and raised her voice. "Dorothy! We've got visitors."

As a woman about Evelyn's age emerged from the house, Mrs. Clark began the introductions. "This is my daughter, Dorothy, and I'm Isolde." Dorothy shared her mother's dark brown hair, although hers was not threaded with silver, and while she and her brother both had brown eyes rather

67

than their mother's green, Dorothy's were caramel rather than chocolate. The biggest difference was their height. Dorothy was an inch or two shorter than Evelyn, while her mother was several inches taller, and Wyatt stood at least six feet tall.

"It's a pleasure to meet you and your daughter, Mrs. Clark."

Wyatt's mother shook her head. "Just Isolde. There's no need for formality here." Like mother, like son, or so it appeared.

Grateful that she wouldn't have to answer to a false name, Evelyn nodded. "I'm Evelyn, and this is Polly." As soon as Mrs. Clark — Isolde, Evelyn reminded herself — released her from the impromptu hug, Polly wrapped her arms around Evelyn so tightly that Evelyn had trouble breathing.

Though there was nothing threatening about either Isolde or Dorothy, with the notable exception of Wyatt, Polly had been shy around strangers from the day she'd arrived at the orphanage. Evelyn had thought it might be the result of the stares her birthmark elicited, but though she'd seen a slight widening of both women's eyes when they noted it, they'd appeared as unconcerned by the stain on Polly's cheek as Wyatt had. That alone would have endeared them to her, but the fact that they both smiled at Polly as if her skin were flawless warmed Evelyn's heart.

Isolde turned to her son. "I'll get our visitors settled while you take care of the horses. And be sure not to dally, because I have a hunch our guests are hungry."

Polly, who'd been listening to the exchange without saying a word, grinned. "I am!"

While Wyatt led his gelding toward the stable, Isolde pointed to the wagon. "Dorothy and I'll help you get your bags out. I imagine you'd like a bath and fresh clothes."

The thought of both excited Evelyn more than the prospect of food had Polly. "A bath sounds heavenly, but we have no other clothes."

Isolde made no attempt to hide her shock. "Why not? Surely you didn't set out on a journey without proper provisions." She pursed her lips and stared at Evelyn, as if she were trying to determine whether her visitor was touched in the head. Evelyn couldn't blame her.

"Our home burned, taking everything we owned. We have a bit of food in the wagon, but that's all." There was no point in hiding that truth.

Dorothy spoke for the first time, her brown eyes filled with concern. "How awful!" As she studied Evelyn, her expression was less critical than her mother's had been a few seconds earlier. "They'll be a bit tight and a little short, but I have a couple dresses that might fit."

Isolde nodded as she led the way onto the porch and into the house. "We'll go into town tomorrow. Ida Downey has some ready-mades at the mercantile."

Though Evelyn had expected Dorothy to agree, she did not. "Oh, Ma, did you forget that the Downeys have been gone? Their inventory is small, and what's left is . . ." She wrinkled her nose rather than complete the sentence. "If we go early enough, we can buy fabric and get something sewn for these girls in time for church."

Evelyn stared at the woman, amazed by her suggestion. It had been ten years since anyone had done so much for her, and then it had been her mother. Isolde and Dorothy were total strangers who owed her nothing, and yet they were being more than kind to her. Their generosity and the genuine caring she saw on their faces as well as their acceptance of Polly solidified her belief that God had led her here.

"I'm not much of a seamstress." Though she could make lace and had, in fact, taught the other orphans to do it, Evelyn was not skilled with a needle and thread.

Isolde did not seem fazed by Evelyn's lack of what was considered a necessary skill for all women. "Don't worry. Dorothy and I are almost as good as Mrs. Steiner."

"She's Mesquite Springs's dressmaker," Dorothy interjected.

"No one can match her hats," Isolde continued, undaunted by her daughter's interruption, "but Dorothy and I can turn out a dress that would rival hers, especially now that we have a Singer." She glanced at the clock that stood at the end of the short hallway and gave a brisk nod. "If we have cold meals tomorrow, we should have just enough time."

The women were kindness and generosity personified, but that didn't mean that Evelyn could let them do this for her. "I don't want you to disrupt your lives for me. You're already doing so much."

A warm, dry place to sleep and a chance to wash their clothes was all that Evelyn had hoped for. Now it appeared that she and Polly were being offered a temporary home and new clothing.

A chuckle greeted Evelyn's protest. "Ma won't mind," Dorothy said with a mischievous smile at her mother. "Cooking is not one of her favorite chores."

71

"But it is mine." Evelyn welcomed the idea of being able to repay her hostesses in some small way. "I love to cook."

Though she said nothing, Isolde regarded her as if she'd sprouted a second head.

"If you're going to sew for me," Evelyn continued, "the least I can do is prepare our meals."

Polly, who'd been silent while the adults spoke, tugged on Evelyn's hand. "You should do it," she said, her expression as solemn as if she were issuing a proclamation. She turned to the Clarks and announced, "Evelyn's a good cook."

Dorothy's grin widened. "There, Ma, you see. It's settled."

While the water for Evelyn's and Polly's baths was heating, Isolde showed them the room they'd share. Twice as large as the chamber Evelyn had had at the orphanage, the room was also lighter, thanks to windows on two sides and pale pink wallpaper with a few deeper pink roses sprinkled over it.

"Pretty!" Polly bounced on the bed, earning a stern look from Evelyn. "It's soft, Evelyn. Not like the other one."

Though anything would feel soft after sleeping in the wagon for so many days,

Evelyn did not dispute the child's claim. The goose down comforter and pillows were far finer than the bedding the orphanage had provided, and the mattress was firm but not hard.

"The tub's ready," Isolde announced as she held out what was clearly a man's chambray shirt. "I'm sorry we don't have anything the right size for Polly, but it's been a while since Dorothy was so small." Dorothy had brought Evelyn one of her dresses to wear while hers was being laundered, pointing out that if she wore one fewer petticoat, it wouldn't be too short.

"I thought Polly could wear one of Wyatt's shirts," Isolde continued.

The little girl stared at the shirt as if it were a princess's gown. "I like it," she announced. "I want Mr. Wyatt to be my daddy."

Chuckling, Dorothy exchanged a look with her mother. "That might be the answer to someone else's prayers."

The slight flush that colored Isolde's cheeks made Evelyn suspect she was like the mothers Mrs. Folger had described who urged their children to marry so they could have grandchildren. That, Mrs. Folger had confided, was often a mistake. "Never marry in haste," she had admonished Evelyn.

"Don't make the mistake I did." Evelyn would not.

She touched Polly's shoulders, then shook her head when the child looked at her.

"I hope you can excuse Polly," Evelyn said to Isolde and Dorothy. "She's still adjusting to her father's death. It's only been a few months." The words were no sooner out of her mouth than Evelyn realized her error. If she and Polly were the sisters she had claimed, she should have said "our father." Papa had been right when he'd told her that lies were dangerous and would trip a person up.

Dorothy's smile faded, and for a second Evelyn feared that she had noticed the slip. But then she said, "My brother might claim that he and I are still adjusting to our father's death, and it's been more than ten years."

That explained why no one had mentioned Mr. Clark. Evelyn had wondered but hadn't wanted to pry. "I'm sorry," she said, hating the inadequacy of the simple words. "It's never easy, is it?" Though the raw pain of her parents' murders had been replaced by a dull ache, the anguish she felt over the deaths at the orphanage was fresh and at times so overwhelming that she had to remember to breathe.

Isolde folded a towel over her arm and led the way to the small room where the now-steaming tub was located. "I told Wilson to stay home that day, but he wouldn't listen. He'd promised to deliver a mare to a neighbor, and nothing I said would convince him to wait." She frowned as she recalled a painful part of her past. "The next time I saw him, he was lying in the back of the neighbor's wagon. A band of marauding Comanche stole the horse and killed him on his way to the other ranch."

Evelyn shivered as she undressed Polly and lifted her into the tub. The girl seemed so entranced by the sight of a tub filled with hot water, a luxury the orphanage had not afforded, that she paid no attention to the adults' conversation. Evelyn, however, could not ignore it. Though Mr. Clark's death was in the past, the story was a reminder that evil knew no boundaries and that she needed to remain vigilant, even in this apparently peaceful spot.

"I don't know what to say."

"There's nothing to be said." Dorothy handed her a bar of sweet-smelling soap. "We simply wanted you to know that we understand what you're feeling. Losing your home so soon after your father's death must have been horrible."

75

Evelyn felt a pang of regret that she couldn't tell the women it had been ten years since her father had died. The weight of lies and omissions weighed heavily on her, but until she was certain — absolutely certain — that she and Polly were safe, she couldn't risk anyone learning her true identity.

"I don't know what your plans are," Isolde said from her post next to the door, "but you're welcome to stay here as long as you'd like."

"Thank you. I don't want to impose on you, but I have to admit that the thought of a night or two in a real bed is appealing." They wouldn't stay longer than that, because no matter how kind these women were, Evelyn needed to find a permanent home for herself and Polly.

She turned to Polly, who'd been splashing in the tub. "Close your eyes now. I'm going to rinse your hair."

While Evelyn dipped the can Dorothy had provided into the water and sluiced water over Polly's head, Dorothy spoke. "How long have you been traveling?"

"About two weeks." At times it had felt like forever; at other times, Evelyn would have said it was only a few hours since they'd left their last home.

Isolde nodded, as if the answer hadn't surprised her. "Where are you headed?"

I don't know. Though the words tickled the tip of her tongue, Evelyn refused to utter them. Not only would that admission raise too many questions, but it would also negate the feeling she'd had earlier today when she'd believed she was close to her destination.

"Mesquite Springs," she said firmly.

"A good choice." Isolde gave her a re-assuring smile. "My children will tell you I'm prejudiced, because this is where Wilson and I started our life together, but to my way of thinking, you couldn't pick a better place to settle."

It made no sense. She hadn't seen the town, but somehow Isolde's words rang true. This was the right place for Evelyn and Polly.

CHAPTER SIX

"You did the right thing by bringing Evelyn and Polly here."

Wyatt turned to smile at his sister. It was unusual for her to join him in the stable instead of helping Ma prepare supper, but he shouldn't have been surprised. Everything about today had been unusual, from the fact that he'd brought two bedraggled females to the ranch to the difficulty he'd had concentrating on the horses. Thoughts of Evelyn and her sister had whirled through his head, displacing everything else, even the need to ensure that Reginald's presence would not disturb the Circle C's horses.

Why was Evelyn unprepared for travel, why had she hesitated when she'd pronounced her last name, and why did Polly's birthmark seem so familiar? The questions formed an endless refrain. Talking to Dorothy might put him back on an even keel.

"Why do you say that?" he asked.

"Those poor girls' home burned down."

As he ran his hand over Emerald's abdomen, checking the position of the foal and trying to guess how long it would be before she delivered, Wyatt nodded. Dorothy had answered one of his questions. "That explains why they had so few belongings in the wagon. I wondered but didn't want to ask."

Dorothy chuckled. "You know Ma. She's not shy."

"That's true." When she was having a good day, Ma could be as blunt as a hammer. Though Wyatt didn't always appreciate her frankness, he much preferred it to the days when she retreated to her room, barely speaking and refusing to eat. Fortunately, today had been a good day. He'd seen her discomfort — oh, why mince words? He'd seen her fear at the sight of strangers invading her home and knew it brought back memories of her early life in Germany, but that had dissipated quickly, her maternal instincts overpowering her ingrained fear of strangers.

"I know I said I hated the ranch, and there are days when I do, but I can't imagine what it would be like to lose our home." Dorothy waved her hand as if to encompass the stable. "It was horrible losing Pa, but at least we had this."

Though Wyatt had not considered it a blessing when he'd had to work so hard to keep the ranch solvent, he knew Dorothy was right. Life would have been even more difficult if they'd had no home.

"You need to be strong to survive losing everything." He hadn't thought about strength at the time. He'd simply done what had to be done. Was that what Evelyn was doing? She appeared strong, but he couldn't forget that she also seemed wary, as if she had secrets she didn't want revealed.

"Did Evelyn tell you her last name?" he asked.

"Not that I recall. Why?"

Though Wyatt had hoped that his question sounded casual, he'd apparently failed. "I just wondered."

"You need a break."

Evelyn looked up from the rolls she was shaping. She'd heard Wyatt's footsteps before he spoke and wasn't surprised that he'd come into the kitchen, since Isolde had admonished him to look after Evelyn and Polly while she and Dorothy went to town.

"These are almost ready for their second rising," Evelyn said as she formed the last bit of dough into a smooth ball. "That gives me half an hour before I have to put them in the oven. Polly and I can take a break."

Though Isolde had invited Polly to accompany her and Dorothy, she'd refused, instead remaining in the kitchen, playing with the doll Dorothy had given her but never letting Evelyn out of her sight. Evelyn wasn't surprised. From the day she'd arrived at the orphanage, Polly had attached herself to Evelyn, and the events of the past two weeks had only deepened her dependence.

"Half an hour will give us enough time."

"Time for what, Mr. Wyatt?" Polly rose, still clutching the doll, and took a step toward him.

"Time for you to meet some of the horses."

A grin split her face. "Goody!" She tugged on Evelyn's skirt. "Let's go."

Evelyn looked down at the child. "Why don't you fetch our cloaks while I wash my hands?" When Polly had left, Evelyn turned to Wyatt. "It was kind of you to remember how much she wanted to see the horses."

He shrugged as if it were of no import that he'd recalled a small child's request. "I thought you'd both like to see a bit of the Circle C. It's your home for a while."

That was what Isolde had said, but no

matter how appealing the idea was, Evelyn knew she could not remain here permanently. The risks were too high. Mrs. Folger had claimed Evelyn was safe at the orphanage, but she had been wrong. Not only had Mrs. Folger perished in the fire that had been meant to kill Evelyn, but so had twenty-two orphans.

"I told your mother we'd stay until I can find a way to support Polly and myself." Evelyn blinked back the tears that surfaced whenever she thought of the fire and covered the rolls with a clean cloth, placing them on the counter next to the oven. The heat there would help them rise but wasn't hot enough to begin the baking process prematurely, giving the rolls the too-yeasty flavor that resulted from a rushed rising.

It was easy to make rolls. If only it were as easy to plan her future. Until they'd reached the Circle C, Evelyn had thought of little beyond getting as far from Logansville as possible. Fear had been her driving force. Now that she'd reached what felt like her journey's end, it was time to focus on the practicalities of everyday life.

She and Polly needed a permanent home, which meant that Evelyn needed a source of income. For the first time in her life, she was solely responsible for herself. Not only herself, but Polly too. It was a frightening prospect for a woman with only one skill.

Before Evelyn could say anything more, Polly burst into the room, her shoes clattering on the wooden floor.

"Hurry, Evelyn. Put on your cloak." She thrust it at her. "I wanna see the horses."

They were magnificent. Evelyn didn't claim to be an expert on horses, but when Wyatt led them to the western paddock, she recognized the sleek lines and proud stance of what the blacksmith in Gilmorton would call "fine horseflesh." Two full-grown horses were racing around the perimeter, while a dozen yearlings grazed peacefully in the center.

"As you can see, Obsidian and Onyx like to run. The others are good, and they'll fetch a good price at the sale, but Onyx and Obsidian are the best. Their foals have turned into champion racers."

Hearing the pride in Wyatt's voice, Evelyn studied the two horses he'd singled out. She couldn't identify specific differences; all she knew was that these two seemed special.

"They're spectacular animals. Are you planning to sell them?"

Wyatt shook his head. "I'm sure some of the buyers will try to convince me otherwise, but Obsidian and Onyx are staying here."

He stared into the distance for a moment, the furrows that formed between his eyes telling Evelyn something worried him.

"What's wrong?"

"Nothing. I just hope I'm doing the right thing by having the sale here."

"Where else would it be?" Evelyn wasn't afraid to admit that she knew nothing about selling horses.

Wyatt's jaw tightened. "Texans are used to going to Fort Worth or another city for a big sale with lots of breeders. That's what I've always done, but when I heard about a man in Kentucky having a private sale at his farm, it sounded like a good idea. He claimed he got better prices than he had at the other sales."

Wyatt shrugged, and Evelyn wondered if he was trying to shrug off his concerns.

"I have more horses to sell this year, so it seemed to make sense. Now I wonder if it's a mistake."

Though she'd never been to a horse sale, Evelyn understood the basics. "How will people learn about it?"

"I plan to place ads in various newspapers. I have records of the men who've bid on Circle C horses for the last five years, so I'll put ads in their local papers."

It was a good strategy, but Evelyn suspected there was a better one.

"Since you know where potential buyers live, have you considered sending them personal invitations? If I received one, I know I'd be more likely to come than if I'd simply seen an ad in the paper."

"That's a great idea." Wyatt's response was instantaneous. "It'll be a lot of work, but you're right — the personal approach is the best one."

"I'll help you any way I can. I may not know much about horses, but I can write invitations. If you give me the list of names and addresses, I'll do the rest." It was the least she could do after the kindness his family had shown her and Polly.

"Are you sure you don't mind?" Though he phrased it as a question, Evelyn heard relief in Wyatt's voice.

"Of course not. I wouldn't have suggested it if I wasn't willing to help."

Bored by the adults' conversation, Polly tugged on Evelyn's hand, then threw an entreating look at Wyatt and pointed at the two large horses. "Can I ride them?"

He gave her a smile as he shook his head. "Not these boys. They're too big, but don't worry, Polly. I have the perfect pony in mind for you. You can ride tomorrow after church."

Wyatt led the way to another paddock where more than a dozen horses grazed peacefully. "These are the mares." He pointed to one who stood by herself at the far corner. "Emerald's due to foal any day now."

The warmth in his voice made Evelyn smile. "The next generation of Circle C horses."

"Yes."

Wyatt was fortunate. His future was clear. If only she could say the same.

The town was prettier than Evelyn had expected, the tree-lined streets wider than she'd seen elsewhere, the buildings well maintained and prosperous looking, the people strolling along those streets equally well maintained and prosperous looking. No wonder Isolde and Dorothy had insisted that she needed a new dress. Her old one was too shabby for church services in a town like this.

The two women had worked industriously all afternoon, the whirring of the sewing machine punctuated by the clicking of shears and brief discussions about the merits of pleats over ruffles. Isolde and Dorothy had paused only to eat the stew and rolls Evelyn had made for supper, and by

86

Polly's bedtime not only had they finished the beautiful blue gown they'd declared would be Evelyn's Sunday dress, but they'd added matching lace to the frock they'd purchased for Polly. Though it was a different shade of blue and a different style from Evelyn's, Polly was thrilled to have a dress so similar to her supposed sister's.

"We match!" she'd crowed with delight. And though Evelyn had feared that the excitement would keep her awake, Polly had fallen asleep almost immediately, leaving Evelyn to thank her benefactresses again for their generosity.

Now the two blue-gowned girls were within minutes of entering the church and seeing whether the townspeople were as friendly as Isolde claimed.

"You don't need to worry," Wyatt's mother said, almost as if she'd read Evelyn's thoughts. "They're good folks."

That might be true, but even good folks had been known to make hurtful comments about Polly's birthmark.

"Since it's Epiphany, Pastor Coleman will preach about the three kings," Dorothy said as she pointed toward the stone building on the corner of Main and River streets. As they'd driven into town, Dorothy had explained that the residents of Mesquite

Springs hadn't been particularly creative when naming their streets. Main was the primary east–west street, while River, which ran north-south, had gained its name from the river at the north end of town.

"Pastor Coleman gives practically the same sermon every year," her mother chimed in. Dorothy and Isolde, who were seated on the rear seat since Isolde had insisted that Evelyn and Polly share the front seat with Wyatt, had kept up a nonstop commentary on the town and its surroundings, leaving Wyatt little chance to say anything.

"Was it like that where you lived?" Isolde asked.

"No." Though Mrs. Folger had conducted a weekly worship service in the parlor, the orphans did not attend church. Mrs. Folger claimed that private services were easier than transporting everyone into town, but Evelyn suspected that they had not been welcome. The residents of Logansville preferred to pretend the orphanage did not exist. Now it no longer did.

"You were lucky."

Evelyn turned toward Wyatt, surprised that he'd joined the conversation. She would not have used the word *lucky* to describe her life in Logansville, but when she spoke, it was with complete honesty. "I feel fortunate to be here. This is a lovely town."

From the backseat, Isolde leaned forward and touched Evelyn's shoulder. "See. I told you you'd like it. Wait until you see the bluebonnets this spring. They're extra special here."

"Ma thinks everything is better in Mesquite Springs than anywhere else in Texas," Wyatt said with a chuckle.

"Well, it is."

" 'The Lord bless thee and keep thee: the Lord make his face shine upon thee, and be gracious unto thee: the Lord lift up his countenance upon thee, and give thee peace.' "

Wyatt raised his head as Pastor Coleman finished the benediction and gave his own private thanks that he could soon leave the church. The familiar sermon and the opportunity to worship his God had not brought him the peace it usually did. The reason wasn't hard to find; it was sitting right next to him.

All morning long he'd been aware of Evelyn in the new blue dress that seemed to deepen the hue of those vibrant eyes of hers. He'd also been aware that the single men in the sanctuary had noticed her and were counting the minutes until the service was over and they could meet her. The ordeal was about to begin.

"Wyatt, glad to see you." Caleb Smith clapped Wyatt on the shoulder the moment he descended the front steps, flanked by Evelyn and Polly. Ma had remained inside the sanctuary, claiming that she and Dorothy needed to speak to Mrs. Steiner.

That had been a ploy to give Wyatt more time with Evelyn. Wyatt knew that his mother was in matchmaker mode as surely as he knew that today was Sunday. Still, there was no point in arguing, especially when spending time with Evelyn was no hardship. The hardship was dealing with the two men who'd been lying in wait for them.

He tried to view them through Evelyn's eyes. Would she be as impressed with Caleb's appearance as most of the single women in Mesquite Springs were? With his dark, almost black hair and eyes as deep a blue as Evelyn's, the blacksmith's son was considered the most handsome man in town.

While under other circumstances, some might call Sam Plaut handsome, his brown hair and eyes seemed to fade next to Caleb's more dramatic coloring, but he made up for that in demeanor. Mesquite Springs's sole attorney was a living, breathing example of confidence. According to Dorothy, women found that as attractive as perfectly formed features. The question was whether Evelyn would be as impressed by these men as they were with her.

"The man's lying." Sam gave Caleb what appeared to be a playful shove. "It's not you he's glad to see. It's the lovely girl at your side. Aren't you going to introduce her to us?"

Before Wyatt had a chance to respond, Evelyn took a step forward. "Good morning, gentlemen," she said, her voice as sweet as honey. Surely it was his imagination that a hint of sarcasm underlaid the apparently ordinary words. "Let me introduce you to Polly." She took the girl's hand and drew her forward. "I thought I was biased, but I'm delighted that you share my opinion that she's the loveliest girl in Mesquite Springs."

Wyatt did his best not to laugh. No doubt about it, Evelyn had won the round. She had probably seen the way both men flinched at the sight of Polly's birthmark and had done what she could to repair the damage to her sister's esteem.

"Now, boys, I thought your mothers

91

taught you better." Ma had apparently finished whatever she was doing in the church and appeared at Polly's other side. "You're supposed to raise your hats when you're introduced to a lady."

"But . . ." Sam's face reddened. Wyatt almost laughed at the way Ma's rebuke had made a man who was noted for his oratory practically speechless. It had been ages since he'd seen Sam at a loss for words.

Caleb shook his head. "You'd better give up before you dig that hole any deeper." He tipped his hat to Polly. "It's a pleasure to meet you, Miss Polly."

The little girl tittered. "Nobody calls me that."

"They should." Sam raised his hat and addressed Polly, although Wyatt noticed that he studiously avoided looking at her cheek. "Who's the lady with you, Miss Polly?"

"That's Evelyn."

This time both men tipped their hats and murmured greetings, grinning like school-boys. Wyatt knew he shouldn't let their obvious fascination bother him, but it did. The day had begun well. The gingerbread pancakes Evelyn had made for breakfast were better than any flapjacks he could recall, and the ride into town had been pleasant, but it had gone downhill after that.

Surely it couldn't get worse.

Wyatt glanced to the left and saw Fletcher heading this way, the gleam in his eye leaving no doubt that he wanted to speak to Wyatt, most likely about running for mayor. The day had just gotten worse.

CHAPTER SEVEN

"This is the best dish I've ever eaten. What do you call it?"

Evelyn smiled. If actions spoke louder than words, and she believed they did, the fact that Wyatt had taken three helpings and cleaned his plate each time confirmed the truth of his words.

"It's chicken fricassee. That was one of the first things my mother taught me to make." Since Saturday, when she'd started doing most of the cooking at the Circle C, Evelyn had experimented with dishes that Dorothy said they rarely or never ate. So far, the experiments had proven successful, and with each success, the possibility Evelyn had begun to entertain for her future seemed more promising.

Dorothy gave her mother a conspiratorial smile. "The first thing Ma let me cook was oatmeal."

Polly, who'd been fiddling with her fork, a

sure sign she was ready for dessert, looked up with apparent interest. "Was it lumpy? Hilda's oatmeal was lumpy."

"Who's Hilda?"

Before Evelyn could deflect Dorothy's question, Polly responded. "A girl at the 'nage."

"The 'nage?" Wyatt, who'd been silent other than praising the food, joined the conversation.

Biting back a sigh, Evelyn realized there was no way around it. His curiosity made it clear that she would have to reveal one part of their past. She couldn't blame Polly for her innocent reference. After all, a child her age wasn't used to keeping secrets. That was why Evelyn had spent two weeks reminding her that they were pretending to be sisters and that their name was Radner, not Radcliffe or . . . Evelyn almost smiled at the realization that Polly was keeping at least one secret. No matter how many times she asked, Polly would not reveal her last name.

Evelyn managed a genuine smile for Wyatt, hoping to put a quick end to this discussion. "That's Polly's way of saying 'orphanage.' She and I lived in one after our parents died."

"Then it was the orphanage that burned, not a house." If Wyatt was surprised by the revelation, he gave no sign of it.

Polly leaned forward so that she was looking directly at him. "There was lots and lots of smoke and stink."

"I imagine so." While her son had given no sign of his feelings, furrows had formed between Isolde's eyes at the unfolding tale. She mouthed the question "Survivors?" and the furrows deepened when Evelyn shook her head. "That's very sad, but you're safe now. I'm glad you found your way here."

"So am I." As if he recognized Evelyn's desire to lighten the conversation, those brown eyes the color of the finest chocolate gleamed with amusement as Wyatt said, "No offense to you, Ma, but Evelyn's a much better cook than you are."

Though she wished she hadn't had to mention the orphanage, this might be the opening Evelyn had sought to discuss her idea. She rose and began to collect the empty dinner plates, hoping the action would help keep her calm. So much depended on the answer.

"I used to cook at the orphanage." She didn't have to tell them that she'd started cooking for groups of people years before that. "I was hoping I could find a job at a restaurant in town, but I didn't see one when we went to church." That had struck her as strange. Surely a town the size of Mesquite Springs had at least one eating establishment.

"You probably didn't notice it, because it's closed," Wyatt said as he passed his plate to Evelyn so that she could finish clearing the table and serve dessert. "Foster's Place used to have good food. Not as good as yours, but good. Folks were upset when the Fosters died."

As the blood drained from her face, Evelyn was thankful that she had her back to the table. No one needed to see how much that simple statement disturbed her or how familiar the story sounded.

"What happened to them?" Somehow the act of slicing the pie helped keep her voice even. There was no reason to believe the Fosters had been killed, just as there was no reason to be alarmed by the similarity in the restaurants' names. There were many restaurants called by the owners' names and "Place." Still, the frisson of fear that slid down her back would not be dismissed.

"Cholera took them." As Isolde continued the explanation, Evelyn began to relax. Cholera was horrible, no doubt about that, but it was a natural cause. Gunshots were not.

"We lost a dozen people to it last sum-

97

mer," Isolde added.

"And Mesquite Springs has been without a place to eat ever since," Dorothy said as Evelyn slid a plate in front of her. "We keep hoping someone will reopen it. Why don't you?"

Why didn't she? There were dozens of reasons, starting with its being a bigger undertaking than Evelyn had envisioned and ending with her lack of money, but the warm feeling that had been flowing through her ever since she'd learned of the now-closed eatery made Evelyn believe that this was part of God's plan.

He'd led her to the Hill Country. He'd seen to it that Wyatt was the one to rescue her and Polly from the storm. And now he'd presented her with an opportunity. It couldn't be coincidence.

"I wish I could afford to buy the restaurant and reopen it, but I don't have any money." Mrs. Folger had paid her a small salary in addition to her room and board, but those savings had been lost in the fire.

Dorothy forked a piece of pie but did not raise it to her lips. "You don't have to buy it. My friend Laura's father owns the building. He used to rent it to the Fosters."

Rent would be better than an outright purchase, but Evelyn would still incur expenses before she was able to open the restaurant. "Most landlords want deposits and a couple months' rent in advance. I doubt I can afford it."

"Leonard Downey is a reasonable man," Wyatt said as he refilled his cup with coffee. "He's not one to brag, but he's the richest man in town and one of the kindest. I feel safe in saying that he'll agree that some money is better than none. You might even be able to persuade him to accept a percentage of the profits instead of rent."

"Like a partner?"

"Exactly."

Isolde, who'd been listening to the exchange, nodded. "I'm not encouraging you and Polly to leave, but the town could definitely use a restaurant, and that particular building could resolve one of your problems. There's an apartment on the second floor. I never saw it, but Nancy Foster said it was more than adequate for her and Harold."

A job and a place for her and Polly to live. If it worked out, this could indeed be the answer to Evelyn's prayers. She let out a breath she hadn't realized she'd been holding.

Dorothy's expression was serious as she laid down her fork. "You'll need help. If you're busy cooking, you'll need someone to serve the customers."

"I can help."

Evelyn struggled to repress her smile at Polly's suggestion. The last thing she wanted was to destroy the child's self-confidence. Remembering how proud she had been when her parents had allowed her to perform simple tasks at Radcliffe's Place, Evelyn said, "I couldn't do it without you, but you'll be in school most of the time the restaurant is open, so Dorothy's right — I will need other help."

"I'd like to try." The four simple words were said with such enthusiasm that Evelyn could not doubt Dorothy's sincerity. "You know I'm not a great cook, and I've never served in a restaurant, but I can learn."

"Aren't you needed here?" Though she liked the idea of working with Dorothy, Evelyn had to ask the question.

Before Dorothy could respond, her mother spoke. "My daughter is always looking for excuses to spend time in town. With Laura gone, she's been at loose ends." Isolde shook her head when Evelyn offered her a second piece of pie. "Neither of my children seem to realize that I can manage on my own."

Evelyn glanced at the man seated next to

her. Though she might have expected surprise, Wyatt appeared stunned by his mother's words. He opened his mouth to speak, then closed it, pressing his lips together as if to keep whatever he had planned to say locked up tightly. A moment later, he gave a firm nod. "It's a good idea. We'll go into town tomorrow."

Evelyn could hardly wait.

As much as he regretted not being able to take Evelyn into town today, Wyatt could not regret the reason. After a long and difficult delivery, Emerald's foal had arrived — a healthy, handsome colt whose conformation was the finest of any animal born at the Circle C. Had Wyatt been a drinking man, he would have toasted the foal's arrival with the finest libation available. Instead, he'd done something better and had offered a prayer of thanksgiving for the successful birth.

"So this is the latest addition to the Circle C."

Wyatt swiveled to stare at the doorway, not bothering to mask his surprise at the sight of Sam standing there, Caleb by his side. Though the two men had approached him — or, more precisely, Evelyn — together on Sunday, it had been years since they'd come to the ranch at the same time.

While Wyatt still counted both of them as friends, their childhood camaraderie had been sundered the day Caleb almost drowned. After that, since Caleb had refused whenever Wyatt suggested they do things as a trio, he'd stopped asking. Yet here they were, apparently united in their desire to see Emerald's foal.

"How'd you hear so soon?"

Caleb shrugged. "I'm surprised you didn't know that Pastor Coleman stopped by here a couple hours ago to officially welcome Evelyn and Polly to Mesquite Springs. It seems little Miss Polly is convinced this is the special pony you promised she could ride and wasted no time telling the reverend about it."

"And he wasted no time in spreading the story." Wyatt was sorry Polly had yet to ride one of the Circle C horses, but circumstances had not cooperated. When they returned from church on Sunday, a cold rain had been falling, leaving the paddocks too muddy for a pleasurable ride. By the time they'd dried, he'd been caught up in the ranch's problems, the latest being Emerald's delivery.

"You got that right. The man likes to talk." As Sam moved closer to the colt, his hand outstretched, Emerald flared her nostrils and whinnied.

"You'd better back off, Sam," Wyatt cautioned. "She's not ready for strangers to touch her son. She had a tough time. At one point, I was afraid for both of them."

"You should have sent for me." Caleb's voice was tinged with anger, or perhaps it was hurt. "I would have helped."

"Next time." Caleb would have to learn, but not on Emerald. "Did you arrange everything with your father?" They'd spoken briefly again after church on Sunday, with Caleb reporting that while he was eager to join the Circle C staff, his father was less enthusiastic.

"Yeah. He wasn't happy, but he finally agreed that I could work here three days a week. We settled on Monday, Wednesday, and Friday."

"Good."

"What's going on?" Sam's displeasure at not being part of the conversation was evident in his stiff posture.

"The Circle C is growing," Wyatt explained. "It's time to bring in someone new."

The look Sam gave Caleb was filled with disdain. "You two and your horses. They're fine to ride, but you wouldn't catch me

103

mucking out stalls and dealing with colic."

"Caleb's going to be doing his share of working with colicky horses, but he won't have to muck out stalls. Not often, anyway." Wyatt shared a conspiratorial smile with Caleb, confirming what they both knew: there were times when everyone was involved in every aspect of work on a ranch.

"Manual labor." Sam's expression left no doubt of his opinion. "I'm glad I don't have to get my hands dirty to earn a living."

Though Caleb seethed, Wyatt refused to take offense. "So long as it's honest work, I don't see anything wrong with raising horses, being a blacksmith, or sitting in an office and giving legal advice."

"That's not all I'm going to be doing."

When Caleb walked to the other end of the stables, Wyatt asked the question Sam expected. "What's going on?"

"Ken's planning to retire, and I'm planning to take his place."

"You're going to run for mayor?" Though he hadn't wanted the job himself, Wyatt had trouble picturing his friend in it. Sam was a fine attorney — everyone in Mesquite Springs agreed about that — but as an only child, he'd never had to share anything. Being mayor involved working with others, persuading rather than ordering them, and those were not things Sam did well. Perhaps he'd learn.

"That's the first step." Sam reached for Emerald's foal again, recoiling when the mare bared her teeth. "I figure that after a couple years as mayor, I can set my sights on the statehouse."

"I always knew you were ambitious." Not only that, but Sam had mapped out his future, which was something Wyatt had failed to do.

"There's nothing wrong with ambition. But the reason I came here today wasn't to tell you that I plan to take Ken's place. It was to buy a horse."

Caleb, who'd rejoined the conversation, let out an exaggerated sigh that made Wyatt suspect that one of the points of contention between his two friends was that Sam could afford multiple horses, while Caleb could not. "Another one? I thought you said three were enough."

"I did, but this is different. This would be a wedding gift for my bride."

"Your bride?" Caleb's face mirrored the astonishment Wyatt felt at the declaration.

"Who's the lucky lady?"

Sam smirked before he answered Wyatt's question. "I've had my eye on your sister, but she says she's not interested in getting married."

"She'll change her mind for the right man." Though Caleb's words could have been innocuous, the way he twisted his lips told Wyatt he intended them to irritate Sam.

Sam took the bait. "Are you saying I'm not the right man?" He clenched his fists and took a step toward Caleb. "You, the man who can't make up his mind what he wants to do with his life?"

It was up to Wyatt to avert a scuffle like the ones that had been all too common when Caleb and Sam had been schoolboys. They weren't boys any longer; they were grown men, and grown men ought to have better control over their emotions.

"Don't blame Caleb. It seems to me Dorothy's the one who said that." Wyatt kept his voice low and even, as if he were dealing with a frightened mare.

As he'd hoped, Sam's anger faded as quickly as it had been kindled. "You're right, and she was right too. Dorothy's not the right gal for me."

"Then who is?" Caleb asked the question before Wyatt could.

Sam's smirk returned. "Evelyn."

CHAPTER EIGHT

What a difference a week made. Evelyn smiled as she climbed into the wagon for the trip to Mesquite Springs. Last Friday she'd been unsure when and where she could finally stop running. Now she was confident that this growing Hill Country town would be her new home. Last week she had had only the vaguest idea of how she would support herself and Polly. Now she was on her way to inspect what might become her restaurant. Last week she'd felt as if she didn't have a friend in the world. Now she considered the Clarks not just friends but almost family. What a wonderful feeling that was.

"Cold or nervous?" Wyatt asked as they turned from the ranch road onto the one that led to Mesquite Springs.

The sun was high in the sky, and though a cool winter sun, it helped warm the air. Still, Evelyn had shivered. "A little nervous," she admitted. Part of that was caused by leaving Polly for the first time since the day of the fire.

Though Dorothy had volunteered to accompany them and entertain Polly while the adults discussed business, Isolde had convinced her to remain at home with Polly. To Evelyn's surprise, Polly had not protested, perhaps because Dorothy had promised her that they could spend the day making clothes for her doll. Still, Evelyn worried about the child who'd become more like a daughter than the sister she pretended she was.

She tried to smile, though she suspected it looked more like a grimace than a genuine smile. "I'm not sure what worries me more — that I'll like the building or that I won't."

Furrows formed between Wyatt's eyes as he considered her statement. "I understand the not liking part, but why would you worry that you *might* like it?"

"Because I might fail." And, if Evelyn failed, Polly would suffer. "It's true that I've cooked for two dozen orphans and the staff there, but I've never owned a restaurant."

Even though she'd helped her mother do everything from cooking and cleanup to taking and serving orders, Papa had never let her see the books, so she had no idea how much he'd paid for supplies or how he'd decided what they should charge for a meal. And offering a variety of dishes to customers was more complicated than serving a single one to the orphans. What would she do if she ran out of food before closing time?

"Stop worrying, Evelyn. I've only known you for a week, but I'm convinced you can do anything you set your mind to."

Evelyn wished she were as confident as Wyatt. What had seemed like a good idea when they'd first discussed it had become the source of seemingly endless concerns. What if no one came? What if they didn't like her food? What if she charged too little to cover her costs? What if Mr. Downey wouldn't rent to her? The questions had chased each other through her brain for days now, keeping her from sleeping and haunting her while she was awake.

"Radner's Place will be a success."

"Radner's Place?" Evelyn startled at the unfamiliar name. She'd been so lost in her own thoughts that she had almost missed what Wyatt had said.

The way he shrugged told her he believed the answer should be apparent. "I assumed you'd want to change the name and make it official that there's a new owner."

"Oh, of course." Radner, the name she'd

invented for herself along with a kinship to Polly. If she was going to succeed with her charade, she needed to remember the stories she'd told.

Feigning a lightness she did not feel, Evelyn said, "I'll change the name. It's just that Radner's Place sounds wrong. Maybe I'll call it Polly's Place." She laughed, trying to cover her discomfort, and hoped Wyatt did not sense how false her laughter was. "I think we're getting ahead of ourselves. We don't know whether I'll like the building and whether Mr. Downey will agree to becoming a partner."

Unfazed by her concerns, Wyatt tightened the reins as they descended a small hill. "We'll have the answers soon."

When they reached the center of Mesquite Springs, Wyatt hitched the horse in front of the empty building that had once been Foster's Place and escorted Evelyn to the mercantile next door. As they entered the store that Dorothy had told her was the largest in the county, Evelyn barely noticed the array of merchandise. Instead, her attention focused on the heavyset man who approached them.

From the time she'd been a child, Papa had taught her to assess people, to determine whether they were honest or whether they'd try to leave the restaurant without paying. Mr. Downey appeared to be in his midforties, his hazel eyes still bright, only a few threads of silver in his reddish-brown hair. Though the paunchy midsection hinted at a fondness for too much food, Evelyn saw no other signs of excess, and she felt herself begin to relax. She'd crossed the first hurdle. Her instincts told her the shopkeeper was an honest man and one who would make a good partner. If he agreed.

When Wyatt had finished the introductions, Mr. Downey nodded at Evelyn. "So you'd like to open a restaurant." The fact that he wasted no time on pleasantries was another point in his favor.

"Yes, sir. I would. I've heard that Mesquite Springs needs a restaurant, and I'm a passably good cook."

The man's laughter echoed through the room, surprising Evelyn as well as one of the customers who'd been inspecting the selection of ribbons. Laughter was not the response she'd expected.

"You're selling yourself short, Miss Radner. From what Wyatt tells me, you're an outstanding cook and just what the town needs." Mr. Downey patted the stomach that overflowed his pants. "I may not need any more food, but I'm sure looking forward to it."

Pulling a key from his pocket, he extended it to Wyatt. "Why don't you two have a look around? Take as long as you like. When you're ready, come back and we'll talk about terms."

Evelyn waited until they were outside before she said, "It sounds like he wants to make a deal." She'd been prepared to answer a host of questions about her qualifications and her plans. Instead, it seemed that Wyatt had paved the way.

"Didn't I tell you not to worry?"

Evelyn nodded, then focused her attention on what might become her place of business as well as her home. Though she had barely glanced at the former restaurant building when they'd entered town, not wanting to raise her expectations in case Mr. Downey did not appear to be trustworthy, she studied it now.

The windows were in dire need of washing, but they were generously proportioned, telling her that the dining room would have enough natural light to make it pleasant. The stone construction was reassuring. While fires were a constant worry in a kitchen, having the building itself made of limestone meant that even if one should occur, it would not be as disastrous as the fire that had engulfed the orphanage. And the front door with its cheerful blue paint seemed to be welcoming her. So far, everything confirmed Wyatt's assertion that there was no need to worry.

"Ready to go inside?" When Evelyn nodded, he unlocked the door and ushered her in.

Evelyn blinked, willing her eyes to adjust to the lower light, then caught her breath as she looked around. "This is more than I expected."

She counted quickly. Eight tables for four, three for two. The Fosters had obviously served more people than her parents had. She walked to the closest table, ran her hand over the back of one of the chairs, then brushed the dust from the table top. Only a few scratches marred the table's surface, and both it and the chairs seemed sturdily built. If the kitchen was equally well equipped, her initial expenses would be minimal.

"All this would need is a good cleaning."

Wyatt surveyed the room. "You might want to paint the walls while you have a chance. I remember Nancy Foster saying they needed freshening."

Nodding, Evelyn walked to the window

113

and fingered the curtains. "I'll probably replace these." The dust would wash out, but the print was too dark for a room with a northern exposure. "I wonder if I can find something the same shade of blue as the door."

As she'd expected, Wyatt appeared to have little interest in interior decorating, but he nodded in the direction of the mercantile. "Ask Ida Downey. Ma claims she can find anything."

"I'll do that." Evelyn almost laughed at her assumption that everything would proceed without a hitch. "I'm glad the building faces north. That way it won't be terribly hot during the summer."

"But the kitchen will be."

This time she did laugh. "Kitchens are hot, no matter which direction they face." The question was whether this one would meet her needs.

As she pushed the swinging door that led to the kitchen, Evelyn's smile widened. "This is perfect!" Larger than the one at the orphanage, the Fosters' kitchen boasted two stoves, both more modern than the one she'd cooked on for the last ten years. A good supply of pots and pans hung from a rack in the center of the room, and the adjacent pantry held a full complement of tableware as well as shelves for foodstuffs.

"Do you like it?" Wyatt asked when she'd completed her inspection.

Evelyn's heart sang with happiness. This was more — so much more — than she'd dared to hope for. "Yes, oh yes. I can picture myself rolling out piecrusts there." She pointed to a long counter.

"And resting your feet there." Wyatt gestured toward the corner where an easy chair with a matching footstool would provide a welcome break for a tired cook.

Evelyn couldn't help chuckling at the idea of sitting and wondered whether the Fosters had ever used the chair. It did not appear very worn. "I can tell you we didn't have one of those at the orphanage. There was never time to sit down." And, to the best of her knowledge, neither of her parents had had the luxury of sitting while their restaurant was open.

Wyatt slapped his hand against the chair cushion, then sneezed at the cloud of dust he'd created. "You'll need to make time to rest, or everything will suffer."

He sounded as if he spoke from experience, making Evelyn wonder if he ever took time off from raising and training horses. She knew that he'd worked on the Sabbath, saying that animals didn't know it was supposed to be a day of rest.

When Evelyn did not reply, he nodded toward the staircase. "Shall we see what the apartment looks like?"

She hesitated, suddenly uncomfortable. "Would you mind if I went alone?" Though Wyatt had been nothing but helpful, showing him the place where she might be sleeping seemed too personal.

"Of course not. I'll look around the dining room to see if we missed anything."

Evelyn climbed the stairs, anxious to discover whether the apartment was as well kept as the restaurant itself. It was. Consisting of three rooms, it had two bedrooms on the south side away from the street and a large sitting room with a table and four chairs in one corner on the north side. Though most apartments would have had a kitchen, there was no need for one here, not with the restaurant's kitchen downstairs.

She took a quick inventory. Other than needing to replace the blankets, since a family of mice seemed to have nibbled on the existing ones, there was little to be done to make this a home for her and Polly.

When Evelyn returned to the main floor, she found Wyatt waiting for her. "Well?"

"It's good. It's better than good. It's great. Polly will love having her own room."

Wyatt's smile said he was almost as pleased as she was. "Then all that's left is talking to Leonard."

More quickly than Evelyn had thought possible, they came to an agreement.

"Are there papers I need to sign?" she asked when they'd outlined the terms of the partnership.

Mr. Downey shook his head. "Sam Plaut will have my head for saying this, but I don't hold with all that legal mumbo jumbo. A handshake's good enough for me."

Evelyn took the hand he'd extended and shook it. "Thank you, Mr. Downey."

"It's Leonard." He gripped her hand tightly before releasing it. "Welcome to Mesquite Springs, partner."

CHAPTER NINE

Thunder. Lightning. Torrential rain. *Not again. Please, God, not again.* Her heart pounding, her hands clenched, Evelyn forced her eyes open as she struggled to escape the twilight between sleep and waking, between past and present. When Polly's even breathing registered, relief washed over Evelyn, anchoring her firmly in the present. She was at the Circle C, not at her parents' home in Gilmorton. She was in a bed, not under it. No one was chasing her. The pounding of heavy rain had wakened her, not screams and gunshots. She had nothing to fear.

Taking care not to waken the sleeping child, Evelyn sat up and breathed in deeply as she told herself there was a logical explanation for her terror. The combination of being in a restaurant after so many years of avoiding them and knowing that she would once again live over one, plus the sounds of the storm, must have triggered memories of the night her parents had been killed. What had wakened her had been a nightmare, nothing more.

Though her pulse had slowed, Evelyn knew she wouldn't fall back to sleep easily. The effects of nightmares could linger for hours. If she'd been at the orphanage, she would have baked a pie. She wouldn't do that here, but perhaps a cup of warm milk would soothe her. Isolde had given her free rein of the kitchen and wouldn't mind if she raided the icebox.

Moving as quietly as she could, Evelyn descended the stairs, trying to convince herself that everything would be fine. There was nothing to fear.

Wyatt sat up suddenly, unsure what had wakened him. As wind-driven rain rattled the windows, the last vestiges of sleep fled, and he reached for his clothes. Horses — at least his — were easily spooked by storms as violent as this one. He'd best check on them.

Within seconds he was dressed and carrying his boots down the stairs, lest the sound of his footsteps disturb the rest of the household. As he reached the first landing, he saw a glimmer of light under the kitchen

119

door. It appeared that someone else had been wakened by the storm.

"Is something wrong?"

Evelyn swiveled at the sound of his question, her eyes widening in what appeared to be momentary alarm. "The storm woke me." Though her voice was even, she acted more skittish than his foals. Perhaps it was because she wore her wrapper and slippers, and her hair was unbound. There was nothing indecent about it, but hadn't Ma told Dorothy that she should never go outside, even to use the outhouse, unless she was properly clad, lest the hired hands see her?

Evelyn raised an eyebrow as she looked at him. "It seems the storm disturbed you too." When Wyatt nodded, she gestured toward the pan that she had placed on the counter. "I was going to warm some milk. Would you like some?"

Wyatt wrinkled his nose. "Warm milk has never appealed to me. Now, if you were to offer hot chocolate . . ." He let his words trail off.

As he'd hoped, the suggestion made her smile. Distraction worked to calm horses, and it seemed to work equally well with Evelyn. "I can do that. Have a seat."

"I want to check on the horses. This is the first time Emerald's colt has experienced a

120

storm." He tugged on his boots and reached for the hat and jacket he'd hung on the hooks near the back door. "I should be back before the milk is warm."

Though he raced across the yard as quickly as he could, by the time he reached the stable, Wyatt's hat was dripping rain, and his jacket was drenched. Fortunately, Ebony was fast asleep next to his dam, and the other horses gave no sign of being fazed by the thunder and lightning. It seemed that only Wyatt and Evelyn had been bothered by the storm.

"Sorry about the mess," he said as he slung the dripping coat over a hook. In the few minutes he'd been gone, the kitchen had filled with the delicious aroma of chocolate.

"Water will dry." Evelyn wrapped a towel around the pot's handle and pulled it off the heat. "How are the animals?"

"Better than we were. The storm didn't seem to disturb them."

"I hate storms!"

It might have been his imagination that Evelyn's hand trembled as she poured the steaming liquid into two mugs, but perhaps it wasn't. Wyatt remembered the fear she'd shown when he found her under the wagon in another storm. At the time, he'd thought that fear was directed at him, but seeing how she reacted tonight made him think it might have been the storm itself that had terrified her. The thought was unexpectedly reassuring.

"I can't say that I'm fond of storms myself — I've seen them cause too much damage — but I can't complain about the one that brought you here."

To Wyatt's surprise, Evelyn's cheeks pinked. How odd! If he hadn't known better, he would have said she was acting like a young girl who'd never had a boy pay attention to her, but that couldn't be the case. A woman as lovely as Evelyn must have had her share of suitors. Not that Wyatt was a suitor. Far from it.

"I see you decided to indulge as well," he said as she took the seat across from him. He hoped small talk would distract him from thoughts of Evelyn and suitors.

"Warm milk sounded boring after you mentioned hot chocolate."

He took a sip, then another, savoring the delicious flavor. After eating the meals she'd prepared, Wyatt had had no doubt that Evelyn would create good hot chocolate, but this was beyond good. "This is extraordinary," he said as he reluctantly lowered the mug to the table. "It has more flavor than

I'm used to. What did you do?" Perhaps she grated more chocolate than Ma or Dorothy did.

As if she had read his thoughts, Evelyn shook her head. "It has the normal amount of chocolate, but I did add a bit of leftover coffee." She pointed to the pot still sitting on the counter. Ma must have had a cup after supper and hadn't bothered to empty the pot.

"Coffee?" Wyatt took another sip, trying to identify the distinctive flavor. "I don't taste it."

Those pretty blue eyes sparkled with amusement. "You aren't supposed to. A small amount of coffee enhances the chocolate flavor, just as a bit of sugar makes gravy tastier. That's why I always add coffee to my chocolate cakes and pies."

"And your hot chocolate."

"Yes."

Wyatt's mouth watered at the thought of chocolate pie. "The town of Mesquite Springs is in for a real treat with your cooking. Once folks taste your food, you'll have to start taking reservations."

Though her eyes lit with enthusiasm, it faded as quickly as it had been ignited, and Evelyn's expression betrayed her doubts. "You're more confident than I am."

Wyatt wondered why she was so hesitant. Admittedly, opening a restaurant was a major undertaking, but from what he'd seen, Evelyn had the necessary skills. Perhaps tonight's doubts were simply the aftermath of the storm.

"I'm confident because I know what the Fosters served and how much better your food is. You have a great future here."

"I hope you're right." Doubt still clouded Evelyn's eyes, and she fiddled with her cup rather than drink the delicious beverage. "It's so hard to know whether I made the right decision."

"I'm sure you have. Your dreams can come true here." Once again, Wyatt felt as if he were calming a nervous filly.

She was silent for a moment, apparently choosing her words. When she spoke, her reply surprised Wyatt. "I'm not sure I have any dreams left. I just want to keep Polly safe."

No dreams? Everyone had dreams, even Wyatt. And safe? It was understandable that Evelyn would have been fearful after seeing her home destroyed, but she and Polly were more than a hundred miles from the orphanage. They were safe here, so why was she afraid that something would happen to her sister?

Though Wyatt longed to ask, Evelyn's expression and the way she quickly offered him another cup of chocolate told him the subject was closed. For now.

"This is it, Polly. This is our new home." Evelyn twisted the key in the bright blue front door and pushed it open, ushering the child into the dining room. She smiled at the thought that this was another Friday. Recently, that seemed to be the most eventful day of the week.

A week ago, she'd reached an agreement with Leonard Downey. That had been followed by the storm that had disturbed both her and Wyatt. Though the moments of terror before she had realized that it was only a storm had been horrible, the time she and Wyatt had spent together had more than compensated for the fear she'd endured. Wyatt had managed to reassure her and had helped restore her belief that running a restaurant was a good idea.

The next day the real work had begun — cleaning, painting, laundering and repairing linens, ordering supplies. It had been exhausting but also exhilarating, and now Evelyn was reaping the benefits, because the restaurant was almost ready.

Though Isolde had urged her to stay on

the ranch at least for a week or two after she opened Polly's Place, Evelyn wanted to ease Polly into their new life. She'd decided that they would have supper here today, spend their first night in the apartment, and then work together on the final preparations. There wasn't much left to do, but Evelyn had left some easy tasks so that Polly could play a role in turning Foster's Place into Polly's Place.

The child didn't yet know about the new name. Painting the sign and telling her about it were the most important activities for tomorrow.

Polly blinked as they entered the dining room, then frowned. "What are all these tables for?"

Her question surprised Evelyn. "I told you that it's a restaurant. We're going to serve food to lots of people." Though they'd discussed Evelyn's plans multiple times, it seemed that either Polly hadn't understood or the reality of the dining room was more than she'd expected.

"Will I have to eat here?" The scowl that marred Polly's face more than her birthmark left no doubt of her opinion of that and reminded Evelyn that there was no way of predicting what would bother a child. Perhaps, though Evelyn saw no resemblance, the dining room reminded Polly of the orphanage. She'd told Evelyn more than once that she was glad they no longer lived there. Though grief continued to ambush Evelyn when she least expected it, Polly showed no signs of missing the other orphans.

"No, sweetie." Evelyn laid a reassuring hand on Polly's shoulder, then drew her close for a quick hug. "You and I have our own special table." When she pushed open the kitchen door, Evelyn pointed to the table and chairs that filled one corner of the room. "That's ours."

Apparently mollified, Polly looked around the kitchen, her eyes lighting at the sight of the two large cast iron stoves. "Two! My papa's house didn't have two stoves."

"The orphanage didn't, either, but we're lucky. We do."

"One for you and one for me."

Evelyn couldn't help laughing. "Maybe. Now, let me show you our apartment." She followed Polly up the stairs.

"There's a table here. I like this one." Polly ran to it and pulled out a chair, as if staking a claim. "I wanna eat here."

Though it meant more work, Evelyn nodded. "We can do that." It wouldn't be difficult to carry their food up on a tray, and if it made Polly happy, it was worth the effort.

Evelyn opened the door to the bedroom she'd decided would be Polly's. "Look. You have your own room. You won't have to share it with anyone." At the orphanage, only Evelyn and Mrs. Folger had had their own rooms. Polly had slept in the girls' dormitory, a medium-sized room that had been crowded with a dozen cots. At the Circle C, she and Evelyn had shared a room. Though Polly was not a difficult roommate, Evelyn was looking forward to having her privacy restored.

Polly gave the room a cursory glance. "I had my own room in my papa's house. It was bigger than this one."

This was twice in less than five minutes that Polly had spoken of her father. When she'd arrived at the orphanage, she had refused to say much, pressing her lips together as tightly as she could whenever someone asked about her family. Perhaps she was finally ready to talk.

"What was your papa's name?"

"Papa." Polly's expression said anyone should have known that.

"What about his other name? His last name."

As she had at the orphanage, Polly shook her head violently. "I can't tell you. I can't never tell nobody."

The poor grammar made Evelyn suspect that the child was quoting someone, and the unmistakable fear in her eyes warned Evelyn not to pursue the subject, even though her curiosity was piqued.

One time soon after she'd arrived at the orphanage, Polly had mentioned that her father had grown cotton. Though Logansville was surrounded by large plantations, Evelyn had assumed that Polly's father was one of the small farmers who eked out an existence by planting a few acres. Perhaps she'd been wrong. It was unlikely that a subsistence farmer's home would have had a large bedchamber for a child.

This was not the time to press for more details. Instead, Evelyn smiled brightly. "Now you have a room of your own again."

But that night Polly crept into Evelyn's room and tugged on her arm. "Can I sleep here? I miss the ranch."

Evelyn patted the pillow next to hers and smiled when the girl climbed into bed. Within minutes, Polly was asleep, leaving Evelyn to her thoughts. Unlike Polly, she wouldn't say that she missed the ranch, but there were things she missed. Like the walks she had taken with Wyatt.

It had been only a week since the storm,

but sharing hot chocolate seemed to have drawn them closer, and they'd fallen into the habit of spending time together after supper. Some days they'd checked on the horses. Others they'd simply strolled across the pasture. What the evenings had in common was that she and Wyatt had talked about everything and nothing, and those talks had become the highlights of Evelyn's days.

She missed them. And, if she were being honest, she missed Wyatt. Evelyn couldn't explain why other than that she'd never had a friend like him.

"The ranch seems empty without Evelyn and Polly." Dorothy split a square of cornbread and buttered it, then frowned as she took a bite.

Wyatt tried not to smile at her reaction to their mother's cooking. While the cornbread was good, it could not compare to Evelyn's.

"It does," he agreed. Though it had been less than twenty-four hours since they'd left, somehow it felt like forever since he'd seen Evelyn smile and heard Polly giggle. Their absence shouldn't have made such a big difference. After all, they'd only been on the ranch for two weeks, but now that they were gone, he felt as if a huge chasm had suddenly appeared in his life.

"I offered to help them today." Ma ate the cornbread with gusto. "Evelyn was planning to paint the sign with the restaurant's new name, and I thought I could help. It didn't make sense to me that she wanted to do it alone, but the girl is independent."

Wyatt knew that from their conversations. Though she was willing to help others, Evelyn was less willing to admit that she needed assistance. The fact that she'd let Ma and Dorothy do all the sewing for the restaurant was a measure of how poor her skills were.

"I said I'd help get everything ready, but she refused me too." Dorothy's expression was just short of a pout, telling Wyatt how miffed she was that her offer hadn't been accepted.

"She's not only independent. She's stubborn." But so was he. Like Evelyn, when Wyatt wanted something, he wouldn't let anyone get in his way. And he wanted something now.

He waited until he'd finished the stew, then rose from the table. "I'm going into town," he announced. "I want to talk to Caleb." Admittedly, the man had been here yesterday and there was nothing Wyatt needed to discuss with him, but it was the only excuse he could think of. In case Ma or Dorothy thought to check, he'd go to the blacksmith's shop, and if he just so happened to stop by the restaurant, he could claim that he wanted to reassure his mother and sister.

As Wyatt strode from the kitchen, the sound of laughter followed him.

CHAPTER TEN

"I don't know why you want to go there today of all days. It's morbid."

His wife's sharp words made Rufus Bauman's perfectly scrambled eggs lose their flavor. Though he was tempted to ignore her, he knew that would have no effect. Instead, he said as mildly as he could, "You visit our son's grave. Why shouldn't I?"

"That's different," Winnie insisted. "I go on his birthday. Today's the day he . . ." She pressed her lips together rather than complete the sentence.

"Died." As painful as the memory was, Rufus wouldn't deny what had happened. "You can't ignore the fact that Isaac is dead or how he died."

He rose from the table, his appetite for what had been a tasty breakfast killed by his wife's continued unwillingness to accept the past. Rufus could forgive many things, but even though it had been ten years, he could

133

not forgive Winnie's refusal to be with their son when he drew his last breath. The sheriff, the hangman, and Rufus had been the only ones to witness Isaac's final minutes on Earth.

Winnie let out an exasperated sigh. "I don't suppose I can talk you out of going."

"No, Winnie, you can't. This is something I have to do." Rufus grabbed his hat and paused at the door. "It's something I want to do."

"At least you don't go to that girl's grave." There was a hint of satisfaction in his wife's voice.

Perhaps he should have kept his mouth shut, but Rufus did not. "I would if she had one."

No one in Logansville had seemed too disturbed by the fire that had killed so many. Someone had erected a simple cross with the matron's name followed by "Twenty-Two Orphans," obviously not believing them important enough to have their names listed.

Winnie's eyes widened in shock. "You went there? Oh, Rufus, when will you learn? That girl is not your responsibility."

But she was. Deep in his heart, he knew that. "I can't help believing that if we'd taken her in, she would still be alive."

134

"Harrumph!"

Rufus strode into the parlor and grabbed his Bible. Each time he visited Isaac's grave, he read aloud the verses that gave him comfort. While he knew Isaac couldn't hear him, the sound of words that had been spoken more than a thousand years before eased some of the pain in Rufus's heart.

" 'In my father's house are many mansions.' " The words from John 14:2 brought tears to Rufus's eyes as he knelt by his son's grave, but the ones that brought peace to his heart were Jesus's words from the cross, "Father, forgive them; for they know not what they do." Rufus had turned to Luke 23:34 so often that the page was dog-eared. He wanted — oh, how he wanted — to believe that God had forgiven Isaac for what he'd done, because if there was one thing he was certain of, it was that Isaac had not known what he was doing.

Evelyn took another sip of coffee, then turned back to her work. Though the sun had not yet risen, she had already been in the kitchen for an hour, getting everything ready for opening day. If all went well, in a month or so she would offer both breakfast and the midday meal with a full bill of fare six days a week, but she'd decided to start simply. For the first few weeks, her plan was to be open from eleven to two and to serve a choice of only two dishes. For today, she'd chosen Wyatt's favorite, chicken fricassee, and a beef pot roast surrounded by carrots, potatoes, and onions. And, even though Isolde had claimed that a single dessert would be sufficient, Evelyn had decided to offer both chocolate cake — again, a favorite of Wyatt's — and oatmeal pecan pie.

"I wanna help make the pie." Polly yawned widely as she entered the kitchen, wearing her school dress with her Sunday shoes. Though Evelyn had informed her that her first day at school was not sufficient reason for good shoes, Polly had obviously hoped that Evelyn would be so busy that she wouldn't notice.

"I wanna roll out the crust."

Though Evelyn hated to disappoint the child again, today's crusts needed to be perfect, and that was something a six-year-old could not accomplish. "Maybe next time."

Polly stamped her foot, then stopped when she seemed to realize that would draw Evelyn's attention to the forbidden shoes. "You shoulda waked me. I coulda helped."

Nodding her agreement, Evelyn set a bowl of shelled pecans on the table. "You can still help me. I need you to make sure there are no shells in the nuts. That's a very important job."

Checking the nuts had been one of Evelyn's responsibilities at her parents' restaurant. And, though it had been years since then, she still remembered how important it had made her feel to be part of creating their most famous dish. While Mama's roast chicken and her fricassee had been popular, folks would come from miles around for a slice of Emmeline Radcliffe's oatmeal pecan pie. That was the reason Evelyn had made that pie today: she'd wanted to honor her parents' memory.

"Okay." Polly began sorting the nuts while Evelyn mixed the eggs, molasses, and other ingredients for the filling.

"Look!" Excitement filled Polly's voice. "I found one!" She held up a large piece of pecan shell, then carefully placed it on the table next to the bowl.

"It's a good thing you were here to help me." Evelyn smiled at the child who'd become so dear to her. Evelyn had deliberately left the shell in the bowl, hoping that would make Polly feel useful. "We wouldn't want someone to bite into a shell, would we?"

"No, ma'am."

Evelyn looked at Polly's shoes. The first day in a new school was an important one, but so was learning to obey. "It's time for you to change your shoes. Come back downstairs as soon as you've done that. We're going to eat breakfast here so I can watch the pies. Then I'll walk you to school."

"I don't wanna eat here, and I don't wanna go to school." This wasn't the first time Polly had insisted that she'd rather stay and work at the restaurant, but like the shoes, it wasn't negotiable.

"Miss Geist is being very kind and will bring you home for lunch so you can see what's happening at Polly's Place." Yesterday after church Evelyn had arranged Polly's schedule with the woman who'd been Mesquite Springs's schoolteacher for three decades.

"Polly's Place!" As Evelyn had hoped, the mention of the restaurant's name had distracted the child. With one of the mercurial changes of mood that seemed so common for her, Polly gave Evelyn a wide grin. "I bet nobody else at school has their very own restaurant."

"Probably not, but you won't know for sure until you ask them."

Polly tipped her head to one side, considering. "Then I gotta go to school."

Evelyn smiled. One problem solved.

It was ten minutes to eleven, ten minutes until Polly's Place opened for its first meal, and the butterflies that had filled Evelyn's stomach were beating their wings with more force than when she beat whipped cream. As planned, Dorothy had arrived at nine to set the tables and help with the final preparations. Now everything was ready.

"I hope we have some customers." Evelyn cut the last of the biscuits and placed it on a baking sheet, ready to slide into the oven.

Dorothy, who'd just finished setting glasses and silverware on each of the tables, laughed. "They're already lined up outside the door. It looks like half of Mesquite Springs wants to see how your cooking compares to the Fosters'."

"Really?"

"Really."

"Then let's open early." Evelyn untied her apron and walked to the front door. Even before she opened it, she could hear the murmur of voices and knew that while Dorothy may have exaggerated the number of customers, there would be enough to fill the restaurant at least once. Still, Evelyn was not prepared for the sight of the man and woman who stood at the head of the line.

"Welcome to Polly's Place." The greeting she called out was meant for everyone who was waiting. She addressed the man and woman more softly. "I didn't expect you."

Isolde kept a firm grip on her companion's arm. "You didn't think we'd miss your big day, did you? My son wanted to be your first customer."

"But being a gentleman, I'll let Ma enter first." Wyatt tipped his hat in greeting. "Don't think I'm rude if I eat fast. I promised to get back to the ranch so Caleb could come." He looked back at the line of people waiting to be greeted. "He won't be happy that Sam got here before him."

Evelyn kept a smile fixed on her face. The two men had made a point of talking to her after church each Sunday, even though she'd done nothing to encourage them. Wyatt must have sensed her discomfort with their attention, because although Caleb was now working at the Circle C three days a week, he did not take his meals with the family. As a result, even while she'd lived there, Evelyn had rarely encountered him.

"Thanks for the warning," she said softly before she turned to her next customer.

"Let me show you to a table." Dorothy's

clear voice carried as she escorted her mother and brother toward one of the tables by the window.

When Evelyn heard Wyatt say, "We'll take that one," she glanced around to see which he'd chosen. Instead of a prime location with a view of the street, he was pointing to the least desirable table, the one nearest the kitchen.

"Why do you want that one?" Dorothy asked.

When Wyatt said nothing, Isolde laughed. "It's closest to the cook."

Trying to ignore the flush that rose to her cheeks, Evelyn continued greeting guests until the dining room was filled. "We'll be with you as soon as we can," she said to the people who were still waiting to enter Polly's Place. Evelyn had thought Isolde was overly optimistic when she suggested placing a bench in front of the building for those who had to wait and had never expected to need it. But she did. At least today.

She moved to the center of the dining room to list the food choices, then returned to the kitchen to begin plating the meals while Dorothy took orders.

"Are you certain you didn't make a mistake?" she asked Dorothy five minutes later. "That's one more meal than we have customers."

"That's because my brother wanted to try everything. I know he'll have both desserts too."

"He'll get indigestion if he eats all that, especially if he rushes."

Dorothy shrugged. "Trust me. I've seen him eat more, especially if it's something he likes. And Wyatt definitely likes your cooking."

So did the other customers. While everyone was eating, Evelyn returned to the dining room to speak to each person. That was something she had learned from her parents, a simple act that made people feel as if they were guests rather than merely customers.

"I hope you're enjoying your meal."

While the man seated opposite him did nothing more than nod, Sam rose and smiled at her. "It's the best food I ever ate. Wyatt was right about that." Sam gestured toward his now-empty plate. "I feel like the luckiest man in Mesquite Springs. No one else has such a short walk to the best meal in town."

Sam turned slightly, as if to remind Evelyn that his office was directly across the street from Polly's Place. "My parents told me that was a good location for my office, and they were right. There are days when it feels like my sanctuary, and now that you're only a minute away, I may even move into the upstairs apartment." Without waiting for her response, he said, "Don't be surprised if you see me here every day. The food is good, and the scenery is even better."

The wink Sam gave her told Evelyn that was meant to be a compliment, so she acknowledged it with a simple nod. Dorothy had warned her that Sam's parents were reported to be pressuring him to marry, and now that he was running for mayor, the pressure would only increase. Mesquite Springs, it seemed, preferred its mayors to be family men, and according to Dorothy, Evelyn was a likely candidate for Mrs. Mayor.

Sam might view her as a practical solution, but Evelyn had no intention of marrying a man simply to further his political aspirations. When she married — if she married — it would be for love.

"I'm glad you liked the roast," she said, her tone as businesslike as she could make it. "You might like the oatmeal pecan pie for dessert. It goes well with the roast."

Though the other man at the table chuckled as if amused by the exchange, Sam's gaze rested on Evelyn's lips. "I have a deep appreciation for sweet things." Another wink punctuated his sentence.

Evelyn had had enough of his winks. "Excellent. I'll have Dorothy bring you a piece."

"Is something wrong?" Dorothy asked when Evelyn returned to the kitchen. "You look a bit flushed."

"Nothing I can't handle." She reached for one of the oatmeal pecan pies and a plate.

Dorothy studied her for a moment, perhaps noting that she sliced the pie with more force than necessary. "Let me guess. Sam was being charming."

"Is that what you call it?" Evelyn had not been charmed.

"He's considered a good catch."

"But I'm not hunting."

Dorothy shrugged as she placed the plate on the tray with the other meals she was prepared to deliver. "Neither am I. I have more important things to do, like" — she paused for a second — "serve pie."

Evelyn couldn't help laughing at Dorothy's response, and as she did, she realized how grateful she was that it was this woman and not a stranger who was helping her. Not only did they work well together, but Dorothy provided a different and welcome perspective on the town and its inhabitants. Even more importantly, she was quickly becoming both a friend and confidante, filling a spot deep inside Evelyn that she hadn't known existed. How wonderful. Sam's unwelcome attentions were of no importance when compared to her friendship with Dorothy.

There were no lulls between customers, and by the time Caleb arrived Evelyn was so tired that she was counting the minutes until she could turn the sign to "closed." Despite her fatigue, she continued to greet each customer.

"Don't tell my ma, but these biscuits sure beat hers." Caleb was as complimentary as the other diners had been. "Once my pa gets a taste of 'em, I can just about guarantee you'll have another regular customer."

Though her feet ached, Evelyn's smile was genuine. "We'd welcome him."

Caleb feigned distress as he spread jam on another biscuit. "What about me? Would you welcome me every day?"

"Of course. Customers are always welcome."

"What about friends?"

"Those too." But Caleb wasn't a friend. Not yet. Perhaps never. Of all the men who'd come in today, only Wyatt deserved that title.

Chapter Eleven

"You need to go." Dorothy looked up from the dishes she was washing, her expression stern. "The Downeys will be insulted if you don't."

"I know you're right." Not only was it common courtesy to accept the invitation, but it would be a way to acknowledge how much Evelyn owed to Ida and Leonard. Leonard had proven to be the perfect partner, never interfering in the running of Polly's Place and providing a substantial discount on the items she ordered for the restaurant.

Though his wife wasn't technically Evelyn's partner, Ida championed the business, encouraging her customers to sample Evelyn's cooking, even promising to pay for their meal if by some chance they did not enjoy it. To the best of Evelyn's knowledge, no one had taken her up on the offer.

No doubt about it. She owed the Downeys

more than she could ever repay. She ought to accept the invitation gratefully, and yet . . .

"It's just that . . ." Evelyn let her words trail off, unwilling to admit the reason for her reluctance to attend what Dorothy claimed was the highlight of winters in Mesquite Springs.

Dorothy rinsed a plate and handed it to her. "Didn't you say you wanted to see what the inside of the mansion looks like?"

Evelyn nodded. Though she passed what was the town's largest and grandest home every day when she took Polly to school, Evelyn had not yet seen the interior.

Dorothy continued, laying out her arguments as carefully as a prosecuting attorney and making Evelyn wonder whether she'd learned that from Sam. The man had lived up to his promise and was an almost daily diner.

"Are you worried that Sam will try to monopolize you?"

Evelyn shook her head. "He and I've come to an understanding." At least she thought they had. "He tries flattery; I ignore it."

"Then it must be clothes. If you're worried about what to wear, don't be. Even before the invitations went out, Ma decided you needed a party dress. She found a

148

length of green poplin that she says will be perfect and has already started cutting it out."

Once again, Isolde was overwhelming Evelyn with her generosity. Thanks to her, Evelyn had a wardrobe that would make any woman proud and one that cost very little. Isolde would allow Evelyn to pay for nothing more than the materials, claiming that the food Evelyn sent home with Dorothy paid for the effort she expended. "It's not clothes."

Dorothy pursed her lips as she scrubbed the last pan. "Surely you don't object on moral grounds. Lent doesn't start until the following Wednesday, so there's no reason we shouldn't enjoy an evening of music and dancing."

"Yes, there is." As embarrassing as it was, Evelyn had no choice but to admit her ignorance. "I can't dance."

"We need to help her."

Wyatt had known Dorothy had an ulterior motive when she insisted on accompanying him on his nightly check on the horses, and he'd assumed that her plea for help would involve something unpleasant. It did not. Of course, that was something he would never admit to his sister. If Dorothy knew that the object of her concern was rarely far from Wyatt's thoughts, she'd subject him to merciless teasing.

He raised an eyebrow and willed his face to look as if he'd just eaten a piece of lemon rind. "The way you explained it, there's no 'we.' You said *I* need to teach Evelyn to polka. What are you doing?"

"I've already done most of it." Dorothy gave him one of those superior looks that she'd perfected over the last year. "I convinced Mrs. Downey to let us practice in their parlor, and I'll play the piano."

Wyatt couldn't fault his sister's logic. The Downeys were the only people in town with both a piano and enough space for a dance like the polka.

"So all I have to do is dance with Evelyn."

"That's it. I've shown her the steps, and she said she and Polly were practicing them, but that's not enough. She needs music and a partner."

"What's this about Polly?" Wyatt couldn't resist teasing his sister. "Don't tell me you expect me to teach her too."

"Of course not. You know the children are asleep by the time the dancing begins."

His lips curved into a wry smile. "We weren't." One of his happiest memories of the time before Pa was killed was sneaking

150

from the Downeys' playroom to watch the grown-ups dance. The image of his parents laughing and looking at each other with obvious love was one he hoped would never fade.

When he thought of marriage — and he had to admit that the thought had crossed his mind more than occasionally ever since Evelyn had come to Mesquite Springs, not that there was any connection, of course — he knew that he would not settle for anything less than that kind of love.

"True. We stayed up way too late those nights and hoped no one noticed. I wonder if they did and just didn't care." Dorothy wrinkled her nose. "You were trying to distract me, weren't you? It won't work. I'm not going to give up until you agree. You'll do it, won't you? You'll teach Evelyn the polka."

"All right." Wyatt feigned reluctance, hoping his sister had no idea of how his pulse raced at the prospect. There were many things little sisters did not need to know, and that was one of them.

Evelyn took a deep breath, trying to calm nerves that were as jittery as if she'd just drunk a full pot of coffee. It wasn't simply being in the most elaborate home she'd ever entered. The parlor where the party would be held was twice the size of the one at the orphanage, even though that had been designed for more than twenty-five people while only three lived here.

The sight of the elegant draperies, the polished oak floor, and the beautifully carved furniture transported Evelyn to a world she'd thought existed only in story-books. That Leonard and Ida Downey, who were as unpretentious as anyone she'd met, lived here amazed her. Mrs. Folger would probably have scoffed at the house, calling it ostentatious, but Evelyn found it beautiful, albeit a bit overwhelming.

The sense that she was an interloper in a dream wasn't the reason for her nerves being on edge. The reason was standing only a few feet away from her, a smile on his face.

"Ready?" Wyatt asked.

"As ready as I'll ever be." Though they were only practicing, and practice by its very nature involved making mistakes, Evelyn said a silent prayer that she wouldn't embarrass herself . . . or him. It was one thing to dance with Polly, quite another to even consider dancing with a man, a very attractive man. Somehow the elegant surroundings enhanced Wyatt's rugged good looks, making him seem even more handsome than he did elsewhere.

He nodded, then fixed his gaze back on Evelyn. Though his expression was serious, the glint in Wyatt's eyes seemed to promise that this would be fun. "Give me your right hand."

As he clasped it in his left hand, the warmth of his palm sent tremors up her arm and left her slightly lightheaded. How silly. She'd never been one to swoon. Of course, there had been no swoon-worthy men at the orphanage.

Seemingly unaware of her reaction, Wyatt continued to prompt her. "Now put your left hand on my shoulder."

Evelyn complied, hoping her face didn't reflect her surprise at how firm his muscles were or how right it felt to be touching him this way. "And now I put my other hand here," he said as he laid it on her left shoulder blade.

Though there was nothing improper about the pose, Evelyn wished no one was watching. She could only hope Dorothy didn't realize how being this close to Wyatt was affecting her. Their hands had touched occasionally when they'd walked around the ranch, but that had been different. Those touches had been accidents. This was deliberate, and it felt oh, so good.

"We're ready." Wyatt raised their clasped hands so that they were at the height of Evelyn's shoulders.

"Don't forget. It's right, left, right, hop, then left, right, left, hop," Dorothy said as she straightened the sheet music.

Though she'd practiced the steps countless times, right now Evelyn wasn't certain she could remember her own name. Being close enough to Wyatt to notice that his breath smelled like the peach cobbler Mrs. Downey had insisted they all taste was turning Evelyn's brain to mush, and that curious feeling of lightheadedness had not disappeared.

"I'll start slowly." Dorothy placed her hands on the keyboard and began.

Though the music sounded odd when played at half speed, Evelyn appreciated the slower pace. It was easy enough to step and hop with Polly at home, but everything was different when there was music playing and she was being held in Wyatt's arms. Though she ought to be counting beats, Evelyn found herself watching the way his lips curved and how a hint of a dimple formed in his cheek when he smiled.

"Just relax and let me lead," he whispered.

And she did. After a few minutes, once Evelyn stopped stumbling and the steps became instinctive, Dorothy played the polka the way Strauss had intended it.

Perhaps it was the days of practice. Perhaps it was Wyatt's skillful leading. Evelyn didn't know, and she didn't care. What mattered was that she was dancing with a man who made her feel both graceful and beautiful, though she knew she was neither. Wyatt, her friend Wyatt, was a wonderful man.

The dance was an energetic one, but even though Evelyn was out of breath by the time it ended, she found herself wishing the music would go on forever. There would never again be a moment like this one. There would never again be another first dance.

Her heart pounding, Evelyn looked up at Wyatt, hoping he'd found some enjoyment in the dance. Her eyes met his, and for a second, she almost forgot to breathe, for the intensity of his gaze mirrored her reaction to the time they'd spent together.

"That was fun," she murmured.

"Yes, it was."

"You're the best dancer in Mesquite Springs."

Wyatt almost laughed at the compliment, coming as it did from Ida Downey. Everyone in Mesquite Springs knew she operated on the premise that honey attracted more flies than vinegar and did her best to make customers at the mercantile feel as welcome as guests in her home. When she hosted a party, her goal seemed to be to make each guest feel that he was the guest of honor.

"Thank you, Ida, but we both know that you're the one who's light on her feet." Ida was an accomplished dancer and followed Wyatt's lead effortlessly, unlike Evelyn, who still hesitated a bit, despite their practice session.

"I've had decades of practice." Ida looked around the room, as if to assure herself that her guests were enjoying the party. "Evelyn doesn't seem to be lacking for partners. You disappointed me, though. I thought you'd ask her to save the first and last dance for you."

The way she said it told Wyatt there must be some significance to those particular dances. He'd planned to be Evelyn's partner for the first — simply to ease her nervousness, of course — but Sam had snagged her for that one, and Caleb had demanded the second. Since then, both men had danced with her twice more, while Wyatt had shared only one polka with her.

There was no reason for him to be counting the number of times Evelyn had danced

156

with other men. There was no reason for him to care. After all, it wasn't as if he had any intention of courting her. The reason he noticed — the only reason — was that he'd enjoyed his dance with Evelyn more than those he'd shared with anyone else. Still, Ida's comment sparked a competitive nerve deep inside him. Foolish as it might be, he resolved then and there that neither Caleb nor Sam would have the final dance with Evelyn.

"I'll take your advice under consideration."

Ida's laugh was light and merry, making her sound more like a young girl than a matron. "You're starting to talk like Sam. And, speaking of Sam, Leonard and I both think you'd be a better mayor. When are you going to announce that you're running?"

"I'm not."

She made no attempt to hide her disappointment. "You should. You're just what Mesquite Springs needs."

But being mayor wasn't what Wyatt needed. The only thing he needed right now was another dance with Evelyn.

As soon as the dance ended, he turned and, spotting the object of his thoughts approaching the refreshment table, he headed

157

in that direction. Though he told himself it was ridiculous, somehow being her partner for the final dance felt like the most important thing in the world.

Wyatt knew he lacked Sam's polished delivery, but he'd find a clever way to ask Evelyn, some pretty words that would convince her to be his partner. But when he reached her side, the pretty words evaporated and Wyatt blurted out the ones that had bounced through his head. "May I have the last dance?"

Evelyn's eyes widened, and for a moment Wyatt feared that his blunt approach would result in a refusal. Hadn't he learned anything from his horses? He wouldn't have demanded something of a skittish colt without first calming it, but he'd given Evelyn no such consideration.

She was silent for a moment, and Wyatt felt his pulse begin to race. This was silly. It was only a dance. And yet it seemed like more than that. At last, Evelyn smiled.

"Yes, of course."

Exultation swept through him. This was the way he felt when he heard that one of his horses won its first race. The same pride and sense of having accomplished something special that buoyed him on those days flowed through Wyatt's veins. A dance, even the last dance, shouldn't have the same importance. It shouldn't make him want to act like a victor, shouting his triumph from the rooftops, and yet it did.

Silly, Wyatt. Silly.

Basil Marlow crumpled the sheet of paper and hurled it across the room, muttering an oath. No matter how many times he added the numbers, the result was always the same. The plantation's expenses were greater than its income.

He strode to the window and stared out at the beautifully landscaped grounds, the terraced gardens that led to the ridiculously expensive fountain that Bart had had imported from Italy simply because Miriam had said she loved fountains, and the flower beds whose carefully clipped shrubs demanded the full-time attention of a dozen slaves. This was the estate he'd wanted more than anything on Earth. It wasn't supposed to cost so much to maintain.

With another oath, he returned to the desk and studied the ledgers once more. Bart had never been one to brag, but when Basil had pressed him, he'd shown him these ledgers a year ago. At the time, Marlow Acres had been turning a good profit, a fact that had caused Basil's stomach to roil.

159

Bart had everything. He always had, while Basil had been second best.

"Why can't you be like your brother?"

Though it had been years since his father had shouted the hateful words, they still echoed in Basil's brain. He couldn't be like Bart. No matter how hard he tried, he hadn't been able to do the things Bart did, and he'd stopped trying.

"It's a shame about the birthmark." He'd heard the women clucking when they'd thought he wouldn't overhear. "At least when his beard starts to grow, it'll hide it."

A beard would have covered the red mark that everyone found so unsightly, but Bart had a beard. If Basil let his grow, he would look like his brother, and that was unthinkable.

He'd kept his face clean-shaven. He'd endured the pitying looks and the cruel comments. He'd pretended that he cared about Bart. And he'd made his plans.

The plantation was beautiful, profitable, and the envy of the county. From the time their father had established it, it had been the local showcase, and under Bart's stewardship, its fame had only increased. There had been no reason to think that anything would change. But it had.

Basil closed his eyes at the memory of his

brother sitting in this same chair, telling him that keeping Marlow Acres running smoothly wasn't an easy task. "Running a plantation is more than a full-time job," his brother had claimed. "It demands every ounce of energy a man possesses."

Basil hadn't believed him. Everyone knew that the slaves were the ones who did the work, but Bart had countered his objection with the smile that had always enraged him, the one that reminded him that Bart was the older brother.

"The slaves do the physical labor," he'd said, "but there's much more to a successful cotton crop than just planting and picking."

Basil hadn't known what Bart meant, and that superior smile had kept him from asking. He'd figured that if it wasn't simple, Bart would have kept notes of all that he'd done, but he hadn't. Now it was too late to ask his brother, and he sure as shooting wouldn't ask any of the other plantation owners. No matter what happened, he would not let anyone know that his boasts of increasing profits weren't true.

Slamming the ledger closed, Basil rose and poured himself a drink. So what if it was only ten o'clock. Whiskey was good at any time of the day. By the time he'd downed half the glass, reassuring warmth filled his stomach. Good old whiskey. There were no problems too big for it to solve. Whiskey and horses were what was important in life, not bolls of cotton.

Grinning at the reminder, Basil pulled out the small book that served as his personal ledger. Yes, indeed. This was what was important. He didn't need the plantation when he had his horses. Everyone knew they were the fastest in this part of Texas, maybe even in the whole state. Others tried, but no one had been able to beat them.

He traced his finger over the result of the most recent bets, his grin widening when he realized that the money he'd won last weekend was more than enough to make up for the plantation's shortfall.

Forget cotton. Horses would make Basil Marlow's name the envy of everyone in the Lone Star State.

CHAPTER TWELVE

"Sundays are the bestest days," Polly announced as she slid to the center of the wagon seat and wrapped her hands around Evelyn's arm. Though the child had not been overly demonstrative when she'd first come to the orphanage, since they'd arrived in Mesquite Springs, she had seemed to crave physical contact with Evelyn. Now, as they left the livery and headed toward the Circle C, she was snuggled next to Evelyn.

"Why do you say that? I thought you liked school and spending Saturdays at Polly's Place."

Polly's initial apprehension over school had vanished, replaced by the excitement of new playmates, and though she occasionally grumbled about not being able to help in the restaurant during the school week, she bubbled with enthusiasm each Saturday, announcing to anyone who'd listen that she was Polly and this was her restaurant.

Evelyn had given the child the same responsibility she'd had at the same age, carrying plates of food that would not easily spill to customers, and had been pleased by how well she'd handled that.

"Oh, I do like them," Polly agreed, "but Sundays we get to see the horses and Mr. Wyatt. I like 'em bestest. Don't you?" She looked up, her expression solemn.

Though Evelyn wasn't certain whether the question referred to the horses or Wyatt, it didn't matter. Like Polly, she liked them both, although she might not have used the word *bestest.*

"Yes, I do like them." And, for her sake as well as Polly's, she was grateful that Isolde had insisted they share Sunday dinners at the ranch. Not having to cook and being surrounded by friends made it a welcome respite from the work week.

"What's your favoritest day?" Polly asked as they crested the hill on the east end of town.

Evelyn had no need to ponder that question. "Saturday."

"How come?" Polly paused for a second before a wide grin split her face. "Oh, I know. It's 'cuz I help you then."

"That's right." Saturdays were always busy. After the first week, Evelyn had decided to serve breakfast on Saturday, reasoning that some of the people from outlying ranches who came into town to shop left home so early that they were hungry again by the time they reached Mesquite Springs. Then there were others, including Wyatt, who came because they wanted a change of fare. Each week Evelyn offered a different variety of pancakes in addition to oatmeal and what had become her most popular item: cinnamon rolls.

Her smile faded as she remembered what had happened yesterday morning.

"Are you sure you won't sell me the whole panful?" Caleb had asked when he'd eaten the two rolls he'd ordered. Unlike Wyatt, who was there each Saturday, this was the first time Caleb had come to the restaurant for breakfast.

"I'm sorry, but I need to save some for other customers."

Sam, who'd reluctantly taken a seat at the same table when Evelyn had explained that it was either share a table with Caleb or wait half an hour, nodded. "I told you she wouldn't agree."

He gave Evelyn the same bright smile that she had seen him bestow on customers when he told them he was running for mayor and hoped they'd give him their votes. "Not only are you a wonderful cook, but you're also a shrewd businesswoman. You don't want to disappoint other customers just to make one man happy." The look he flashed at Caleb left no doubt that Sam did not consider him worthy of special treatment.

He turned back to Evelyn, his smile once again firmly in place. "These are the best rolls I've ever tasted. No question about that, but it seems a shame that someone as pretty and as smart as you is burning her fingers to make food for strangers." He touched her hand, pointing to the inflamed spot where she'd bumped against a hot pan.

Evelyn pulled her hand away. She could handle compliments, even when she sensed that they were little more than flattery, but it was unseemly for a man to touch her, particularly here in public. Choosing to address the second part of Sam's statement, she made a show of looking around the dining room. "I don't see any strangers here. These are friends and neighbors."

"But not family. You ought to be cooking for a husband and children of your own."

Caleb shook his head. "If she did, you wouldn't get any at all."

"How do you figure that?"

This time Caleb smiled. "If Evelyn marries me, even if she keeps the restaurant open, there won't be any rolls left, because I'd eat them all."

This conversation was becoming more absurd by the second. Though she was tempted to walk away and let the two men who were acting more like squabbling boys than adults work it out between themselves, Evelyn was concerned that they might disturb the other customers.

"What makes you think she'd marry you?" Sam's face darkened with what appeared to be anger, and the way he clenched his fork made Evelyn wonder if he planned to stab Caleb rather than his pancakes. "I have more to offer her. I'm going to run this town."

Enough was enough. While she'd made it a rule to be polite to every customer, Evelyn had her limits, and they'd both passed them. "I hate to disappoint you gentlemen," she said firmly, "but I have no plans to marry for a long time, if ever."

Sam's smile was little more than a smirk. "That's what all the ladies say. They like to play hard to get, but when the right suitor comes, they change their mind. You will too."

But Sam was not the right suitor, and neither was Caleb. As for changing her mind, as she returned to the kitchen, Evelyn admitted to herself that she might do that someday, but it wouldn't be until she found a man who loved her the way Papa had loved Mama and who'd treat Polly like his own child.

"I still like Mr. Wyatt the bestest." Polly's words brought Evelyn back to the present. "I wish he was my papa. He'd be a good one."

"Yes, he would." A good husband too . . . for someone.

"He's everything I had hoped for." Wyatt gestured toward the midnight black colt that was gamboling around the paddock. A second colt, slightly larger than Ebony but dark gray rather than black, followed him. "His conformation is close to perfect, and his spirit . . . just look at him. He's only a month old, but he already wants to race. Ebony's a born leader."

Wyatt's enthusiasm was contagious. Though Evelyn knew very little about horses, there was no mistaking the pride in Wyatt's voice as he watched the new colt, just as there had been no question that he'd wanted her to accompany him when he checked on his horses.

For once, Polly had not pleaded to join

them. Though she'd been adamant about wanting to ride a horse today, when Dorothy had offered to help her make a new dress for her doll, all thoughts of horses seemed to flee, and Polly had grabbed Dorothy's hand, leading her to the corner of the parlor where she'd placed her Singer sewing machine.

The Mechanical Monster, as Isolde had nicknamed it, was not only one of the reasons she and Dorothy had been able to make so many clothes for both Evelyn and Polly but was also one of the reasons Polly looked forward to her visits to the Circle C. Though she was often distracted at home, she seemed content to spend an hour with Dorothy and the Singer, giving Evelyn time alone with Wyatt.

Evelyn's gaze moved from the man to the horse. "How can you tell that he's a leader?"

"See the way he holds his head. How would you describe that?"

She was silent for a moment, trying to choose the best adjective. "Regal," she said at last.

"Exactly. He's younger than Marble, but Marble already treats him like he's the one who's in charge. See how Marble watches and imitates what Ebony does."

Resting her hands on the fence rail, Evelyn studied the two horses, observing the subtle differences in their behavior. "It's fascinating. I never knew horses had such different personalities."

"That's because you didn't see Reginald in a herd. Horses are like people. There are leaders and followers."

"And Marble is a follower."

Wyatt nodded. "He'll probably be almost as fast as Ebony, but he'll be easier to train. Leaders are easily bored, and they can be stubborn. That makes them a challenge to train."

"And you love it."

Wyatt shrugged as if the answer were of little importance. "I'll admit that there's satisfaction in knowing that Circle C horses are considered some of the best racers in the state and that their agility makes them such good mounts for the Rangers. I'll probably regret not knowing who buys Ebony."

Though his voice was neutral, Evelyn saw a flash of something that might have been pain or perhaps only confusion in Wyatt's eyes. "Why wouldn't you know that?"

Once again his face bore the stoic expression she had seen so often. "I shouldn't have said anything. Can you erase that last sentence from your memory?" When she

170

shook her head, he continued. "Ma warned me that speaking without thinking would get me into trouble, and I guess she was right. Even if you can't forget what I said, I'd appreciate your keeping it to yourself."

As a light breeze blew a lock of hair from her chignon, Evelyn brushed it back. She didn't want or need any distractions, not now when she felt on the verge of learning something important about Wyatt.

"I can keep a secret." Look at how many of her own she was holding. "But there's a price." Though Wyatt's eyes widened with surprise, he waited for her to name it. "I promise not to tell anyone if you explain why you think you won't be here."

He nodded slowly. "Fair enough. I plan to leave Mesquite Springs just as soon as I know that Ma and Dorothy will be cared for."

If he'd told her he intended to sprout wings and learn to fly, Evelyn would not have been more surprised. "Why?" It made no sense that Wyatt would willingly leave a life he so obviously enjoyed. "Where would you go?" He had a home — a wonderful home — and a family. Surely he wouldn't abandon that. Evelyn knew she would never have left Gilmorton if her home and family hadn't been torn from her.

"I don't know where I'll go." Wyatt's hands tightened on the fence rail, silent witnesses to his discomfort. "There are times when I think I want to see the Atlantic Ocean, others when the gold mines of California beckon. Where I go doesn't really matter. What matters is being free to wander."

He spoke as if the ranch were a burden, not the source of satisfaction that he'd already admitted it was, and that confused Evelyn. "I don't understand. You have what looks to me like a wonderful life."

As he stared into the distance, Wyatt said, "It's true that the horses bring me satisfaction, but it's not as if I chose to raise them. That was my father's dream. I do it to honor him and as a way to take care of my mother and Dorothy."

He paused for a second, his frown deepening. "Pa was happy here. His dreams came true when he met my mother and they built the ranch, but he wasn't always happy before that. He told me that when he still lived in Virginia, he knew he wanted a different life. That's why he left everything and headed West."

Wyatt turned and looked at Evelyn, his eyes asking for understanding. "I feel the same way. There's something missing in my life, and I want to discover what it is."

Though she wasn't sure she understood completely, Evelyn's heart ached at the pain she heard in Wyatt's voice. They'd both lost parents, but their lives afterward had been vastly different. While Evelyn's life had not been easy after her parents' deaths, she had not had overwhelming responsibilities thrust upon her. To the contrary, Mrs. Folger had sheltered her from the world outside the orphanage, letting her continue to do the work she knew and loved: feeding others. And while Wyatt was still searching for a future that would fill the empty spots inside him, she felt as if she'd found hers.

"There are times when I'm afraid I'll never be able to leave. It seems like every time I get close, something comes up." He let out a mirthless laugh. "Now folks think I should run for mayor. Can you imagine that?"

Evelyn studied the man who'd become her friend in such a short time. He might not have Sam's legal training, but she knew he possessed an innate sense of justice, and the fact that he'd sacrificed his own dreams for his family was evidence of a deep-seated commitment to service.

"I think you'd be a good mayor," she said firmly, "but it needs to be something you want to do."

"And I don't want to do it. Besides, I wouldn't run against Sam. He's my friend."

Evelyn bit back a smile at the indication that Wyatt wasn't as opposed to the idea as he claimed. "Competition is good."

"So I've heard, but not between friends. I'll let someone else run against Sam."

The finality in Wyatt's voice told her the subject was closed. Evelyn wasn't sure what to say next. Somehow, talking about the horses seemed wrong, so she stepped away from the fence and headed back toward the house, more disturbed than she'd expected by Wyatt's revelation that he wanted to leave Mesquite Springs. The beautiful Sunday afternoon had lost its sparkle.

"I have a question for you," Wyatt said as he joined her. "Are there times when the fact that you're responsible for Polly weighs on you? It's not like she's your daughter."

It was a fair question, and it deserved an honest answer. "That's true. She's not." Polly wasn't even Evelyn's sister, although no one here knew that.

Evelyn wanted to confide in Wyatt as he'd confided in her, but fear kept her silent. Until she was certain — absolutely positive — that danger had not followed her and that she and Polly were safe, she would say nothing. She could, however, offer Wyatt the comfort of knowing that he wasn't alone in his feelings.

"You're right in thinking that there are times when I feel overwhelmed. Every time I make a decision, I ask myself if it's the right one for her." Their pace had slowed, and now they were stationary. Evelyn looked up at Wyatt, hoping her next words would not sound accusatory. "I haven't had the responsibility as long as you have, but I've never considered abandoning Polly."

Wyatt flinched as if Evelyn had struck him. "I wouldn't be abandoning Ma and Dorothy. Don't you see that I've waited this long to ensure that the ranch has consistent profits and that they'll be well cared for? I'm putting everything in place to protect them. Besides, they're not children. Dorothy's old enough to be on her own, and Ma . . ."

As he hesitated, Evelyn completed the sentence. "Your mother's a strong woman. She can manage by herself, but that doesn't mean that she wouldn't miss you or that leaving the ranch is the best thing for you."

Though it had been only a couple minutes since he'd introduced and dismissed the idea of running for mayor, Evelyn found herself intrigued by it. While he might deny it, Wyatt would be good in the role.

"Then you think I should stay."

She shook her head. "Only you can make that decision. All I'm saying is that if you leave, you'll leave holes in others' lives. You'll be missed."

Her words seemed to surprise Wyatt, and he gave her a long appraising look. "Would you miss me?"

"Yes."

A strong woman. Evelyn's words continued to echo through Wyatt's brain, though it was more than a day later. Why had she said that? Strong was not an adjective he would have applied to his mother. Of course, Evelyn had not seen Ma after Pa was killed. He knew women grieved differently from men, but Ma's grief had been extreme, or so it had seemed. She wouldn't eat for days and would barely talk to him or Dorothy. Instead, she'd lain on the bed she'd shared with Pa, clutching his pillow as if somehow that would bring him back.

Wyatt shook his head as Thunder neighed in apparent sympathy. He wouldn't think about Ma today. Instead, he'd think about what waited for him in Mesquite Springs: another meal at Polly's Place and another chance to talk to Evelyn.

When he reached the center of town, he pulled out his watch and nodded. As he'd expected, he had plenty of time to make another stop.

"What can I do for you today?" Theo Smith asked as he entered the blacksmith's shop. "Thunder throw a shoe?"

Wyatt shook his head as he blinked to help his eyes adjust to the relative darkness and the smoke that always filled the small building. "I just wanted to make sure you were still okay with Caleb working for me."

Caleb's father nodded as he pumped the bellows to fan the fire. "Yep. It pains me to admit it, but the change seems to be good for my boy. I just hope he doesn't lose interest the way he always does." Theo's face darkened. "Augustina says she doesn't think that'll happen. She claims she's never seen him so happy."

And that must have hurt his father. Wyatt knew that Theo had planned for Caleb to take over the smithy just as his other son had assumed responsibility for the livery. The expectation was that each son would raise at least one son who'd become the third generation of Smiths to own the business.

"Caleb's got a way with horses," Wyatt told the older man. "They trust each other.

But how about you? Have you had to turn anyone away?" One of Wyatt's fears had been that the blacksmith's business might suffer if Caleb wasn't there every day.

"Not so far." Theo inspected the fire, then gave the bellows another pump as he said, "The days Caleb's here, he works harder than ever. It's almost like he's makin' up for the time he's away. I can't complain about that."

Relief washed over Wyatt. "I'm glad to hear that. I didn't want to cause you any trouble."

Though he kept his attention on the barrel rib he was firing, Theo continued to speak. "I reckon the only trouble we're gonna have is when he gets hitched. The wife warned me it would happen, and it has. That boy of mine is fixin' to get himself a bride. There's no telling what he'll want to do then."

Wyatt tried to hide his surprise. "That's the first I've heard of it."

"Don't feel bad, son. He ain't said anything to his ma or me neither, but Augustina is sure of it. She calls it women's intuition."

"Who's the lucky lady?" There was only one woman Wyatt could imagine that might have caught his friend's eye.

Theo shrugged as if the answer should have been obvious. "The gal that runs the restaurant."

Evelyn. Of course. A strong woman. A talented woman. A beautiful woman. What more could a man want?

Wyatt was still reflecting on the blacksmith's revelation when he opened the door to Polly's Place. To his relief, the restaurant was emptier than usual, and he wouldn't have to share a table with someone else. Though he didn't normally mind the company, today he needed time to himself.

Memories of his conversation with Evelyn were still bouncing through his head, seeming to taunt him. It was more than her assertion that Ma was strong; what disturbed him most was Evelyn's declaration that he'd be a good mayor. That was becoming a refrain — an unwelcome refrain. Fortunately, Theo Smith had said nothing, although encouragement to run for office would have been more welcome than the idea of Caleb's courting Evelyn.

"Good afternoon, brother dear," Dorothy said with a mischievous smile. "Welcome to Polly's Place . . . again." As she led him to a table in the center of the room, she added, "We're having beef stew or roast chicken with chocolate pie for dessert."

"No oatmeal pecan pie?" Wyatt had spent part of the ride into Mesquite Springs thinking about what had quickly become his favorite dessert, eclipsing even Evelyn's chocolate cake.

"We ran out already. Evelyn thought it would be a slow day, so she only made two today. Then Mr. Downey's cousins from San Antonio arrived for a visit, and they all insisted on second helpings."

"I see." It was downright silly to be so disappointed. He could come back tomorrow and have the pie then. "I'll take a bowl of stew and a piece of the pie that you do have." With some luck, the food would help settle his thoughts.

Twenty minutes later, the woman who dominated his thoughts appeared at Wyatt's table with a slice of chocolate pie. "I'm sorry that we ran out of the oatmeal pecan pie."

It might be his imagination that Evelyn looked prettier than usual today. Although her apron was as spotless as ever, a few tendrils had come loose from her braid, evidence that she'd had a busy morning. Her cheeks were flushed, probably from the heat of the kitchen, making those sapphire eyes appear more brilliant than ever, and her smile seemed especially welcoming, as if he were more than a customer. He shouldn't care about that. After all, unlike Caleb, he wasn't planning to court her.

Wyatt forced his attention back to the pie. "I'm sure this will be delicious, especially if you put a bit of coffee in it."

Her smile widened. "I'm surprised you remembered that I do that."

Wyatt remembered a lot of things Evelyn had told him, but he wasn't going to admit it. If he did, he'd sound like Sam, trying to flatter her. Instead, he said, "I remember your saying that you planned to serve oatmeal pecan pie every day, but you never told me why." When she didn't respond immediately, he added, "Knowing you, there must be a reason."

"There is." Evelyn looked around, almost as if she were worried that someone would overhear her. That made no sense, though. Surely there was nothing secret about a pie.

Tipping her head to one side, she said softly, "My mother used to serve oatmeal pecan pie every day. It was a favorite with the customers."

"Customers?" Though Evelyn had mentioned her parents several times, she'd said nothing about customers, yet now she was acting as if they were part of some dark secret. Apparently, there was more to Evelyn's past than she'd admitted so far. Much more.

"Yes." She lowered her voice again, forcing Wyatt to lean forward to hear her. "My parents owned a restaurant. I started helping in it when I was Polly's age."

Though he could not imagine why that simple fact was causing Evelyn such distress or why he'd seen what appeared to be fear flitting across her face, Wyatt kept his voice low as he said, "No wonder you're doing such a good job here. It must be in your blood." When she managed a smile, he added, "Your parents would have been proud of you."

She met his gaze, her eyes moist with unshed tears. "I hope so."

CHAPTER THIRTEEN

"Wait until you hear this. It's the silliest one yet." Dorothy giggled as she opened the book that had been delivered two days ago. Ever since she'd arrived at the eastern finishing school, Dorothy's friend Laura had sent her monthly packages. Initially, they'd included things that she hadn't seen in Texas, like an assortment of seashells, but the most recent one contained three books that Laura said the other girls touted as the best stories ever written. Dorothy had begun reading excerpts to her after the restaurant closed and they'd completed the cleanup.

"Sillier than the one where the hero declares that he loves the heroine because she's the only woman he knows who can bone a trout faster than he does?"

While they'd both laughed at that, Evelyn had wondered if there wasn't some truth to the adage that the way to a man's heart was through his stomach. Would either Caleb or

Sam have mentioned marriage — even jokingly — if she had burned the roast and made tough piecrusts? She had no romantic interest in either of them, and so it didn't matter, but the possibility that any man found her attractive only because she was a good cook was disturbing.

"Much sillier. This time the hero writes a sonnet to her eyebrows." By the time she finished reading the poorly rhymed poem to Evelyn, Dorothy was laughing so hard that the words were barely intelligible. "Isn't that dreadful?"

When she finally stopped laughing, Evelyn nodded. "I don't know what's worse — the fact that some publisher paid money for it or that anyone thinks that's the way a woman wants to be courted. If someone composed a sonnet to my eyebrows, I'm afraid I'd laugh at him."

"So would I." Dorothy closed the book and slid it into her bag, preparing to leave.

Evelyn felt a pang of regret that their time together was over for the day. She had known Dorothy less than two months, but in that time, she had become much more than a trusted employee. They did more than share responsibilities, rub salve on each other's burns, and bandage each other's cuts. They also laughed together, and though Evelyn had no idea how it had happened, they seemed to know each other so well that they had begun completing each other's sentences. More quickly than she had thought it possible, Dorothy had become Evelyn's best friend, what one of the silly books Laura had sent called a bosom buddy.

Right now, that bosom buddy was grinning. "At least you don't have to worry about Sam or Caleb wooing you with poetry. I can't imagine either of them doing that."

Sam, Caleb, and courtship. Evelyn had no desire to discuss any one of them, but Dorothy's comment deserved a response. "They'd be wasting their time, and they know it. I told them both I wasn't interested."

"But if you were," Dorothy persisted, "how would you like to be wooed?"

Evelyn doubted her answer would satisfy her friend, but it was the truth. "I don't know."

"This is mighty fine pie."

Evelyn smiled at the man who was praising her raisin pie. Today was the first time she'd served it, the first time the mayor had come to Polly's Place, and the first time she'd sat with a customer. Though it was contrary to her policy, when the older man asked her to join him for a cup of coffee, Evelyn found herself unable to refuse. There was something in his plea that touched her heart, and so she told Dorothy she'd be in the dining room longer than normal. Fortunately, it was almost closing time, and the restaurant was not busy.

"I'm glad you're enjoying it, Mr. Mayor."

The man who'd led Mesquite Springs for longer than Evelyn had been alive shook his head. "Just call me Ken. I reckon I need to get used to the idea of someone else being Mr. Mayor."

Evelyn wasn't sure what he expected her to say, but before she could form a response, he continued. "I never thought I'd retire — always figured I'd die in the office — but once Sally was gone, nothing felt the same. It lost its flavor." He gestured toward his slice of pie. "Kinda like raisin pie without the raisins. The most important ingredient is missing."

And if he stopped being mayor, what would be left in his life? Evelyn had to ask the question. "Do you think your wife would have wanted you to retire?"

The mayor grinned. "You're the first person who's asked me that. The ladies at church ask me if I've thought about marrying again, as if Sally was a broken teapot that could be replaced, but no one's asked me about retiring."

He took a bite of pie, chewing carefully before he spoke again. "Funny thing is, for the last five years Sally kept telling me it was time to slow down. I was too stubborn to listen. Now I wish I had. We could have done all those things we kept promising each other we would — long walks, picnics among the bluebonnets, trips to Austin or San Antonio. Now all I have are regrets."

Evelyn knew that wasn't true. "You have much more than that. You have memories."

He pursed his lips, as if considering her words, then nodded. "You're right. I have memories — years and years of memories." He shook his head when Evelyn offered to refill his coffee cup. "Will you listen to some advice from an old man? Life is shorter than you think. Don't waste a single minute. If you find someone to love the way I loved Sally, don't let him go. You hear me?"

"I do." But that didn't mean she was ready to marry. Not yet.

"One more thing. See if you can convince Wyatt to run for mayor. A bit of competition would do Sam Plaut a lot of good."

"The mayor certainly stayed a long time,"

Dorothy said a few minutes later when Evelyn returned to the kitchen, bearing his empty plate and the coffee cups. "I never realized he was such a talker."

"I think he's lonely. It was clear that he loved his wife deeply."

Dorothy slid the dishes into the soapy water. "I wonder if he'll remarry. When Pa was killed, folks kept telling me Ma owed it to Wyatt and me to find a new husband."

"But she didn't." Though Evelyn had trouble picturing either of her parents marrying again if one had died before the other, she knew that many widows and widowers did, especially if they had children. Two parents were better than one, or so everyone said.

"She wouldn't even consider it." Dorothy was silent for a moment. "Sometimes I wish she would have. It might have been easier on Wyatt."

The wistfulness in Dorothy's voice made Evelyn wonder whether she knew of Wyatt's desire to leave Mesquite Springs, but she had no chance to ask, for Dorothy posed a question of her own. "What else did Mr. Mayor say?"

"He thinks Wyatt should run for mayor."

"So do I. That would give him the change he wants, but he wouldn't have to go away."

It appeared that Dorothy was aware of Wyatt's discontent. When Evelyn did not respond immediately, Dorothy continued. "You don't look surprised. That tells me Wyatt confided in you." She narrowed her eyes. "I wonder how much he told you. My brother doesn't usually talk about himself, but he's been different since you came."

Dorothy stared at the wall for a few seconds, obviously lost in thought. "It seems to me that you're the one to do it."

"Do what?"

"Convince Wyatt to run for mayor."

It was the perfect day to train a horse — the air cool enough that neither horse nor trainer would have to stop from heat exhaustion, clouds covering the sun and preventing shadows that might spook the horse, the ground fully dry after the last few days' rain — and Caleb was taking full advantage of it.

Wyatt leaned on the fence, watching his friend work with Granite. His instincts had been right: Caleb had an affinity for horses and a knack for training them. Granite, who'd been skittish around everyone except Wyatt, had accepted Caleb almost immediately. Now the horse was following his commands, moving in the directions Caleb

189

indicated without hesitation.

"Good job!" Wyatt called as Caleb returned from taking Granite back to the stable.

The man grinned, then gave Wyatt a sly smile. "I still say you oughta let me work with Charcoal. After all, I've had my share of experience with real charcoal."

"And you think that qualifies you to train what will probably be one of my best horses?" He'd assigned Caleb to Granite, knowing that the horse would be good but probably not great. From the time he was born, Granite had shown an agility superior to half the other horses, and his stamina was excellent, but he lacked the short-term speed of a racer. If Caleb made mistakes with him, they would not be disastrous.

Caleb shrugged. "A man can hope, can't he?" He gazed at the smaller paddock, his eyes brightening at the sight of the new foals chasing each other as if they were racing. "I can see why you love ranching so much. Being here with the horses is even better than I'd thought. No wonder you don't want to run for mayor."

Wyatt schooled his expression to remain neutral. There it was again, the suggestion that he was the right man to lead Mesquite Springs. Why did people think that? They were wrong. Being the mayor wouldn't fill the empty spots inside him.

Brushing those thoughts away, Wyatt reminded himself of what a good job Caleb had done. The man deserved a reward. "Seems to me you've earned a break. What do you say to a piece of oatmeal pecan pie?"

"Evelyn's?" Caleb's eyes, almost as deep a blue as Evelyn's, lit with pleasure, either at the prospect of the pie itself or the fact that Evelyn had made it. The suspicion that it was the latter left a sour taste in Wyatt's mouth, but he said only, "Ma claims no one else in Mesquite Springs will even try to bake one, because they're sure to fall short, so yes, it's Evelyn's. She sent a couple pieces home with Dorothy yesterday. Something about not wanting them to get stale."

"You don't have to convince me. She's a mighty fine cook." As he matched Wyatt's strides toward the house, Caleb added, "I can't figure out why some man hasn't snatched her up before this, but I'm sure not complaining that she's still single. It gives me a chance."

It appeared that Caleb's mother was right. "So, you're thinking about getting married?" Wyatt could have kicked himself when the words came out of his mouth. He should have let the subject die by refusing to respond to it as he had with the idea of his running for mayor. But, no, he'd had to ask, and now Caleb would tell him what he did not want to hear.

"Who wouldn't be with a woman like Evelyn in town?"

Who? Wyatt for one. Marriage was for other people, not for him. "Are you sure you're ready for the responsibility? Taking care of a wife is a lot of work." Much more than training a horse.

They'd climbed the steps to the back door, but before Wyatt could open it, Caleb grabbed his shoulder and spun him around to face him, his expression making it clear that he thought Wyatt was crazy. "I reckon you'd better not say anything like that to my ma. She'd tell you she's the one doing all the work. I can't count the number of times she's said how much easier her life was before she had Pa and me to take care of."

That made no sense. Everyone knew that men had all the responsibility. They were the ones who had to keep their families safe and ensure that they had a warm, dry home and enough food to eat. Rather than argue with Caleb, Wyatt simply said, "She seems happy enough now."

"I reckon they both are. I got to tell you,

Wyatt, sometimes it's downright embarrassing the way those two carry on. You'd think they were our age. Now, where's that pie?"

Five minutes later, as he scooped the last bite onto his fork, Caleb grinned. "I could eat this every day."

"And that's why you want to marry Evelyn — so you can have pie every day?" Wyatt could think of better reasons, like the smile that made a man feel ten feet tall and the way she listened — really listened — when he spoke. Then there was her obvious love for her sister, her courage in leaving the only home she knew, her strength of mind. The list was endless.

Caleb washed the last of the pie down with a swig of coffee before he said, "Of course that's not the only reason. She's also mighty easy on the eyes."

Another stupid reason. Evelyn deserved more than that. She deserved a man who saw her for what she was — a caring, talented woman. She deserved a man like . . . Wyatt stopped abruptly, unable to complete the sentence.

CHAPTER FOURTEEN

The scream wakened her. Evelyn sat up, her heart pounding as she tried to convince herself that it had been only a dream. But when the terrified shriek was repeated, she knew she had not been dreaming. Memories of the night the killer had invaded her parents' house and she'd cowered beneath the bed mingled with those of the smoldering orphanage, and she began to tremble. Somehow the Watcher had found her. Worse yet, Polly was in danger.

Heartsick at the idea that she had brought peril to the little girl she loved so dearly, Evelyn ran the short distance to the other bedroom and flung the door open. *Please, dear God, keep her safe,* she prayed silently as she barreled into the room. Her prayers were answered, and relief rushed through Evelyn when she saw no intruder. Though Polly was tangled in her sheets, she was still asleep but whimpering in the aftermath of her nightmare.

"It's all right," Evelyn said as she perched on the side of the bed and drew the girl into her arms, hoping to wake her gently. "It was just a dream."

Polly's eyes flew open. After a moment of confusion while she struggled with whatever had terrified her, she wrapped her arms around Evelyn's waist, clinging so tightly that Evelyn could barely breathe. "I'm scared."

"It's all right, honey. You're safe here." Evelyn prayed that was true. "You're safe," she repeated as she stroked Polly's back and murmured words of comfort.

When Polly's trembling subsided, Evelyn pressed a kiss on her head as she said, "Why don't you put on your slippers and a robe, and we'll make some hot chocolate?"

"Okay." Polly followed Evelyn into her room, waiting while Evelyn donned her robe, then clutched Evelyn's hand again as they walked toward the stairway. "Cook used to make hot chocolate. She was nice to me."

It was rare for Polly to refer to anything about her past, and the fact that she did so now made Evelyn wonder if something in the past had triggered her nightmare. She waited until they'd reached the kitchen before she spoke. Then, as she pulled out a saucepan and poured milk into it, she asked as casually as she could, "Was someone not nice to you? Is that what scared you?"

Polly nodded. "I don't wanna go to school today."

The answer surprised Evelyn. Other than the first day when she'd been reluctant to attend classes, Polly had seemed to enjoy school, frequently coming home with stories of what she'd learned and what she and her friends had done during recess.

Though Evelyn had worried that the children might either shun or make fun of Polly because of her birthmark, Sarah Geist had assured her that she could handle that. And she had. Before anyone could comment on Polly's face, she had told the class that the strawberry mark was an angel's kiss. Polly had returned from school that day, radiant with the knowledge that even if she couldn't remember her mother, she had a permanent reminder that an angel had loved her.

She wasn't radiant now.

"Would you find the chocolate?" While Polly was searching the cupboard for it, Evelyn asked the question that was foremost on her mind. "Was someone not nice to you there?"

Polly nodded as she held out the chocolate, tears filling her eyes. "They laughed at me and called me a dummy."

Knowing that either one could be devastating to a child Polly's age but not knowing which one had hurt her the most, Evelyn decided to address the easier taunt. "You're not dumb, Polly. You're a very smart girl."

She'd recognized the child's intelligence the day she'd arrived at the orphanage. Though Polly had been clearly distressed by being left there and had hardly spoken, her eyes were bright, and the way she'd studied her surroundings told Evelyn that she was cataloging everything.

Without being asked, Polly retrieved the grater, yet another proof of her intelligence. "That's what Papa said. He said I was smart like my mama, but Maisie told me not to let anyone know."

Evelyn grated the chocolate into the milk, then added sugar and began to stir it. "Why don't you sit at the table?" When Polly did, Evelyn continued. "Who's Maisie?" This was the first time Polly had mentioned that name. As fear crossed the child's face, Evelyn said softly, "You can trust me. You can tell me anything."

Polly stared at her for a long moment, her

indecision evident. Then she said, "Maisie was my mammy. She's the one who took me to the 'nage. She said I could never tell . . ." Once again, fear appeared to overwhelm Polly's natural instinct to confide in someone.

"Tell what?" The little she had revealed tonight had challenged Evelyn's belief that Polly's father had had only a few acres of cotton. While small growers might have had field slaves, it was unlikely they'd have been able to afford a mammy for their children.

Polly shook her head violently. "I can't tell you. If I do, something bad is gonna happen."

Nodding as if this were a normal conversation when it most definitely was not, Evelyn said, "That's fine, but you can tell me what happened at school, can't you?"

As the scent of melting chocolate began to fill the room, Polly shrugged. "Miss Geist asked us to write our names, but I couldn't remember."

"You didn't remember how to spell Polly?"

"Not that one." Polly looked at Evelyn as if she ought to have understood. "My last name. I couldn't remember the one you told me, so I started to write the other one. That's when I remembered what Maisie said." A shudder wracked Polly's small frame. "I wiped the slate clean. When Miss Geist came to me, I pretended that I didn't remember."

"And someone laughed at you." Though an adult would have shrugged off the incident, it would have mortified a child.

"They all did. That's why I can't go back." As a tear made its way down her cheek, Polly brushed it away. "Ever."

Though she suspected that there was more to the nightmare than feeling humiliated at school, Evelyn knew this was not the time to pursue it. "You can stay with me today," she agreed. It was Friday, and by Monday Polly should have forgotten the dream.

Evelyn poured the now-steaming chocolate into two cups and set them on the table. When she'd taken the chair opposite Polly, the girl's mood lightened. "Can I help Miss Dorothy serve? I like it more than she does."

"Why do you say that?" Dorothy had never given any indication that she did not enjoy being part of the restaurant, although Evelyn realized she had never actually asked her.

Polly took a big slug of cocoa, leaving her lips coated with the sweet beverage as she said, "She doesn't smile the way you do."

Twelve hours later, Evelyn had to admit

that Polly had seen something she'd missed. While Dorothy smiled at every customer who entered the restaurant and was unfailingly polite, even when someone complained, she did not appear to be as happy as she had when Polly's Place had first opened.

Evelyn waited until the restaurant was closed and Polly was upstairs playing with her doll before she broached the subject.

"Are you happy working here, Dorothy?" she asked as she handed a freshly washed and rinsed plate to her assistant.

Blood rushed to Dorothy's face, and she fumbled with the plate. "Why would you think I'm not?"

Evelyn, who'd been watching her reaction carefully, reflected that Dorothy seemed more chagrined by the possibility that someone had discovered her secret than shocked by the very idea. The fact that she countered with a question rather than answering Evelyn's directly corroborated the validity of Polly's observation.

"Because you don't seem as enthusiastic as you did a month ago. Back then, there was a spring in your step. It's gone now." Perhaps it had happened so gradually that she hadn't noticed the change, but now that Polly had alerted her to it, it was clear to

Evelyn that something was wrong.

"Are you unhappy with me? Do you want me to quit?" Once again, Dorothy was sidestepping the underlying question.

"No, of course not." Evelyn continued to wash and rinse plates, sensing that Dorothy needed the rhythm of drying dishes to help settle her thoughts. "I can't imagine running the restaurant without you, but I want you to be happy."

"I am. It's just . . ."

"Just what?"

Dorothy studied the plate she was drying as if the explanation were painted on it. "It's not what I expected. I'm like Wyatt. I couldn't wait to leave the ranch. Everything is so boring there." She frowned and laid the plate on the stack in the cupboard. "I thought it would be different here, but . . ."

Evelyn was beginning to understand the problem. "The novelty wore off, and it's routine."

"Exactly." Dorothy pursed her lips. "Don't you get tired of cooking the same things every day?"

"No."

"Well, I do." Without waiting for Evelyn's response, she said, "I know the problem is me. I can't seem to help being easily bored." She frowned again. "People say that about

201

Caleb, that once he masters a thing, he wants to do something else."

Evelyn had heard several customers speculate that Caleb would soon lose interest in working at the Circle C, but so far she had seen no indication of that. Every time they spoke, he was enthusiastic about working with the horses.

"I don't think either you or Caleb are wrong. I think you haven't yet discovered what you're meant to do." Just as Wyatt was struggling to identify what would make him happy. Despite what he'd said, Evelyn was not convinced that he would be satisfied with an itinerant lifestyle. "My mother once told me that each of us is put on Earth for a reason, and once we find that purpose, we'll be happy."

Evelyn handed Dorothy the last plate, then dried her hands on the towel she'd tucked into her apron waistband. To her surprise, Dorothy shook her head as if refuting Evelyn's statement.

"I know what I want to do, but it'll never work out."

The despair in her voice wrenched Evelyn's heart. "What do you want to do?"

"Write." Dorothy closed the cupboard and turned to face Evelyn. "All my life I've wanted to be a writer. That's why Laura sent those books. She's convinced I can become another Jane Austen."

Evelyn looked at her friend, trying to picture her with a pen in hand. It wasn't difficult to conjure the image, but somehow it felt wrong. "Is that what you want to write — novels about manners and people's places in society?"

Dorothy shook her head again. "I want to make a difference in the world and change the way people think about important things, the way Harriet Beecher Stowe did."

Though Evelyn had not read *Uncle Tom's Cabin,* she'd heard enough about it to know that anything similar would not be well received, even here where there were no slaves. "What would you write about?" she asked.

"That's the problem. I know that I want to do something important with my life, and I feel that writing is the way, but I don't have any ideas for a book."

No wonder she was frustrated. Evelyn thought quickly. "Fiction isn't the only way to influence people. What about writing for a newspaper?"

Though a spark of interest lit Dorothy's eyes, it faded quickly. "That's hard to do when there isn't one in town."

Evelyn heard Polly moving around upstairs and realized her time alone with Dorothy was limited. There had to be a way to encourage her. "I'm surprised Mesquite Springs doesn't have a paper. Surely there are enough people to support it." Evelyn had been impressed with the prosperity of the town that was now her home and the fact that it continued to expand. The two things it was missing were a newspaper of its own and a hotel.

Dorothy's lack of enthusiasm was palpable. "I suppose there are enough people, but no one seems interested in starting a paper. Even if I wanted to run one — which I don't — it takes a lot of money to buy a press."

This discouraged, almost despondent, woman was not the Dorothy Evelyn had come to know and love. "What about writing articles and sending them to other newspapers? That doesn't take much money." Evelyn saw another faint glimmer of hope in Dorothy's eyes and tried to fan it. "Don't abandon your dreams. Life is too short to waste a single minute."

"But how do I find the time? There aren't enough hours in the day for everything I need to do."

"If being a writer is truly important to you, you'll find a way."

■ ■ ■ ■

Something was bothering her. Wyatt had seen it as she and Polly slid into the pew. The look she gave Dorothy was filled with concern; the smile she bestowed on Ma seemed strained; and she'd given him no more than a perfunctory nod. This was not the Evelyn who greeted her customers enthusiastically and who somehow managed to hide her deepest feelings.

The knowledge that something was wrong nagged at him throughout the service, and by the time Reverend Coleman pronounced the benediction, Wyatt knew what he had to do. He turned to his mother as they followed Evelyn and Polly out of the church.

"Don't wait for me. I'll ride with Evelyn."

Ma's grin told him that visions of weddings and grandchildren had begun to float through her brain. She couldn't have been more wrong. Caleb and Sam were the men who wanted to court Evelyn. A man who planned to brush the dust of Mesquite Springs from his bootheels as soon as he could had no business even thinking about marriage.

"Good idea, son." Ma touched Dorothy's arm to get her attention. "There's no time to dawdle today. I'm worried that the roast might be overcooked."

Seeming not to notice the flimsy excuse, Dorothy fixed her gaze on Wyatt, who'd started to walk away. "Aren't you coming with us?"

"Don't worry about me. I'll be there."

He looked around the churchyard. While Evelyn talked to the schoolmarm, Polly sat under an oak, her arms clasped around her knees, her expression leaving no doubt that she was unhappy about being alone. Though his primary concern was for her sister, Wyatt hated the idea of Polly feeling abandoned.

"Where are your friends?" he asked as he approached her.

"Don't got any." She laid her head on her arms, as if trying to make herself invisible.

The pieces were starting to fit together. If Polly had had problems at school, it made sense that Evelyn would be concerned and would speak with her teacher. But if that was the reason for Evelyn's distress, why had she looked at Dorothy the way she had?

Wyatt crouched next to Polly. "I don't believe you. Girls as friendly as you always have friends."

"That's not true, Mr. Wyatt. They laughed at me."

And that was painful. Wyatt remembered

206

the cruelty children could inflict on each other, but he also recalled how quickly situations changed.

He pointed toward the little girl who had been sharing secrets with Polly a week ago. "Melissa's not laughing now." The child stood a few feet away from her mother, looking for all the world as miserable as Polly herself. "She seems lonely. I think she needs a friend."

Polly's eyes brightened. "Really?"

"Really. Could you help her?"

"Maybe." Polly stared at her erstwhile bosom buddy.

"It would be a nice thing to do."

"Okay." Apparently convinced, Polly jumped to her feet and scampered off. Within seconds, the two girls had their heads together and appeared to be giggling.

"How did you manage that?" Evelyn asked as she approached Wyatt. "I was afraid I'd have to drag Polly to school tomorrow."

The look Evelyn gave him made Wyatt feel as if he'd accomplished something significant, not simply convincing a little girl to stop pouting.

"I pointed out that her friend was lonely. It seems that compassion overpowered the humiliation of being laughed at."

"She told you what happened?" Evelyn

sounded surprised.

"Not the details. Just that the others laughed. It was pure luck that I remembered Melissa's name."

"And I'm grateful that you did. You made it sound easy, but in just a couple minutes, you accomplished what I haven't been able to do in two days." Evelyn looked at the girls who were now holding hands and skipping across the grass. "I wish there were a way I could repay you."

It was the opening Wyatt needed. "There is. You can give me a ride home. Ma and Dorothy have already left."

Though Evelyn appeared surprised that he'd been left behind, she nodded. "Of course. Let's give Polly another five minutes."

The smile that lit Evelyn's face as she looked at her sister did not erase the underlying discomfort he'd seen all morning, leaving Wyatt with the question of whether he should ask her about it here or wait until they were on the road.

"Why don't I get Reginald for you?" There'd be no one to overhear them when they were in the wagon, and that might make her more likely to confide in him. "That'll give Polly a little more time with her friend."

"That's a good idea."

Once again, the smile Evelyn bestowed on him made Wyatt's heart sing. Surely whatever was bothering Evelyn couldn't be too serious if she smiled like that.

When he returned to the churchyard with Reginald hitched to the wagon, Polly abandoned her friend and raced to his side as he climbed out. Evelyn, who'd been conversing with Ida Downey, made her way toward him.

"What are you doin' with Reginald, Mr. Wyatt?" Polly demanded, her hands fisted on her hips.

"Your sister offered me a ride to the ranch."

"Goody!" All traces of the despondent child had disappeared. This was the Polly whose enthusiasm had infected everyone at the Circle C. "Can I sit in back?"

Wyatt waited until Evelyn nodded before he agreed. "You sure can." Having her in the back would give him and Evelyn more privacy, and that was good.

When they were settled in the wagon, Evelyn turned to Wyatt. "Would you prefer to drive?"

He shook his head. "I'm feeling lazy today." The truth was, he wanted to watch her expression when they spoke. Wyatt waited until they were outside the town itself before he broached the subject that had been weighing on him. "You can tell me to mind my own business if you feel I'm overstepping, but I couldn't help noticing that something seems wrong."

Evelyn glanced over her shoulder, seeming to relax a bit when she saw that Polly was staring at the countryside as she sang to herself. "I hadn't realized it was obvious, but the truth is, I'm worried about your sister."

"Dorothy?" That would explain the strange looks Evelyn had given her, but try though he might, Wyatt could not imagine what had caused Evelyn to worry.

She gave him a mischievous smile. "Do you have another sister?"

"No. I'm simply surprised. Why would you be worried?"

"She's not happy."

The day was bright and sunny, a cool but perfect Sunday morning in one of the most beautiful parts of Texas. Ma would probably say it was a day for rejoicing, but Wyatt could not rejoice, not when Evelyn's words had destroyed his equilibrium. He'd thought — no, he'd been convinced — that his sister was content with the changes in her life.

"That makes no sense. She spends her

days with you." He'd known that Dorothy wanted to leave the Circle C, and she had, at least for most of the day. "Why wouldn't she be happy?"

"Because working at Polly's Place is not her dream."

"Then what is? She didn't like being on the ranch, and she's gotten off it." Which was more than he could say for himself.

A sudden gust of wind tugged a lock of Evelyn's hair loose. She brushed it from her face as she said, "Dorothy dreams of being a writer."

A writer. Wyatt shook his head, trying to clear his thoughts. He wasn't certain what disturbed him more: the fact that he hadn't known Dorothy as well as he thought he did or that his sister seemed to have a clearer view of her future than he did.

"What kind of writer?" By some small miracle, his voice sounded as calm as if they were discussing a particularly fine stretch of weather, not the fact that his sister hadn't trusted him enough to tell him her dreams.

"Someone who changes the world with her words. She envisions herself as another Harriet Beecher Stowe and is frustrated because she doesn't have any ideas as . . ." Evelyn paused, obviously searching for the correct word. "Important," she said at last.

211

"I suggested she might write for a newspaper."

And that idea, Wyatt knew, presented its own challenges. "Mesquite Springs doesn't have a paper."

"Not yet, but that doesn't mean it never will. A town this size needs one." Though she'd been watching the road, Evelyn turned toward him, apparently waiting for his response.

"I agree." While he hadn't spent a lot of time thinking about it, Wyatt admitted that his hometown would benefit from a newspaper. "Ken McBride has been a good mayor, but one thing he could have done better was to encourage someone to start a paper. We need a more reliable source of news than the grapevine."

Evelyn's lips curved into the sweetest of smiles. "That's something you could do if you were mayor."

Despite himself, Wyatt laughed. "I thought we were talking about Dorothy, not me. You already know I have no intention of running for mayor."

"Not even if it could help your sister's dream come true?"

Wyatt shook his head. "It's only a temporary dream. She'd have to give it up when she married." Dorothy may have claimed that she had no intention of marrying, but Wyatt hadn't believed her. It was only a matter of time before his sister found the man with whom she wanted to share the rest of her life.

"Why?"

He didn't have to ponder the question. "A married woman's place is in the home, not in a newspaper office."

Evelyn's smile faded and her hands tightened on the reins. When Reginald reacted, she loosened her grip and turned back toward Wyatt. "So, if I were married, people would expect me to close the restaurant?"

"Probably." Wyatt couldn't imagine either Sam or Caleb wanting his wife so tired from working in a restaurant that she didn't have time for him or their children. Everyone knew that taking care of a house, preparing meals, and raising children was enough to keep a woman busy from sunup until sundown.

"I thought both Fosters worked in the restaurant the way my parents did in theirs." Evelyn's voice was firm, reminding him of his mother's when he'd said or done something foolish.

"You're right," he admitted. "Nancy Foster worked alongside Harold."

"Like partners."

Suddenly, Wyatt felt as if he were on trial, being cross-examined by a particularly difficult attorney. "That's one way to describe it." One way to describe Wyatt was uncomfortable. This conversation had taken unforeseen turns. If only he'd never begun it.

"That's what marriage is, Wyatt. Not all couples work together like the Fosters or my parents, but if they truly love each other, they both have a part in decision making. They consider the other person's needs and their dreams."

"You believe that, don't you?"

Evelyn's blue eyes flashed, and anger had turned her cheeks rosy. "Yes, I do. The question is, why don't you?"

The answer was simple. "Because my parents' marriage wasn't like that." He thought of the way Ma had depended on Pa, the way she'd asked his opinion of everything. That wasn't his idea of a partnership. And yet, what if there was some truth to what Evelyn had said? What if Ma had done those things because she wanted to be certain that Pa was happy?

"Are you sure about that?"

At the moment, Wyatt wasn't sure about anything other than that Evelyn was mighty pretty when she was riled.

CHAPTER FIFTEEN

Someone was watching her. The hair on the back of Evelyn's neck rose, alerting her to the danger just as it had the times she'd gone to Gilmorton. Someone's gaze was following her every move. Hers and Polly's.

Willing herself not to show her distress, she tried not to tighten her grip on Polly's hand. No matter how worried she might be by the knowledge that the Watcher had followed her to Mesquite Springs, Evelyn would not willingly communicate her fears to the child, just as she did her best not to let Polly see the tears that sprang to her eyes whenever she thought of Mrs. Folger and the orphans and that horrible night when the orphanage had been destroyed.

"What do we do now?" It was more than a rhetorical question. They'd reached the intersection of Main and River.

"We look both ways."

"That's right." Each morning as they

walked to school and each afternoon as they returned, Evelyn had tried to drum into Polly's head the importance of watching for traffic before they crossed the street. "What do you see?"

Polly's head swiveled as she looked first to the right, then to the left. "I see a wagon with Mr. Sam in it."

The sight of Sam was not unusual. He often arrived in town about now, but he rarely brought the wagon, preferring instead to simply ride. Was he the one watching them? Though Evelyn did not dismiss the idea, she thought it unlikely. She knew Sam, and while his flirting occasionally caused a mild discomfort, she had never felt threatened as she did this morning.

She fisted her hands, then released them in an effort to calm herself. There was no one else on the street, but the Watcher could be in one of the buildings, peering out from behind curtains. No matter how carefully she'd studied the streets of Gilmorton, she had never been able to identify the Watcher's location. It would be no different here. All she could do was try to ignore the prickling feeling and the fear that though she had thought she'd be safe here, Mesquite Springs might not be the haven she'd expected.

Evelyn kept her eyes on Polly. "What do we do?"

The girl giggled and recited the admonition she'd heard so often. "We wait until he's gone before we cross."

"Exactly."

But instead of passing by and heading toward the livery where he boarded his horse while he was at work, Sam stopped next to them and doffed his hat. "Can I offer you two lovely ladies a ride?" Though he'd included Polly in the invitation, he'd hardly glanced at her.

"Thank you, but we're only going as far as the school. We'll walk."

He shrugged as if he'd expected her response. "All right. I'll see you later."

As he drove away, Evelyn and Polly crossed Main and turned right onto River. To Evelyn's relief, as they approached the school, Melissa raced toward them, skidded to a stop, then whispered something in Polly's ear. Within seconds, the two girls had their arms wrapped around each other's waists and were giggling.

Just as quickly, the sensation of being watched faded. It must have been her imagination, Evelyn told herself, fear triggered by the memory of Polly's nightmare the other night. Sam was no threat.

217

A partnership. Evelyn's assertion that that was the characteristic of the best marriages echoed through Wyatt's brain. He'd been thinking about their conversation, replaying it mentally, when he'd fallen asleep last night, and it had been his first thought this morning. Even the unexpected revelation that Dorothy had dreams she had not shared with him had paled in comparison to the possibility that he'd been wrong about his parents' marriage.

Wyatt searched for the currycomb and began to groom Thunder. Though he needed a brisk ride to clear his thoughts, there was no time for that. Caleb would arrive within the next few minutes, ready to continue training the horses Wyatt planned to sell this year. Nothing — absolutely nothing — could interfere with that.

"You want to run too, don't you, boy?" Wyatt asked as he rubbed the spot on Thunder's forehead that always relaxed the gelding. "Maybe later."

And maybe later he'd talk to Ma. Only she could answer the questions that continued to plague him. Asking Ma made sense. Wyatt knew that just as he knew Thunder wanted to gallop. He needed to learn whether his memory was faulty or whether he'd misinterpreted what she and Pa had said and done. If he asked her, Wyatt knew Ma would tell him the truth, so why was he hesitating? He had no answer.

The day passed quickly, as most Mondays did, with the dining room filled to capacity the entire time it was open. Fortunately, they had not run out of anything, and there had been no disgruntled customers. But by the time the last dish was dried, Evelyn was more than ready to walk Polly home from school and simply relax. The early morning fear had drained her more than she'd realized. Now all she wanted was to curl up in a chair and watch Polly play with her doll.

She closed and locked the front door behind her, startling when she heard a man's voice only a few inches away from her.

"You wouldn't accept a ride this morning, but I hope you'll accept this."

Sam held out the most beautiful crystal vase Evelyn had ever seen. Intricately cut, it was obviously the work of a master craftsman, its many facets creating rainbows where the sun hit them. And then there were the flowers. Red, pink, and white roses vied with each other for the title of most fragrant. By any standard, it was an extravagant gift.

"I don't understand," Evelyn said, overwhelmed by Sam's gesture. "Roses don't bloom in February."

His smile verged on a smirk. "They do if you have a greenhouse. My mother loves flowers, so Father had one built for her."

That was a luxury beyond Evelyn's wildest dreams, as was the gorgeous vase. Though the thought of having the bouquet in her home was tempting, she knew there was only one possible response.

"I'm sorry, Sam, but I can't accept your gift."

"Why ever not? Mother assured me that flowers, books, and candy were proper gifts for a courting couple."

Mrs. Folger had said the same thing right before she advised Evelyn not to fall into a smooth-talking man's trap. "That's true," Evelyn agreed, "but there are two problems. First of all, we are not courting, and secondly, even if we were, the vase is far too expensive a gift for anything but a wife."

The flash of anger that crossed Sam's face was quickly replaced by what appeared to be disappointment. "I'm sorry you feel that way, but I respect your opinion, even though

I don't agree with it. I'll keep the vase in my office until you're ready to accept it."

He placed it on the bench beside the entrance to Polly's Place as if it were no more valuable than a tin can filled with wildflowers.

"At least let me escort you this afternoon." Sam bent his arm so that she could place her hand on it. "I know you always bring Molly home from school. I thought we could walk together."

Evelyn wasn't certain which bothered her more, his assumption that she would one day welcome his courtship or that he didn't know Polly's name.

"Polly."

"Polly what?"

"That's her name." Evelyn turned to point toward the sign on the front of the restaurant. "I named it for her."

Sam had the grace to look abashed. "Oh, of course. Polly. I hope you won't hold that slip of tongue against me. I really would like the pleasure of your company, even if it's only for a short walk."

It would be churlish to say no, particularly after she'd refused his extravagant gift, and so Evelyn did not. "Certainly," she said as she placed her hand on the crook of his arm.

"I realize I may have been premature in

giving you the vase," Sam said as they made their way toward the corner. "I didn't mean to put you in an awkward position. It's simply that the last time I was in Fredericksburg, it caught my eye. I found it exquisite, just like you."

No one had ever called Evelyn exquisite, and for a second she felt a rush of pleasure at the compliment, but it faded as quickly as it had blossomed. This was Sam, the man folks claimed had been born with a silver tongue. He didn't mean anything by the pretty words.

"Thank you, but . . ."

Sam didn't appear to hear her protest. "The truth is, I worry about you."

"Why would you do that?"

"I've seen how hard you work. A lovely lady like you shouldn't have to work." Sam glanced around, as if ensuring that he would not be overheard. "It's no secret that I earn a good living and that my family has plenty of money. Not as much as the Downeys, but enough that my wife would never have to work. I'd even hire servants so she could have an easy life."

Once again, the conversation was going in a direction Evelyn had no desire to travel. "I hope you and your wife will be very happy together," she said as they crossed the street. Perhaps if she increased her pace, they'd reach the school before he could say anything else.

Sam laid his other hand on top of hers and gave it a quick squeeze. "Don't be coy, Evelyn. It's not becoming in a lady of your stature."

Evelyn bristled at the idea that this man felt the need to lecture her as if she were a mischievous schoolgirl. Though she tried to pull her hand away, he held it firmly.

"You know I don't have a wife yet, but I'm hoping to change that soon. The citizens of Mesquite Springs expect their mayor to have a wife at his side, and there's no one I'd rather have at my side than you."

Any pleasure she may have felt from his earlier compliments was gone, replaced by indignation that Sam was treating marriage as if it were a case to be argued and won.

"In summary," he said, cementing her belief that his emotions were not engaged, "I would like to court you."

She hadn't walked quickly enough. Sam had said more than she wanted to hear, and now she had to reply. Though her first inclination was an angry retort, informing him that his need for a wife meant nothing to her, Evelyn stifled that. Her parents had taught her the importance of civility, and so she said only, "Marriage is a big step. I'm not ready for it."

Once again, Sam squeezed her hand. "I could make you happy. I know it."

Before Evelyn could reply, the school door opened and children raced out, with Polly leading the rush. She ran across the school-yard as if pursued by an angry javelina, then skidded to a stop in front of Evelyn.

"Look, Evelyn. I did it." She held out her slate so that Evelyn could read the neatly printed letters: Polly Radner.

"Wonderful!" Evelyn gave the girl a hug, then straightened up. "Now, remember your manners and say hello to Mr. Sam."

Looking more than a little crestfallen, Polly raised her eyes and said dutifully, "Hello, Mr. Sam."

"Nice to see you again, Molly."

She probably should have been mending the hem that Polly had torn, but Evelyn was too tired to think about it. Instead, she leaned her head against the back of the chair and closed her eyes, grateful that Polly was so immersed in a conversation with her doll that she didn't need to be entertained. Evelyn wouldn't sleep, of course, but she could try to relax. She was doing exactly that when she heard a knock on the back door.

Please, don't let it be Sam. She'd had more than enough of him today. Though she was tempted to ignore the knock, she couldn't.

"I'll be right back," Evelyn told Polly as she descended the stairs and unlocked the door. It wasn't Sam. This visitor was a welcome one. Far from raising her hackles, the sight of the tall man with chocolate brown eyes made Evelyn's heart beat erratically. How strange. She'd never reacted this way. It must be fatigue or perhaps relief that was making her pulse race and her heart flutter.

"What are you doing in town so late?" The words escaped before Evelyn could censor them.

Wyatt's grin said he wasn't offended by her curt greeting. "It's nice to see you too."

"I'm sorry, Wyatt. That was rude of me." Evelyn felt her cheeks warm with embarrassment. "Only this afternoon I had to remind Polly of good manners, and now I've been remiss myself. I *am* glad to see you — just surprised by the timing."

As she ushered him into the kitchen, Wyatt explained that his mother had hurt her ankle. "It swelled up so much that she thought it was broken, so I brought her in to see Doc Dawson."

"Is she all right?" Evelyn could not picture

Isolde being unable to walk. Every time she saw the woman, she was bustling somewhere.

"It turns out it was just a bad sprain. Doc wrapped it and handed her a cane." Wyatt gave Evelyn a mischievous grin. "You can imagine how Ma liked that. She says it makes her feel like an old lady."

His grin widened. "I suspect it was as much to defy the doctor's orders that she take it easy as that she needed something, but she decided to visit the mercantile. She talked Ida Downey into keeping it open late just for her. If I know Ma, she'll be there for at least half an hour."

"And you didn't want to help her choose calico and lace."

"Not when there was a chance you might have a piece of pie left over."

"Now the truth comes out. It wasn't the pleasure of my company you sought, but my pie."

It felt so good to be bantering with Wyatt. Evelyn had never before had a friend who made her laugh as often as he did, and on a day like today, laughter was a welcome diversion.

"There's no pie left, but I have some chocolate cake. Would you like a piece now? I'll pack up three more for you to take home for later."

"You know I'd never refuse anything you cook."

When Evelyn gestured toward the table, Wyatt took a seat and watched as she pulled out a plate and fork and began slicing the cake. "Would you like coffee or milk to go with it?"

"Coffee."

Footsteps clattering on the stairs announced Polly's arrival.

"Mr. Wyatt! You came to see me!" She started to pull out a chair, then stopped when she spotted the cake. "Can I have some?"

"*May* I have some," Evelyn corrected her.

"Sure."

Not bothering to hide his amusement, Wyatt turned to Polly. "I think what your sister is trying to tell you is that if you want a piece of cake, you need to say 'may I.' "

Though she wrinkled her nose, Polly gave Evelyn her most persuasive smile. "May I have cake?"

"A small piece."

"And coffee?"

"A glass of milk." Evelyn pulled the bottle from the icebox and started to fill a glass.

"What are you having?" Wyatt asked. "Milk or coffee?"

227

"I wasn't planning to eat."

"Just watching doesn't sound like much fun to me."

Evelyn placed the glass of milk in front of Polly, then turned to pour a cup of coffee for Wyatt as she considered his statement. Fun was not a word she would have used to describe her life, but maybe it should be.

"Coffee and cake sound good," she admitted and cut a third piece of cake.

It *was* good, she reflected a minute later. There was no denying how pleasant it was to sit here with Wyatt and Polly. Her fatigue and the faint uneasiness that had plagued her all day had disappeared, but though Wyatt was clearly enjoying the cake, he still appeared tense.

"Are you worried about your mother?"

"Not really. She's in good hands with Doc Dawson."

"Then what's wrong?"

Wyatt wrinkled his nose. "Trying to ferret out my secrets, huh? It's not much of a secret that I'm still worried that the sale won't go well. So much is riding on having a lot of men bidding on each horse."

Competition would increase the prices and Wyatt's profits. The key to that was making sure every potential buyer knew about the Circle C sale.

"Do you think you need more than the ads and invitations?"

Wyatt forked another piece of cake. "Maybe. The problem is, I don't have any other ideas."

Polly slurped the last of her milk, obviously bored by the conversation. "Can I be excused?"

"You may." This was not the time to correct Polly's grammar. It was the time to help Wyatt and possibly his sister. "Ads are good, but there's another way to reach people, and it costs a lot less."

"What's that?"

"Articles. I remember my father saying that when he and Mama opened their restaurant, the local newspaper ran an article about them. It told a little bit about how they met and why they decided to establish a restaurant."

Evelyn paused long enough to take a sip of coffee. "The article brought in a lot of folks, and when the papers in the neighboring towns reprinted it, they started drawing customers from the whole county."

Wyatt's lips curved into a mischievous smile. "Let me guess. You think Dorothy should write the article."

"Of course. It'll give her an opportunity to see if this is something she enjoys. If it succeeds, you both win. If not, you haven't spent much money, and Dorothy has still had a chance to chase her dream."

"All right." Wyatt swallowed the last bite of cake. His smile broadened as he laid down his fork. "You could give Sam a run for his money when it comes to persuasion. You know that, don't you?"

What Evelyn knew as she looked across the table was that she didn't want to talk or even think about Sam. Wyatt was the one she cared about, and it appeared that he was relaxing. The furrows that she'd thought had taken up permanent residence between his eyes had begun to fade, and he was leaning back in the chair, clearly comfortable.

Evelyn smiled. Sam had said she worked too hard. Perhaps she did, but Wyatt worked much harder. It was good to see him relaxing. Helping him had been fun.

"I can't believe you convinced him." The smile that wreathed Dorothy's face told Evelyn as clearly as her words that Wyatt had asked his sister to write an article about the horse sale. "I never thought he'd admit that I could do anything more than muck out stalls or curry the horses."

Dorothy twirled around, her skirts flaring, her cheeks flushing with enthusiasm. "I

230

know it was your idea. Wyatt told me, but even if he hadn't, I would have known you were behind it. Thank you, thank you, thank you."

She flung her arms around Evelyn and hugged her so tightly that Evelyn feared she might crack a rib. "I'm so glad you came to Mesquite Springs."

So was Evelyn. Seeing Dorothy's happiness on top of Wyatt's relief filled her with satisfaction and a sense that all was right. This was where she was meant to be.

Wyatt looked around the churchyard, trying to do something — anything — other than grit his teeth. He'd known Ida Downey his whole life. He liked the woman, but now she seemed downright annoying, talking about the latest letter she'd received from Laura and about the young men Laura had met at a cotillion. If the stories were supposed to make Wyatt jealous, they failed. Like drinking overly sweet tea, being with Laura's mother made his teeth hurt.

He stared into the distance for a long moment. Ida talked and talked and talked. It didn't seem to matter that he didn't always respond. She just kept talking.

This conversation, if it could be dignified by that term, was nothing like the one he had shared with Evelyn. Wyatt smiled, remembering how he'd relaxed as he'd eaten cake in her kitchen. For the space of half an hour, he'd been able to put his worries aside, and thanks to her suggestion, he now had a happy sister. This was different, filling him with tension and the desire to escape.

Matchmaking mamas were one of the reasons he needed to leave the Circle C and Mesquite Springs. He wanted a life where he owed nothing to anyone, not even a few minutes of polite conversation. It would be good to leave. No responsibilities, no . . . Wyatt paused as the word *Evelyn* popped into his brain.

He must have been thinking of her because he'd seen her standing on the other side of the churchyard, talking to Dorothy and his mother. Yet somehow the knowledge that he'd be leaving Evelyn as well as his unwanted responsibilities took some of the luster off his shiny future life.

While Ida continued to talk about the chess pie Laura had made and how her teacher claimed it was the best she'd ever tasted, Wyatt's thoughts continued to whirl. He hadn't planned on it, but somehow Evelyn had become part of his life. An important part.

Perhaps it was because she was the most interesting woman he'd ever met. Perhaps it was because she made him think about the world differently. Perhaps it was because she expressed her opinions so freely.

She was open and honest and yet . . . Despite her apparent honesty, Wyatt couldn't shake the feeling that she was hiding important parts of her life from him. The question was, why.

CHAPTER SIXTEEN

"I wanna make my own pie!"

Evelyn tried not to sigh as Polly punctuated her words with a thump on the table. Normally on Saturday mornings Polly was happy to be able to help in the kitchen, but today she was cranky, undoubtedly the result of last night's nightmare. Though they'd become less frequent, this one had been particularly intense, and Polly had wakened Evelyn with her screams of "I want my papa!" It had taken Evelyn the better part of an hour to soothe the girl enough that she would sleep. Now they were both paying the price for Polly's lack of sleep.

"I'm sorry, Polly, but the pies are all in the oven. I don't have any more pans." She did, however, have some leftover pie crust dough. Pointing to it, she smiled. "Let's make cinnamon twists." Polly had enjoyed doing that several times. Perhaps it would placate her now.

It did not.

"No!" Polly banged her foot against the chair leg. "I wanna make a pie. You let Ginny make pies at the 'nage."

Evelyn hadn't realized that Ginny had confided in Polly. The other girl was two years older than Polly and had been at the orphanage since birth. When she'd been born with one leg noticeably shorter than the other, her parents had abandoned her on the front porch with nothing more than a note saying they could not care for a crippled child.

Though Ginny had learned to walk at the same age as most children, her limp made her much slower than the others, and she was excluded from their games. As a result, she spent many afternoons in the kitchen with Evelyn, pretending that she didn't mind being shunned, while Evelyn pretended that her heart didn't ache for the child, when the truth was that she longed for a way to make Ginny feel special.

Jubilant when she had discovered a small round pan with steep sides in the back of the pantry, Evelyn had planned to make an individual cake for Ginny, but the girl had insisted that it was a pie pan and that she would make her own pie.

Ginny had patted crust into the pan, then

surprised Evelyn by dumping in brown sugar, a few chunks of butter, and a bit of milk and declaring it ready to bake. Even without mixing the ingredients, the pie had turned out to be edible. More than edible. Ginny had been thrilled with the result and had christened it Ginny's Sugar Pie. Now Polly wanted her own version of it.

"You're right. I did let Ginny make a pie, but I don't have an extra pie tin here." Evelyn pointed to the dough that was waiting to be rolled out, spread with butter, sprinkled with cinnamon and sugar, then cut and twisted. "That's why I'm going to let you make cinnamon twists."

Normally cheerful Polly shook her head. "It's not the same. I want pie!"

"Not today."

Polly glared at her, then flung herself out of the chair. "I hate you!" she shouted as she raced upstairs.

Wyatt smiled as Polly brought the piece of cake he'd ordered. He didn't have time for a whole meal. The truth was, he didn't have time for a trip into town today, but he hated the thought of not having at least a few minutes with Evelyn. He hadn't admitted to himself just how much he enjoyed their Sunday afternoons together until he'd faced the fact that she wouldn't be having dinner at the Circle C tomorrow. And so, though he had horses to train, he was here, sitting in the corner of Polly's Place, hoping Evelyn would follow her sister into the dining room.

Polly did not return his smile as she plunked the plate in front of him. Instead, she fisted both hands on her hips and frowned. "Evelyn's mean to me, Mr. Wyatt," she announced.

Though he kept his expression neutral, Wyatt couldn't believe the little girl. If anything, he would have said that Evelyn was overly protective of her. This must be some kind of childish pique.

"What did she do?"

"She won't let me make my own pie." Polly pushed her lower lip forward in a classic pout.

Though he doubted Polly wanted to hear it, Evelyn's stance sounded reasonable to Wyatt. A child her age could easily burn herself if she tried to bake a pie.

"She lets you serve here," he reminded her. "That's important."

"It's not fair! She let Ginny make pies."

Hoping he wasn't fueling the fire, Wyatt asked, "Who's Ginny?"

" 'Nother girl at the 'nage. She was there

237

a long, long time before me, and she tole me Evelyn gave her a special pan and let her bake pies in it, but Evelyn won't let me, and that's not fair." The story came out in a rush, leaving Polly breathless at the end.

Wyatt wasn't breathless; he was confused. If Evelyn and Polly were sisters, surely they would have arrived at the orphanage at the same time, yet it sounded as if Evelyn had been there for years before Polly. That made no sense unless Evelyn had been lying and Polly wasn't actually her sister.

A horrible fear assailed Wyatt. Was this the reason Evelyn sometimes hesitated when she called Polly her sister? Was this the reason for the fears she'd tried so hard to hide? Was she worried someone might uncover her deception? Polly's comments had raised even more questions. Who was this child, and how had she come to be in Evelyn's care? Surely Evelyn hadn't kidnapped her.

It might be wrong to probe, but Wyatt was going to do it. He wanted — no, he needed — to learn the truth.

"Maybe Evelyn let Ginny bake a pie because she was at the orphanage longer than you."

Polly gave him a tentative smile. "You think so? Ginny tole me her parents didn't want her 'cuz her leg wasn't right. They left her at the 'nage when she was a baby." The smile turned upside down. "That's mean, isn't it?"

"Very mean." The fact that he was now almost certain that Evelyn and Polly were not related made Wyatt wonder if Polly had been abandoned because of her birthmark. Perhaps Evelyn had befriended her because of her birthmark just as she had done special things for crippled Ginny. If, as seemed to be the case, they were the only two to have survived the fire, it made sense that Evelyn would not abandon Polly. But why was she claiming they were sisters?

"My papa wasn't mean," Polly declared. "He loved me."

The fact that she had memories of her father told Wyatt Polly had not been abandoned as an infant, and yet it opened more questions. Why did she never refer to her mother?

"I'm sure your mother loved you too," he said, hoping to learn more about the girl who'd captured the hearts of everyone on the Circle C.

Polly shrugged. "Papa said she went to live with the angels when I was borned."

It was an innocent remark and one that confirmed Wyatt's belief that she and Evelyn were not sisters. Evelyn had lied. There was no doubt of that. The questions were, why had she lied, what other lies had she told, and what should Wyatt do now?

"Thank you so much for inviting us to dinner, Mrs. Smith," Evelyn said as she slid the final piece of peach cobbler onto her fork. It had been a delicious meal, made all the more special because she hadn't had to cook it.

The food had been good, the company even better. Though she'd met them both at church, this was the first opportunity she'd had to spend time with Caleb's parents, and she was enjoying it.

It was easy to see where Caleb had gotten his good looks, for Augustina Smith was one of the most beautiful women Evelyn had ever met. She had the same almost black hair and deep blue eyes as her son, but unlike Caleb, she was shorter than average.

Caleb's father, the source of his height, was a fairly ordinary man in terms of appearance, but the welcome he'd given Evelyn and Polly was not ordinary. With his warm smile and kind words, he'd made them feel like honored guests.

"I would have invited you sooner," Mrs. Smith said, "but I was afraid my cooking wouldn't meet your standards. I've heard so much about your meals from Caleb and Theo."

"I get to serve Mr. Caleb when he comes," Polly announced, the straightening of her shoulders conveying her pride as much as her words.

Caleb's mother gave Polly a sweet smile. "I heard about that. I also heard you do a very good job."

"Polly's a big help." While the child smiled at Evelyn's praise, Evelyn continued. "We're both happy to be here. It's a treat to have someone else cook."

Though she would not say anything to disparage Isolde's culinary skills, there was no doubt that Augustina Smith was a superior cook. The fried chicken and mashed potatoes had been delicious, and the biscuits rivaled any Evelyn had eaten. Even better than the food itself had been the fact that conversing with new people had helped keep her mind off today's sermon.

A shiver had run down Evelyn's spine when Pastor Coleman had opened his Bible to the eighth chapter of John and had read the thirty-second verse. "Listen, carefully," he had said, "because this is important. 'And ye shall know the truth, and the truth shall make you free.' Are you enslaved by lies?"

Though she'd wanted to hide under the pew, certain that everyone in the church knew he had directed his question to her, Evelyn had remained seated while inwardly she cringed. Oh, how she hated the web of lies she'd spun! More than anything, she wished she could undo them, but how could she do that and ensure that she and Polly would remain safe? The answer eluded her. Fortunately, conversing with the Smiths had kept her fears at bay.

"What do you think of our springs?" Caleb's father asked as he set his empty cup back on the table.

This was a safe subject, far from lies and their consequences. "I must confess that I haven't seen them. I've been so busy that there hasn't been time."

Caleb frowned. "That's terrible. You've been in Mesquite Springs over two months. Why, the sheriff might arrest you for failing to see our namesake landmark." The twist of his lips made it clear that he was joking.

As Evelyn debated her response, Mrs. Smith took charge of the conversation. "We'll ride out there this afternoon," she said firmly. "It's walking distance, but maybe not for those with shorter legs." With

242

a fond smile at her husband, she added, "This will give us a chance to take Caleb's carriage."

"You have a carriage?" Evelyn hadn't thought a single man would have a need for one.

"Not exactly."

"My son is modest," Mrs. Smith said as her husband headed out of the house and toward the livery that their other son ran. "He likes to make new things, so when Joshua noted that business was trailing off, Caleb decided we needed an unusual carriage to rent out. Once you see it, you'll know why it's our most popular one."

When Mr. Smith returned a few minutes later, Evelyn understood his wife's pride in their son's creation. It was obvious that a man who enjoyed working with metal had designed it, for the first thing that caught Evelyn's eye were the high iron wheels and the simple frame.

She'd seen wagons with two benches, but most of them were like the Clarks' and had sides that spanned the entire length, making it difficult to climb in. She'd seen carriages with two seats, but most of those were elaborate and had seats facing each other. This vehicle was striking in both its simplicity and its beauty.

It boasted two comfortable-looking uphol-
stered seats, both of which faced forward.
The sides were designed to make entrance
and exit easy, although the height meant
that a woman would need assistance. And
then there was the top. While wagons had
none and most carriages had heavy roofs
that wrapped around the back, protecting
passengers from some of the elements, this
one had a simple flat roof held up by four
seemingly delicate iron poles. Passengers
would be protected from the sun but would
have the pleasure of an open-air ride.

"Oh, Caleb, this is wonderful!"

His cheeks pinked with pleasure. "I like
making things," he admitted.

Though Evelyn's attention had been
focused on the carriage, Polly's was directed
at the handsome bay in front of it.

"A horse! I like horses!"

Mrs. Smith laid a restraining hand on her
shoulder, keeping her from racing to the
horse's side. "Then you'll sit in front with
Mr. Smith and me. You'll be closer to
Mildred that way."

And so Evelyn found herself in the rear
seat next to Caleb. As his father flicked the
reins and Mildred began to move, Caleb
smiled at Evelyn. "I'm glad you could come,
even if Ma's food isn't as good as yours."

"It was nice not to have to cook."

Caleb's smile faded. "You seem to work awfully hard."

"And you don't? I knew you were working at the smithy and at the Circle C, but I didn't know you also made carriages for the livery. That sounds tiring to me."

"I only made this one carriage, and that was a couple years ago, but creating things from metal is fun." He ran his hand up and down the closest pole.

As Polly continued to chatter to Mr. and Mrs. Smith, an idea popped into Evelyn's head. "Have you ever made pans for cooking and baking?" Her voice was little more than a whisper, because she did not want Polly to overhear.

"I can't say that I have."

"Would you try?" Lowering her voice even more, Evelyn explained what she wanted.

When she finished, Caleb grinned. "For you? Sure."

Within minutes they arrived at the spring. Though the town itself was attractive, the area around the spring was beautiful. Evelyn's heart skipped a beat as she remembered her mother speaking of a green cathedral. Mama had never been to Mesquite Springs, so she'd never seen this particular spot, but the tall trees that ringed the bubbling water and the ferns that covered much of the ground were as majestic as the pictures Mama had shown Evelyn of the great cathedrals in Europe.

"Looky, Evelyn!" Polly raced toward the water and thrust her hands into it, then pulled them out a second later, shrieking. "Cold!"

Evelyn wasn't surprised. Even though it was mid-March and less than a week before the official start of spring, the tree-shaded water would have had little chance to warm.

"Horse!" Polly wiped her hands on her skirts before hurrying back to the carriage. Mildred, it seemed, was more interesting than cold water. When the elder Smiths indicated that they'd watch Polly, Evelyn and Caleb walked around the spring. Though Evelyn was tempted to trail her hands in it, she remembered Polly's reaction and did not.

"This must be a wonderful place during the summer — refreshing and cool."

Caleb nodded. "You're right. Summers aren't as hot here as in some parts of Texas, but they're still hot."

Though the site was peaceful now, Evelyn imagined it became crowded and noisy during July and August. "It looks like it would be an ideal swimming hole."

His face darkening with something akin to pain, Caleb clenched then released his fists. "It is," he said, "unless someone decides to hold you under the water." The way he phrased the sentence left no doubt that Caleb had been the one who'd been dunked.

"Was it part of a childhood prank?" Evelyn had seen the boys at the orphanage engage in what they thought were playful antics, never realizing how dangerous they could be. Surely that was what had happened to Caleb.

He shook his head. "That's what he said. He apologized the next day and claimed he only wanted to scare me, but it felt like he wanted to kill me."

Evelyn closed her eyes, not wanting to picture the scene that had taken place only yards away from her. She knew all too well how terrifying it was to realize that someone wanted to kill you, but she'd been fortunate. The man who'd murdered her parents hadn't found her. Caleb had been closer to death than she had.

She opened her eyes and fixed them on him. "Who?"

He was silent for a moment, clearly debating whether or not to tell her. At last he spoke. "Sam."

CHAPTER SEVENTEEN

Evelyn reached for her cloak. Though Polly was sleeping, more tired than usual from the afternoon's adventures, Evelyn knew that slumber would elude her. She wouldn't go far, but perhaps walking would help settle her nerves. Thoughts she'd tried to dismiss had been whirling through her brain faster than leaves before an autumn storm. Pastor Coleman's sermon and the lies she'd told haunted her, as did Caleb's revelation.

Though she wanted to believe that the enmity he claimed Sam harbored toward him had been a momentary madness, Evelyn wasn't certain that was the case. She'd seen the hostility between them. And while she didn't know what had provoked Sam, she now knew why Caleb didn't trust him. The question was what, if anything, she could do to mend a rift that was more than a decade old.

And then there was the question of

whether she should even try. The day Evelyn had intervened in two boys' fight and had wound up being punched by both of them, Mrs. Folger had warned her of the dangers of meddling, telling her she couldn't mend all the world's ills. Perhaps this was another time when it was best to do nothing.

Evelyn nodded as she closed the door behind her and headed right on Main, planning to turn around when she reached Mesquite. Back and forth for one block was enough. It wasn't as if she were looking at anything. All she wanted was the exercise and a chance to clear her thoughts. Fortunately, at this time of day, there were few people out, so she didn't have to worry about making polite conversation.

What should she do about her lies? What could she do about Caleb and Sam? The questions formed a refrain, keeping time with her footsteps. At first, Evelyn barely noticed the approaching horseman, but as he drew nearer, she recognized him and her heart leapt. Why was Wyatt in town on a Sunday evening?

"I didn't expect you to be out," he said as he reined in Thunder and slid from his back. "I thought I'd have to knock on your door."

249

Wyatt had come to see her. Though part of her was pleased by the thought, the other part wondered why he'd come at this particular time. Right now, she wasn't fit company for anyone, even Wyatt.

His expression was solemn, leading Evelyn to ask, "Did something happen to your mother or Dorothy?" The last time he'd made an unexpected visit had been when Isolde had sprained her ankle.

"No. They're fine, and so are the horses." But something was wrong. Evelyn could hear the strain in his voice.

After he tied Thunder's reins to the hitching post, Wyatt gestured toward the bench in front of Polly's Place. "Shall we sit for a while?"

The smile he gave her seemed forced, sending a shiver of apprehension through Evelyn. Even though she wasn't certain she was ready for the answer, she had to ask. "What's wrong, Wyatt? I can tell that something's bothering you."

"It is." He crossed his ankles, a gesture Evelyn had noticed he often did when he wanted to buy time before speaking. For what seemed like an endless moment, he stared across the street. Then he turned his gaze back to her. "The truth is," Wyatt said, stressing the noun, "I can't get today's sermon out of my mind. I want the truth to set us both free."

"What do you mean?" She had wrestled with the sermon's message, but surely Wyatt wasn't keeping secrets the way she was.

His eyes were solemn, his expression pained as he said, "I know Polly isn't your sister."

Evelyn gasped. Before she could respond, Wyatt said, "What I don't know is why you're pretending she is."

"How did you find out?" Asking another question was easier than answering one.

"Polly told me. Oh, not in so many words, but her stories didn't match yours. What's the real story, Evelyn?"

Fear of the Watcher and what he might do if he learned where she was battled with the desire to share the truth with Wyatt. As Pastor Coleman's sermon echoed through her brain, Evelyn knew what she had to do. Her heart told her she could trust Wyatt.

"I hated lying," she said, "but I didn't think I had a choice."

"We always have choices." A hint of censure colored Wyatt's words, making Evelyn cringe. He was right.

"That's true. I had a choice, and I made the wrong one. My conscience has been telling me that all along, but I was too afraid to stop lying."

Wyatt extended his hand palm up, urging her to place hers in his. "Afraid of what?" he asked when she'd accepted his peace offering.

"My parents didn't die. They were murdered." The words hung between them, more ominous than a thundercloud. "A man shot them one night while they were still downstairs in the restaurant. It was late, and I'd gone to bed, but the shots woke me." She shuddered at the memory. "Then I heard him. He was coming up the stairs, calling out for me, and I knew he was going to kill me too."

Somehow Evelyn managed to tell the story without breaking down in tears. Even though a decade had passed since that horrible night, simply saying the words brought back memories that tore her heart to pieces.

"I hid under my bed, and for some reason, he didn't look there." Evelyn closed her eyes, trying to block out the image of her younger self trembling as the heavy footsteps echoed on the stairs before entering her room. "Afterward, the minister told me God had protected me, but for the longest time, I couldn't imagine why."

She looked up at Wyatt, willing him to understand. "You know what it's like to lose a parent, so you know how awful that time was. I felt as if my world was shattered. My whole family had been taken away, and I had no idea why. As far as I knew, my parents had no enemies. Here it is, ten years later, and I still don't know why anyone would kill them. All I know is that I was left alone."

Wyatt's expression had changed, softening as she recounted the events of the night that had changed her life irreparably. "Didn't you have any relatives?"

"No. That's why I was sent to the orphanage." The orphanage that was now nothing more than rubble, its inhabitants gone, all because of Evelyn.

Wyatt was silent for a moment, as if trying to absorb all that she'd said. "It may have seemed cruel at the time, but maybe you were sent away to protect you. You were safe at the orphanage, weren't you?"

Evelyn nodded, remembering how Mrs. Folger had taken her under her wing and given her increasing responsibilities so she would feel useful. "I always felt safe there, but every time I went to Gilmorton — that's where my parents and I had lived — I knew someone was watching me. It was frightening, Wyatt. I didn't know who he was, but I knew he had his eye on me."

Wyatt closed his hand around Evelyn's, the warmth of his clasp helping dispel the fears her story had resurrected.

"Of course it was frightening, especially if the killer was still on the loose."

"The sheriff told me they'd found and hanged the man, but it was hard for me to believe that when I was in Gilmorton. That's where Polly and I were the day the orphanage burned. Reginald threw a shoe, making us late getting back."

Even now the memory of the charred ruins and the acrid smell of smoke made Evelyn's heart clench. "If we'd been on time, we would have died too."

"But you weren't. God protected both of you that day." Wyatt uncrossed then crossed his ankles again. "Was the fire an accident?" The way he phrased the question made Evelyn realize that he suspected the truth even without her confirmation.

"No. When I heard people say they found empty kerosene cans, I knew what had happened. The killer had come for me. He didn't care how many others he killed." She trembled, remembering the stench of the scorched wood, the terror that had swept through her when she'd realized there were no survivors, and the grief that still had the power to overwhelm her.

"All I knew was that I had to get away. I had to keep Polly and me safe. Changing my name and saying she was my sister seemed like the easiest way to avoid attention, because I was sure the Watcher wouldn't be looking for a woman and a child."

Wyatt appeared to focus on one aspect of her story. "You changed your name? You're not Evelyn?" He tightened his grip on her hand as he waited for her answer.

"Evelyn's my real name, but Radner isn't. I'm Evelyn Rose Radcliffe, the daughter of Herman and Emmeline Radcliffe."

"Evelyn Rose Radcliffe." Wyatt pronounced the words slowly. "It's a pretty name."

Evelyn had always thought so, but that wasn't what mattered now. "Do you understand why I did what I did?"

When his gaze met hers, she saw more than understanding. She saw empathy. "Yes. I probably would have done the same thing."

Now came the most important question. "Can you forgive me for lying?"

Wyatt's reply was instant. "Of course. You didn't do it to hurt anyone. You had no way of knowing who you could trust." He paused for a second. "I hope you know you can trust me."

"I do." Relief flowed through Evelyn, leaving her bones feeling limp. "Oh, Wyatt, I wanted to tell you so many times, but I was afraid."

"And now?"

"Now I feel free. The Bible is right. Truth does set you free."

CHAPTER EIGHTEEN

Wyatt leaned forward as he urged Thunder into a gallop. Though he rarely raced his horse, tonight he needed speed, the feeling of chasing the wind, to help him deal with what he'd learned. His instinct that Evelyn had been hiding something had been accurate, but so had the instinct that she was strong. Only a strong woman could have survived what she had without being more deeply scarred.

He smiled as Thunder lengthened his stride, continuing past the turnoff to the Circle C as if he shared his master's desire for a long ride. One of the many things Wyatt liked about Thunder was that the gelding reacted to his moods so easily. "All right, Thunder. Let's go."

Ten minutes later, he tightened the reins, slowing the horse. It was time to return home. He'd composed himself enough that neither Ma nor Dorothy should be able to tell that he'd had such an eventful evening.

Though he didn't like keeping secrets, when Evelyn had asked whether it was necessary to tell everyone her real name, he'd surprised himself by saying that no one else needed to know, at least not now. Countless people had changed their names when they came West, wanting a new start for their lives. There was no reason Evelyn should not do the same.

Wyatt still had many questions to ask her, like why she'd stayed at the orphanage so long and what she knew about Polly's parents, but those could wait for another day. When he'd seen how difficult it was for Evelyn to tell him the truth, he hadn't wanted to overwhelm her with the host of questions that whirled through his head. Even though he'd wanted to delve into her past, to learn everything he could about this fascinating woman, he'd known there would be time to learn the rest of the story. What was important was that Evelyn — Evelyn Rose Radcliffe — trusted him.

What a heady feeling that was.

"One of the customers wants to talk to you."

Evelyn turned from ladling stew into a bowl, surprised by Dorothy's anxious tone. As long as Evelyn didn't expect her to cook,

Dorothy seemed unflappable, but something about this customer had upset her.

"Which one?"

"The stranger. He wants the pie recipe and wouldn't believe me when I said you won't share it."

As she let out an exasperated sigh, Evelyn untied her apron. "All right. I'll talk to him." Fixing a smile on her face, she approached the middle-aged man with graying blond hair and pale blue eyes.

"Hello again, Mr. Shepherd." Though it had been a busier than normal morning, Evelyn had followed her routine and had spoken with each of her customers as they ate their main course.

When he started to rise, she shook her head. If he remained seated and felt a bit awkward about not standing for a lady, the conversation might be shorter. "I heard you enjoyed the oatmeal pecan pie."

Mr. Shepherd nodded and gestured toward the empty plate. "That was the best pie I've ever eaten, and that's sayin' a lot. I'm a travelin' salesman, you see, and I make it my business to eat in a different place every day. I've had me some mighty good meals, but nothin' like your pie."

He kept his gaze fixed on her as he continued. "I don't reckon I'll be back here, but I sure hate the idea of not ever tastin' that pie again. That's why I'd be much obliged if you'd let me take the recipe to my wife. She's a mighty good cook, and I reckon she could make it taste almost as good as you do."

Though the man sounded sincere, there was only one possible answer. "I'm sorry, sir, but I have a firm policy. The recipe is a family secret, and it's going to stay that way."

"I can promise my wife won't share it with anybody. You can trust me."

"Be that as it may, the answer is the same."

"I'll pay whatever you ask."

Evelyn almost smiled at the salesman's belief that if he refused to admit defeat, he would make a sale or, in this case, a purchase. "I admire your persistence, but the recipe is not for sale."

"No chance?"

"No chance." Sensing that his disappointment was genuine and flattered by the lengths to which someone would go to eat her pie again, Evelyn decided it was time to make an exception. "I can't give you the recipe, but I will do something I haven't done before. I'll sell you a whole pie. If you take it home, your wife may be able to figure out the recipe."

A glimmer of hope lit Mr. Shepherd's eyes. "I reckon that's better than nothin'. Thank you, ma'am."

"That was a nice thing you did," Dorothy told Evelyn that afternoon after she'd turned the sign to "closed" and had returned to the kitchen to help Evelyn with the dishes. "Mr. Shepherd was happy."

And so was Evelyn. It had felt right to send the pie home with him. "Just don't tell Sam or Caleb. They've both asked to buy whole pies and pans of cinnamon rolls, and I've refused."

"I know." Dorothy reached for a knife and began to scrape slivers of the soap into the dishpan. "If you ever get tired of running a restaurant, you should open a bakery. Mesquite Springs could use one."

Though she knew that the absence of a bakery contributed to the popularity of Polly's Place, Evelyn still wondered why there wasn't one. While Gilmorton was no larger than Mesquite Springs, it had a bakery. "The town has so many shops and businesses, but it's also lacking some basics."

"Like a newspaper." Dorothy had been excited about writing an article about the horse sale and had shared her remarkably good first draft with Evelyn. Now she had

261

begun to hope someone would start a paper in Mesquite Springs.

"We need a hotel too," Evelyn pointed out. "Where are the men who come for Wyatt's sale going to stay?"

As she poured water into the pan and watched the suds form, Dorothy explained Wyatt's plan. "He's going to turn the barn into a bunkhouse for the first to arrive. Martha Bayles has a couple empty rooms at the boardinghouse, and she's putting some pallets in her attic. Folks in town have offered to take in anyone who can't find a room otherwise. They're all determined to show Mesquite Springs in the best light."

Evelyn didn't doubt that. Ida Downey had told her she was ordering extra merchandise in case some of the men brought their wives, and Mrs. Steiner had begun work on a couple summer bonnets that she planned to have on display the week of the sale to attract any wives who might come.

"What about you?" Evelyn asked Dorothy. "Will you be boarding anyone?"

When Dorothy shook her head, Evelyn smiled. "I think you're wise not to do that. There will be so much other work that having guests would be overwhelming. Besides, you'll have Polly and me there."

When Evelyn had heard that Wyatt wanted

to serve meals to everyone who came for the sale, she had volunteered to prepare them. But even if she did the actual cooking, Isolde and Dorothy would still be responsible for setting up tables, ensuring there were enough dishes, and cleaning up afterward. And, on top of that, they'd have Evelyn and Polly staying with them, for Isolde had insisted they come to the ranch the night before the sale.

"It's not the extra work as much as we're not sure Ma could handle having strangers in her house."

The unexpected response made Evelyn blink in surprise. "But you took in Polly and me. We were strangers." And Wyatt had shown no hesitation in bringing them to the Circle C.

As if she'd read Evelyn's mind, Dorothy said, "Wyatt knew he was taking a risk, but he did it anyway."

"What do you mean?"

Dorothy continued washing plates, as if this conversation were an ordinary one. "Ma had a hard time after Pa was killed. I'm not sure why, but she couldn't handle his death. For the better part of a year, she stayed in her room. She hardly ate anything, and she didn't do any of the work around the ranch. She absolutely refused to go near the horses and left the room whenever Wyatt asked her advice about them. Even after she got better, she was wary of strangers."

Evelyn gasped as she tried to reconcile Dorothy's description with the energetic woman she knew. "What did you do?"

Though the subject was grim, Dorothy let out a short laugh. "I tried to feed us, but I was an even worse cook then. You can imagine what my meals were like. The truth is, I didn't do much. Wyatt did everything. He even made our meals." Dorothy looked around the kitchen and shook her head. "It wasn't like this. Lots of times we had either beans or oatmeal, but at least we didn't starve."

She was silent for a moment, as if reliving that obviously difficult part of her life. "I don't know how Wyatt did it all. Looking back on it, I realize he must not have slept more than a couple hours each night, but somehow we scraped through. The horse sales brought in enough money to keep the ranch, and eventually Ma got better."

Evelyn's heart ached at this new revelation. She'd known that Wyatt had felt unprepared to take over the ranch and turn his father's dream into reality, but she hadn't realized that Isolde had been a burden rather than a help. His dream of a life with no responsibilities began to make more sense.

Evelyn forced herself to continue drying the dishes as if the revelation hadn't shocked her. "It must have been difficult for Wyatt, having all that responsibility thrust on him."

"It was," Dorothy agreed. "I didn't realize it at the time, though, because he never complained. He's never been a complainer."

No. Wyatt wouldn't complain. Instead, he'd act. He wasn't complaining now. Instead, he was making plans to escape. Evelyn couldn't blame him. As much as she dreaded the thought of Mesquite Springs without Wyatt, she knew why he wanted to leave and why he wouldn't consider running for mayor. For Wyatt, Mesquite Springs and the Circle C were filled with memories — unhappy ones.

"Got time for a cup of coffee with a friend?"

Wyatt didn't. He'd come into town to mail announcements of the sale along with Dorothy's feature article to every town in Texas that had a newspaper. Wyatt's plan had been to simply do the mailing, then return to the ranch. He hadn't even gone into Polly's Place, but the slightly plaintive note in Sam's voice told him this was no casual invitation.

265

"Sure." He strode into the law office and tossed his hat onto the rack Sam had installed near the front door. As his eyes adjusted to the relative darkness, Wyatt's gaze was snagged by a large ornate vase.

"Pretty fancy for a business, isn't it?"

Sam shrugged as he filled a mug with coffee and handed it to Wyatt. "I bought it for Evelyn, but she claims she's not ready to accept it. Says it's too expensive for a couple that's not officially courting."

The bolt of pleasure that speared him surprised Wyatt by its intensity. He shouldn't care that Evelyn had refused Sam's gift, and yet he couldn't deny his relief. He wanted Evelyn to be happy, and if Sam would make her happy, he'd dance at their wedding, but Wyatt couldn't dismiss the feeling that Sam was not the right man for Evelyn.

"You still want to court her." He made it a statement, not a question.

"Of course. I can't think of anyone who'd make a better mayor's wife."

Wyatt did his best to keep his expression impassive. While he knew some marriages were arranged for practical reasons, if he ever married, it would be because he loved a woman and couldn't imagine his life without her. Surely Evelyn sought — and deserved — that kind of love.

"That's one of the things I want to talk to you about," Sam continued. "I wondered whether you had any ideas of how best to court Evelyn. I know I'm going to win the election. Even if someone else decides to run, I'm practically guaranteed the job. Everyone knows that lawyers have special qualifications."

"Like modesty."

To Sam's credit, he laughed at the barb. "That's not a requirement for becoming mayor, but a pretty wife who cooks the best meals in town would definitely help. I know that, and I'm sure you do, so how do I convince Evelyn?"

Wyatt took another slug of coffee to buy himself time. "I'm the wrong person to answer that. I've never courted a woman — haven't even considered it." Although the thought of marriage had flitted through his brain more often in the past few weeks than ever before, he had no intention of telling Sam that.

"Why don't you ask one of the men who've gotten married in the last year or so?" Wyatt listed three names, but Sam dismissed them.

"I can't ask them."

Pride and the unwillingness to admit that

he did not have all the answers were the only reasons Wyatt could imagine for Sam's reluctance.

"You said courtship was one of the things you wanted to discuss. What are the others? Maybe I can help with them."

Sam drained his mug and refilled it before he turned back to Wyatt. "What changes do you think I should make once I'm elected?"

Wyatt tried not to let his surprise show. Even he, who had no intention of running for mayor, had ideas of how to improve Mesquite Springs, but Sam appeared not to have considered anything other than the honor of the title. As much as he hated to admit it, Wyatt was beginning to think that someone should run against his friend.

"What's so amusing in that there newspaper? I ain't seen you smile like that in months."

Rufus laid the paper aside and forced himself to give his wife a smile. There'd been a time when they'd both smiled as they'd greeted each new day. They'd had a routine. After spending a few minutes in prayer, they would remind each other how blessed they were to have each other and two healthy children. But then everything had changed. For years now, they'd been alone, their children no more than memories.

Rufus had believed that he'd healed as much as a man could after losing both of his children in such tragic ways. He'd begun to smile again, and he started reminding Winnie of their blessings each morning. And then the orphanage had burned, taking with it all desire to smile.

Winnie didn't understand — she claimed he was a foolish old man — but he was still haunted by the knowledge that the girl had died. Today, however, he'd been intrigued by the article in the paper.

"Some rancher in a place called Mesquite Springs is having a horse sale at the end of June. He claims his quarter horses are winners."

Winnie raised an eyebrow, her skepticism evident. "Racehorses?"

"Yep. Says they're fast and agile — good mounts."

His wife's skepticism turned to disapproval. "You ain't thinking of buying one, are you? You know we ain't got the money to waste on tomfoolery like that."

"I know." Rufus wasn't a betting man, so he'd never attended a race, but that didn't stop him from admiring good horseflesh. "Don't worry, Winnie. I'm not going to

Mesquite Springs."

But, oh, how a part of him wished he could.

270

CHAPTER NINETEEN

"Are you ready to leave?"

The hint of exasperation in Ma's voice told Wyatt he needed to hurry. If there was one thing Ma hated, it was being late for church. He didn't like the stares tardy parishioners received any more than she did, but there were times when no matter how hard he tried, he couldn't finish his work quickly enough for them to be seated before the first hymn.

That was one of the reasons he'd hired Caleb — to take some of the responsibility. So far, it had worked, but everything was different today. Because it was Good Friday, the service would begin at noon rather than eight. And it would last for three hours instead of the normal one. As a result, everyone's schedule had had to be adjusted.

Dorothy had gone into town earlier than usual, because Polly's Place would open at ten rather than eleven, giving those who'd traveled from distant ranches a chance to eat a cinnamon roll or a second bowl of oatmeal before the lengthy service. The restaurant would be closed while everyone was in church, but, because some people might not have eaten before the service, Evelyn had decided to reopen for an hour afterwards and serve a simple meal of stew and biscuits.

It would be a long day for her and Dorothy, and it had already been a long day for Wyatt. He'd stayed up far too late, reconciling the ranch's accounts and figuring out the minimum he could accept for each horse in order to leave Ma and Dorothy with enough money for the next two years. Two years would give him enough time to explore the country and Caleb enough time to prove his mettle.

Though Wyatt expected Caleb to do well with the horses, he didn't want him to have the same worries he'd had when Pa died. Wyatt's savings would give Caleb a measure of security, knowing that any mistakes he might make would not result in Ma and Dorothy losing the ranch.

"I want to do a final check on the horses," Wyatt told his mother as he strode into the kitchen. She'd already tied her bonnet strings and stood near the door.

"I thought Caleb did that."

"He did, but . . ." Wyatt couldn't explain why he felt compelled to visit the paddock again. All he knew was that it seemed important.

"You and those horses." The refrain was so familiar that Wyatt barely noticed it.

As he left the house, he heard Emerald whinny and knew that he'd been right to worry. That was not her normal sound. Something was upsetting his prize mare. His heart pounding with fear of what he might find, Wyatt sprinted toward the paddock, fear turning to dread at the sight of Emerald's foal. Ebony lay on the ground, rolling from side to side, his eyes radiating pain and panic. The last time Wyatt had seen a horse like this, he'd . . . He wouldn't think about that. Ebony was not going to die.

"It'll be all right, boy. We'll get you up."

Heedless of the dirt that would coat his Sunday suit, Wyatt raced into the barn for a rope. It was vital to get the colt on his feet and walking before it was too late. Ebony's violent rolling might have already twisted his gut, and if it had, Wyatt's favorite foal might die.

"Please, Lord, let me be in time," he prayed as he slid the rope over Ebony's head and began to hoist him. Emerald watched her foal nervously, then when she realized what Wyatt was doing, she moved to Ebony's flank and began to nudge him. Together, they got the young horse to his feet and began to walk around the paddock. Wyatt murmured soothing words as he led the colt, while Emerald kept pace, her snorts and whinnies encouraging her son.

"What's going on?" Ma appeared at the edge of the paddock and stared at Wyatt.

"Colic. At least I hope that's all it is." Though anger had bubbled up inside him like the oil Ma used to make fritters, Wyatt kept his voice calm. "I saw some moldy hay the other day. Caleb was supposed to get rid of it, but Ebony may have eaten some of it before he did." Or maybe Caleb hadn't cleaned the stall completely. That possibility was one Wyatt didn't want to consider.

"What can I do?" Ma's voice was warm with worry. Though she avoided the horses whenever she could, she knew how much each of them meant to Wyatt.

"Pray." Both he and Ebony needed that. "And make my excuses to Pastor Coleman." There was no way Wyatt could leave the ranch today.

"Should I tell Caleb what happened?"

Wyatt shook his head as he tugged on

Ebony's lead. Though the colt was showing signs of wanting to lie down, Wyatt could not allow that. "There's nothing Caleb can do now." And Wyatt needed time for his anger to dissipate. Even if Caleb had disposed of the bad hay, he should have seen the signs of Ebony's distress when he let the horses out of the stable this morning.

"Don't be angry, son. People make mistakes."

Wyatt turned to face his mother. "Believe me, I know that. I'm the one who made the biggest mistake." What a fool he'd been to think he could leave the ranch!

The last of the customers had left, and Evelyn was about to turn the sign to "closed" when she saw Caleb hurrying toward the restaurant, a brown-wrapped package under his arm.

"I know you're busy, but I gotta talk to you," he said as he approached Polly's Place. Though his face was flushed from the exertion, his eyes were solemn.

Evelyn opened the door and ushered him inside, grateful that since Dorothy and Polly were in the kitchen, there was no impropriety involved in inviting a single man to join her. It was only afterwards that she had realized she might incur censure for the day she and Wyatt and Polly had shared cake in the kitchen without a chaperone nearby. Since then, she'd been extra careful.

"Let's sit here." Evelyn chose a table in the middle of the room, far enough from the window that passersby wouldn't spot them but close enough to the kitchen that Dorothy could see but not hear what was going on.

"Thank you." Caleb laid the package on one of the empty chairs before sitting down. "I know you heard what happened to Wyatt's horse." When Evelyn nodded, acknowledging that, like Caleb, she'd been close enough to overhear Isolde telling Pastor Coleman why Wyatt wouldn't be at church, he continued. "I'm sick at the thought that I might be responsible. I can't help thinking that I missed something because I was preoccupied."

That didn't sound like Caleb. Hadn't his mother told her that while he didn't necessarily persist with any endeavor once he'd mastered it, he devoted his full attention to it initially?

"Isolde didn't say that Wyatt blamed you."

"But he will." There was a fatalistic note in Caleb's voice. "I've known Wyatt all my life, and I know that he expects perfection. The problem is, I'm not perfect."

"No one is."

"Try telling that to Wyatt. I wanted to go out there and explain, but his mother told me it wasn't a good idea. Not today, anyway."

Evelyn looked at the man Dorothy had called the handsomest male in Mesquite Springs and wondered why he'd come here this afternoon. Did he expect her to plead his case with Wyatt? It almost sounded as if that was his intention, but why would he believe Wyatt would listen to her? While it was true that he'd accepted her suggestion that Dorothy write about the sale, he'd soundly rejected the idea of running for mayor every time Evelyn had raised it.

Deciding to change the subject, Evelyn leaned forward ever so slightly as she said, "You mentioned being preoccupied. What was on your mind?"

Caleb pulled the package from the chair and slid it toward her. "This. I kept trying to think of ways to make it more special." When she stared at it, trying to guess what was inside the clumsily wrapped package, he nodded. "Go ahead. Open it."

As she untied the twine and unfolded the paper, Evelyn discovered that the packaging hid the shape of the contents. Inside what had appeared to be a square parcel was a small pie pan. She picked it up and studied it from every angle, smiling when she saw that it wasn't what she'd expected. It was something far better. Though she'd envisioned nothing more than a small version of her pie pans, Caleb had added a wide rim with scalloped edges. Even without showing it to her, Evelyn knew Polly would love it.

"It's perfect!"

Caleb seemed unconvinced by her praise. "I know it's not exactly what you described, but when I looked at my mother's pie tins, I thought this might be better." He pointed to the rim. "I wanted that to be big enough for a child to hold."

It was that and more. Besides adding beauty to a utilitarian pan, the scalloped edges would help prevent it from slipping from Polly's hands.

"This is a much better design. I don't know how to thank you, Caleb."

He leaned forward and laid a hand on one of hers. "No thanks are necessary. Surely you know I'd do anything for you." The intensity in his expression underscored his words and left Evelyn feeling uncomfortable. Had she made a mistake when she'd asked Caleb to craft a pan? Though she'd thought he had believed her when she'd told him and Sam she was not ready for marriage, the looks he was giving her said otherwise. She needed to get this conversation back on the right track.

"The pan is absolutely perfect, Caleb. I can't wait for Polly to see it." Without pausing, Evelyn raised her voice. "Polly, come see what Mr. Caleb made for you."

Still carrying a dishtowel, Polly raced into the dining room and skidded to a stop next to Evelyn, her eyes widening as she spotted the pan. "Is that for me? My very own pie pan?"

"Yep. What do you think?" The hesitation that Caleb had shown over Evelyn's reaction had disappeared, and he seemed genuinely interested in Polly's opinion.

Polly picked the pan up, holding it as carefully as if it were made of the finest crystal. "It's boo-tee-ful." She ran her fingers over the scallops and grinned. "Can I make a pie right now?"

Evelyn shook her head. "We'll do that tomorrow morning." When Polly's smile turned into a sulk, she added, "The pan isn't ready for the oven. You need to wash and dry it very carefully, but before you do that, what do you say to Mr. Caleb?"

"Thank you, Mr. Caleb." With the social amenities complete, Polly clasped the pan to her chest and ran back into the kitchen.

279

"Miss Dorothy, look what I have!"

"You made a little girl very happy," Evelyn told Caleb when the sound of Polly's excited chatter drifted into the dining room.

He frowned ever so slightly as he looked at her. "I was hoping to make a big girl happy."

Evelyn tried not to flinch at the longing she saw in his eyes, and for a second she was convinced that she had indeed made a mistake by asking Caleb to make the pan. But the memory of Polly's happiness told her she'd do it again, regardless of the uncomfortable scene her request had created.

Caleb sighed. "I can see you're not ready to hear what I want to say. I'd be lying if I said I wasn't disappointed, but there's nothing I can do about that other than wait. I'm good at waiting."

"Would you mind staying with Polly for a few minutes?" Evelyn asked Dorothy when they'd finished the dishes. "I want to take a piece of pie to Mrs. Steiner."

Though the real reason for the visit to the dressmaker was to pick up the bonnet Mrs. Steiner was making to go with Polly's new Easter dress, Evelyn would not say that while Polly was within earshot.

"No problem. Polly and I have lots to do, don't we?"

The girl nodded. "Miss Dorothy is gonna help me pick out the right 'gredients for my first pie."

"I was thinking about sauerkraut and molasses," Dorothy declared solemnly.

As she'd intended, Polly shrieked her protest while Evelyn climbed the stairs to their apartment to retrieve her hat and gloves. A minute later as she left the restaurant, she blinked in surprise at the sight of Caleb entering Sam's office. As far as she knew, the men ignored each other as much as possible. Why was Caleb initiating a meeting?

Telling herself it was none of her business, Evelyn continued down Main Street to Mrs. Steiner's shop, but when she returned, Polly's new hat carefully stowed in a box that would elicit no curiosity, she could not ignore the curses that emanated from the law office nor the unmistakable sound of glass shattering. Were the men fighting?

Though she had no idea how she'd stop them, Evelyn flung the door open and entered the room, expecting to see two angry men, perhaps pummeling each other. Instead, the office was empty except for a now-silent Sam, who was staring at the remains of his crystal vase as if perplexed by the puddle of water and the bruised flowers that mingled with the glass shards.

"Are you all right?" Evelyn asked. The expression in his eyes was one she'd never seen before, a wild ferocity competing with bewilderment.

Sam shook his head as if to clear it. "I must apologize for my language. I know it wasn't fit for a lady's ears, but I was upset when your vase tumbled off the table and broke. It was one of a kind, like the pie pan Caleb gave you."

So that was why Caleb had come. He'd wanted to gloat over the fact that Evelyn had asked him to make a pan. If only she hadn't been so impetuous. And yet, Evelyn knew it wasn't impetuosity that had led her to request the pie tin; it was the desire to make Polly happy.

"The pan was for Polly, not me." Though she owed Sam no explanation, Evelyn hated the fact that what she had done, albeit for the best of reasons, had caused someone pain.

"It's all right." Sam looked at the mess on the floor. "Accidents happen."

But this had been no accident. The curses had preceded the glass shattering, and the gouge in the wall confirmed that the vase had not slipped off the table. It had been hurled.

CHAPTER TWENTY

"How's Ebony?"

Wyatt turned at the sound of Evelyn's voice. When he'd had supper with his mother and Dorothy, neither one had mentioned that she might be coming to the ranch. And, knowing that she didn't like traveling after dark, her appearance surprised him. While he knew Evelyn felt an affinity to Emerald's son, Wyatt hadn't expected her to make a special trip out here just to check on him. Still, he couldn't deny the warmth that spread through his veins at the knowledge that she had cared enough to come.

"He's all right." Wyatt gestured toward the foal who was now back in his stall, looking for all the world like a healthy colt, not one who'd been writhing in pain not long ago. "It turned out to be nothing more than colic. Once I got him on his feet, he started looking better. I learned a long time ago that walking helps calm horses, and being calm is the first step toward recovery."

He stroked Ebony's neck, watching as the horse eyed Evelyn, hoping for the carrots she sometimes gave him. "Sorry, boy. No carrots for you tonight." Turning back to Evelyn, Wyatt continued his explanation. "It took longer than I'd expected, but his digestive system is working again." There was no need to tell her all the unpleasant details of colic and the methods he'd used to unblock Ebony's intestines.

Evelyn remained standing a foot outside the stall. "I'm glad. I know how special he is to you." She paused, then added as if it were an afterthought, "Caleb was upset when he heard what happened."

So that was why she was here. She'd spoken to Caleb. Had he tried to sweet-talk her the way Sam did every time he was near her? Caleb might not be as wealthy as Sam, but according to Dorothy, his good looks made him Mesquite Springs's most eligible bachelor. Was it possible Evelyn harbored tender feelings for him?

The idea bothered Wyatt more than it should have, and so his voice was gruffer than normal as he said, "I told Ma not to say anything to Caleb."

"She didn't." The reply came so quickly

that it was almost like a retort. "He over-heard her explaining to Pastor Coleman what had happened. Caleb wanted to come out here to see you, but your mother con-vinced him that wouldn't be a good idea."

Ma was right. "So he sent you instead."

To Wyatt's surprise, Evelyn bristled with apparent annoyance. "No one sent me. I came because I was worried about you."

"I'm fine." Even as he pronounced the words, Wyatt knew they were a lie.

"You don't look fine to me. You look angry."

Realizing that their discussion was upset-ting the horses, Wyatt gestured toward the stable door. Only when he and Evelyn were outside did he speak again. "Wouldn't you be angry if a simple mistake endangered something you cared about?"

Wyatt had been more than angry; he'd been furious as well as frightened by the possible effect that mistake might have had. Though he'd resolved that it would never be repeated, the implications of that resolu-tion only fueled his anger.

"I would be, but I also know that every-one makes mistakes." Evelyn brushed aside the curl that the light breeze had loosened from the knot at the back of her head. Though it softened her face, it did not lessen the intensity of her gaze. "I hope you can forgive Caleb."

She didn't understand. No one did. "It wasn't Caleb who made a mistake. It was me." Wyatt spat the words, challenging her to deny them. "I should have known better. The horses are my responsibility, mine alone. I should never have let someone else care for them."

Evelyn took a step backward, as if repelled by the ferocity of his reply, and her eyes widened in surprise. A second later, she closed the distance between them and put a hand on his arm. "Oh, Wyatt. You can't do everything yourself. It's not wrong to share responsibilities with someone else."

As the warmth of her hand penetrated the thickness of his sleeve, he felt himself begin to relax. What she said made sense, and yet she didn't fully understand. "It is wrong when it endangers my horses. I saw that moldy hay. I should have pitched it right then, but I didn't. I thought I could trust Caleb."

She tightened her grip, as if she feared he'd bolt like a frightened foal. "I doubt he'll make that mistake again."

"He won't, because I won't let him."

Evelyn waited until Wyatt met her gaze

before she asked, "Are you going to fire him?"

"I don't know." That had been his first thought, but now he wasn't so sure. After all, as he'd just told her, the ultimate responsibility had been his own. "What would you suggest?"

"Give him a second chance. We all deserve that." Though she said nothing more, Wyatt knew Evelyn was thinking about her own life and how she'd escaped not only the murderer but also the fire. God had given her a second and a third chance at life. What she asked for Caleb was far less than that. How could he refuse?

"All right. You've convinced me."

The smile that lit her face was brighter than a summer sun. "You're a good man, Wyatt."

He wasn't. Wyatt knew that. But knowing that Evelyn cared made him want to do everything he could to be one.

"He is risen."

Basil kept a smile fixed on his face as the minister continued his sermon, talking about the miracle of the risen Christ. What else could you expect on Easter Sunday? It was a waste of time being here. Basil knew that as surely as he knew there would be

288

ugly gossip if he didn't attend Easter morning services, and so he'd donned his best suit and seated himself in the second pew where everyone would see the master of Marlow Acres.

At least today's service was early enough that he could make it to the races this afternoon. His own horse was lamed during last week's race and couldn't run today, but he'd heard that Finley was going to be there. It would be interesting to see if his entry from the Clark stables was as good as he claimed.

Basil stopped himself from frowning as the minister droned on. He was planning to buy two or three horses this year and wanted at least one to be from Clark's. Those he'd seen at last year's sale in Fort Worth had practically taken his breath away. Big, beautiful, fast. Basil had wanted one more than almost anything he could recall, but Finley had outbid him because Bart refused to advance him any more money. That was when he'd decided that Bart's days were numbered.

"Oh, Mr. Marlow, I'm so glad to see you here today." The overweight matron stopped Basil as he tried to exit from the church after the endless service finally came to a close. "Isn't this the most glorious Easter

Sunday?" she continued, snagging her daughter's hand and pulling her so that Basil couldn't miss her.

Basil gave the woman whose name he could not recall his broadest smile, hoping that would satisfy her. The only good thing he could say about her and her daughter was that neither had flinched at the sight of his face. The men at the races didn't care that his left cheek was marked with a blemish, but most women averted their gaze when they saw the strawberry-colored mark. Perhaps it was time to let his beard grow. Who cared if it made him look like Bart? Bart was six feet under.

The woman's smile widened in response to Basil's. "I was just saying to Mr. Gibson that you must be lonely all by yourself in that big old house of yours."

Gibson. That's right. Harold and Frances Gibson. Basil thought quickly, trying to recall everything he'd heard about them. Fairly wealthy. Only one child. What was her name? Sue something. SuEllen. That's right. The daughter was SuEllen.

"I hope you'll join us for dinner today," Mrs. Gibson continued, oblivious to the detours Basil's thoughts had taken. "You know I'm not one to brag, but our cook makes the best ham in the county."

The women in this congregation were exceedingly persistent. Every time Basil attended church, one of them invited him for a meal. It wasn't Christian charity, he was certain, but the fact that each of them who issued an invitation had an unmarried daughter.

Basil gave this one an appraising look. Blonde hair, blue eyes, curves in all the right places. SuEllen Gibson was pretty enough. The problem was, she didn't stir his blood the way Miriam had.

"Thank you kindly, Mrs. Gibson. I would surely enjoy your company and that of your lovely daughter, but sadly, I have another engagement today."

"Perhaps next week."

"Perhaps." Basil said his farewells and strolled to his carriage. "Let's go, Whistler," he said as he settled himself onto the deeply padded seat. One of the few good things he could say about Bart was that the slave he'd chosen to drive his carriage knew how to handle one.

When they reached the open road, Whistler flicked the reins, and the horses began to trot. Speed was just what Basil needed to settle the thoughts that had begun to float through his brain. Was he making a mistake? He was over thirty now, well past the age most men married. While Miriam had been alive, he'd refused to even consider another woman, but now . . .

Now he needed a wife to give him a son and heir. He could do worse than SuEllen. The Gibsons weren't as wealthy as everyone believed Basil to be, but the truth was, they probably were richer than he was now that the plantation was suffering. He could use an infusion of money from SuEllen's dowry, and if he snuffed the candles, perhaps he could pretend that she was Miriam.

CHAPTER TWENTY-ONE

Evelyn smiled as the minister concluded the benediction. It was Easter Sunday, her favorite day of the year, and her heart was filled with joy at the story that never grew old, no matter how often she heard it. Even Polly, who frequently fidgeted during the sermon, had paid attention when the minister had recounted the women's astonishment at the empty grave. But now that the service was over and they'd emerged into the bright sunshine, she tugged on Evelyn's sleeve.

"I wish my papa would come out of the grave," she said, her light blue eyes solemn. "I miss him."

"I know you do. I miss Mama and Papa too." And it had been much longer since their deaths, not to mention that she'd been older than Polly and better able to deal with grief when they'd been taken from her.

"I want a new papa."

"How about a big brother? Would that be almost as good?"

Evelyn turned, startled not only by the sound of Sam's voice behind her but by the fact that he was being attentive to Polly. Gone was the angry man who'd smashed an expensive vase. In his place was a charming, seemingly gentle one.

Though Evelyn hadn't noticed Sam during the service, he'd obviously been there, for here he was, accompanied by an elderly couple whom Evelyn hadn't seen before. Sam's resemblance to the man left no doubt that he was a relative, perhaps his grandfather. They shared the same muscular build and the same warm brown eyes, although the man's hair was now fully gray rather than brown.

Sam turned to the silver-haired woman who leaned heavily on a cane. Perhaps an inch or so shorter than Evelyn and more than a few pounds heavier than most women, she had eyes almost as light blue as Polly's. Those eyes appeared to be assessing Evelyn.

"I'm sorry, Mother."

This was Sam's mother? Evelyn tried not to let her surprise show. His parents must have been at least forty when he'd been born, and while it wasn't unusual for a couple to have children at that age, it was unusual for their firstborn to make his appearance then.

"I forgot my manners for a moment," Sam continued. "Evelyn, I'd like you to meet my parents, Adam and Eve Plaut. Father and Mother, let me introduce you to Evelyn Radner and her sister Molly."

Evelyn sighed. Though Sam's mood had changed, one thing had not. Before she had a chance to correct him, Polly took charge. "Polly." She stomped her foot. "My name is Polly."

Mrs. Plaut took a step forward and smiled at Polly. "Why, so it is. And that's a lovely name." To Mrs. Plaut's credit, she did not flinch at the sight of Polly's birthmark. Instead, she turned her attention to Evelyn. "I'm pleased to meet you at last. Sam has said so much about you."

"The pleasure is mine. Sam intrigued me with the story of your love of flowers and how Mr. Plaut gave you a greenhouse."

"Then you must come see it." Mrs. Plaut tightened her grip on the cane. "I know you have other plans for today, but I do hope you and Polly will come for supper some evening."

She lifted her cane, giving Evelyn a good view of her hand. The twisted fingers and enlarged knuckles told their tale. "As you can see, I suffer from arthritis. That makes it difficult for me to come into town very often, but I would like to get to know you better and, of course, show you my flowers. Perhaps this Wednesday?"

Before Evelyn could respond, Polly, who'd been listening more patiently than normal, looked up at Mr. Plaut. "Do you have horses?"

"You bet we do. Some of the best in the county."

That was all Polly needed to hear. She gripped Evelyn's hand and looked at her with pleading eyes. "Can we go?"

There was no way Evelyn could resist. "Yes." Turning to Sam's mother, she asked, "Would you like me to bring a pie?"

Mr. Plaut gave his wife no time to reply. "There's no need. We have a cook."

"Don't be rude, Adam." With another smile for Evelyn, Mrs. Plaut added, "I'd be most grateful if you did. Sam has said so much about your cooking that I'm eager to taste your pie."

And so Evelyn found herself riding with Polly and Sam to his ranch Wednesday afternoon.

Located south of Mesquite Springs, the Plaut ranch was situated on what Sam

296

claimed was some of the best cattle ranching land in the Hill Country. "Others like the hills, but my father thought cattle would thrive on flatter ground." He pointed to the dark specks that dotted the countryside. "That's only a few of them."

Polly gave them a cursory glance. "Where are the horses?"

Her question was answered when they approached the sprawling one-story building whose wide porch left no doubt that this was the main house. Half a dozen horses were grazing in a paddock on the west side, eliciting Polly's enthusiastic cries.

"Horses!" she cried.

As she walked to the edge of the porch to greet them, Mrs. Plaut gave Polly a warm smile. "Sam, we don't want to disappoint Polly, do we? Why don't you show her the horses? I'd like a chance to get acquainted with her sister."

As Sam and Polly walked toward the paddock, Polly scampering to keep up with his longer stride, Mrs. Plaut led Evelyn into the house and ushered her into the parlor, saying they'd visit the greenhouse later when Polly could accompany them.

While less formal than the Downeys', the Plauts' parlor boasted finer furnishings than anywhere Evelyn had lived. No expense had been spared on the horsehair settee and chairs or the china figurines that decorated the side tables. Evelyn suspected that the delicately crocheted antimacassars had either been made by someone else or dated from the time before arthritis had crippled Mrs. Plaut's fingers.

"I hope you don't mind my frankness," Sam's mother said once she and Evelyn were seated, "but I'm curious about you. I've never seen Sam so taken with a woman before."

Evelyn tried to keep her expression non-committal. She couldn't — she wouldn't — tell Mrs. Plaut that she was not taken with her son and that she was concerned about his outbursts of anger.

"As you can imagine, Adam and I are anxious for Sam to settle down and give us some grandchildren. Now that he's going to be Mesquite Springs's mayor and perhaps someday a senator, he has an even greater need for a wife." It was another comment that Evelyn had no intention of answering. Fortunately, Mrs. Plaut's next question was less fraught with emotion. "How old are you, Miss Radner?"

"Twenty-three."

The older woman nodded. "I thought so. I'd been married for five years by the time I was your age." She pulled a small painting of a newly married couple from the table and showed it to Evelyn. "That's us on our wedding day. Unfortunately, the good Lord didn't bless us with Sam until we'd been married more than twenty years. We'd just about given up hope, but like Abraham and Sarah in the Bible, God gave us a son in our old age."

Realizing some response was expected, Evelyn murmured, "You must be very proud of him."

"Oh yes." Mrs. Plaut's face turned rosy with pride. "We couldn't have asked for a better son. Even when he was mischievous the way all boys are, we never had to discipline him. Sam was always so genuinely sorry that neither of us could bear to do more than remind him not to do it again."

She set the portrait back on the table. "I know there are some in town who claim we spoiled him, but they're wrong. Look at the way he turned out. Sam's a fine, upstanding man. Any woman would be proud to marry him."

Evelyn's discomfort grew. While she understood Mrs. Plaut's desire to see her son settled, she had no intention of becoming his bride. If she married, it would be to a man who loved her for herself, not because she was a good cook or because his family believed he needed a wife. She wanted a man who remembered Polly's name, a man like . . . Evelyn paused as an image floated before her. If she married, it would be to a man like Wyatt.

Ever since Reverend Coleman's sermon about the freedom truth provided, Wyatt had known that he had to have this conversation, even though it meant dredging up the worst year of his life.

"Is something wrong, son?" Ma looked up from her mending.

"No. Not really. I just wanted to talk." He settled in the chair across from her so that he could watch her expression. He'd never known Ma to lie, but there were times when he suspected she hadn't told the whole truth. He wouldn't let that happen today.

"About what?"

"Why do you hate horses?" Wyatt gulped. That wasn't the question he'd planned to ask. He'd wanted to ask why she'd fallen apart after Pa was killed, but the other question had popped out unbidden.

Ma laid down the sock she was darning and faced him, her expression troubled. "I don't hate horses."

"You rarely go to the stable, and when I

talk about them, I feel as if you're closing your ears." A distant memory assailed him. "It wasn't always that way. When Pa was alive, you used to help him train the horses, and you were always there when a mare was foaling." How had he forgotten that?

The clock on the mantel chimed, a reminder of the passage of time. Wyatt had believed the past indelibly etched on his memory, but he'd forgotten at least one important thing. What other memories had he lost?

When she spoke, Ma's voice was so soft he struggled to hear it. "I love horses. I always have."

"Then what changed?" Even as he posed the question, Wyatt knew the answer. Everything had changed the day Pa had died. That had been the last day Ma had spent any appreciable time in the stable.

"Did you know your father wanted to raise sheep?"

Wyatt shook his head, as much from confusion over the question that seemed to have no bearing on the subject as the fact that he could not recall anyone discussing sheep.

Ma stared into the distance for a moment, tears welling in her eyes. "You and Dorothy have heard how my family emigrated from

Germany and how your father became my lifeline after my parents died on the journey from Galveston to here. What you don't know is that your father's family expected him to be a farmer. Clarks had farmed for generations, and Wilson was expected to follow the tradition."

Wyatt tried and failed to imagine his father being happy behind a plow. He'd grumbled every time he'd had to clear the ground for Ma's garden, although he'd enjoyed the vegetables she'd grown.

"We were young and thought we could do anything," Ma continued. "Wilson told me he wanted to raise animals, not wheat or rye, and I agreed. Where we disagreed was over what animals he should raise."

"He wanted sheep," Wyatt guessed.

Ma nodded. "I couldn't abide those smelly creatures, but I love horses. The only thing I missed about Germany was my mare."

"And you convinced Pa that horses were better than sheep." Was this what Evelyn meant when she'd described his mother as a strong woman? Only someone who was strong and determined could have overruled Pa's wishes. But maybe it hadn't been a matter of one person winning and the other losing. Perhaps the decision had been a shared one, evidence of the partnership

302

Evelyn claimed was the hallmark of a good marriage.

The tears that had hovered on Ma's eyelids trickled down her cheeks. "It wasn't hard to persuade him, especially once he saw what quarter horses were like, but oh, Wyatt . . ." The trickle turned into a flow. "If I could undo one thing in my life, it would be that. I should have let Wilson have his sheep."

Pa had once told Wyatt that no man could understand how a woman's mind worked. This conversation was surely proof of that. "But he loved raising horses." That was an incontrovertible fact.

"And they killed him." Ma shook her head so violently that a hairpin tumbled to the floor. "That's not true," she said, contradicting herself. "It wasn't the horses. I was the one who killed him. Don't you see, Wyatt? It was only because of the horses — the horses I urged him to raise — that he was on the road that day. I killed him as surely as if I'd shot the arrow."

It made no sense. Pa could have been killed going into town on an errand; if he'd raised sheep, he could have been taking a ram to a neighbor; and yet Ma's words explained so much. No wonder she'd withdrawn from the world. If she believed herself guilty of causing her husband's death, her grief would have made even normal activities unbearable. And her beloved horses were nothing but a reminder of her mistake.

Wyatt rose and went to his mother's side. Drawing her into his arms, he murmured, "You weren't to blame. We'll never know why God let Pa be on the road that day, but I do know it wasn't your fault. Pa loved you; he loved being a horse rancher; and he died doing what he loved. He wouldn't have wanted you to blame yourself."

Ma brushed the tears from her face as she said, "I know that now. And I know how much I hurt you and Dorothy." She cupped Wyatt's cheeks. "I'm sorry, son. I never meant to hurt you, but I was lost when Wilson died. I loved him so much that when he was gone, I felt as if half of me had been torn away. I didn't want to live without him."

The anguish in his mother's voice wrenched Wyatt's heart. If only he had had this conversation with Ma when she was in the depths of her depression, perhaps he could have helped her. He dismissed the thought as quickly as it appeared, knowing neither he nor his mother had been ready then.

"It was selfish of me." Ma fixed her gaze on Wyatt. "You and Dorothy loved him too. You were as lost without him as I was. I should have stood with you, but I didn't. Can you forgive me for that?"

Wyatt pressed a kiss on his mother's forehead. "There's nothing to forgive." As he pronounced the words and felt his heart lighten, Wyatt knew that the minister had been right. Truth did bring freedom. It had taken more than a decade, but Ma's revelation had freed Wyatt from his own burden of guilt and the belief that he could have done more to ease his mother's pain.

"Thank you, son." Her face wreathed in a radiant smile, Ma said, "I know that if he were here, your father would say the same thing I do. You're the best son anyone has ever had."

He wasn't, but the praise filled an empty spot deep within him.

"Promise me one thing." It appeared Ma wasn't finished. "Promise me that if you find a woman you love as much as I did your father, you won't let her go."

CHAPTER TWENTY-TWO

"Miss Dorothy said we're going on a picnic today. What's a picnic?" Polly bounced up and down on the bench in front of the restaurant, her yellow skirts fluttering as she and Evelyn waited for Wyatt and his family to arrive.

Though Evelyn was surprised that Polly wasn't familiar with the word, she reminded herself that since Polly's mother had died when she was born, perhaps there had been no one to introduce her to the simple pleasures of a picnic.

"It's when we take special food and eat outside."

Polly was silent for a moment, digesting Evelyn's explanation. "Like the horses? I don't wanna eat grass."

Evelyn bit back a smile. "Don't worry. We'll have people food, but we'll be able to eat most of it with our fingers."

Her eyes widening, Polly stopped bouncing and stared at Evelyn. "But you said that's rude."

"The rules are different for picnics."

"Then I like picnics." A wide grin underscored Polly's opinion.

"So do I."

After the awkwardness of the evening with Sam's parents when Evelyn had felt as if she were being evaluated as a potential bride for their son, she needed the comfort of Sunday dinner with Wyatt's family. They had no unrealistic expectations of her. Instead, they accepted her for who she was.

And yet Evelyn could not ignore the apprehension that mingled with anticipation. Would Wyatt sense that her feelings for him had changed and that she no longer regarded him as nothing more than a friend? Oh, how she hoped he would not. It would be horribly embarrassing, for he'd never been anything but a perfect gentleman, an ideal friend. Somehow, someway, she would keep her emotions under control.

Fortunately, Polly helped. When the Clarks' wagon approached, she jumped off the bench and grabbed the small basket Evelyn had filled with peach turnovers. "I can carry it," she announced. "Look what I got, Mr. Wyatt," she said as he lifted her into the wagon. "Food. Did you bring some?"

The smile Wyatt flashed at Evelyn was warm, friendly, and slightly amused. Perfectly normal. She began to relax.

"He didn't, but someone else did." Dorothy gestured toward the two large baskets that shared the back of the wagon with several blankets. "I made enough fried chicken to feed a dozen hungry men."

"Yummy! I like fried chicken."

It was hard to resist Polly's enthusiasm, and no one tried. "Wait until you see how good it tastes cold," Isolde said with a broad smile.

Her skepticism evident, Polly wrinkled her nose. "Cold?"

Dorothy nodded. "Everything for this picnic is cold."

Polly started to protest, then looked at Wyatt. "Do you like cold chicken?" she demanded.

"I sure do."

Her frown turned upside down. "Then I do too."

As everyone chuckled, Isolde announced that she and Dorothy would sit on the backseat with Polly, leaving Evelyn to join Wyatt in front. It was their normal arrangement, no reason for her to be nervous, and yet Evelyn could not help noticing that, even though she sat a proper distance from him, the scent of Wyatt's bay rum drifted toward her. She'd smelled it before, but somehow today it seemed more . . . She struggled to find the correct adjective, settling for "tantalizing." And that was ridiculous. She needed to think about more prosaic things.

"Where are we going?" she asked as Wyatt turned the wagon around, then headed north on Mesquite. There was nothing even remotely romantic about that question.

And there was nothing romantic about his answer. "It's not too far — about ten minutes. Dorothy found this spot one spring when she decided to run away from home. I don't remember why she ran off, but when she discovered it, she thought it was so pretty that she came back home to tell us about it. She never ran away again, although," Wyatt said, raising his voice ever so slightly, "sometimes I wished she would."

"I heard that, big brother."

His grin confirmed that he'd known she was listening to their conversation. "Then you know exactly what I mean. We were hoping you'd find another good picnic spot."

"A likely story!"

The gentle bantering changed the tenor of

Evelyn's longing. How she wished she'd had siblings!

"Is something wrong?" Though Wyatt spoke softly, there was no need, for Dorothy and his mother were now engaged in a lively conversation with Polly about the merits of cold food.

Evelyn shook her head, regretting that her expression must have revealed her emotions. She didn't want anything to spoil this day, especially not her past. "I just hope you realize how fortunate you are to have a sister."

Wyatt gave her a penetrating look, as if he understood more than she'd said. "You have Polly now."

"Yes, but . . ."

"You wanted someone closer to your age. You're more like Polly's mother than her sister."

Evelyn nodded. "She needed one. Oh, Wyatt, I saw a number of children during the years I was at the orphanage, and most of them had tragic backgrounds, but none touched me the way Polly did. From the first day, I knew she was special."

Struggling to keep her voice from cracking, Evelyn continued. "I wish I knew her story, but she won't even tell me her last name. I suppose it shouldn't matter, but somehow it seems important to know who she is."

"You mean who she was." Wyatt kept his voice low. "You know who she is now — your sister of the heart."

Evelyn smiled at the phrase that captured her relationship with Polly so well. "You're right, but . . ."

"You still want to know who abandoned her and why." Wyatt was silent for a moment. "I wish I could help you. I know I've seen a man with a similar birthmark, but I can't remember where, and that's frustrating. It's a long shot, but he might be a relative."

Evelyn didn't believe that was likely. "I doubt she has any living relatives. She said it was her mammy who took her to the orphanage after her father died."

"You never know. Some people aren't cut out to be parents." Wyatt turned his attention from the road back to Evelyn. "We can't solve that today, so let's enjoy our picnic."

"I agree."

Only minutes later, Wyatt pulled off the road into a field covered with flowers so deep a blue that it looked as if the sky had turned upside down.

Evelyn's breath caught, and she pressed

311

her hand to her chest to slow her heartbeat. "This is incredible. It almost looks like water." The flowers were so abundant that they grew in wide meandering masses that mimicked the flow of a stream.

"Looky, Evelyn." Polly poked her head between Evelyn and Wyatt and pointed at the flowers. "Miss Dorothy says they're bluebonnets. Can I touch them?"

"Of course. These are wildflowers." Evelyn had cautioned Polly about picking flowers in town, reminding her that people had spent a lot of time growing them, but these were different.

"Goody!" Polly took Evelyn's words as an invitation to enjoy the beauty and raced across the ground to one of the largest masses of bluebonnets. Kneeling, she bent to sniff, then began to pick them.

While Wyatt tended to the horses, Evelyn and Dorothy spread out the largest blanket and were arranging the food in the center of it when Polly returned, her hands full of flowers.

"Look, Evelyn. I picked you a boo-key."

"Bouquet." Evelyn corrected her as she accepted the bluebonnets.

"That's what I said. Ooh, that's pretty." Polly grinned when Evelyn tucked half the flowers into her hatband, then slid the remainder into Polly's sash. A second later, apparently losing interest in the bluebonnets, she tugged on Evelyn's hand. "Can we eat now? I'm hungry."

"Since you're so hungry, it seems to me you should be the one to give thanks for the food," Isolde said when Polly had plunked herself onto the blanket between her and Wyatt.

Shock turned Polly's face white, then red. "You mean say the blessing?"

"Yes." Isolde's voice was kind but firm. "You're a big girl now. You can do that."

To Evelyn's amusement, Polly seemed to puff with pride.

"Okay." She bowed her head. "Jesus, I know you're listening, 'cuz Evelyn says you hear everything, but she didn't say you could smell things. I hope you can, 'cuz this chicken smells good. Evelyn says we can eat it with our fingers. I hope that's okay with you. Amen." She paused for a second. "Oh, I forgot. Thank you for the chicken and the turnovers. Don't be mad, but I don't like coleslaw, so I ain't gonna thank you for it. Amen."

When Evelyn opened her eyes, she saw that Wyatt could barely control his mirth over the unorthodox blessing. The slow wink he gave her sent warmth flooding through her, warming her from the top of her head to her toes, and she winked back, then began passing the containers of food.

The meal was delicious. As Wyatt had predicted, Polly enjoyed the cold chicken and even managed to eat the spoonful of coleslaw that Evelyn insisted she take, despite her prayer. When they'd devoured the last of the peach turnovers and had cleared the dishes from the blanket, Wyatt rose.

"I don't know about you ladies, but I could use a walk to settle all that fine food. Can I convince any of you to join me?"

When Evelyn nodded, Isolde exchanged a look with Dorothy. "Not me," she said. "The shade of that pecan tree looks more inviting."

Dorothy laid her hand on Polly's shoulder. "Do you want me to show you how to make a crown of flowers for your doll?"

"Yes, ma'am."

"Then I guess it's just you and Evelyn." Though Isolde's words were noncommittal, the gleam in her eye told Evelyn she was pleased with the outcome.

Evelyn wouldn't admit it aloud, but she was too, and so it seemed was Wyatt, for he grinned as he said, "That's fine with me."

CHAPTER TWENTY-THREE

It was more than fine, a fact that Wyatt suspected his mother and sister knew quite well. He hadn't been alone with Evelyn since the day of Ebony's colic, and oh, how he missed those special times with her. It didn't matter what they discussed; simply being with her brought him pleasure and something even less expected — peace. When they were together, he managed to put the cares of the day aside or at least view the problems from a different perspective. Though there was no way he could repay her for that, today he wanted to share a special place with her. And maybe, just maybe, if the time felt right, he would also share his innermost feelings.

Wyatt bent his arm, enjoying the warmth that flowed through him when Evelyn placed her hand on it.

"I hope you're up for a bit of a walk, because there's something I want to show you. I have no guarantee that it'll be there, but if it is, it's worth the walk."

She smiled and nodded. "I don't suppose you'll tell me what this elusive thing is, will you?"

"And spoil the surprise? Of course not."

By unspoken consent, they skirted the swaths of bluebonnets as they crossed the meadow toward a stand of live oaks, not wanting to crush the blossoms beneath their feet. In any other season, the majestic trees would dominate the landscape, but today they shared the glory with the vibrant flowers.

Evelyn's smile grew as they walked, enjoying the sunshine, talking about ordinary things. She'd seemed relaxed before, but with each step she took, she seemed to blossom. Bringing her here had been a good idea.

A second later, she stopped and pointed at the ground. "Red flowers! What are they?" Standing a bit taller than the bluebonnets, from a distance the flowers appeared to be pure red, but closer inspection revealed creamy centers on the crimson petals.

"They're Indian paintbrush."

"They're beautiful." Evelyn's eyes glowed with enthusiasm as she bent down to finger one of the petals. "Is this what you were looking for?"

"No. We have to be on the opposite side of the trees to find that."

Evelyn looked up from the flowers. "I never saw anything like this in Gilmorton."

It was the first time she'd mentioned the town without frowning. Perhaps he should remain silent, but Wyatt wanted to learn more about her past, for the past was what had made Evelyn the woman she was today.

"What was it like?"

When he stretched out his hand to help her stand, Evelyn laid her hand against his palm. "I always thought it was a nice, friendly town," she said as she rose, "but after my parents' deaths, I hated going there. Those monthly trips were the hardest thing I've ever done."

Wyatt kept her hand in his as they approached the live oaks. It might not be the approved way of walking, but he was enjoying the sensation of skin touching skin. Evelyn had removed her gloves when they'd eaten and hadn't drawn them on again. He wasn't complaining, and if the shy smile that crossed her face was any indication, she wasn't either.

Forcing his attention back to the conversation, he asked, "Why did you go if it was so painful?"

Her smile faded. "I had no choice. Mrs. Folger needed someone to sell the lace the children made. She claimed I was the logical person, since I'd once lived there and knew the shopkeepers."

That made sense, but Wyatt suspected there had been another motive. "Did you tell her your fears?"

"Yes. She said that facing them would make me stronger. You'd think that after ten years, I'd have gotten over my fears, wouldn't you, but I didn't."

And yet Mrs. Folger had insisted that Evelyn return. If the matron were still alive, Wyatt would have been tempted to give her a lesson in fear.

"You *are* strong, but if she was that cruel to you, why didn't you leave once you were of age?"

Evelyn closed her eyes for a second, as if reliving some part of her past. "I thought about it, but where would I go? I was safe at the orphanage. Mrs. Folger made sure of that."

Perhaps. But perhaps she had been manipulating Evelyn. "Who did the cooking before you were sent there?"

"Mrs. Folger." Evelyn wrinkled her nose. "She wasn't very good."

318

And so she made certain the one person who was very good felt that she had no choice but to stay. She probably also kept Evelyn from meeting men who might have tried to woo her away. Though he hated the idea that Evelyn's freedom had been curtailed, Wyatt couldn't complain about the fact that Mrs. Folger's iron rule meant that Evelyn was still single.

"I don't think I would have liked her."

Evelyn seemed surprised. "She was very kind to the children and made everyone feel special in some way."

If that was true, he needed to change his opinion. "How did she do that with Polly?" He'd never once heard the child mention the matron.

"She told her she was the only one she trusted to help me."

Kindness or manipulation? Wyatt wasn't certain. "And that made Polly happy."

Evelyn nodded. "Me too. Oh, there are times when she hinders more than helps, but she's such a sweet child that I don't mind." Evelyn ducked her head to avoid hitting a tree branch. "I give thanks every day that she was with me when the orphanage burned."

"It was a blessing for both of you." As they emerged from the trees, Wyatt squinted to let his eyes adjust to the sunshine, then stared into the distance. "It's still here." He turned to Evelyn. "Close your eyes and let me lead you. I want it to be a surprise."

Her hand felt so good clasped in his, softer and smaller than his own, but still strong. It may not have been due to Mrs. Folger, but Evelyn had more strength than she realized.

He led her for a few yards before stopping. "All right. You can look now."

As she opened her eyes and gazed in the direction he was pointing, he heard her gasp. "What is it?" She took a step forward, wanting to confirm what she'd seen. "It looks like a bluebonnet, but it's white. A white bluebonnet?"

He nodded, enjoying her sense of wonder at the discovery. "As strange as it sounds, that's exactly what it is. I've heard they're very rare, but I normally see a few here each year." He'd wanted to share the flowers' beauty with her, just as he wanted to share so many other things.

Evelyn dropped to her knees to study the rare blossom. "I'm tempted to pick it, but I won't. It needs to drop its seeds here so that there'll be flowers again next year." She caressed the white flower's petals, then rose and smiled at Wyatt. "Thank you for sharing this with me."

That was the opening he wanted, the perfect opportunity to share what was in his heart, but as he glanced at the sky, Wyatt frowned. The cumulus clouds that had been an innocent white a few minutes ago now had black underbellies, and the wind was picking up.

"I wish we had more time, but it looks like a storm is brewing." He pointed to the sky. "We'd better hurry if we don't want to get drenched."

Hand in hand, they hurried back to the picnic site, and with each step, Wyatt felt an increasing sense of urgency. The sky had turned ominously dark, the temperature dropping precipitously. The storm was close now. Dangerously close. He could only hope that his mother and Dorothy had loaded the wagon and were ready to leave.

When he and Evelyn arrived, Wyatt saw the two women standing next to the wagon, their posture leaving no doubt that they understood the danger of the impending storm.

"I was hoping you'd get here soon," his mother said as he and Evelyn practically ran the last few yards.

Dorothy glanced at them for a second,

then looked around as if searching for something.

"Where's Polly?"

CHAPTER TWENTY-FOUR

The new hat had been a good idea, Rufus realized when he saw how Winnie preened as she inserted the final hat pin. She had smiled more since he'd given her the combination of lace and feathers, asking how he'd guessed which one she wanted. There'd been no doubt, because she'd talked about it so often that he'd known this was the one she wanted on her head on Easter Sunday.

Rufus didn't understand the appeal. It wasn't big enough to shade her from the sun, and heaven only knew what would happen if a drop of rain fell on it, but Winnie was happy — or at least happier — and that was what mattered.

Today she'd even agreed to visit the cemetery with him and had brought two small bouquets, one for each of their children's graves. Surely that was a good sign, a sign that she was beginning to accept what had happened. She needed to put the past behind her, and so did he.

If only he'd spoken to the girl before it was too late.

The chill that made its way down Evelyn's spine owed nothing to the impending storm. She shook her head, trying to dispel the fear that Dorothy's question had instilled.

"I thought she was staying with you."

"She was, but she got bored quickly." Dorothy gestured toward the row of oaks. "You were still on this side when she said she wanted to join you, so I agreed. I lost sight of her when she went into the trees."

Wyatt kept Evelyn's hand clasped in his, as if he knew how much she needed the reassurance of his touch. "We didn't see or hear her."

And that wasn't normal for Polly. Though she'd been a silent child when she first arrived at the orphanage, since they'd been in Mesquite Springs, she'd become increasingly vocal. If she was following them, Evelyn would have expected her to call out to them.

"She must have gotten distracted." It was the only answer. "If she saw a bird or butterfly that caught her attention, she might have chased it." And she would have been as quiet as possible, since Evelyn had warned her that unfamiliar sounds would frighten an animal.

"We'll find her." Wyatt's voice was infused with confidence. He looked at his mother and sister. "You two go left. Evelyn and I'll search to the right."

They all ran, shouting Polly's name, but there was no answer, and the sky grew darker with each minute.

"We'll find her." Wyatt repeated his re-assurance, but it did little good. The feeling of dread, the sensation — no, the knowledge — that something was seriously wrong gripped Evelyn and would not let go.

"Polly! Polly, where are you?" It didn't matter how many times she called. There was no answer. Evelyn's eyes searched the ground, looking for a small figure chasing something. But there was nothing. And then she saw a spot of yellow in the middle of a swath of blue.

"That's Polly's dress," she cried as she broke away from Wyatt and began to run toward the brightly colored patch. "Polly! Polly!" Had she fallen and hurt herself? If so, why wasn't she answering? The dread that had lodged in Evelyn's throat, making both swallowing and breathing difficult, increased. Not even Wyatt's presence helped.

"Oh no!" For a second, everything turned black as Evelyn stared at the child she loved so dearly. Polly lay with her right leg extended. Her white stocking was torn, but that wasn't what made Evelyn's heart stutter. Polly's leg was swollen to twice its normal size, and though her eyes brightened with recognition when Evelyn knelt next to her, her breathing was so labored that she could not speak.

"What happened?" Evelyn asked Wyatt.

He pointed at Polly's leg. "Snakebite." He scooped the child into his arms and began to run toward the wagon, spitting out the words as he raced. "If we'd gotten here sooner, I would have tried to suck the venom out, but it's too late now. The poison has spread through her body."

Evelyn didn't need Wyatt to tell her how serious the situation was. Snakebites were dangerous, fatal more often than not.

"We've got to get her into town." Somehow, though he was running so quickly that Evelyn had difficulty keeping up with him, Wyatt managed to speak. "Doc Dawson may be able to help."

"May?" That wasn't what she wanted to hear. Though her head knew it was possible, Evelyn's heart couldn't bear the thought of Polly dying. Surely God hadn't spared her from the fire only to let her die here.

"There's no telling with snakes. Some of their venom is more poisonous than others." He shouted for his mother and Dorothy, telling them to meet at the wagon.

The women were already there when Wyatt and Evelyn arrived.

"Snake," he said. As Isolde and Dorothy shuddered, Wyatt laid the now-unconscious Polly in the back of the wagon, then helped Evelyn climb in. Without waiting to see that she'd cradled Polly's head in her lap, he practically shoved his mother and sister onto the bench before taking his place behind the reins.

"Hold on tight. We're going as fast as we can."

The drive was silent, save for the thunder that grew closer and closer. Though lightning split the sky, no rain fell. And for that, Evelyn gave thanks. Silently, she prayed for the child she held in her lap while Isolde and Dorothy murmured prayers of their own. Surely God would answer them. Surely he would spare Polly's life.

As they approached Mesquite Springs, Wyatt spoke again, directing his words at his mother. "You and Dorothy need to head for the ranch. I'll find a way back home once we know what Doc thinks." He gave the sky an appraising look. "You can probably outrun the storm."

"Are you sure we can't help here?"

He shook his head. "Make sure the horses are inside. You know how skittish they are in storms."

Evelyn's heart sang with the realization that Wyatt was willing to stay with her, even though she knew that his mother and sister were less experienced with the horses. "Thank you," she said softly as he halted the wagon in front of the doctor's office.

"You and Polly are more important than horses," he said, his words bringing tears of relief to Evelyn's eyes as he lifted Polly into his arms and strode to the front door. She wouldn't be alone.

"Doc!" Wyatt cried as Evelyn opened the door. "Where are you?"

Doc Dawson, whom his friends called "Andy" when they were not consulting him on medical matters, emerged from what Evelyn assumed were his living quarters at the rear of the building. Though the freckles that covered his face and complemented his red hair and green eyes gave him a boyish air, there was nothing juvenile about the way he appraised Polly.

"What do we have?" He directed his question at Wyatt.

"Snakebite. I didn't see it, but it was probably a rattler."

Frowning, the doctor opened the first door on the right and gestured to the table in the center. "You can lay her down there."

Though his movements were unhurried, his expression radiated concern as he inserted the earpieces of his stethoscope and laid the disc on Polly's chest. When he'd finished, he gently opened her eyelids to study them, then inserted a wooden stick into her mouth to examine her throat.

It took less than a minute, but for Evelyn that minute seemed to last forever. When the doctor placed his instruments on the small table behind him, he shook his head slowly. "It's too late," he said, his voice heavy with regret. "There's nothing I can do."

It was unthinkable, positively unthinkable. "There must be something."

A lock of auburn hair bounced as the doctor shook his head. "I wish there were. I've seen close to a dozen snakebite cases like this, and the patients all died. It's worse for children, because they're smaller. That means that the venom is more concentrated." He ran a hand through his hair. "Maybe someday someone will find a way to counteract the effects, but for now all I can do is advise you to pray."

The finality of Doc Dawson's words chilled Evelyn, loosening the tears that she'd been battling to control. "I can't lose her. I can't."

She turned her gaze to Wyatt, who nodded. "We'll pray."

When the doctor left, Evelyn and Wyatt pulled chairs next to the examining table and sat on opposite sides, each holding one of Polly's hands, taking turns praying aloud. Evelyn had no idea how much time passed or how often Doc Dawson returned. She remembered him lighting the lamps and offering them food. What he hadn't offered was hope, and that was what she needed.

They'd both refused the food, though Wyatt had agreed with the doctor that Evelyn needed a cup of hot tea with double the normal amount of sugar in it, because her voice had become hoarse.

"It'll be soon," she heard him say to Wyatt when he brought a tray with two cups and a pot of steaming tea. There was no reason to ask what he meant by "it." Evelyn knew that the doctor didn't expect Polly to last through the night, but though she respected his professional opinion, she could not accept it. God would not be so cruel.

She drank the tea; she continued to pray;

she took comfort from Wyatt's presence. Those were easy to do. But, no matter what the doctor said, she would not — she absolutely would not — lose hope.

As the hours passed, Polly's breathing grew more labored, and with each tortured breath, Evelyn's heart clenched. How much more could the child endure? How long would she suffer? Were she and Wyatt wrong to pray for Polly's life if it meant that she had to undergo such pain?

Evelyn closed her eyes and took a deep breath, wishing with all her heart that she could give that breath to Polly. If she could, she would take Polly's place on that table. She would give her life so that the little girl could live.

"Lord," Evelyn said, her voice cracking with emotion, "I know you've heard our prayers just as you heard Polly's prayer before we ate. I know you can heal her the way you healed Simon Peter's mother-in-law and the centurion's servant." She took another breath before she continued. "I also know there are others you did not heal. I don't pretend to understand your reasons. The Bible tells us that your ways are not our ways, and I accept that. But still I pray that you will heal Polly."

Evelyn paused, knowing there was more

she had to say. This was the hardest part and the most important. "I pray that you will heal Polly, if it is your will. Your will, Lord, not mine."

"Amen." Wyatt ended the prayer.

They sat silently, their prayers exhausted. Once again, Evelyn lost all sense of time. All she knew was that she had done everything she could. She had protected Polly from the storm that brought them to Mesquite Springs; she had tried to give her a home and a good life; she had prayed that God would spare that life. It was his decision now.

"Please, Lord, don't let her suffer any longer." Though she had thought her prayers were finished, Evelyn could not bear the sound of Polly's rasping. "Please, Lord, have mercy."

The troubled breathing stopped.

"Oh, Wyatt." Evelyn laid her hands over her face, not wanting him to see the anguish that contorted it, the river of tears that flowed down her cheeks. "I had hoped . . ."

Though he said nothing, Evelyn heard Wyatt moving and lowered her hands so that she could watch him. He'd risen and had tipped his head so that his ear was close to Polly's mouth. When he raised his head, Evelyn had never seen such unfettered joy.

"She's breathing, Evelyn. She's breathing normally." He sprinted to the door and shouted down the hallway, "Doc! Come here!"

The doctor appeared, his expression leaving no doubt that he expected to pronounce Polly dead. When he saw Wyatt's grin and Evelyn's relief, he mimicked Wyatt's actions and pressed his ear close to Polly's mouth. A second later, he straightened up and grinned.

"I'd say you've got yourselves a miracle."

Her heart filled with happiness and a peace that overwhelmed her with its power, Evelyn lowered her head. "Thank you, dear Lord. Thank you." When the doctor left, she turned to Wyatt. "Thank you too. You gave me strength when I faltered."

"And you buoyed me when I was weak."

They smiled at each other, relief and something more sparking between them. Afterwards, Evelyn could not say who moved first. All she knew was that she found herself in Wyatt's arms, and a second later, his lips were pressed to hers.

CHAPTER TWENTY-FIVE

"I'm hungry, Evelyn. I wanna eat breakfast."

Polly punctuated her words with a tug on Evelyn's braid, waking her from what had been a disturbed and far too short sleep. For a second, Evelyn stared at the little girl, her still-muddled brain trying to understand why Polly was in her room, balancing carefully on one leg. Then memories flooded through her, and she gave silent thanks that the child Wyatt had called Evelyn's sister of the heart was alive. It had been a miracle, an answer to prayer.

Evelyn sat up, a quick look at her watch confirming what she'd feared: she was late. "We'll have oatmeal this morning."

"I don't want oatmeal. I want pancakes."

On another day, Evelyn might have cringed at Polly's whining. Today she smiled, for it was proof that the child was recovering. Truly, God was good. Not only had he spared Polly, but the ordeal had brought Evelyn and Wyatt closer. Heat flooded her cheeks as she remembered just how close they'd been.

"It's oatmeal today," she said firmly. Since she'd slept much later than normal, it would be a challenge to be ready to open the restaurant on time.

When they'd brought Polly back here, Wyatt had suggested that Evelyn let it remain closed today, but she hadn't wanted to. People were depending on her. She couldn't disappoint them any more than she could forget what had happened in Doc Dawson's office. But now was not the time to moon about like a love-struck girl.

Evelyn turned to Polly, giving her a coaxing smile. "If you eat oatmeal, I'll let you help me." Though the swelling in Polly's leg had subsided, Doc Dawson had cautioned Evelyn to keep her as inactive as possible. She'd give her tasks that allowed her to sit at the table rather than try to stand on her still-sore leg.

"Okay!" As Evelyn had expected, the lure of being able to help in the restaurant had turned Polly's whining into eager anticipation.

The next few hours passed in a whirlwind of activity. There hadn't been time to make pies, and Evelyn had chosen her simplest —

and fastest — main courses, but at least she'd be able to offer her usual Monday customers a choice of meals. By the time Dorothy arrived, the pots of stew and chili were simmering, and the biscuits and cornbread were ready to be slid into the oven.

"You look tired," Dorothy announced as she tied her apron strings.

"I am." But it was a fatigue unlike any she'd experienced. Evelyn was both exhausted and exhilarated.

"Wyatt looked pretty tired too."

"I'm not surprised. It was a long night." And the way it had ended . . . Evelyn hoped Dorothy would believe that the color that had risen to her cheeks was caused by the heat of the stove. It seemed that she blushed every time she remembered the wonderful kiss she and Wyatt had shared.

Only a few months before she'd died, Mama had told Evelyn that the right man's kisses would stir her senses, that they'd taste sweeter than honey. At the time, her advice had been nothing more than words. Kisses happened to someone else. But now Evelyn knew the truth of her mother's words. She'd experienced the sweetness, the power, and the excitement of being kissed. The kiss had lasted only a few seconds, but it had changed everything.

Dorothy took a step closer to Evelyn and studied her. "Are you feeling all right? You look flushed, and your eyes are brighter than normal."

"I'm just tired."

"Of course." Though Dorothy nodded as if agreeing, her expression said she hadn't believed Evelyn's explanation. That was the problem with friends. They saw too much.

"What do you want me to do today?" Caleb asked as he approached the paddock where Wyatt was watching his yearlings engage in their early morning antics. Each day they raced around the perimeter, as if testing their speed, before settling down to grazing.

Wyatt nodded at the two he expected to bring the highest price at the sale. "I want to see how Anthracite and Acanthus do against each other. We've got less than three months to get them ready."

That was true, but more than training the horses, Wyatt wanted the challenge of racing to help clear his mind. All he'd been able to think about since he'd wakened was how good it had felt to hold Evelyn in his arms and how sweet her kiss had been.

He'd tried telling himself that it had been nothing more than a reaction to the ordeal they'd shared, the simple relief that their prayers had been answered and that Polly would live, but Wyatt knew he was lying to himself. What had happened was caused by more than relief.

Though he'd tried to deny it, his feelings for Evelyn had been growing, changing from friendship to attraction to something more. At first, the change had been almost imperceptible, but he could no longer ignore the way she made him feel. The kiss was the culmination of all the tender thoughts he had for her.

Now, the question was what he should do next. Courting Evelyn would mean abandoning his dream of leaving the ranch and Mesquite Springs. As much as the idea of exploring new parts of the country beckoned to him, Wyatt knew he couldn't ask Evelyn to close the restaurant and uproot Polly again. That wouldn't be fair. Nor would it be fair to expect her to wait until he returned, especially since he had no idea when that would happen.

Caleb's eyes gleamed with excitement. "I'm ready to race."

"Think you can beat me?" Though Caleb was a good rider, the horses didn't know him the way they did Wyatt.

"It's worth a try."

As they saddled the horses, it wasn't only

Caleb who was excited. Anthracite and Acanthus were bred to race, and they knew what the lighter saddles meant. Soon they'd be able to show the world just how fast they were. They chafed as Wyatt and Caleb walked them to the main road, tossing their heads with impatience.

"See the live oak down there, the one whose branches almost reach the road?" Wyatt asked when he and Caleb had reached the road to Mesquite Springs.

Caleb nodded and patted Anthracite's neck.

"That's a half mile," Wyatt continued. Though quarter horses had gained their name because of their speed in quarter mile races, he wanted to challenge his horses as much as he challenged himself.

"We'll call that the finish line." Wyatt looked at his friend. "Ready?" Another nod was his answer. "Okay. Ready. Set. Go."

It was a feeling like no other, having a powerful animal responding to his commands. As he and Acanthus raced toward the oak, Wyatt felt as if nothing mattered but reaching the finish line first. They'd do it. He knew they would. But, to his surprise, Caleb beat him.

"Great ride." Wyatt straightened and began to walk Acanthus back to where they'd started, Caleb and Anthracite keeping pace next to him. "I thought Acanthus was faster, but you two proved me wrong. Let's try it again."

As they approached the junction in the road, a thought made its way into Wyatt's brain. It was one he hadn't considered before but one he needed to explore.

"Let's see how you do with Acanthus." He dismounted and handed his horse's reins to Caleb, then swung himself into Anthracite's saddle. "Ready?"

Once again, they raced to the oak, and once again Caleb and his mount won, this time by an even greater margin than when he was on Anthracite.

"You keep surprising me," Wyatt said as he stroked Anthracite's neck. He lifted his head and studied Caleb. "I'm a good rider." There was no pride in it, simply a statement of fact. "But you're better. Much better." As Caleb's shoulders straightened at the unexpected praise, Wyatt continued. "I've never seen you ride like that."

Caleb grinned. "I've never had a horse like either of these." He was silent for a moment, his expression saying that he was choosing his next words carefully. "It's the first time I've felt like this."

"Like what?"

"Like this is what I was born to do." Caleb appeared almost embarrassed by the confession, but his words touched a chord deep inside Wyatt.

What was he born to do?

"Are you gonna be my daddy?"

"You'd be a good mayor."

"Competition is good."

"Promise me that if you find a woman you love as much as I did your father, you won't let her go."

"You gave me strength when I faltered."

The memories swirled through his brain, pulling him in opposite directions, making him feel like a leaf tossed by the wind.

"Have you ever felt that way, like you were born to do something?" Caleb asked.

Wyatt grinned as the pieces suddenly fit together. "Yes."

His questions had been answered. He knew what he would do next.

"Your mail, sir." The tall slave bowed obsequiously as he laid half a dozen envelopes on Basil's desk, then left the room. Basil had made certain that Sager and the other slaves knew that he did not speak except to command them.

Settling back in the chair that Bart had claimed was so comfortable, Basil steepled

341

his hands. He should be able to forget what had happened on Sunday, but he couldn't. He'd been so certain that Prince would win that he'd bet more than ever on the first race. That race was supposed to be the answer to his problems, a way to win enough money to satisfy the lenders. But Prince had come in second, beaten by Carnelian, a mare from the Circle C stables.

Bah! Basil still couldn't believe it. Not just that Prince had lost, but that he'd lost to a mare. Everyone knew the female of the species was weaker than the male. That was a simple fact of nature. So, how could a mare have beaten Prince? That red chestnut had cost Basil a pretty penny.

Letting out a curse, he reached for the first envelope. More bills, just what he didn't need. The stack of unpaid bills was already too high, and thanks to that blasted mare, it wasn't going to diminish any time soon.

He riffled through the envelopes, his attention caught by a heavy cream-colored one inscribed by an unfamiliar hand. It looked like a woman's penmanship, probably one of the ladies from church asking him to dinner. Resolutely, he slit the envelope and withdrew the card. As he'd expected, it was an invitation. What he hadn't expected was that it was to a horse sale. The Circle C Stables announced their annual sale.

Basil kept reading. Mesquite Springs. A sale in Mesquite Springs? Didn't Wyatt Clark know that sales were held in cities, not on individual breeders' ranches? The arrogance of the man, believing his horses were special enough to deserve a private sale.

Basil pounded his fist on the desk, wishing it were Wyatt Clark's face he was hitting. Arrogance. Unbridled arrogance. Unfortunately, Clark wasn't just arrogant. He was right. His horses were special enough that buyers would come to him.

"Sager! Get in here!"

The man, who knew better than to venture a foot past the door without permission, rushed inside the office. "Yes, sir."

"You ever hear of Mesquite Springs?"

"No, sir."

"Figure out where it is. I'm going there."

Wyatt dipped his head under the spigot. Though the water was still cold, he needed to wash off the day's dirt before he changed into a clean shirt.

"Going somewhere special?" his mother asked five minutes later as he descended the stairs.

"Town." He'd waited until he'd finished the most important work at the ranch and until Polly's Place had closed for the day, but now it was time.

His mother gave him an appraising look, then grinned. "I figured that when I saw you were all spruced up."

"I want to make sure Polly's all right." Though he was a grown man, his mother somehow managed to make him feel as if he owed her an explanation.

"Dorothy said she was well."

The slight twist to her lips made Wyatt suspect his mother was teasing him. He should have ignored her, but instead he said, "I want to see for myself."

"Of course." The skin around Ma's eyes crinkled with her amusement. "Of course. Be sure to say hello to Evelyn for me."

Wyatt nodded and made a hasty exit before Ma could say anything more. He'd take horses over inquisitive mothers any day.

Thunder needed no urging to trot, making the ride into Mesquite Springs blessedly short. This was where he wanted to be, where he needed to be, Wyatt reminded himself as he hitched the horse in front of Polly's Place. So, why were his palms sweating?

He wiped his hands on his pants as he walked to the rear of the building. It was silly to be nervous, and yet he was. So much hung on Evelyn. Wyatt thought he knew what she'd say, but he wasn't certain. Pulling the bell cord, he waited, his heartbeat accelerating when he heard her footsteps descending the stairs.

"Wyatt, what a nice surprise!" Her face turned a rosy pink as she ushered him into the kitchen. "I imagine you came to check on Polly."

As she started to turn toward the stairs, Wyatt laid a hand on her arm. "Yes, but not yet. I want to talk to you first." It was probably inappropriate for him to be alone with her, but right now he didn't care.

Evelyn looked at him, obviously startled by his comment. Was she remembering their kiss? He saw her gaze linger on his lips for a second, then dart away. Did she feel the same urge he did to repeat it? He wanted to, oh how he wanted to, but first they needed to talk.

"Yes, of course." Evelyn seemed to regain her composure. "Would you like some coffee? I didn't make any pies today, but there's some spice cake left." The words came out more quickly than normal, as if she were as nervous as he was. Somehow, the thought encouraged Wyatt.

"Later, maybe. Right now, I just want to talk."

She gestured toward the table, waiting while he pulled out the chair for her. When he'd settled into the one next to her, she turned toward him. "Is anything wrong? You look serious."

"Nothing's wrong. In fact, everything feels right." Now that he was here, it did. He still didn't know how today would end, but he knew that he was in the right place at the right time.

"What happened yesterday made me reconsider a lot of things," he said. "Seeing Polly so close to death made me realize how short life can be and that we need to live each day to the fullest."

Evelyn placed her hands on the table, the right one on top of the left. Though he wanted nothing more than to take one of those hands in his and press a kiss on it, Wyatt remained stationary.

"I feel that way too," she admitted. "I knew that I loved Polly, but until yesterday I hadn't understood how much I did." Evelyn closed her eyes for a second and shuddered. "I don't want to think about life without her."

Just as Wyatt didn't want to think about

life without Evelyn.

"You won't have to. You've created a good life for her here, and God kept her alive to enjoy it."

Though Evelyn nodded, her smile was tremulous. "But I haven't given her what she wants most."

As color rose to Evelyn's cheeks, Wyatt knew she was thinking but didn't want to say that she hadn't found a new daddy for Polly.

"That's one of the things I want to talk about," he told her. Forcing his suddenly jittery hands to remain still, he took a deep breath and continued. "Until you and Polly came to Mesquite Springs, I never thought of myself as a father, certainly not one with a ready-made family. Now it's almost the only thing I think about. I want . . . I'd like . . . Would you . . ."

He paused, trying to gather his scattered wits. Though he wasn't normally tongue-tied, this was the first time he'd done anything like this.

"What I'm trying to say is, I'd like to court you."

Evelyn's eyes widened, and the color that had stained her face receded. "So that Polly can have a daddy?"

"Yes. No." As Evelyn stiffened, Wyatt re-

347

alized what he'd done. "I'm messing this up, aren't I? Let me start over. Yes, I want Polly to have a father, and yes, I believe I could be a good one, but that's not the main reason I want to court you."

Ever so slightly, Evelyn's shoulders relaxed. Thank goodness. He couldn't afford to make any more mistakes.

"I care about you, Evelyn. I've never been in love, so I can't be certain, but I believe what I feel for you is love." The pain that had filled her eyes began to recede, giving Wyatt hope that he'd be able to make amends.

"What about traveling? I can't envision Polly and me not having a home, but I know that leaving Mesquite Springs and seeing the country has been your dream for a long time. I can't ask you to abandon that dream for us."

Though he hadn't thought it possible, Wyatt's love for Evelyn deepened with the realization that her first thought was for his wishes. What a wonderful woman! Now it was up to him to convince her that she was the right woman — the only woman — for him and that he was the right man for her.

"It's taken me a while," he said, choosing his words carefully, "but I've come to understand that the reason I wanted to travel was to fill an empty spot inside me." He gazed into her eyes, hoping she'd see the sincerity in his. "That spot's no longer empty. You and Polly have filled it."

Evelyn was silent for a moment, her thoughts inscrutable.

"Dare I hope that you might have feelings for me?" Wyatt couldn't let the silence continue, not when his heart was aching at the thought that she might not feel the way he did.

"Yes." Though she nodded, she said nothing more.

"Yes, I can dare, or yes, you have feelings?" There was a huge difference between them.

This time he got more than a nod. Evelyn favored him with the sweetest of smiles. "Yes to both. I'm like you, Wyatt. I've never been in love. After living with Mrs. Folger for ten years and hearing her view of marriage, I never thought I'd have a husband and children." Her smile turned wry. "I seem to have done this in reverse order. I have Polly, who's like my child, but I don't have a husband."

Once again, color flooded to Evelyn's cheeks, making her look even more appealing than she had a moment ago.

"I do have feelings for you. They're strong

and tender at the same time."

Though her words sent waves of happiness flooding through him, Wyatt said nothing, for he sensed that Evelyn was not finished.

She paused and turned her right hand palm up, as if inviting him to take it in his. When he did, she continued. "Until I met you, I felt like a flower seed planted deep in the earth, waiting for rain before it began to sprout. You've been that rain. You've given me what I needed to grow."

Her words mirrored his own thoughts, deepening his conviction that Evelyn was the woman God intended for him. "You've shown me that loving someone doesn't mean being burdened. It's a gift that opens our hearts to new possibilities."

Wyatt hadn't thought he'd imbued his final words with any special inflection, but apparently he had, for Evelyn's eyes widened. "The way you said that makes me think there's more to your story."

He wrapped both hands around hers, wanting the warmth of them as he told her of the decision he'd made. "We're not even married, and you're reading my mind. That's a little scary, Evelyn, but you're right. I've thought about everything you said, and

I realized you're right. I'm going to run for mayor."

CHAPTER TWENTY-SIX

"I don't know how you did it, but I'm glad you did." Dorothy grinned as she tied her apron. "Now that he's decided to run for mayor, my brother looks happier than I've seen him since our father died."

It had been two days since Wyatt had made his decision, and while the town was still buzzing with excitement that the race for mayor was being contested, Evelyn knew there was more to Wyatt's happiness than that. They'd both been almost delirious with happiness at the realization that the tender feelings they harbored for each other were returned.

For the first time in her life, Evelyn felt complete, as if she'd discovered the one thing that would fill the emptiness inside her: Wyatt's love. The kisses they'd shared had been sweeter than taffy, made all the more wonderful by the knowledge that before summer ended, they'd be man and wife, sharing a life as well as the sweetest of kisses.

But Dorothy knew none of that, and so Evelyn kept her attention focused on the biscuits she was cutting, lest Dorothy discover the truth from her expression. It was almost impossible not to grin when she thought of Wyatt.

"I can't take the credit," she told Wyatt's sister. "He's the one who decided to run, but I have to agree that he'll make a good mayor." A better one than Sam, who saw being mayor as nothing more than a stepping-stone.

Dorothy raised an eyebrow before continuing to load napkins, silverware, and cups onto a tray in preparation for setting the tables. "If he wins. Sam may be Wyatt's friend, but he'll be a formidable opponent. He's determined to be mayor and wasn't expecting to be opposed."

"Competition is good."

"Says the woman who runs the only restaurant in town. Who's your competition?"

Evelyn couldn't help laughing at the hint of indignation in Dorothy's voice. "Every woman in Mesquite Springs. People don't have to eat here, but I'm glad they choose to." She cut the final biscuit and placed it on the baking sheet. "Now, what are we going to do to help your brother win?"

"You're going to take sides?" Dorothy sounded surprised.

"Why not? I believe Wyatt will be good for the town, and being mayor will be good for him." There'd been a new spring to his step and a lightness to his voice that hadn't been there before that special night. While neither one of them thought it would be easy to win the election, they'd both been enthusiastic about his candidacy. Evelyn had even laughed privately that, though it certainly wasn't the way Sam would have envisioned it, she just might wind up being the mayor's wife.

"You may lose customers," Dorothy cautioned her.

"That's a risk I'm willing to take."

Dorothy smiled and laid the now-filled tray on the table. "Good. Here's what I was thinking . . ."

"You're amazing." Wyatt clasped Evelyn's hand in his and led her outside. It was Sunday afternoon, the first time he'd seen her alone since the evening they'd declared their love and he'd announced his intention to run for mayor. While he wanted nothing more than to kiss her once, twice, a hundred times, there were things he needed to say first. "Handing out those flyers to your customers was a great idea."

"Thank your sister. It was her idea. She's the one who wrote them, and she's the one who gives them to customers."

How typical of Evelyn. She wouldn't take credit for anyone else's work. "But your allowing her to do that says you endorse me."

"Why wouldn't I? Some might say I'm prejudiced, but the simple fact is, you're the better candidate."

Whether or not that was true, the fact that Evelyn believed it warmed Wyatt's heart. "And you're amazing." He tightened his grip on her hand as he repeated his declaration. "You're the only woman I know who'd put winning an election over being courted."

She'd been the one who'd suggested they not make their courtship public until after the election, and while he'd protested at first, wanting to shout the news from the rooftops so that everyone would know that he was the most fortunate of men, eventually Wyatt had agreed with Evelyn's logic.

"I want you and the town to focus on the race for mayor without any distractions." It was the same argument she'd made that evening.

"What if I like being distracted by you?"

When she was this close, it was difficult to think of anything other than how much he loved this woman. Wyatt looked around. They'd reached the corner of the barn and were no longer in sight of the ranch house. Unable to wait any longer, he pulled Evelyn closer and pressed his lips to hers.

"If that's what you call a distraction," she said when they broke apart, both a little breathless, "I like it."

"So do I. So do I." He kissed her again. This time it was Evelyn who ended the kiss with a sweet smile and the reminder that they'd agreed to keep their courtship secret.

"I think my mother and Dorothy may suspect we're more than friends." Both of them had been giving him speculative glances ever since he'd returned from Mesquite Springs and had announced his candidacy, almost as if they expected him to admit there was more than one reason for his enthusiasm.

"Caleb may too. The last time he was in the restaurant, he mentioned that you've been looking happier this week. I told him it's because you're doing something new and exciting."

Wyatt wasn't surprised by Caleb's suspicions. He'd spent hours on end with him, and even though they talked about the horses, Wyatt knew that his thoughts drifted to Evelyn more often than ever, making him appear absentminded.

"What about Sam? He hasn't spoken to me since I announced my candidacy."

Though he'd known that being opponents would put a strain on their friendship, Wyatt hadn't expected total silence. His first act after officially entering the race by filing a form in the mayor's office had been to tell Sam. The man had stared at him for a long moment, his face registering shock and, for a second, anger. Then he'd shrugged as if Wyatt's announcement were of no import.

"You'll lose," he'd said. "Now, get out of here."

Evelyn's eyes radiated sympathy. She'd warned him that Sam wouldn't take the news well. "He comes to the restaurant as often as he did before, only now he talks to more people. He goes from table to table, greeting each customer. Dorothy wanted to stop him, but I wouldn't let her. I thought that might hurt you."

"You're right. It would have." Once again, Evelyn had shown a deep understanding of human nature. "I keep saying it, but it's true. You're amazing."

And soon, if everything went the way he

hoped, this amazing woman would be his wife.

Evelyn smiled as she watched people gathering in the park. The past three weeks had gone by more quickly than she'd thought possible. The bluebonnets had begun to fade, and temperatures were increasing, including those of Mesquite Springs's citizens. As the first mayoral contest in a generation approached, the town had split into two camps, those supporting Wyatt and those favoring Sam.

Predictably, heated discussions had erupted, with each side convinced that its candidate was the only one who could lead the town. Even as they shared meals at Polly's Place, it seemed that residents believed that the way to convince others was to speak more loudly. More than once, Evelyn had asked customers to lower their voices, and more than once she'd received an angry rebuke.

Today, though, it would be the two candidates who did the majority of the talking. When he'd realized how divided the town had become, Mayor McBride had arranged a debate and had chosen the afternoon of the last Sunday in April, reasoning that most of the voters would be in town for church that morning. They could bring picnic lunches, then stay to hear Wyatt and Sam try to convince them to vote for them.

It was a good plan and one that the town endorsed. There'd been no angry outbursts while everyone had eaten their lunches, and smiles had outnumbered frowns. Not knowing what might happen during the debate itself and not wanting any distractions, Isolde and two of the other women had volunteered to keep the children entertained at the far end of the park while the adults listened to the candidates.

"I'm worried about Wyatt," Dorothy whispered as she settled onto the blanket next to Evelyn. "He's not as polished a speaker as Sam."

"True, but he's sincere. People will see that." While there was no denying Sam's eloquence, he'd always struck Evelyn as glib.

She looked around the park, wondering who would support Wyatt and who was firmly in Sam's camp. It was hard to tell, and from what Dorothy had said, some people were wavering. Today might help them make a decision.

"Good afternoon, ladies and gentlemen," Mayor McBride said after he'd mounted the crate that had been turned into a make-shift platform. "Y'all know why we're here, and it's not just to share a meal with neighbors on a beautiful Sunday afternoon. Y'all want to hear these two men tell you why they deserve your vote."

He continued for another minute, reminding the audience of the need to remain silent while the candidates spoke and stressing that this was to be a friendly debate. "Sam was the first to declare his candidacy, so he'll begin." Gesturing to the man who stood ready to take his place in more ways than one, the current mayor said, "Ladies and gentlemen, please welcome Sam Plaut."

"Thank you, Mayor McBride." Sam gave the retiring magistrate a smile that failed to reach his eyes, then addressed the group gathered on the lawn. "Let's give a round of applause to our mayor. He's done a good job of leading this town for over thirty years. We owe him thanks for that."

When the clapping and cheers faded, Sam straightened his shoulders and adopted a sober mien. "As good a job as our current mayor has done, I promise you that I will do better. I will root out the evils that threaten our town — evils like horseracing."

At Evelyn's side, Dorothy gasped. "What a hypocrite! He bets on every race in the county."

"We need to start at the root," Sam continued. "If I'm elected, I will make it illegal for anyone in Mesquite Springs to raise racehorses."

This time it wasn't only Dorothy who gasped. Sounds of shock mingled with soft murmurs as the implications of Sam's proposal registered. He was trying to put the Circle C out of business. Even though Wyatt had expanded and was selling horses to Rangers and others, at least half of his sales were to men who intended to race.

"Yes," the candidate said, "I will eradicate the seeds of evil and keep you safe. I will . . ."

As Sam spoke for another half hour, enumerating the ways Mesquite Springs had taken wrong turns and the way he proposed to right those wrongs, the crowd began to grow restive.

"Aren't they supposed to be limited to fifteen minutes?"

Dorothy's shrug was an eloquent answer to Evelyn's question. "They were, but no one's willing to stand up to Sam, not even Mayor McBride."

And so Sam spoke for another fifteen minutes. "I'm sure you'll agree that I'm the best man — no, not just the best man, the only man — who's qualified to lead Mesquite Springs."

As the crowd applauded, Evelyn couldn't help wondering whether the applause was for Sam's speech or the fact that it had ended. Now it was Wyatt's turn. She had no idea what he planned to say, because when she'd asked if he'd prepared a speech, he'd looked at her as if she were speaking a foreign language.

"Thank you all for coming here today," Wyatt said after the mayor had introduced him. "I know you have other ways to spend your day of rest, so I promise not to take much of your time."

Laughter and a spattering of applause greeted his words and warmed Evelyn's heart. In only two sentences, he'd clearly established the differences between himself and Sam.

"I'm not a trained orator like my opponent," Wyatt continued. "What I am is a plain-spoken man. You won't hear any fancy words from me, but I will tell you the truth. Always."

He paused for a second, letting them absorb his promise. "I'm proud to call Mesquite Springs my home. It's a good town populated with good people that I'm proud to call my neighbors. There are so many good things about this town."

To Evelyn's surprise, Wyatt began to name

each of the businesses in town, including a short anecdote about each. "And that's only the beginning. There are all you ranchers and farmers who contribute so much." Again, he cited each by name.

It was, Evelyn realized, a masterful touch. Wyatt was making it clear that the election was about the people themselves, not about him.

"Together you've made Mesquite Springs the finest town in the county." He stopped and shook his head, feigning embarrassment. "No, I was wrong. It's the finest town in the Hill Country." Another pause, this one accompanied by a grin. "Why stop there? This is the finest town in all of Texas."

By now, everyone in the audience was either grinning or nodding.

"If you honor me with your vote and I become the next mayor of the finest town in Texas, I promise you that I will do everything in my power to continue this town's tradition of excellence."

Wyatt made a point of looking at the crowd, making eye contact with everyone he could. "I won't claim that I have all the answers. I don't. But I can and will listen to those of you who have suggestions for ways we can become even better. Together we can — and will — do anything."

He smiled again. "Thank you."

There was a moment of silence followed by thundering applause. A second later, one man rose. Others joined him, and soon almost everyone was on their feet, clapping, whistling, and shouting encouragement.

Evelyn's heart overflowed with pride. The man she loved had proven how honorable he was. Not once had he attacked his opponent. Instead, he'd done everything he could to mend the rifts that threatened to divide the town.

Evelyn hummed as she walked down the street. It was Saturday afternoon; Polly's Place was closed until Monday, and Polly herself was spending the day with Melissa, giving Evelyn a rare few hours alone. As much as she loved the little girl, she had to admit that it felt good to be on her own for a bit.

She smiled, thinking of how blessed she was. So much had changed in four months. Though waves of grief still washed over her whenever she thought of Mrs. Folger and the children who'd died, her life was living proof of the truth of Romans 8:28. God had taken a terrible event and brought good from it. Though Evelyn hadn't thought it possible at the time, good had come out of the embers of the orphanage. She had built a new life for herself and Polly here.

Opening Polly's Place had been a way to honor her parents' memory, but it had become more than that. Somehow, though Evelyn couldn't explain it, the restaurant made her feel closer to them than she had in all the years they'd been gone.

It was a wonderful feeling. So too was the knowledge that she and Polly were safe in Mesquite Springs. The Watcher hadn't followed her. There was nothing to fear. She was safe, and so was the little girl who'd be thrilled by the parasol Evelyn had just ordered for her. Mrs. Steiner had assured her that Polly would be the envy of all the other girls when she carried it to church next week.

"You look happy."

Evelyn smiled at Sam, who'd emerged from his law office at the same time that she walked by. Coincidence? Perhaps. Or perhaps he'd been waiting for her. He normally closed his office at the same time that she closed the restaurant and headed for his parents' ranch soon after.

"I am happy," she admitted. "I was thinking about how glad I am to be in Mesquite Springs."

"Not as glad as I am that you're here."

He crooked his arm. "This is too nice a day to spend inside. Let's take a walk." When she started to hesitate, he gave her his most persuasive smile. "There's something I want to talk to you about, and this isn't the place."

A feeling of unease swept over Evelyn. "Where do you want to go?"

"To the park. Please, Evelyn. It's important."

The unexpected pleading tone touched her heart, leaving her unable to resist. "All right."

Though she laid her hand on his arm, Evelyn set the pace, walking quickly rather than strolling.

"This isn't a race." Sam sounded annoyed.

"That's right. You don't believe in racing anymore, do you?" She couldn't resist the jab.

He placed his hand on top of hers and stopped abruptly, leaving her no choice but to stop as well.

"Don't tell me you hold that against me. A man says what he has to to win. I needed to take a stand against my opponent."

"Who's also your friend." Evelyn forbore pointing out that Wyatt had not attacked Sam or his profession.

The town's attorney shrugged. "Someone

said 'all's fair in love and war.' "

"What does that have to do with running for mayor?"

"More than you might think."

When they reached the park, Sam led her to a bench on one side. Though she'd expected him to take the seat next to her, he remained standing in front of her, then dropped to one knee.

Oh no! The unease Evelyn had felt turned into apprehension. There was only one reason she knew that a man would adopt that pose. Why, oh why? She had given Sam no encouragement. To the contrary, she'd made it clear that she was not interested in being courted by him. She sighed. This was her fault. If she hadn't insisted that she and Wyatt keep their courtship secret, Sam would know that he had no chance.

Though Sam reached for her hands, Evelyn kept them folded in her lap. While his lips thinned briefly, he gave a short nod. "I can't wait any longer," he said. "You know how I feel about you. I've made no secret of that. I want to marry you. I want to give you the life you deserve. You'll be an excellent mayor's wife."

His final sentence sent understanding flooding through Evelyn. Sam was nervous about the election, and for some reason he believed that marrying her would help him win. What would he do if he knew she was promised to Wyatt? Though part of her wanted to tell Sam, the other part knew that she had been right in telling Wyatt that their love had no bearing on the election.

Sam laid his right hand on top of hers. "Say yes, Evelyn." It was a command, not a plea.

She shook her head, more convinced than ever that she'd made a mistake in coming here. She didn't love Sam, and she didn't believe he loved her. Though he'd asked — or ordered — her to marry him, he'd never mentioned the word *love*. All he cared about was becoming mayor.

"I'm sorry, Sam, but I can't marry you."

"Why not?"

There was no point in dissembling. He needed to know the truth. "Because I don't love you."

He shrugged as if her protest were immaterial. "You'll learn to love. My father told me that love grows."

"That may be true, but first there needs to be a seed."

"I'll plant it."

He sounded so assured of himself that Evelyn's temper began to rise. "It doesn't work that way, Sam. I don't love you, and I never will." The words were harsh, but she doubted he'd understand anything else. Trying to soften her refusal, she added, "I'm sorry."

He rose, his face flushed with anger. "Sorry. That's right. You'll be sorry."

CHAPTER TWENTY-SEVEN

"I'm glad it's a sunny day." Dorothy's words were positive, but the furrows between her eyes told Evelyn that worry wasn't far away.

"Me too. I've always heard that more people turn out on nice days." And, according to Wyatt, he needed every possible vote.

Evelyn wrenched her attention back to the piecrust she was fitting into the pan. It wouldn't do to serve anything but the best today. At times, the campaign had seemed endless, but now that it was June 3, Election Day, she felt as if the weeks had passed in the proverbial blink of an eye.

"He's done everything he can," she said, more to herself than to Dorothy. "Surely Mesquite Springs's voters will agree that he's the better candidate."

As much as she wanted to believe that, Evelyn knew that public opinion could change in an instant. It had been difficult to ignore Sam's slurs when he'd tried to paint

Wyatt as a man out of touch with the town and its needs.

"His whole life has been spent on the ranch," Sam had told anyone who'd listen. "The man knows nothing but raising race-horses." He'd accompanied the last word with a frown, reminding people of the evils of gambling.

Though Dorothy had fumed and advised retaliation, Wyatt had refused to counter those claims, at least not with words. Instead, he'd spent the last five weeks calling on every single person who lived in town or on the surrounding ranches. Some had turned him away, but others had listened to him. More importantly, Wyatt claimed, many had told him what they liked and didn't like about the town they called home.

By eight o'clock tonight, Wyatt would know whether he'd succeeded in convincing the majority of the town's voters that he should become mayor. Evelyn prayed that he would, because as the weeks had passed, she'd become more and more convinced that Sam was not the right man to lead Mesquite Springs.

Though he'd been nothing but cordial to her, despite her refusal of his offer of mar-riage, she felt prickles of apprehension whenever she sensed that he was watching her. It wasn't the same fear she'd experienced in Gilmorton, knowing the Watcher was there, but it still left her uneasy.

Dorothy loaded a tray with silverware, napkins, and glasses, then returned a minute later after laying them on the tables. "I peeked outside, and it looks like there's a good turnout already." Voting was taking place at the mayor's office across the street from Polly's Place.

"I thought there would be." And, since many people would stay in town until the results were announced this evening, there was a good likelihood that they'd want a meal. "I expect us to be busier than usual today." That was the reason Evelyn had made more of everything. Even though she hadn't advertised it, she was prepared to remain open an extra hour if there were people still waiting at her normal closing time.

"Once we open the door and everyone smells the fried chicken, I wouldn't be surprised if people decide they'd rather eat than vote."

"They can do both. They'd better do both, because your brother thinks it's going to be a close race." And Evelyn didn't want to consider the possibility that he'd lose.

Within minutes of opening, Polly's Place

was filled with men who'd come to vote and wives who'd come to either encourage their husbands or to take advantage of the shops.

"You won't believe who's here," Dorothy said as she returned to the kitchen with the first round of orders. Without waiting for Evelyn to guess, she said, "Sam's parents. I didn't think they'd come, since everyone knows I've been handing out flyers for Wyatt."

"Maybe they're planning to campaign the way their son does." In truth, Evelyn was as surprised as Dorothy. She hadn't thought that the Plauts would want to associate with the woman who'd refused their son's offer of marriage, but perhaps he hadn't told them.

"Did Sam come too?"

"No. He's across the street, talking to everyone who's in line." Dorothy made it sound like a crime.

"Isn't Wyatt doing the same thing?"

"Yes, but . . ." Dorothy stopped abruptly and chuckled. "You're right. That's what candidates do."

As Evelyn made her way around the dining room, greeting each of her customers, she watched Sam's parents from the corner of her eye. They sat at a table for two and didn't appear to be engaging with other customers.

"It's good to see you again," she said when she reached their table. Though she had no desire to marry their son, she had enjoyed her time with the elder Plauts.

"I couldn't pass up an opportunity to have another piece of your pie while we wait to congratulate our son." Mrs. Plaut acted as if the result of the race had already been determined.

"He'll be a fine mayor," her husband announced, "just like he's been a fine lawyer and son."

"He'll make a fine husband too." The look Mrs. Plaut fixed on Evelyn confirmed her belief that Sam had not mentioned his proposal and her rejection.

She simply nodded and turned to the customers at the next table.

"We've got a dozen people still waiting," Dorothy told her as the clock in the kitchen chimed twice.

Evelyn nodded. It was what she'd expected. "I'll talk to them."

She walked to the front of the store and opened the door, smiling broadly at the people who stood outside. To her surprise, the majority were women. Perhaps their husbands were in line at the polls.

"I'm sorry you've had to wait."

The two women closest to the door looked at each other, then back at Evelyn. "I guess we should have come earlier," the elder of the two said.

"That's what I told you, Mabel." Her companion's tone was chiding. "We'll have to see what victuals Mr. Downey has in the mercantile."

"You can certainly do that," Evelyn agreed. "I recommend the canned peaches, and I've also heard that the tinned beef is good, but if you'd prefer to eat at Polly's Place, we should have a table for you in ten or fifteen minutes."

"You mean you're not closing now?" The second woman was clearly surprised by Evelyn's statement.

Though Evelyn addressed her reply to the two women, she raised her voice enough that everyone in line could hear her. "We'll stay open until all of you have been fed." As murmurs of thanks rose, she continued. "I have two whole pies waiting for you."

Mabel nodded. "That's mighty nice of you, Miss Radner. Like I told my Henry, this is a fine place to call home."

Two hours later, the last of the dishes had been washed. With nothing to do other than wait, Dorothy had acceded to Polly's pleas and had gone upstairs to play with her. Not wanting to disturb them, Evelyn settled in the easy chair and closed her eyes. She wasn't certain whether she'd dozed, but the sound of a knock on the door roused her.

As she opened the door, she smiled. This man was welcome at any time of the day or night.

"Is there any food left?" Wyatt asked as he doffed his hat.

"I have some chicken and biscuits I could reheat. Or you could eat them cold."

"Cold is fine. I don't want to be gone for too long, but my stomach was grumbling so loudly that it was drowning out everything I wanted to say."

Though she suspected he was exaggerating, Evelyn pretended to take his words at face value. "We wouldn't want the town's next mayor to faint from hunger."

She pulled a plate from the cupboard and filled it with three pieces of chicken and four biscuits. A jar of peach jam and a tall glass of buttermilk completed the impromptu meal.

"Now I won't faint. Thanks." Wyatt took a large bite of the chicken and washed it down with a slug of milk.

"Do you have any idea how the voting is going?"

"None." His immediate hunger sated,

Wyatt split a biscuit and spread a generous helping of jam on it. "Almost everyone's been friendly, but they've been friendly to Sam too."

"It's a friendly town." That was one of the things Evelyn liked best about Mesquite Springs, and she hoped that no matter who won, that wouldn't change.

"Would you like a piece of pie?" she asked when he finished the last of the chicken.

He shook his head, his regret evident. "I can't afford the time away. Will you save it for later?"

"Celebratory pie. Why not?"

Wyatt rose and laid his hand on her cheek, giving it a light caress. "No matter whether I win or not, I'll be celebrating, because starting tonight, I'll have time to spend with you."

"But you will win." He had to.

The sun had yet to set when Mayor McBride announced that the polls were closed. "I know y'all are anxious — especially two of you — to hear how the voting went." He grinned as his gaze moved from Sam to Wyatt and then to the crowd that had assembled outside his office. Clapping the sheriff, who stood at his side, on the shoulder, he said, "It shouldn't take Fletcher and me more than half an hour to count the ballots. Y'all need to be patient a little while longer."

Twenty-eight minutes later, the two men emerged from the mayor's office. At the sight of their solemn expressions, a shiver of apprehension made its way down Evelyn's spine. She had expected the mayor and the sheriff to be smiling, but they showed no sign of emotion.

Mayor McBride stood silently, waiting until the crowd quieted. "In accordance with our normal procedure, Fletcher counted the ballots and recorded the results. Without telling me the counts, he passed the ballots to me. I counted them and recorded what I found; then we traded papers."

The mayor paused, and for the first time, his face broke into a grin. "I'm happy to tell you that your sheriff and I count the same way. Y'all know it was a hotly contested election between two fine men, but the results are clear." He paused again, this time to ensure he had everyone's attention.

"Sam Plaut received 133 votes." Another pause. "Wyatt Clark received 207."

Excitement and a sense of rightness swept through Evelyn. The town had confirmed what she knew, that Wyatt was the best man to lead them.

"Our next mayor is Wyatt Clark." Mayor McBride extended his hand to Wyatt. "Congratulations."

When a round of cheers greeted the mayor's announcement, Wyatt waited until the crowd was once again silent before he began to speak. "Thank you, ladies and gentlemen." He gave them a conspiratorial grin. "Yes, I know you ladies weren't able to cast a vote, but I also know that you had your say in this election."

Several women laughed, while a number of men nodded, acknowledging their wives' influence.

"I'm grateful to all of you for your support, and I'm honored that you've chosen me as your mayor. I promise you that I will do my best."

When the applause subsided, Wyatt continued. "And now let's have a round of applause for my opponent. He and I didn't agree on everything, but I think we all can agree that Mesquite Springs is fortunate to have him as our attorney. I'm proud to call Sam Plaut my friend."

Though a smile crossed Sam's face, Evelyn could see that it was a false one, and when his gaze met hers, his expression sent chills down her spine. Never before had she seen him look like that. She could understand anger, but what frightened her was the other emotion that blazed from his eyes. Hatred.

CHAPTER TWENTY-EIGHT

"What's the occasion?" Curiosity shone from Winnie's eyes.

"Do I need a special occasion to take the woman I love out for a meal?"

Her eyes widened as his words registered. "Do you love me?"

"Of course I do." The question was preposterous, and yet . . . Rufus paused, trying to recall the last time he'd told his wife he loved her. What a fool he'd been! He'd blamed her for the coolness between them when he was equally to blame.

Thank you, God, he said silently. *I see your hand in this.* At the time, he couldn't explain why he'd awakened with an urge to eat at Ma's Kitchen. The meals weren't as good as they'd been when the Radcliffes had owned it, although Ma's pot roast was excellent.

There was no reason to go there today. He had other things to do, but Rufus had been unable to suppress the feeling that it was important that they dine there. Now he realized that it gave him an opportunity to do something nice for Winnie. She'd seemed happier this past week, as if she'd turned a corner, and he wanted that to continue.

She giggled, a sound he hadn't heard in months, perhaps years. "If you're trying to sweet-talk me, it's working."

"That's good." He laid a hand on her shoulder and squeezed it, remembering that she'd once craved his touch. "You deserve a meal you haven't had to cook."

Winnie smiled again. "Thank you, Rufus."

When they arrived at the restaurant, it was as crowded as he'd expected. High noon was the most popular time at Ma's Kitchen, but he'd chosen it because Winnie had once told him she liked watching other diners.

"Your table is ready, Mr. Bauman," the waitress said as soon as they'd entered the building.

Winnie's eyes widened. "You reserved a table?"

It had cost him an extra two bits, but he'd done it gladly. "Why not? I didn't want you to have to stand in the sun." For as long as he'd known her, Winnie's one vanity had been her pale skin. Other than that silly hat she'd wanted for Easter, she wore bonnets with extra wide brims and avoided going outside when the sun was at its zenith.

"That's mighty thoughtful of you, husband."

Rufus grinned as she gave his arm a little squeeze. It had been years since she'd called him that. "I made sure they were serving pot roast today." That was her favorite dish.

"You're a good man, Rufus."

And he was going to do his best to be a better one. He kept his attention focused on his wife as they ordered and began to eat their meal. Though he was aware that two men he'd never seen before occupied the table next to them, he paid them no attention until the waitress offered the strangers dessert.

"I don't suppose you have any oatmeal pecan pie, do you?" the first one asked, his voice a clear baritone.

"No, sir. That's one dish we don't serve, but we do have plain pecan pie."

Baritone's disappointment was palpable. "I was afraid of that. It's been more than ten years, but I still miss the pie the Radcliffes made."

Rufus nodded silently. Though it was trivial compared to the tragedy of the Radcliffes' deaths, he knew that many in town regretted the fact that Ma hadn't been able to re-create their famous pie.

The baritone's companion, a tenor, joined the conversation. "You like oatmeal pecan pie?"

"It's my favorite. Like you, I travel a lot. I used to go out of my way to eat here back when the Radcliffes were alive. Since then, I keep looking, but I haven't found anything to compare to theirs."

"This is my first time in Gilmorton," the tenor admitted, "so I don't know what that pie tasted like. I'd never even heard of oatmeal pecan pie until I had a piece a month or so ago, but that pie was the best thing I've ever eaten."

The tenor leaned across the table and dropped his voice to a conspiratorial level. "I tried to talk the cook into sharing her recipe, but she wouldn't. Claimed it was a family secret. The only thing I could talk her into was selling me a whole pie." He shrugged. "My wife's still trying to figure out what made it special."

Baritone was clearly intrigued. So was Rufus.

"Where was this?" Baritone asked the question that was on the tip of Rufus's tongue. It was unlikely — highly unlikely — that there was any connection between this pie and the Radcliffes, but unlikely things did happen.

"The Hill Country. A town called Mesquite Springs. If you go there, you can't miss the restaurant. Polly's Place is the only one in town."

Polly. Not Evelyn. Not Radcliffe. Rufus swallowed deeply, wishing he could dismiss his disappointment as easily as he swallowed the bite of tender pot roast.

"Maybe I can talk Polly into selling me more than one pie." Baritone appeared to be a persistent man.

"Not Polly. The woman you want to talk to is Evelyn."

Exultation, pure and powerful, flowed through Rufus's veins. It couldn't be a coincidence that a woman named Evelyn was making what used to be the Radcliffes' most popular pie. This was why he'd felt compelled to come here today. He didn't know how it was possible, but Evelyn was alive. Not only alive but apparently settled in a new life doing the same thing her parents had.

Thank you, God. Now that he knew where she was, there was only one thing to do. He needed to see her once more. This time he'd do more than watch from afar. He'd talk to her. He'd explain what had happened and why. And then he'd ask her forgiveness.

Rufus turned to his wife, who'd been listening as intently as he. "What do you say we take a trip?"

"Where?"

"Mesquite Springs."

Winnie frowned, the lighthearted mood that had sustained her all morning seeming to evaporate. "You think she's the one, don't you? You think she didn't die in that fire."

Rufus nodded. As improbable as it seemed, he could not dismiss the conviction that Evelyn had survived.

"And you want to go to that town so you can see that girl again?"

It was more than wanting. "I need to." There were things he should have said ten years ago. At the time, he'd told himself that she wasn't ready to hear them, but the news of the fire had changed everything. That day he'd realized that he was the one who hadn't been ready. Since then, he'd lived with regret that he had been a coward. Now that he'd been given a chance to do what he should have a decade ago, he had no intention of squandering it.

Winnie laid down her fork and glared at him. "You may need to go, but I don't. If you go, you'll go alone." She closed her eyes and pursed her lips, her anger apparent. A moment later, her face softened, and she looked at him. "I wouldn't mind it if you brought back a pie for me. I always did like it."

Rufus grinned at the evidence of another answered prayer.

"What a beautiful day!"

It was the first Sunday after the election, and as had been their custom for months, Evelyn and Polly had gone to the Circle C for lunch. Now she and Wyatt were strolling around the ranch. They'd visited the horses and were making their way to the stand of oak trees on the far end of the pasture.

"The day can't compare to you." Wyatt reached over to take her hand in his. "I'm thankful that the election is over and we can spend more time together."

His palm was warm, firm, and so comforting that it scrambled her brain. How could she think about ordinary things when she was with Wyatt, when being near him made her dream of a life together?

Evelyn inhaled deeply, trying to compose her thoughts. "Now you can concentrate on getting everything ready for the sale." It was less than a month away, and though they'd finished a fair amount of preparation, there was still work to be done.

Wyatt shrugged his shoulders, as if the sale

were of no import. "What I want is to concentrate on courting you. I want to convince you that I'll be a good husband and father."

He sounded so unsure of himself that Evelyn wanted to do nothing more than press her lips to his, showing him that she had no doubts. A lady wouldn't do that, even though they were far enough from the ranch house that no one would see them, so she settled for saying, "You don't need to convince me. I already know that, and Polly has wanted you as her daddy from the first day she met you."

"I suspect she was desperate for a father. She probably reacted the same way to every man she saw."

Once again, Wyatt seemed to doubt his appeal, and once again Evelyn sought to reassure him. "She didn't. Oh, it's true that she was always searching for a daddy. She'd look at every man she saw the same way she examines stick candy at the mercantile, trying to pick her favorite, but she always shook her head. You were the first and only one she's liked."

As they meandered across the meadow, Wyatt paused to let Evelyn admire the prickly pear blossoms that covered one of the spiny plants. "Do you suppose I resemble her father, and that's why she was drawn to me?"

She thought for a second. "I doubt it," she said. "I don't see any similarity between you two. Why don't you admit it, Wyatt? Polly loves you because you're lovable."

Surely that wasn't a blush that colored his cheeks. "Lovable? You're the first person to call me that."

"Well, it's true."

Wyatt waited until Evelyn turned her gaze back to him before he spoke. When he did, his eyes radiated sincerity. "Until I met you, I never thought much about love. Now it seems to be on my mind all the time."

He took both of her hands in his, his touch sending more shivers of delight along her spine. "I told you I wasn't sure what I felt for you was love, but now I know that this is love, and it's real. I love you, Evelyn."

The words were sweeter than any she'd ever heard, filling her heart with such happiness that she thought it might overflow. This was the answer to her prayers. The man she loved loved her. And he loved Polly. They would become a family, brought together seemingly by chance but united by the most powerful of emotions. This was what she had sought for so long, the one thing that would make her life complete. If there was anything better in life than to give and receive love, Evelyn didn't know what it might be.

"I love you, Wyatt. More than I can ever say. You're my hero, the man of my dreams."

His lips curved into a smile that made Evelyn's blood race, and the way he stared at her lips made her long for more than a smile.

"Oh, my darling." As if he'd read her thoughts, Wyatt reached forward, drawing her into his arms, and pressed his lips to hers.

Evelyn had thought nothing could compare to her first kiss, but this one was even more wonderful. It filled her with a sense of homecoming, as if this was where she was meant to be, a sense of rightness, as if this was her destiny.

Nothing could harm her. Nothing could destroy this feeling of perfection. This was what she wanted. This was what she had longed for all her life. The happiness that had threatened to overflow its banks did, turning her legs into jelly, and she moved closer to Wyatt, glorying in his strength.

Crack!

Evelyn's head jerked backward, breaking the kiss, at the same instant that Wyatt pushed her to the ground, sheltering her with his body.

A gunshot. There was no mistaking the sound. She'd heard it that horrible night, and no matter how many years passed, she would never forget the terror it brought. Even now, though she was surrounded by sunshine, she was drawn back into the vortex of memories. Rain against the roof, thunder growing ever closer. The acrid smell of lightning, the unmistakable scent of blood. The shouts, the shots, the terrifying silence when she realized her parents were no longer breathing.

She had thought she had escaped. She had thought she was safe. But she wasn't.

"He's found me," she whimpered. "The Watcher has found me."

Wyatt rose slowly, scanning the horizon. When he saw no sign of the shooter, he extended his hand to Evelyn. "He's gone. You're safe."

She shook her head, still trembling from shock. "No, I'm not." Though she stood next to him, her eyes moved rapidly from side to side.

Remembering what Evelyn had told him about her parents' deaths and the fear she'd felt whenever she'd been forced to go to

Gilmorton, Wyatt knew she was reliving that terror.

"I thought I was safe, but I'm not." Her teeth were chattering, her face unnaturally pale. He needed to calm her, to protect her.

Wyatt led Evelyn to the nearest tree. After sinking to the ground, he reached for her, pulled her onto his lap, and wrapped his arm around her. If the shooter was still nearby, it would be difficult to hit them here.

"It's all right, Evelyn," he said, using the voice that rarely failed to soothe a frightened horse. "It must have been a hunter."

That wasn't the case, and Wyatt knew it. There was no reason for someone to be hunting in this area. Furthermore, the shot had come so close to them that it was obvious they were the targets. Questions tumbled through his brain. Who? Why? Why now?

"If it wasn't a hunter, most likely it was someone gunning for me." That was just as plausible as the idea that the Watcher had come here. More plausible, actually, the more Wyatt thought about it.

"It wasn't a hunter, and the shooter wasn't looking for you." Her voice was stronger now. This was the old Evelyn, the one who didn't back down from anything. "It was the man who killed my parents."

Though Wyatt knew she believed that, he wasn't convinced. If the Watcher, as she called him, had wanted to kill Evelyn, he'd had ten years to do so. There was no reason for him to have waited and to have traveled all the way to Mesquite Springs when he'd had so many other opportunities.

"What if it wasn't that at all?" he asked. "What if it was someone who wanted to hurt me?" They'd been so close together that the shooter could have been aiming for either one of them.

"Who?"

There was only one person Wyatt could imagine who might have fired that shot. "Sam. He wasn't happy when he lost the election." Though he'd shaken Wyatt's hand in apparent congratulations, Wyatt had known that was all for show. Sam had been seething with fury that night, and though he normally greeted Wyatt after church, today he'd kept his distance.

Wyatt didn't want to believe his friend would have resorted to murder, but perhaps the shot hadn't been meant to kill or even wound. Perhaps it was simply meant as a warning. Sam was an expert shot. If he'd wanted to kill Wyatt, he would have.

Evelyn appeared to consider the possibility. "You might be right about it being Sam, but I could have been the target. He's not very happy with me, either."

This was the first Wyatt had heard of that. "Why?"

Evelyn shifted so that she was facing him. "I told Sam I wouldn't marry him. When I explained that I didn't love him, he said I'd be sorry. Maybe this is what he meant."

Wyatt inhaled sharply. That put a new spin on the shooting. Maybe it had been Sam, but he hadn't been fueled by anger over losing the election. Though Wyatt had known Sam was interested in Evelyn as a potential bride, he hadn't realized he'd proposed to her. Being rejected and then finding the woman kissing another man might have unleashed his anger, but that still raised the question of why he'd been in the woods.

"Very few people say no to Sam," Wyatt said, trying to make sense of what had happened. Sam's parents had pampered him, and he'd always been strong enough that none of the other boys would challenge him. While Wyatt would not have called him a bully, there was no doubt that Sam was accustomed to being the leader.

"I can see why he'd have been angry, but I can't believe he'd try to harm you." It was one thing to consider that Sam might have tried to warn Wyatt away, quite another to picture him killing someone.

"Sam's not a violent man," he assured Evelyn.

She shook her head. "He broke a valuable vase when he was angry, and Caleb said he tried to drown him at the spring."

Wyatt flinched as yet another shock registered. "When we were boys?" Evelyn nodded. "I was there that day," he told her, trying to reconcile his memory of the afternoon with Caleb's allegation.

"The three of us went swimming. I decided to see if I could find the source of the spring, so I kept diving as deep as I could. When I came up one time, I saw Sam's hands on Caleb's shoulders. Something looked wrong, so I swam over to them."

Wyatt tried to recall exactly what he'd seen and what his friends had said. "Sam told me Caleb was drowning, and he was pulling him out of the water."

"Caleb said he was pushing him under."

The way Sam's hands had been positioned, it could have been either. Wyatt realized that, and yet he found it difficult to believe that Sam had wanted to harm their friend. "Caleb never told me what happened." But he'd told Evelyn.

As if she sensed how much that knowledge rankled, Evelyn tipped her head to one side and gave him a smile meant to reassure him. "I don't think he meant to tell me. It simply slipped out, and I could tell that he regretted saying anything."

Her smile faded a little. "Caleb didn't say why he'd never told you, but I suspect he didn't want to come between you and Sam. He did say that Sam apologized the next day, claiming it was only a prank and that he'd meant to scare Caleb but not hurt him. I think Caleb forgave him and tried to put the incident behind him."

"That sounds like Caleb. He's a good man."

The question was, was Sam?

CHAPTER TWENTY-NINE

Evelyn's trembling began to subside. Wyatt was right; they were safe. After that first terrible blast from the rifle, there'd been no further sign of the shooter. At Wyatt's urging, she'd risen, and with his arm wrapped around her waist, she'd managed to put one foot in front of the other as they headed back to the ranch house. Her heart had stopped pounding, and the way the birds were once again warbling in the treetops confirmed that the threat was gone.

They walked toward where the shot was fired. After searching the grass for a few moments, Wyatt bent down and plucked a shiny object from the grass.

"What's that?"

He eyed it carefully before responding. "A shell casing. One of Sam's."

Though they'd both thought it likely, the proof that Sam had been the shooter turned Evelyn's legs to jelly again. "Are you sure?"

Wyatt nodded. "The rest of us use ones Leonard Downey stocks, but Sam orders his from some place back East. He and I've gone hunting many times, and he never misses an opportunity to show me his fancy shells."

"Then there's no question."

His eyes solemn, Wyatt shook his head. "Only why."

When they reached the house, Isolde and Dorothy were waiting on the porch, their faces filled with anxiety. Since there was no sign of Polly, Evelyn guessed the women had found a way to keep her indoors and gave silent thanks that the child would be spared listening to the story.

"We heard a gunshot." Isolde's accent was heavier than usual, a measure of her distress. "What happened?"

"Sam shot at us." Wyatt's words were matter-of-fact, but the way he tightened his grip told Evelyn he was as affected by the shooting as she.

Dorothy stared at her brother, her shock obvious. "Are you sure?" When Wyatt pulled the shell casing from his pocket and held it out to her, Dorothy's lips tightened. "That's Sam's, all right."

"Why did he shoot at you?" The question burst from Isolde's lips, her anger that someone had dared to threaten her son so strong that Evelyn began to tremble again as the memory of those horrible moments washed over her.

Wyatt led her to the porch swing and waited until everyone was seated, she and Wyatt on the swing, Dorothy and Isolde on the wicker settee next to it, before he spoke. "Possibly because I won the election."

"Or because I wouldn't marry him." Evelyn would not discount that motive.

The look Dorothy flashed at her told Evelyn she understood. "He doesn't like being refused." When Isolde raised both eyebrows in a question, Dorothy continued. "Yes, Ma. Sam asked me to marry him last year. When I refused, he said he'd kill me before he let me marry someone else."

Evelyn felt Wyatt's arm tighten around her, as if he were more determined than ever to keep her safe. "He didn't even have the decency to ask my permission to court you, and you didn't tell me?" Wyatt spat the words at his sister.

"What would you have done? You would have refused him because you know how I feel about him, and that would have only made him angry at you. I knew his anger would fade. It always does."

Dorothy gave her mother a quick hug,

clearly trying to reassure her, but she fixed her gaze on Wyatt. "Sam's like a firecracker. There's a lot of noise, but it only lasts a second or two, and he's always remorseful afterwards."

As she thought about the day he'd broken the vase, Evelyn realized there was much truth in Dorothy's observation.

Wyatt, however, seemed surprised by his sister's insight. "Sam's been my friend for as long as I can remember, but you seem to know him better than I do."

"He shows different sides to different people."

That was true. Evelyn had seen many sides to Sam — charming, thoughtful, angry, even absentminded. "What do we do now?" she asked. Her terror had subsided, replaced by the conviction that Sam had to be stopped. While he hadn't hurt anyone this time, there was no telling what he might do in the future, particularly when she and Wyatt announced their plans to marry.

"*We* don't do anything," Wyatt said with a frown. "*I'm* going to see Sam."

Though she hated the idea of a confrontation with a man whose anger was easily aroused, Evelyn would not let Wyatt do this alone. "I'm part of this too. Don't forget that he shot at both of us."

Wyatt turned to his mother and sister. "Can you talk any sense into her?"

Isolde shrugged. "She sounds sensible to me. Dorothy's right. Sam's anger fades quickly. I don't believe either of you are in any danger now." As if she'd read Evelyn's mind, she added, "We'll keep Polly occupied until you return."

Moments later, Evelyn and Wyatt were in the wagon, headed toward the Plaut ranch and their conversation with Sam.

"I don't know where he is," Mr. Plaut said when they arrived. "We haven't seen him since he left for church."

"He has to be somewhere. The question is, where." Wyatt frowned as he helped Evelyn back into the wagon.

"Let's try in town. He might have gone back to his office for something." After all, he'd once told her it was his sanctuary. It made sense that if he hadn't gone home, that was where he would be.

But Sam wasn't in his office. Not yet. As they drove along Main into the heart of Mesquite Springs, Evelyn and Wyatt saw Sam walking from the church toward the law office, Pastor Coleman at his side.

Though Sam appeared dejected with his shoulders slumped, his head bent forward, when he spotted the wagon, his posture became military. "Looking for me?"

"Yes." It was one word, but Wyatt imbued it with such ferocity that Sam took a step back.

"Let's all go to the parsonage," Pastor Coleman suggested as he put his arm around Sam's shoulders. "Sam has some things to say to both of you."

Evelyn looked around as the minister ushered them into his parlor. The worn furniture, the almost threadbare carpet, and the walls devoid of all decoration save an exceptionally fine oil painting of Jesus with the children left no doubts about the Colemans' priorities. She took a seat on the settee, gesturing to Wyatt to sit next to her, while Sam and the minister sat on the straight-backed chairs on the opposite side of the low table.

When they'd all declined Mrs. Coleman's offer of tea or coffee, Sam leaned forward, as if trying to breach the distance between them. The nervousness Evelyn had noticed from the moment he'd spotted them had only increased, and though she could not forget the fear she'd felt when she'd heard the shot, her heart ached for Sam's obvious distress.

"I don't know where to start other than to say that I'm sorry." His words were clearly enunciated, but his expression betrayed his nervousness.

"About this?" Wyatt held out the shell casing.

"Yes." After swallowing deeply, Sam looked directly at Wyatt. "I didn't mean to hurt you. You've got to believe that, Wyatt. You too, Evelyn."

Though his words rang with sincerity, they didn't explain his actions. "Then why did you shoot at us?" she asked.

"I was angry. It seemed as if you were taking everything I wanted. It was bad enough that Wyatt was going to be mayor, but when I saw the way you looked at him after church, I knew you were going to marry him." His eyes darkened. "You never looked at me that way, and it made me furious. I had to do something to let the anger out."

Sam turned to Pastor Coleman, waiting until the minister nodded before he continued. "I can't explain it, but sometimes the anger is so strong that I feel like one of those people in the Bible who were possessed by evil spirits. I've tried, but I can't fight them."

Wyatt was clearly not convinced. "Do you expect me to believe this? Evil spirits?"

"It's the truth." The minister paused, his gray eyes filled with sorrow. "When he realized what he'd done and that he might have hurt you or Evelyn, Sam came to me. We've talked and prayed, and we believe we have an answer."

"What kind of an answer can there be?" Though his own anger seemed to be diminishing, Wyatt sounded dubious.

"Pastor Coleman knows of a place back East, a hospital that works with people like me. I'll go there unless you report me to the sheriff and I wind up in jail."

Evelyn laid her hand on Wyatt's arm, silently urging him to agree. The most important thing was to get Sam away from Mesquite Springs. While she wasn't certain anyone could drive the demons out, it was obvious Sam needed help.

Wyatt was silent for a moment before he addressed the minister. "You really think those people can help Sam?"

As Pastor Coleman nodded, Wyatt looked at Evelyn, wordlessly seeking her opinion. When she nodded, he said, "That sounds like a good plan to me."

Though both Sam and the minister appeared relieved, no one spoke for what felt like an hour but was probably no more than a minute.

"Thank you, Wyatt." The reason for Sam's silence was obvious in his choked voice. He'd been trying to regain his composure.

"You have every right to hate me after the campaign I ran and now this."

"I don't hate you. I was sincere when I called you my friend on Election Day."

His eyes suspiciously wet, Sam managed a small smile. "Again, thank you." He turned to Evelyn as he said, "You were right to refuse me. He's the better man."

"For me." There was no question about that. "There's a woman waiting for you, Sam. I'm sure of that." A week ago, she couldn't have said that, but Evelyn was convinced that the contrite man sitting across from her was the true Sam. Though she didn't know what the hospital would do, she had to trust that Pastor Coleman was right and that they could help Sam control his anger.

Wyatt stretched out his hand to clasp Sam's. "I have only one question: when will you be back?"

CHAPTER THIRTY

For the next few days, Mesquite Springs was buzzing with the news that Sam had gone East to care for some distant relatives who had complicated legal affairs. Though Wyatt had told his family the full story, they'd all agreed there was no reason to share that with anyone else. The truth was, both he and Evelyn were so busy that they had little time to dwell on what had happened. They had no idea how long Sam would be gone or who — if anyone — would take over his law practice while he was away.

Wyatt tried to dismiss his worries as he saddled Thunder and headed toward town. Evelyn was safe. He knew that, and yet he couldn't help feeling that he was missing something, that perhaps the danger remained. That was part of the reason he tried to see Evelyn every day, even though with the sale in only a few days he couldn't spare the time away from the ranch. The time he and Evelyn spent together might be brief, but it was the highlight of his days, reassuring him of her safety and reminding him how blessed he was to have found her. The woman he loved was one in a million.

"Mr. Wyatt! Mr. Wyatt! You came!" Polly jumped down from the bench in front of the restaurant where she and Evelyn had been sitting and raced toward him, hugging his legs as soon as he'd tied Thunder to the hitching post.

"Of course, I did. I can't go a day without seeing my favorite ladies." He lifted Polly into his arms and twirled her around as he did each day. It was, he'd soon discovered, one of the things Polly enjoyed most.

"I love you, Mr. Wyatt. I want you to be my daddy."

As he placed the child back on the ground, Wyatt shared a smile with Evelyn. "We'll have to see about that."

Though that was what he wanted as well, he and Evelyn had agreed not to rush their courtship. Today he wanted to talk to her without Polly overhearing, and so he continued addressing the little girl. "I heard you were the best swinger in your class. Will you show me how high you can swing?"

"Sure." She grabbed his hand and began

to lead him toward the street, not bothering to wait for Evelyn to join them. "Let's go." Once they'd crossed the street, as Wyatt had expected, Polly skipped ahead, heading for the schoolyard swings.

"Nicely done." Evelyn flashed Wyatt one of those smiles that made his heart skip a beat as she tucked her hand into the crook of his arm. "You're going to be an excellent father."

"I hope so." Though they had a few moments before they reached the school, he wasn't ready to tell her his concerns. "How was your day?"

Evelyn laughed, as if the answer should be apparent. "Busy. A few people have already arrived for the sale, but even without them, I had more customers than usual. It seems like everyone wants a piece of pie." She slowed their pace and looked up at him, her gaze piercing him. "I don't think that's what you really wanted to ask."

"You're right." It was eerie the way she seemed to read his thoughts. Was this what marriage would be like, communicating without words? Wyatt thought he could get used to it.

"I keep thinking about your parents' deaths, the Watcher, and the fire, and I can't help thinking we're missing something."

"I've had the same feeling. I know someone was watching me during all those years, but I can't explain why he waited so long to try to kill me and why he was willing to let so many other people die in the fire just to get to me."

Her thoughts mirrored his own, making Wyatt wonder whether Evelyn had come to the conclusion he had. "Unless the fire wasn't connected to you."

When her eyes widened, Wyatt realized that Evelyn's thoughts hadn't traveled the same path as his.

"Maybe you weren't the target," he said softly. Polly had reached the schoolyard and was headed for the swings. There was no danger of her overhearing, and yet he didn't want his voice to carry.

"Who could it have been?" Evelyn frowned, as if she were recalling an unpleasant incident. "Not everyone in town liked having orphans nearby, but I can't believe they would have set the fire. And while it's true that some people didn't care for Mrs. Folger, I don't think she had any real enemies. I can't imagine that any of the orphans did, either."

Wyatt hated the concern that colored Evelyn's expression, but he couldn't dismiss his suppositions so easily. "Are you sure?"

"If there were enemies, why did the killer wait? Everyone had been there for a while." She paused, and this time Wyatt knew she had reached the same conclusion he had. "Except Polly," she said slowly. "She came only a month earlier."

Evelyn's feet stopped as if of their own accord, and she gazed up at Wyatt, her blue eyes filled with fear. "Oh, Wyatt, do you think it's possible? Why would anyone want to kill Polly?"

As much as he hated feeling ignorant, he had to tell her the truth. "I don't know."

"I'm the bestest swinger, aren't I, Mr. Wyatt?"

Though Evelyn tried to smile at Polly's enthusiasm, she could not dismiss the fear that clutched her heart. If Wyatt was correct — and she believed he was — precious Polly might be in danger.

"You sure are." Wyatt ruffled Polly's hair, nodding when Evelyn gestured toward the schoolhouse steps. They'd agreed that it was imperative to learn Polly's name. Once they had that information, he would ask the sheriff to make inquiries.

"Why are we going here?" Polly demanded. "School's closed."

"I know it is," Evelyn said, "but Mr. Wyatt

410

and I need to talk to you. We'd like to sit down." Evelyn didn't want to frighten Polly by having two adults towering over her while they questioned her.

"We have something very important to ask you," she said when they were seated on the top step, Polly sandwiched between her and Wyatt. "We know your name is Polly, but what's your last name?"

"Radner." The satisfied smile she gave Evelyn told her she was proud not to have repeated the embarrassing moment when she'd forgotten her new name.

"Not that one." Evelyn kept her voice gentle. "The name you had before. Your daddy's name."

Alarm drained the color from Polly's cheeks, and she shook her head violently, pressing her lips together. "I can't tell you. Maisie tole me bad things would happen if I tole anybody."

As he laid a hand on Polly's head to calm her, Wyatt said, "We're not anybody. Evelyn's your new family. You can trust us."

Polly shook her head. "But Maisie said Papa was in the ground and couldn't keep me safe. That's why I had to go away and never, ever, ever tell anybody my name."

Evelyn's heart ached at the realization that Polly had had to deal with danger at such a young age. "Maisie was Polly's mammy," she told Wyatt when she saw his perplexed expression. Turning back to Polly, she said, "Maisie was right then, but everything is different now. I'll keep you safe, and so will Mr. Wyatt, but we need to know your name."

Still dubious, Polly looked at Wyatt. "Do I have to tell you?"

"Yes, but Evelyn's right. You're safe with us. You don't have to worry."

Evelyn prayed that was true. Surely whoever had set the fire believed everyone had died in it and had no reason to be looking for Polly.

"What's your name?" she asked again.

The child squeezed her eyes closed, as if trying to block some image, then opened them again. "Marlow," she said so softly that Evelyn had to strain to hear her.

As she looked at Wyatt, Evelyn knew he felt the same tremor of fear she did. One of the invitations she'd written had been sent to Basil Marlow.

The town was as dreadful as he'd expected. Basil kicked an acorn aside as he strode down the miserable excuse for a main street. There was no decent place to stay — he, Basil Marlow, would have to share a room with three other travelers — and only one place to eat.

"Yer in luck," the owner of the disreputable boardinghouse told him with a grin that revealed three missing teeth. "They're keepin' the restaurant open for supper. Don't normally happen, but this here's a special week. You kin eat at Polly's Place tonight."

Polly's Place! It figured that the only eating establishment in this godforsaken town would bear the one name he hated more than any other. If his stomach hadn't been protesting the lack of food, he'd have forgone supper, figuring that he could eat his fill tomorrow after the sale. One good thing was that Wyatt Clark had promised a meal to everyone who attended. But Basil's stomach wouldn't wait that long. Polly's it was.

He fingered his beard. It still felt odd, but at least it had grown long enough that it was no longer bristly. That was good, and so was the fact that he no longer had to endure strangers' stares. What wasn't good was that he did a double take every time he glanced in a mirror. With the beard, he looked almost identical to Bart, and if there was anything he didn't want, it was to be reminded of that brother of his, the man who had stolen the woman he loved and then let her die in childbirth.

No matter what anyone said, Basil knew that his brother had killed Miriam as surely as if he'd stabbed her. Others claimed it was the storm that kept the doctor from reaching her in time, but Basil knew better. The fault was Bart's. He should have sent for the physician days earlier, just to be sure that Miriam had the care she deserved. But Bart hadn't, and Miriam had died.

It was Bart's fault. He'd killed Miriam, and so he had had to die.

Basil chuckled as he walked toward Polly's Place. Bart had died all right. Though he'd feigned sorrow when he'd heard the news, Basil had had but one regret: that he wasn't there to watch his brother draw his last breath. He could only hope that the stories were true and that poisoning was a painful way to die. That was what Bart had deserved — a long, agonizing death.

"Dinner for one?" an attractive young woman asked as Basil entered the restaurant.

Perhaps this place wasn't as bad as he'd thought. The delicious aromas that had assailed him when he opened the door had encouraged him, and the sight of a woman who was almost as pretty as Miriam made him grin. Maybe he ought to consider staying around for an extra day or two.

"Yes," he said shortly. "What's the best thing to eat?"

As she escorted him to a table for two, the waitress gave him a practiced smile. "Anything Evelyn serves is delicious."

"Evelyn? I thought this was Polly's Place."

"It is. Polly's her sister."

Basil felt the tension that had knotted his neck begin to ease. It was foolish of him — downright ridiculous — to have been worried about a name. This wasn't the same Polly. It couldn't be. Polly Marlow had been an only child, and she was dead.

"All right. I'll have the chicken."

The waitress nodded and headed to the back of the restaurant to place his order. As she opened the door to the kitchen, Basil caught a glimpse of another young woman with a child at her side. The light was good, but even without it, he'd have known her anywhere. That blonde-haired girl had the same tilt to her head as Miriam, and as she turned to address the woman, he spotted the strawberry birthmark.

Rage surged through him, and for a second the world turned black. It couldn't be! She was supposed to be dead. She would be dead.

Chapter Thirty-One

"That's odd." Dorothy frowned as she reentered the kitchen bearing a full plate of fried chicken, mashed potatoes, and creamed peas.

Evelyn looked up from the six plates she was preparing, grateful that this table had made it easy for her with everyone ordering the same thing. Thanks to all the people who'd come to Mesquite Springs for the sale, it had been a hectic day. As if preparing supper as well as lunch weren't enough, Polly had turned cranky when Evelyn wouldn't let her help serve. The child was too excited by the prospect of spending the night at the Circle C to pay attention to something as mundane as carrying plates of pie, and Evelyn did not need her spilling food on a customer.

"What's odd?" she asked.

Dorothy gestured toward the plate in her hand. "The man's gone. He ordered his food, then left."

"Could he be outside smoking?" Though the policy hadn't been popular at the beginning, Evelyn did not allow men to smoke inside Polly's Place, explaining that the smell of burning tobacco masked the aromas of her food.

"I looked, but there was no sign of him, and the other man at the table said he bolted like a spooked horse."

Evelyn had no time to worry about eccentric customers. "If he comes back, don't ask why he left. There's no reason to make anyone uncomfortable."

Though she nodded, Dorothy's expression radiated skepticism. "It seems awfully strange. This has never happened before."

"My mother used to say there was a first time for everything."

"Including Wyatt's first home sale. Oh, Evelyn, I hope it'll go well."

"It will."

Rufus grinned. Though it had taken longer than he'd expected, thanks to the rain that turned the roads into a muddy mess, he'd made it to Mesquite Springs. God was definitely looking out for him. Not only had he arrived safely, but apparently for the first time ever, Polly's Place was open for supper. He'd thought he might have to wait until tomorrow to see Evelyn and confirm his belief that she was Evelyn Radcliffe, but if he hurried, he could get a meal and possibly a glimpse of her.

"One for dinner?" The waitress who greeted him when he entered the restaurant was not Evelyn, but Rufus hadn't expected her to be. She'd be in the kitchen preparing meals or at least overseeing their preparation.

He nodded in response to the question. His stomach craved food, and he craved the opportunity to confirm that the Evelyn he sought was indeed the proprietor of this place.

"I'm afraid I can't give you a table by yourself." The waitress gestured around the crowded dining room. "We're extra busy tonight because of the horse sale tomorrow. Mesquite Springs has never seen so many people. Is that why you're here?"

"Yes. I saw an article in the local paper, and it interested me." That was partially true, though it was not the principal reason he had come. Still, the way the waitress's eyes lit with pleasure told him he'd said something right. "I don't mind sharing a table."

"I'll put you with Mr. Saylor. You'll like

418

him. He's one of our regulars." She led him to an empty chair at one of the center tables.

"Howdy, stranger, and welcome to Mesquite Springs." The burly man gave Rufus a warm smile. "I reckon you came for the sale."

"That and the oatmeal pecan pie. I heard it was good."

"Good ain't a good enough word to describe it. That pie is better than anything I've ever tasted." Mr. Saylor waited until the waitress had listed the evening's meal choices and Rufus had ordered before he continued. "I sure hope she don't close this place when she gets hitched."

"Polly's getting married?" Though Rufus knew that the proprietor was not named Polly, he saw no need to admit what he knew about the restaurant and the woman who ran it.

"Not Polly. She's the little sister."

Sister. Disappointment threatened to drown Rufus. His Evelyn was an only child. Either Mr. Saylor was mistaken or Rufus had made the trip for naught.

"The gal who runs this place is Evelyn." Mr. Saylor continued the story. "She ain't been here all that long, but I heard she and our new mayor are fixin' to get hitched."

"Is he a good man, your mayor?"

419

Rufus asked the question to be polite, but all the while thoughts churned through his brain. He'd been so certain this was his Evelyn. After all, how many women in Texas could there be who were named Evelyn and who ran a restaurant that served exceptionally fine oatmeal pecan pie? The discouraged part of his brain told him there could be dozens. The optimistic side said otherwise. Still, there was the sister.

Rufus knew next to nothing about orphanages, but he supposed it was possible that the children referred to each other as brothers and sisters. Maybe that was the case with Evelyn and Polly. There was only one way to find out.

Mr. Saylor nodded in response to Rufus's question. "The mayor sure is a good man. I reckon you'll meet him tomorrow. He's the one what's runnin' the sale. Name's Wyatt Clark."

A good man and a horse ranch. If this was Rufus's Evelyn, she'd done well for herself. As he and Mr. Saylor dug into their plates of delicious-smelling food, Rufus smiled. "If the pie is as good as I've heard, I'd like to meet Miss Evelyn."

"Most days she comes out and talks to her customers, but I ain't seen her today. I reckon she's extra busy cookin', what with all the new folks in town."

Rufus's disappointment must have shown, for Mr. Saylor continued. "If you miss her tonight, she'll be out at the Circle C tomorrow."

But Rufus didn't want to wait. He'd come back once the restaurant closed.

"Are you sure you have everything?" Wyatt asked as he loaded what seemed like the hundredth crate from Evelyn's now-closed kitchen into the back of the wagon. While he ought to be filled with anticipation of tomorrow's sale, his heart was heavy over the news he had received.

He must be hiding his worries well, though, because Evelyn chuckled. "Don't worry, Wyatt. This is all I need. I know you said you were expecting fifty, but I'm making enough food to feed a hundred."

"You really think there'll be that many?" If so, the sale would be more successful than he'd thought possible, and that was good. What wasn't good was the telegram the sheriff had shared with him.

Evelyn nodded as she accepted his help climbing into the wagon that he'd parked in the alley near the back entrance to the restaurant. "You didn't see how crowded we were today. There were extra customers at lunch, and far more than fifty strangers came in for supper."

Though he hated to destroy her enthusiasm, Wyatt had to warn her. As he took his place on the bench next to her, he said, "That's good. But promise me that even if you're missing something, you won't come back tonight." He'd made certain there were no strangers lurking near Evelyn's home, but there was no telling what might happen once the sun set.

Evelyn's carefree expression sobered. "What did Fletcher learn?"

"A man named Bart Marlow owned a cotton plantation around twenty miles from the orphanage in a town called Hambryton." When Evelyn nodded, Wyatt knew she recognized the name. That was the address he had for Basil Marlow. "Bart Marlow died last fall."

The light breeze wafted the aroma of fried chicken through the air, remnants of the many meals she'd cooked today, but Wyatt doubted Evelyn noticed.

"What about children?" she asked.

"He had one, a daughter named Polly Alice who was around five or six. The mother died in childbirth." So far everything confirmed the details Polly had shared with Evelyn.

The way Evelyn clasped her hands to-gether made Wyatt think she might be pray-ing. "Polly claimed her father grew cotton. At first, I thought he had a small farm, because she was wearing clothes more suited to a slave than a plantation owner's daughter, but some of her stories sounded as if he was wealthy."

She paused, clearly distressed by the memories. "I couldn't imagine why a well-to-do family would have abandoned her. It still doesn't make much sense, but it seems that the sheriff found Polly's family."

"Maybe." Wyatt hated the next part of the story. "The girl died a month or so after her father. She's buried between him and her mother."

The gasp that greeted his words mirrored his own shock when he'd read that part of the telegram. "Then, who is Polly?" Evelyn demanded, her bewilderment obvious. "Did Fletcher ask about the birthmark?"

Wyatt shook his head and urged the horse to pick up his pace. The sooner they reached the safety of the Circle C, the better. The birthmark was one detail the sheriff hadn't thought to mention when he'd sent the telegram to Hambryton.

Evelyn was clearly not convinced by the report of Polly's death. "It's hard to believe she made up the whole story. Children her age have vivid imaginations and tell the same story over and over, but they forget the details, so the second time you hear it, it's different. Polly's story was remarkably consistent."

When Evelyn continued, her voice was fervent. "I believe Polly's telling the truth. She's Bart Marlow's daughter."

Wyatt couldn't disagree. "If that's true — and I agree that it probably is — someone went to a lot of trouble to make it look like she died."

"Whoever did that was trying to protect her." Evelyn nodded, as if the pieces of a puzzle were fitting together. "It must have been Maisie. That would explain the thread-bare clothes Polly was wearing. Polly said she was her mammy." Concern colored Evelyn's eyes. "Maisie must have been incredibly brave. I hope no one ever found out what she did."

Wyatt shared her fears. Though he had no firsthand experience with slavery, he'd heard tales of overseers' and masters' brutality. A slave who defied her master by whisking a child away to the relative safety of an orphanage was risking death.

"Why would Maisie think Polly was in danger? She must have to have done what she did."

There was only one answer Wyatt could imagine. "Money. From what Fletcher learned, Bart Marlow was a wealthy man. When he died, his estate would have gone to Polly if she was still alive."

"And if she wasn't?"

"His brother, Basil."

"The one we sent the invitation to."

Wyatt nodded as he looked in all directions, reassuring himself that they were not in imminent danger. "He must be the reason I thought Polly's birthmark looked familiar. There can't be two families with the same birthmark. If Basil has one — Fletcher's checking on that tonight — it would explain a lot."

Shuddering at the thought that he might have led to Polly a man who wanted her dead, Wyatt continued his explanation. "I met Basil Marlow at last year's sale. According to my records, he didn't buy a horse, but he bid on one. That's why I had his name."

Wyatt had spent the past few hours berating himself for not recognizing the connection earlier, and yet how could he have? He'd only learned Polly's full name a few days ago.

"Do you think he's coming for this sale?"

That was the big question. "He might be. As I recall, he was furious when he didn't get the horse he wanted last year, so I wouldn't be surprised if he tried again tomorrow. Fletcher's on the lookout for him, but so far he hasn't seen anyone matching Basil Marlow's description."

"I need to be careful." Evelyn's expression confirmed that she recognized the danger to Polly if a man who wanted her dead saw her.

"Very careful."

He'd waited long enough. Once the sun set, Rufus slipped out of the house where he was spending the night and headed for Polly's Place. By now the last of the customers would be gone, and Evelyn would be either washing dishes or relaxing in her apartment. Rufus's temporary landlady had been free with the information that Miss Evelyn and her sister lived above the restaurant.

He walked quickly along Main Street, determined not to waste another minute. Winnie would probably scoff, reminding him that it had been more than ten years and that another few minutes or even hours wouldn't matter, but they mattered to Rufus. He didn't want to wait another day to discover whether this was his Evelyn and, if she was, whether she would forgive him.

No lights shone from the restaurant, but he hadn't expected any. While he'd eaten the best meal he'd had in years and a piece of the pie that was every bit as delicious as he recalled, he'd observed that the kitchen was in the back of the building, separated from the dining room by a solid wooden door. Even if light seeped under the door, it would not be visible from the street.

Almost giddy with relief at all he'd discovered, Rufus made his way along the alley to the back of the building. It appeared that God had answered his prayers, leaving him happier than he'd been since Isaac had returned from that horrible Mexican prison. He and Winnie had begun a new chapter of their lives, and if all went the way he prayed it would, he'd be able to close the most painful one. The future looked good. Very good.

As he rounded the corner of the restaurant, Rufus blinked in surprise at the realization that someone else had come to visit Evelyn. He hadn't counted on that.

He paused for a few seconds, watching the man who stood in front of the back door. Something wasn't right. Even from this distance, Rufus could see that the man wasn't knocking on it or ringing a bell. He had a piece of metal in his hands and was trying to pry the door open. This was no innocent visit.

"Stop!" Rufus surged forward, determined to stop the would-be intruder. "What are you doing?"

The man ignored him as if his shouts were no more important than a gnat's buzzing. A second later, the stranger abandoned his efforts to pry the door open and began to beat on it with the metal bar.

"Stop!" Rufus cleared the distance between them in three swift lunges. He couldn't let the man harm Evelyn. Not now. If the stranger succeeded, everything Rufus had done for the past ten years would have been in vain.

He grabbed the man by the shoulder and spun him around. "You can't do that!"

"Can't I?" More swiftly than Rufus had thought possible, the man swung the metal bar at him. Though he tried to duck, it was too late.

The world went black.

CHAPTER THIRTY-TWO

"I doubt this is the way you envisioned being courted."

Evelyn smiled at the man she loved so dearly, wondering if he'd believe her. It was true that the stable wasn't the most romantic setting in the world and that checking each of the horses, feeding one a carrot, another a dried apple, wasn't the way most women would choose to spend their evening, but she wasn't complaining. These were things that had to be done, and doing them together made them special.

Then, too, the mundane tasks helped defuse the tension that the sheriff's telegram had generated. Polly was in the house with Isolde and Dorothy, safe from Basil Marlow, and Evelyn was here with the man who'd sworn to keep both her and Polly safe. There was no reason to be afraid.

The horses were restive, perhaps sensing how nervous everyone around them was today, perhaps simply reacting to the strangers who'd invaded the Circle C. The barn was already filled with prospective buyers, their rowdy shouts clearly audible here. Because Wyatt was insistent that no one have an advantage, he'd decreed that the horses would be sequestered until the start of the sale.

He and Caleb had brought them into the stable before the first guests had arrived, and Caleb would remain all night, guarding them. But Wyatt, being Wyatt, had wanted to say good night to each of his animals, knowing that after tomorrow he would not see many of them again. Though he said nothing, it had to be a bittersweet moment for him, and Evelyn was grateful that he'd asked her to share it.

She took a deep breath, exhaling slowly as she chose the words to explain her views of courtship.

"Courtship wasn't something I spent a lot of time thinking about," she told him. "Mrs. Folger made me feel that the only place I was safe was at the orphanage, so whenever I thought of marriage and a family, I tried to brush those thoughts away."

Wyatt didn't seem convinced. "You must have dreamt of romantic walks, of a man who'd shower you with flowers, books, and candy. Dorothy told me that's what every woman wants, but all I've given you is —"

"Everything I ever wanted." Evelyn wouldn't let him finish his sentence. She couldn't allow him to believe that he'd disappointed her. "Have you forgotten the walks we've taken? What about the white bluebonnets you showed me?"

He still looked skeptical, and she realized she hadn't addressed all the items he thought she craved. "I don't want books or candy, and I don't need you writing sonnets to my eyebrows."

Wyatt blinked, his brown eyes reflecting confusion and perhaps amusement. If the latter, Evelyn had accomplished her goal.

"Where did that come from?" he demanded. "Sonnets to your eyebrows?" He stared at hers, as if trying to imagine why someone would compose a poem about them.

"Dorothy found it in one of the books Laura sent to her. We both thought it was the silliest thing we'd ever heard of."

Wyatt appeared relieved. "Good, because I'm no poet. And, even if I were, I can't imagine myself writing about your eyebrows. I might say that your hair is the color of good hay and that your eyes remind me of the August sky, but that might make you

431

believe all I cared about was how you look."

Evelyn opened her mouth, but before she could protest, he held up a cautionary hand. "Hear me out."

He moved away from the stalls, drawing her toward a bale of hay. When she'd taken the seat he indicated, Wyatt continued. "You're the most beautiful woman I've ever met, not because of your hair or your eyes or those lips that make me think about kissing every time I look at them."

He paused for a second, his gaze meeting hers. "You're beautiful to me because of what's inside you. You're a woman who cares about others, who puts her needs aside to help someone else, who surmounts her fears to keep others safe. You're the woman who believed in me from the beginning and who challenged me to be a better man. That's the Evelyn I love."

"Oh, Wyatt." Tears of joy filled Evelyn's eyes, and she blinked furiously to keep them from falling, lest he misunderstand. "You make me sound much better than I really am."

He slid his arm around her shoulders and squeezed gently. "I'm simply telling you what I see."

It was time for turnabout. "You know what I see? I see a man with a deep love for

432

his family and friends. I see a man committed to protecting others and making the world a better place. I see the man I love." She flashed him a saucy smile. "And, while you may deny it, I see a man with the heart of a poet."

His eyebrows rose. "You think so?"

"I know so."

"Do you want to hear what I know?" Without waiting for a response, he said, "This man who is *not* a poet wants to kiss you."

And he did.

Rufus woke to the worst headache he could recall and the sight of bars. If he hadn't known there was no reason for being incarcerated, he might have believed he was in jail.

"Where am I?"

Firm footsteps announced the approach of a man with a star affixed to his shirt and confirmed Rufus's first impression. For some reason, he'd wound up in jail, though he'd done nothing other than try to foil a break-in. Where was the other man? He was the one who'd been committing a crime.

The sheriff glared at Rufus, his expression so intimidating that Rufus suspected criminals confessed simply to escape his scrutiny.

"I'm glad to see you decided to wake up." The sheriff stood a foot away from the cell, one hand on his six-shooter, as if he thought Rufus might attempt a breakout. "You've got a lot of explaining to do, starting with who you are and why you broke into Evelyn Radner's home."

"Radcliffe." Though Rufus doubted the sheriff wanted to be contradicted, he couldn't let the error stand. Even though he hadn't seen her, his instincts told him that the Evelyn who ran Polly's Place was Evelyn Radcliffe. The pie she'd served tasted exactly like Emmeline Radcliffe's had.

"All right, Radcliffe. I'm Sheriff Engel. Why did you break into Evelyn's home?"

"My name isn't Radcliffe; it's Bauman. Rufus Bauman. Evelyn's the Radcliffe."

The frown Engel gave him might have caused others to recant, but Rufus wasn't backing down. "I don't know how you managed to hit your head like that, but it appears to have scrambled your brains. Everyone in Mesquite Springs knows her name is Radner."

There was no point in arguing about Evelyn's name, especially since he had no proof of it. Still, if she was hiding after the fire, it made sense that she would choose a name close to her real one. But Engel didn't want

434

to hear that.

Rufus tried another tack. "Look, Sheriff, I wasn't breaking into the restaurant. I was trying to stop another man from doing that."

Judging from the sheriff's expression, the stranger had succeeded in entering Evelyn's home and had done some damage. But since Rufus hadn't been accused of injuring her or worse, it seemed that Evelyn had escaped. *Thank you, Lord.*

"I went around back 'cuz I wanted to talk to her, but the other fella was already there." Rufus continued his explanation. "He was using a metal bar to pry the door open. When I tried to stop him, he must have hit me."

His eyes narrowed, Engel studied Rufus. "You expect me to believe that?"

Rufus winced as he touched the lump on his head. "How else would you explain this lump on top of my head? I couldn't have hurt it by falling, and I sure didn't do it to myself."

"Hmmm . . ." For the first time, the sheriff appeared to be considering Rufus's statement. "What did this other fellow look like?"

"Shorter than me — less than six feet, I'd say." Rufus looked at the man who held his immediate fate and perhaps Evelyn's in his hands. "Maybe an inch or so taller than you.

Heavier, though, with brown hair and a beard. I couldn't see his eyes."

Another *hmmm* greeted Rufus's words. The sheriff stared at the far wall of the cell for a second, then returned his gaze to Rufus. "Why did you want to talk to Evelyn?"

"It's a long story." And the man might not believe it.

"I've got all night." Engel dragged a chair closer to the cell and sat down.

"It started more than ten years ago."

When Rufus finished, the sheriff was silent for a moment. "That's quite a story. I'm inclined to believe you, if only because I can't imagine anyone inventing something so far-fetched."

"Then I can leave?" Rufus had never liked small spaces, and this cell was definitely small. The only good thing he could say about it was that one side had bars instead of a wall, so he wasn't completely closed in.

"Not so fast. I don't reckon the sheriff in Gilmorton is still in his office, but I'll send him a telegram and see what he has to say."

Mesquite Springs's lawman gave Rufus a look that stopped short of being friendly but was at least conciliatory. "Make yourself comfortable. You're not going anywhere until he vouches for you."

That wasn't the answer Rufus wanted. The lump on his skull and the headache that wouldn't stop were living reminders that someone wanted to harm Evelyn. "What about Evelyn?" he demanded. "If the other man didn't find her . . ."

"He didn't. She's staying at the Circle C tonight."

The sheriff acted as if that ensured her safety. Rufus didn't believe it. "She's still in danger."

Engel nodded. "I'll get a message to Wyatt first thing in the morning."

Rufus could only pray that that wouldn't be too late.

CHAPTER THIRTY-THREE

"Mornin', Wyatt."

Wyatt turned, surprised to see Fletcher at the Circle C. Neither of them had thought there would be any need for lawmen at the sale, since while bidding often became heated, fights were rare at the sales themselves. It was only afterwards when men who'd been unsuccessful in buying the horses they wanted imbibed too heavily at the saloon that Fletcher and his deputy's intervention might be needed. And, while Wyatt and Fletcher had discussed the possible danger to Polly, Wyatt had assured the sheriff that he could keep her safe at the ranch.

"Did you change your mind and decide to bid on a horse, or are you just admiring them?"

"Neither, I'm afraid." Fletcher lowered his voice. "I'm here as your sheriff." He looked around, watching men emerge from

438

the barn while others had begun arriving by wagon or on horseback. Though the sale wouldn't start for another hour, anticipation was building.

"Is there somewhere we can talk privately?"

Dread snaked its way down Wyatt's spine, but he kept his voice even as he said, "There shouldn't be anyone other than Caleb in the stable. I can spell him for a while."

"Keeping the horses under wraps?"

"So to speak. We'll bring them out one at a time, saving Anthracite and Acanthus for the last."

"I wish I could afford one of them, but until Mesquite Springs raises its pay for sheriffs, I'll have to stick with my old nag."

Wyatt knew that Fletcher was merely making conversation, pretending this was nothing more than a friendly visit. Apparently, he didn't even trust Caleb, because he waited until they were alone before he said, "I won't mince words. Someone broke into Evelyn's apartment last night."

The sheriff paused, letting Wyatt absorb the impact of his words before he continued. "As far as I can tell, nothing was taken. It didn't look like the place was searched, so I eliminated robbery as a motive."

Trying desperately to swallow the fear that

threatened to steal his breath, Wyatt nodded. "You think someone was looking for her." Had he and Evelyn been wrong in thinking she was safe, or was the threat directed at Polly?

"Possibly. Leonard saw that the door to the restaurant was open when he went back to the mercantile, so he called me." Fletcher lowered his voice again, even though no one was within earshot. "I found a man inside lying at the foot of the stairs, unconscious. At first glance it seemed he was the intruder and that he'd fallen down the stairs, but when he came to, he spun me an almost unbelievable tale."

Fletcher removed his hat and scratched his head. "It checked out. If I were a betting man, I'd bet that this fellow is innocent and that his story of seeing another man trying to break in is true."

"Do you have a description?"

A shrug was Fletcher's first response. "About my height, but heavier with brown hair and a beard."

"That could be almost anyone." Wyatt understood the sheriff's discomfort with the description. "My guess is that it's Basil Marlow looking for Polly."

"That's a definite possibility. I sent another telegram to Sheriff Cassidy in Ham-

440

bryton. He reported that Marlow hasn't been seen for the last week. That's no proof of anything, but he could be here."

And that was what Wyatt feared. The man wanted more than a horse. Somehow he'd learned that Polly was not in the grave between her parents and he'd tracked her here. Wyatt had no idea how Basil Marlow had done that, but he would take no chances.

"I'll alert the men. We'll keep a lookout."

"So will I. I'm not going anywhere until the sale is over." Fletcher plunked his hat back on his head. "One more thing. Cassidy said Bart Marlow died of poisoning. He suspects Basil, but the man was out of town when Bart died, so he can't prove it." Fletcher's brown eyes darkened as he said, "Y'all need to be careful."

"We will be."

"I wanna go outside and see the horses."

Evelyn bit back a sigh. Polly had had a restless night, perhaps because of the different surroundings, perhaps because she'd sensed Evelyn's worries. Whatever the reason, she was pouting this morning and had flatly refused to drink her milk.

"Not now. There are too many people out there." Even though it was still early, the

441

men who'd bunked in the barn were milling around, leaning on the rails surrounding the paddock and watching the foals and mares. While none of those horses was for sale, they gave prospective buyers a good idea of the quality of the Circle C's animals. Though she saw nothing alarming about any of the strangers, until they had all left, Evelyn would not let Polly out of her sight.

"You're mean." The pout appeared on the verge of turning into a tantrum.

"Maybe so, but that doesn't mean I'm going to change my mind. You are not to leave the house without me."

Polly started to protest, then bit back the cry as Wyatt entered the kitchen.

"That's right, Polly," he said smoothly. "You need to listen to Evelyn."

Though he smiled, the concern Evelyn saw reflected in his eyes made her heart thud. Something was wrong.

"If you're good," Wyatt continued, "I'll let you ride Thunder with me this afternoon."

With the mercurial change so common for children her age, Polly's frown turned into a radiant smile. "I'll be good, Mr. Wyatt." Unbidden, she took a seat at the table and lifted the milk glass to her lips.

"Bribery?" Evelyn accompanied her question with a smile.

"Whatever it takes." Wyatt stood at her side, his back to Polly and his voice so low that she could not overhear him. "The situation is worse than we feared. We need to talk."

Isolde and Dorothy were outside, directing the placement of the long tables where the guests would eat, leaving Evelyn with little choice but to keep Polly occupied.

"I have a very important job for you," she told the child. "I need you to stir the oatmeal and make sure it isn't lumpy. Can you do that?"

"Yes!" Polly's shout of glee was followed by the sound of her chair being dragged to the stove.

Once Polly stood next to the stove, stirring the pot of oatmeal as if the fate of the world depended on its being free of lumps, Evelyn moved to the corner of the kitchen. "That'll keep her occupied. Now, what's wrong?"

"A man broke into your apartment last night. The sheriff thinks he was looking for either you or Polly."

"Basil Marlow?"

"That's my guess. Whoever it was was bearded, so a birthmark wouldn't be visible." Wyatt laid a hand on Evelyn's cheek, caressing it as he said, "Be careful, Evelyn."

"I will."

"Sold to the gentleman with the green bandanna."

Caleb whistled softly as Wyatt announced the tenth sale of the morning. "This is going even better than you hoped, isn't it?"

"Yes." They had more potential buyers than he'd expected, with the result that the bidding had lasted longer and gone higher than any previous sale. No doubt about it: having a private sale had been a good idea. Under other circumstances, Wyatt would have been overjoyed by the success, but today that satisfaction was shadowed by the fear that Basil Marlow was here.

Wyatt had studied the crowd, searching for the man who might be looking for Polly, but far too many men met the description Fletcher had given him. Even though he knew Marlow hadn't had a beard when he'd seen him last year, he'd thought he might recognize him, but no one looked familiar.

"We're down to the final two." He'd deliberately kept Anthracite and Acanthus to the end. As his fastest horses, they were the ones that would command the highest prices. If Basil Marlow was here, Wyatt expected him to bid on one or maybe both of them.

"That'll take at least another two hours," Caleb said. Like Wyatt, he'd been assessing the crowd, but for different reasons. He was trying to pinpoint the most likely bidders for each horse.

Wyatt pulled out his watch and frowned at the realization that it was later than he'd thought. No wonder the men were starting to become restless.

"All right, gentlemen. There's going to be a slight change of plans." He waited until the low murmurs ceased before he continued the explanation. "I promised you a meal once the sale was over, but if your stomachs are like mine, you probably don't want to wait that long."

"Spending this much money works up an appetite," said the man with the green bandanna.

"I need something to eat before I buy Anthracite," another announced.

The man next to him poked him in the ribs. "What makes you think you'll get him? I'm planning to bid on him, and I've got deep pockets."

Food might stop the argument from escalating. "Here's what we're going to do. Caleb will put Anthracite and Acanthus through their paces so you can see just how

445

good these horses are. I'm going to make sure the food is ready. We'll eat first, then see who buys my finest horses."

As Wyatt had expected, his plan was met with shouts of approval.

Evelyn slid the tray of biscuits into the oven, then turned at the sound of familiar footsteps. Why was Wyatt here now? The plan had been for her to serve lunch in an hour when the sale was finished.

"Is something wrong?"

"No." Though he shook his head, Evelyn saw the signs of strain on his face. "The sale's going well, but it's taking longer than I expected. Folks are getting hungry. How soon can we eat?"

Fortunately, everything other than the biscuits was ready to be served. "Fifteen minutes if we rush; otherwise, half an hour."

"Let's make it half an hour. Caleb's showing off Anthracite and Acanthus now. That'll keep the men occupied and thinking of something other than their empty stomachs."

Evelyn's stomach wasn't empty. It was churning with worry. "Have you seen him?" Though Polly was in the next room, helping Dorothy and Isolde fold napkins, Evelyn saw no reason to pronounce the man's name.

"No, but my gut tells me he's here." Wyatt's frustration was apparent in his frown. "I want to mingle with the crowd now. Maybe I'll recognize him if I'm closer."

"Be careful."

Wyatt shrugged. "I'm not the one he wants." He pressed a quick kiss on Evelyn's lips, then strode out the door.

Seconds later, Isolde entered the kitchen, followed by Polly. "What was Wyatt doing here?"

"He wants the meal ready in half an hour."

Isolde looked as if she'd expected that. "Dorothy and I'll start setting the tables now. Dorothy!"

"I can help." Polly tugged on Isolde's hand to add more drama to her plea.

"No, Polly. I need you to help me cut more biscuits."

"No!" Polly stomped her foot. "I want to go with Mrs. Isolde."

"You're staying with me." Evelyn gripped Polly's hand as Dorothy and Isolde headed outside, their arms filled with checkered tablecloths and matching napkins. Though the child was pouting, Evelyn would not let her leave the house until Wyatt was certain that Basil Marlow was nowhere to be seen.

447

"You need to wash and dry your hands before you cut the biscuits." She gestured toward the small basin of water and the towel that she kept on a stool where Polly could reach it.

Defiantly, Polly splashed water onto the floor as she wiggled her fingers in the bowl. When she'd completed her sketchy ablutions, she picked up the basin to empty it into the bucket just outside the door. It was something she'd done a dozen times when they'd lived here, her chest puffing with pride that she could carry the bowl without spilling any water. This time was different. Polly had no sooner pushed the door open than she began to shriek.

"Papa! You came back!" The door banged behind her as she ran across the yard.

No! Oh no! Her heart pounding, her legs propelled by terror, Evelyn raced outside. And suddenly, though she knew she was running faster than ever before, everything seemed to happen in slow motion. Polly was shouting with pure joy as she ran toward a bearded man, a man whose face bore no smile, only a grin that turned Evelyn's blood to ice. If evil had a face, it would be this one.

Slowly, ever so slowly, the man pulled his gun from the holster and pointed it at the girl she loved so dearly.

"No!" If it was the last thing she ever did, Evelyn would stop him from killing Polly.

With every ounce of energy she possessed, she sprang forward, covering the remaining distance in one lunge. Though Polly shrieked in annoyance, Evelyn wrapped her arms around the child's waist and knocked her to the ground, landing on top of her at the same instant that a gunshot rang out.

There was a moment of silence, a moment when the world went black. A second later the noise rushed back, assaulting Evelyn's senses, leaching the last bit of strength from her. And then she saw the blood.

CHAPTER THIRTY-FOUR

A gunshot! Fear raced through Wyatt's blood faster than a wildfire through dry grass. He spun around, all rational thought fleeing at the sight before him. Evelyn lay on the ground, and even from this distance, he could see blood. Was that her lifeblood draining out? *No, dear God, no.* What would he do without her? And where was Polly?

From the corner of his eye, Wyatt detected unusual motion. While the men who'd come to buy horses were either stationary, stunned by shock, or hurrying toward Evelyn, this one was not. Wyatt swiveled and spotted a man running in the opposite direction. The shooter. It had to be. That miserable excuse for humanity was trying to escape.

For a second, Wyatt remained paralyzed, his heart urging him to race to Evelyn while his head shouted that he needed to stop the shooter. A second later, Ma rushed toward Evelyn. The woman he loved would be in good hands. Now it was up to Wyatt to capture the man who'd hurt her.

He sprinted after the shooter, mentally cataloging his description. Dark hair, a beard. Although half the men at the sale fit that description, none of them had any reason to shoot Evelyn. Basil Marlow didn't either, unless Evelyn had been protecting Polly. The man's motive didn't matter now. All that mattered was catching him.

Though Wyatt would have expected the shooter to head for the entrance to the ranch where everyone else had left their horses and carriages, Marlow was running away from the house, away from the crowd, heading toward the stand of oak trees. This was no impulsive shooting. It appeared to have been carefully planned after he hadn't found anyone at the apartment. Leaving his horse by the oaks meant he was less likely to be apprehended.

Wyatt took a shallow breath, trying to ease the fear that even now coursed through him. He couldn't let Marlow escape, especially after he'd hurt Evelyn, but Wyatt was making no progress in catching him. Marlow had a head start and was surprisingly fast for a man who spent his days issuing orders rather than doing anything physical.

He won't get away. I won't let him. Wyatt

gritted his teeth as he reminded himself that he had three advantages. His legs were longer, he was accustomed to physically demanding work, and — most importantly — he was determined that the man who had hurt Evelyn and possibly Polly would not escape.

His heart pounding, Wyatt sped forward. He couldn't let Marlow get away. He *wouldn't* let him get away. A horse's whinny told him Marlow was close to escaping. Once he was on horseback, Wyatt would have no chance of catching him.

"Stop!" he shouted.

Marlow turned, his expression little more than a sneer. Though Wyatt was tempted to shoot him where he stood, he had no proof that Marlow was the shooter other than his attempt to run away. The man's expression was menacing, but he made no move toward his gun, and so Wyatt kept his holstered.

"You!" The sneer turned into a snarl. "I might have figured that. The town's brand-new mayor. Heard you're planning to marry the gal who's looking after my brother's whelp. Want the money, do you? Now that she's dead, it goes to me."

The man didn't seem to care that he was incriminating himself with every word. It was arrogance, pure arrogance, and Wyatt would use that arrogance against him.

"Polly's not dead." At least Wyatt hoped she wasn't. The fact that he hadn't seen her made him believe Polly was either inside the house or protected by Evelyn's body. If he were a betting man, he'd bet on the latter.

Marlow's face contorted with fury. "You're like that brother of mine, thinking you know more than me. You're wrong. Dead wrong." When his right hand moved toward his holster, Wyatt was prepared. Marlow wasn't an experienced gunman; he had to think about pulling his gun. In the instant that it took him to reach for the gun, Wyatt lunged forward, knocking him to the ground.

"No!" The cry was instinctive as Marlow realized that he'd lost his advantage. He cocked the gun, but before he could pull the trigger, Wyatt wrestled it from his hand and flung it into the grass. A second later, he heard the sound of hoofbeats.

"That was quite a race you two had." Fletcher sounded almost amused as he reined in his gelding. "For a while it looked like you were trying to run faster than your horses."

The sheriff dismounted and strode toward Wyatt and his captive, pulling out his handcuffs. As a volley of curses greeted him,

Fletcher scowled. "Sounds like a little boy who needs his mouth washed out with lye soap."

Wordlessly, Wyatt flipped Marlow onto his stomach and yanked his arms behind him, waiting until Fletcher had secured Marlow's wrists and tied a rope around his shoulders before he rose.

Fletcher tugged the shooter to his feet, then turned to Wyatt. "I reckon there's a lady you want to see. Why don't you take my horse? Mr. Marlow and I can walk. We've got a lot to talk about, starting with how much time he's gonna spend in jail."

Raising his voice to be heard over Marlow's curses, Wyatt said, "Thanks, Fletcher." The truth was, he didn't want to wait another minute to see Evelyn. Though he'd never thought of himself as a violent man, the memory of her blood seeping into the ground made him wish he'd pummeled Marlow's face and broken a rib or two.

"I should be thanking you, Mr. Mayor. You're the one who caught this guy." Fletcher yanked on the rope and began to lead Marlow away. Ignoring the man's anger at being treated like a wayward steer, Fletcher winked at Wyatt. "Now, get back to

Evelyn. I know that's where you want to be."

It was indeed.

"Ouch! You're squishing me, Evelyn."

Waves of relief washed over Evelyn as she realized that Polly sounded unharmed. But if she wasn't hurt, why was there blood on the ground? She hadn't seen the bullet, but surely the blood meant that it had hit something. As Evelyn pushed herself to the side, trying to free Polly, sharp pain speared her left arm. How had she not noticed that? There'd been pain when she'd knocked Polly out of the shooter's way, but she'd ignored it, focusing on keeping the girl safe.

A quick glance at her arm made Evelyn look away. She'd been shot. There was little doubt, for blood had soaked through her sleeve and was continuing to leak out. She'd been shot. Her head felt light as the thought reverberated through it.

"Here, let me help you." As if she recognized how weak Evelyn was, Isolde knelt next to her and slid her onto her right side, releasing Polly.

The child leapt to her feet, then shrieked at the sight of Evelyn's arm. "You're hurt!"

Though the world threatened to turn black as she tried to sit up, Evelyn forced a reassuring smile onto her face. Whatever she did, she couldn't add to Polly's alarm, lest the child suffer from nightmares the way Evelyn had after her parents' deaths. "It's only a scratch."

"That's one way to describe it." Isolde pulled a large handkerchief from her apron, tied it around Evelyn's upper arm, then looked at her daughter. "Help me get Evelyn up, but be careful of that arm."

As they maneuvered her upright, Evelyn realized that a crowd had gathered. Gunshots weren't on the day's agenda, and it appeared that everyone wanted to be the first to learn what had happened.

"She'll be all right, gentlemen, but lunch will be delayed a bit." Isolde's voice was firm as she shooed the onlookers away. "Caleb, I need you to carry Evelyn into the parlor."

It was odd being carried like a child, and yet Evelyn knew Isolde was right. Her legs felt as limp as overcooked carrots, and the sound of the gunshot echoed through her head, making it difficult to concentrate on anything. Caleb was gentle, his arms strong, but he was not Wyatt. Where was Wyatt?

As Evelyn started to ask, Isolde, who'd been walking at her side, pursed her lips, tipping her head toward Polly. For some reason, Isolde did not want to discuss her son in front of the child. New fears assailed Evelyn, but she dared not voice them. Not yet.

Within a minute, she was lying on the sofa with Polly hovering over her while Isolde retrieved bandages and Dorothy filled a basin of water.

"Did you see him?" Polly demanded, her voice more excited than Evelyn had ever heard it. "Papa was here. He got out of that box in the ground, just like I knowed he would. Papa loves me. That's why he came to take me home."

Evelyn tried not to wince at the throbbing that continued to intensify, despite the tourniquet Isolde had fashioned. She had to keep her wits about her while she burst Polly's bubble of hope. "That wasn't your father, Polly. I think the man was your uncle Basil."

"It was Papa," the child insisted. "I know it was, 'cuz Uncle Basil doesn't have a beard."

"Men can grow beards."

"Oh." Polly was silent for a moment, considering Evelyn's statement. "I don't think Uncle Basil liked Papa. I heard him shouting at Papa."

Evelyn wasn't surprised. From everything

she'd learned, Basil Marlow was a man so obsessed with money that he'd stop at nothing — not even murder — to gain it.

"Let's let Evelyn rest." Isolde placed the water and bandages on the table in front of the sofa, then turned to her daughter. "You and Polly can put the finishing touches on the meal. Unless I'm mistaken, there are biscuits in the oven."

Evelyn blinked, surprised that she'd forgotten. "Yes, there are."

"Once they're ready, we'll serve the meal," Isolde continued.

As soon as Polly left the room, Evelyn asked the question that had been weighing so heavily on her heart. "Where is Wyatt?"

"Caleb said he went after the shooter."

"Of course." Wyatt wouldn't let the man escape if he could help it. And Basil Marlow had already proven that he had no compunction about killing.

Once again, Isolde seemed to read Evelyn's mind. "He'll be all right. I haven't heard any other shots." She sat on the chair next to Evelyn. "Now that Polly's gone, I want to look at your arm." She pulled out a pair of sewing scissors and began to cut Evelyn's sleeve. Only seconds later, she loosened the bandage and slid the sleeve off Evelyn's arm.

"The bleeding has subsided. That's good." Isolde studied the wound site for a moment, turning Evelyn's arm so she could see the underside. Though the pain was severe, Evelyn said nothing, knowing this was necessary.

"It looks like the bullet went straight through," Isolde said. "That's very good. I'll clean the wound and stitch it shut. It'll be sore for a while, but in a few days, you'll be back to rolling piecrusts."

She had just finished the sutures and was tying the new bandage when the kitchen door slammed.

"Where is she?"

Relief swept through Evelyn with the force of a whirlwind. The prayers she'd been offering while Isolde cleaned and stitched her wound had been answered. Wyatt was safe. "In here, Wyatt."

The man she loved stormed into the parlor, his face as threatening as a thundercloud. "How badly did that monster hurt you?"

Evelyn heard the fear in his voice and sought to allay it, while Isolde, realizing her son needed time alone with Evelyn, slipped out of the parlor and closed the door behind her. "Your mother says it's a flesh wound and that the bullet went all the way through.

Now, sit down. You're making me nervous towering over me like that."

When Wyatt took the chair opposite her, leaning forward so they were only inches apart, Evelyn continued. "What happened to the man? Was it Basil Marlow?"

"It was Marlow, all right. Fletcher's got him in custody. He said the sheriff in Hambryton is anxious to get him back there. It seems everyone liked Bart, but Basil hasn't made many friends."

Evelyn nodded. Though she'd never met the man, she agreed with Wyatt's description of him as a monster.

"They may never be able to prove that he killed his brother," Wyatt continued, "but he'll spend the rest of his life in jail for trying to kill Polly. Juries don't look kindly on men who harm little girls."

"But she's safe now." Evelyn frowned, realizing they'd probably never know the whole story. She could surmise that the slaves were aware of Basil's evil streak and that Maisie must have planned the fake burial, deciding that the child would be safer at the orphanage and dressing her in some of her own children's clothes to help disguise her.

"Do you suppose Basil was responsible for the fire?"

"It seems likely. Fletcher's going to send some more telegrams to Hambryton and Logansville to see if anyone saw or heard anything suspicious. He also said when you're feeling up to it, he'd like you to come into town. There's someone you need to meet, and don't worry. It's not Basil Marlow."

That was good, because Evelyn had no desire to speak to the man who'd tried to kill Polly. Once again, she thanked God that she'd been able to save the child she loved so dearly.

"Then who is it?" she asked. The pain in her arm seemed less severe now, perhaps because she knew that Wyatt was safe and that Basil Marlow would never again threaten anyone.

"I'm not sure, but it could be the man who saw Marlow breaking into your apartment last night. Fletcher said he was looking for you."

Evelyn nodded slowly, knowing that whoever it was, she had to talk to him, if only to learn why he wanted to meet her. She fixed her gaze on Wyatt. "I'll go this afternoon, once the sale's over. Will you come too?"

"You couldn't keep me away, even if you wanted to." Wyatt's eyes darkened as he gazed at her. "I feel like I aged ten years when I heard that gunshot and saw you lying on the ground. It was the worst moment of my life, worse even than the day the neighbors brought Pa's body home. I don't want to let you out of my sight ever again."

Poor Wyatt. She hadn't thought about how difficult the shooting must have been for him. Trying to lighten the mood, Evelyn gave him a wry smile. "That's going to make it hard to do our jobs, isn't it?"

"I'm glad you can smile. All I could think about was how short life is and how I don't want to waste a single day." Wyatt paused long enough to take both of her hands in his. His eyes were serious, still tinged with the fear that had assailed him. "If we're going into town, what do you think about stopping at the parsonage and seeing if Pastor Coleman will marry us today?"

She understood his urgency, and part of her shared it. Being faced with possible death made a person reassess her life, discarding everything except the most important, most life-affirming parts. What could be more life-affirming than to join their lives in marriage, giving Polly the father she longed for and perhaps creating a new life? That was what Evelyn wanted, and yet . . .

"It's a wonderful idea, but . . ." She let

her voice trail off as she sought the right words to help Wyatt understand why she couldn't accept his proposal.

"But what?"

He looked so bewildered that Evelyn almost agreed to his wish for a wedding today, but she couldn't. She knew that if she did, she'd always regret it.

"I love you, Wyatt, and there's nothing I want more than to be your wife, but today's not the right day." Her declaration of love seemed to relax him, so Evelyn continued. "I wasn't lying when I told you that I hadn't spent much time thinking about courtship — I hadn't — but some of my earliest memories are of sitting in my mother's lap and describing my wedding to her."

He nodded, as if he understood. "It wasn't a rushed affair, was it?"

"No. I want everyone I care about in the church when I walk down the aisle toward you, and I want Polly to have a new dress and to walk with me. After all, you may be marrying me, but she's part of the deal."

Another nod told Evelyn Wyatt agreed, but his lips curved into a smile. "You drive a hard bargain, Evelyn. If not today, how soon can you be ready?"

"Three weeks."

"One."

She couldn't help laughing at his attempt at negotiation. "How about two?"

"All right." Though his eyes were fixed on her lips as if he wanted to seal the agreement with a kiss, Wyatt made a show of shaking Evelyn's hand. "Two weeks from today."

"And right now you have a horse sale to finish."

Wyatt was still grinning as he left the house and headed toward the makeshift tables where his customers had gathered. What man wouldn't grin when his wedding to the most wonderful woman in the world was only fourteen days away?

"I saved you some food," his mother said, uncovering the plate she'd tried to keep warm.

His mouth watered as the delicious aromas of fried chicken and gravy tantalized his senses. "Thanks, Ma. I'm hungrier than I realized." Perhaps chasing a would-be killer had sparked his appetite, but Wyatt suspected it was the relief of knowing that Evelyn's life was not in danger that was responsible.

He laid the plate on the closest table, then whistled to get everyone's attention. "I'm sure you're wondering what happened," he said when the crowd had quieted. "The man who shot Evelyn is in jail and likely to spend the rest of his life behind bars."

"Somebody oughta string him up," one of the men shouted.

Wyatt shrugged, although the thought had occurred to him more than once when he'd been chasing Basil Marlow. "That's for the judge to decide. What's important is that he's no longer a threat and . . ." He paused for emphasis. "Evelyn will be able to cook again within a couple days."

A loud round of hurrahs greeted his announcement.

"It looks like you've finished your food. Give me ten minutes, and then we'll see who's going to take Anthracite and Acanthus home today."

"Are you gonna do a private sale again next year?" another man asked after the cries of "I'm gonna get him" ended.

Wyatt turned to Caleb, who'd come to his side. When the man nodded, he said, "Yes. We'll have another dozen horses ready for sale next June."

The men's cheers left no doubt that they approved of the decision.

CHAPTER THIRTY-FIVE

"Are you certain you feel well enough to do this?"

Wyatt stopped at the side of the wagon and faced Evelyn, a question in his eyes. Though she appreciated his concern and realized it was evidence of his love, there was only one answer. "Yes. My arm hurts, but that's no reason not to go into town. I'm not feeling dizzy any longer." And she was anxious to meet the man who'd come to her home last night.

Wyatt nodded as he placed both hands on her waist and lifted her into the wagon. "Maybe we should stop by Doc Dawson's just to make sure Ma did everything right."

"You can stop worrying and tell me about the sale. Was it as successful as you'd hoped?" Though Evelyn had wanted to watch at least part of it, fear for Polly's safety and then her own injury had prevented that.

"Even better," Wyatt said with a wide grin. "The fact that there were no other breeders' horses was more of an advantage than I'd expected. We had a lot of excitement, and that translated into high prices."

Good news. Excellent news, in fact. "Does that mean you can stop worrying about money?"

Wyatt's grin widened. "Now I can focus all my worries on you and Polly. I may even have time to think about what improvements Mesquite Springs needs."

"I don't doubt that you'll continue to worry." Evelyn softened her words with a laugh.

"And you'll continue to tell me how useless those worries are."

Evelyn winced as the wagon hit a rut and her attempt to steady herself shot pain up her arm. "I feel like a hypocrite," she admitted, "because I'm sitting here, worrying about the man Fletcher wants me to meet. Are you sure he didn't tell you anything about him?"

"Just that Basil Marlow knocked the man unconscious when he went to see you last night."

"I can't imagine who he is."

Wyatt laid a reassuring hand on hers. "You'll have your answer soon."

When they arrived at the sheriff's office, Wyatt opened the door and let Evelyn precede him. She looked around, blinking her eyes to help them adjust to the relative darkness and tried but failed to tamp down her worries. Soon. Soon she'd know who the man was and what he wanted.

The main part of the sheriff's office was devoid of decorations other than "wanted" posters. Fletcher sat behind a battered desk, while one of the three chairs in front of it was occupied by a man with his back to the door. At the far end, the closed door that marked the entrance to the jail where Basil Marlow now resided failed to muffle his curses.

"Good afternoon." As Fletcher rose, so did the other man. "Evelyn, this is Rufus Bauman," the sheriff said. "The man with Miss Radner is Wyatt Clark, our new mayor."

The introductions barely registered as Evelyn stared at the man who had wanted to talk to her. Tall and almost scarecrow thin, he had steel gray hair and pale blue eyes. She would have sworn that she'd never seen him before, but as he stared at her, his eyes somehow reflecting both joy and pain, she felt it, and her knees began to buckle.

"You need to sit down." Wyatt pulled out

the chair and helped her into it.

He was right. Sitting did help. Evelyn took a deep breath, exhaling slowly as the same sense of being watched that had frightened her every time she'd gone into Gilmorton swept over her. But this time was different. Though she couldn't explain it, she knew she had nothing to fear. This man meant her no harm.

"Do you live in Gilmorton?" The words burst out of her, unbidden.

Both Wyatt and Fletcher seemed surprised by her question, and why wouldn't they? It was hardly the normal response to an introduction.

"I do." Rufus Bauman acted as if he found nothing odd about her question. A smile teased the corner of his lips. "I'm grateful you agreed to see me, Miss Radcliffe. Until just now, I wasn't certain you were the woman I sought." He paused for a second before saying, "I didn't know whether you'd remember me. I didn't eat at your parents' restaurant very often."

Evelyn studied his face again, searching for something to trigger a memory, but finding nothing. "I'm afraid I don't remember you, Mr. Bauman. You don't seem at all familiar, and yet being in the same room with you feels as if it's happened before."

469

"The Watcher?" Wyatt, who'd pulled his chair close to hers, asked softly.

Evelyn's response was equally low. "I think so." She turned back to Rufus Bauman. "Every time I went to Gilmorton, I felt as if someone was watching me. That was you, wasn't it?"

"Yes."

One simple word, but the memories it evoked were anything but simple, and for a second she was the girl who cowered under the bed while a murderer climbed the stairs. "I was so frightened," Evelyn said when the memories faded and she was once again a grown woman who'd managed to overcome her fears. "I thought whoever was watching me was the person who killed my parents and that he wanted to kill me too."

Blood drained from Mr. Bauman's face as his expression radiated horror. "I never meant that to happen. Never! You must believe that. It's true I was watching, but it was because I wanted to make sure you were safe." His voice trembled with emotion. "I would never, ever hurt you."

Fletcher spoke for the first time since he'd made the introductions. "I think she needs to hear the story you told me, Bauman."

The man who'd watched her for so many years nodded. "That's why I came. I should

470

have done this years ago, but I wasn't strong enough." Regret tinged his words. "When I heard about the fire, I thought I'd lost my last chance to beg for your forgiveness, but when I heard about a woman named Evelyn who owned a restaurant and served oatmeal pecan pie, I knew I'd been given a second chance. I had to come here to see if you were the same Evelyn."

Dimly, Evelyn registered the second half of his explanation, but her mind focused on one word: forgiveness. "Why would you think that I needed to forgive you?" He had no way of knowing how much anguish his watching her had caused.

"Because I didn't stop my son."

Evelyn's eyes widened as she tried to understand where this was leading. As if he sensed her distress, Wyatt reached over and took her hand between both of his, the warmth of his palms helping to settle her nerves.

"I knew the time in that Mexican prison had changed him, but I didn't know he would become violent." Mr. Bauman's face contorted with agony.

"What are you saying?" Evelyn asked.

"My son killed your parents."

The words hung in the room, as if daring someone to contradict them. Evelyn stared

471

at the man who'd watched her from afar. For so many years, she'd feared him. For so many years, she'd mourned her parents' deaths, not knowing why they'd been killed. Now, she had the opportunity to have her questions answered.

Praying that she could keep her voice steady though everything inside her was trembling like a dried leaf clinging to its branch in a windstorm, she asked, "Is he the one they caught and hanged? I never knew his name." The sheriff hadn't mentioned it, and Evelyn hadn't asked. Knowing the killer's name wouldn't have brought her parents back.

"Yes, that was Isaac."

Isaac Bauman. She rolled the name around in her head, wondering if she'd ever heard it, but like Mr. Bauman himself, it triggered no memories.

"Why?" The question that had haunted Evelyn for ten years came out with more force than she'd intended. "What did they do to him that he wanted to kill them?"

The killer's father shook his head, his eyes reflecting more pain than Evelyn had ever seen. "Nothing. It was all in his mind." Mr. Bauman paused for a second as he struggled to regain his composure. "My son saw unthinkable cruelty while he was imprisoned. He wouldn't talk about it, but I heard from another man who survived that they were forced to watch their fellow soldiers die in front of a firing squad."

Evelyn flinched at the image Mr. Bauman's words evoked, wondering how she would have reacted if she'd been there. An experience like that would have created scars, perhaps wounds so deep that they never had a chance to heal. As horrible as her parents' deaths had been, at least she had not had to watch their lifeblood draining away.

"I think that's why rainstorms bothered Isaac so much," his father continued. "Thunder sounds like rifles."

And there'd been a thunderstorm the night of her parents' deaths. "Your poor son." Evelyn's hands trembled with emotion as, for the first time, she felt sympathy for the man who had ended her parents' lives. He might not have borne physical scars, but he'd been wounded.

While the other men remained silent, Mr. Bauman kept his eyes focused on Evelyn. "I'll never know whether he might have recovered from what happened in the prison, but when Isaac came home and discovered that Rose was gone, he went into a wild rage. He wouldn't believe that she'd died."

"Who was Rose?" Wyatt asked the question before Evelyn could.

"My daughter. Isaac's little sister." Tears filled the older man's eyes. "She died of scarlet fever while Isaac was in Mexico. He was convinced that we were lying and that someone was hiding her from him."

Mr. Bauman brushed away the lone tear that had trickled down his cheek, clearly embarrassed by the display of emotion. "Rose didn't look like you, but she had the same color hair. The best I can figure it out, Isaac must have seen you go into the restaurant and thought you were Rose. The thunderstorm must have triggered something that made him go looking for her."

Evelyn bit the inside of her cheek, trying to rein in her emotions as she remembered the night that was indelibly etched on her memory. She'd been right. The killer had been looking for her.

"He kept shouting, 'Where is she?' I was terrified he'd find me, so I hid under the bed."

"Isaac wouldn't have hurt you."

"You don't know that." Wyatt hurled the words back at Isaac's father.

"You're right," the man admitted. "I don't

474

know that, but I don't want to think that he would have harmed Evelyn. If he'd been in his right mind, Isaac would never have killed anyone. Sadly, he did."

Mr. Bauman was silent for a moment. Then he fixed his eyes on Evelyn again. "I know it's a lot to ask and more than I deserve, but can you forgive me for not stopping him?"

Her heart aching as she realized that she wasn't the only one who'd been hurt by her parents' deaths, Evelyn nodded. "You did nothing wrong, Mr. Bauman. There's nothing to forgive."

She closed her eyes for a second, reflecting on all that she'd heard and praying for the right words to comfort this man who'd suffered as much as she had. He'd lost two of his children and spent more than ten years blaming himself for two other deaths. The poor man.

"Isaac is the one who needs forgiveness." When Mr. Bauman nodded as if he agreed with her, Evelyn spoke quickly. "I forgive him, but I believe he's already been forgiven. I believe that when Jesus spoke from the cross saying, 'Father, forgive them, for they know not what they do,' he was asking forgiveness for people like your son."

Once more, Mr. Bauman's eyes glistened

with tears. "I tell myself that every day, that God saw Isaac's heart and forgave him." His voice husky with emotion, the Watcher reached forward and touched Evelyn's hand. "Thank you, Evelyn. You've given me a gift beyond price."

He turned his gaze from her to Wyatt, then smiled as he fixed his eyes on her again. "I worried about you for ten years, but I can see that I don't have to worry any longer. I can go back to Gilmorton knowing you found love and happiness."

"I did." As tears of relief filled her eyes, Evelyn looked at Wyatt. "It's over."

CHAPTER THIRTY-SIX

It's over. Evelyn's words echoed through Wyatt's mind, and his stomach knotted at the sight of her tears. He'd guessed that Bauman's revelation had been a turning point for Evelyn, that the knowledge of how tortured the man who'd ended her parents' lives had been might have forced her to reevaluate her own life, but until they spoke, he couldn't be certain of what she was feeling.

Wyatt rose and extended his hand to Evelyn. There was nothing more to be said here. She'd made her peace with Bauman; now it was time for them to talk. But not here. He wanted privacy. Wyatt waited until they reached the crest of the hill outside Mesquite Springs before he stopped the wagon. This was his favorite spot between town and the ranch, providing a view of Mesquite Springs in one direction, the Circle C in the other.

"What's wrong?" Furrows formed between Evelyn's eyes. "Why are we stopping?"

"I wanted to make sure that you were all right before we went back to the ranch. It's been quite a day for you." An emotionally draining one, he was certain.

She nodded and brushed aside the tears that even now were welling in her eyes. "I'm not sad, if that's what's worrying you." As new tears welled, she shook her head. "Not sad, though I am sorry that Mr. Bauman suffered so much, and even though it's over, I can't forget what it was like going to Gilmorton and feeling as someone was watching me."

"But now you know why." Wyatt wished he were the poet Evelyn claimed he was. Perhaps if he were, he could find the words to reassure her, but he wasn't. All he could do was say, "You don't need to fear anymore."

"No, I don't. I no longer have to wonder why my parents were killed or that I might be next. That chapter of my life is over."

When Evelyn laid her hand on his arm, he placed his on top of hers, hoping to give her the reassurance she seemed to need. "I'll keep you safe."

"I know you will. Now it's time to start a

new chapter" — she gazed into his eyes, her expression so full of love that his breath caught at the wonder of it — "with you."

Wyatt's heart overflowed with joy at the evidence of Evelyn's love. It was as strong as an oak tree, as rare and beautiful as a white bluebonnet.

"I like the sound of that new chapter," he said, letting the corners of his mouth curve into a mischievous smile as he phrased his question. "Are you sure we have to wait two weeks to get married?"

She matched his smile. "Are you trying to renegotiate our deal? It won't work. We agreed on two weeks."

He shrugged, savoring the return to normalcy. "You can't blame a man for trying, but you're right. I did agree to wait for the wedding." His smile broadened. "But I never agreed to wait any longer for this."

Slowly, as if they had all the time in the world, he drew her close and pressed his lips to hers. This was what the next chapter would bring: hugs, kisses, and a lifetime of love with Evelyn. A man couldn't ask for anything more.

"You look purty, Evelyn."

Evelyn smiled as she looked at her reflection in the cheval mirror Mrs. Steiner had loaned her for this special day. Ensconced in a corner of her bedroom, it gave Evelyn a full-length view of her gown.

Polly was right. She did look pretty. She'd followed Queen Victoria's example and had chosen a white dress for her wedding, but Isolde had insisted on embroidering bluebonnets around the high collar, the cuffs, and the hem. The result was the most beautiful dress Evelyn had ever owned.

"So do you," she told Polly. The child's dress was bluebonnet blue with a single white bluebonnet embroidered on the bodice.

The sound of footsteps on the stairs told Evelyn that Dorothy had arrived. She'd arranged to meet them here, then walk across the street to the church with them.

"Wyatt's already there, and Mr. Downey is anxious," she said after she'd admired both dresses. "Are you ready?"

"Yes." Evelyn wouldn't keep either her groom or the man who'd volunteered to walk her down the aisle waiting. Though the past two weeks had gone quickly, she was just as anxious as Wyatt to start the next phase of their lives.

"Papa Wyatt." Polly looked up at Dorothy. "That's his name."

Both women smiled. An attorney in Ham-

bryton had done all the necessary paper-
work for Evelyn and Wyatt to adopt Polly as
soon as they were married and had started
the process of selling Marlow Acres to a
neighboring planter. Though Basil had
squandered most of his brother's cash, the
Gibsons had offered a fair price for the
plantation itself, making Polly a relatively
wealthy girl.

She was too young to understand all that,
but there was one thing Polly had no trouble
understanding. She was finally getting the
daddy she wanted. She'd been so excited by
the idea of having Wyatt as her father that
she'd already begun calling him Papa Wyatt.

"That's right: Papa Wyatt." Evelyn
doubted Polly would ever call her Mama
Evelyn, but she didn't mind. In her heart
she knew that Polly was part sister, part
daughter, a little girl she couldn't love more,
even if she'd borne her.

As they crossed the street and headed for
the church, Evelyn smiled at the sight of so
many wagons and carriages parked along
Main. Everyone in town had been invited
to the wedding, and it appeared that most
had come.

When they entered the church, Polly and
Evelyn remained near the door with Leonard Downey while Dorothy took two steps

forward and nodded at the pianist. A moment later as triumphant music filled the church, Dorothy began to walk slowly down the aisle, followed by Polly. When they'd reached the front of the sanctuary, Evelyn took Leonard's arm and began her processional.

She knew every pew was full, for everyone in Mesquite Springs wanted to witness their new mayor's wedding. She heard murmurs as she and Leonard proceeded down the aisle, but she didn't try to distinguish the words. All that mattered was the man standing in front of the altar, Caleb on one side, Pastor Coleman on the other.

This was the man who'd helped dispel her fears, the man who loved Polly as much as she did. This was the man God intended for her, the man she loved more than anything on Earth. This was Wyatt, the man who'd showed her that happily ever after was possible.

Evelyn didn't know what the future would bring, but she did know that she and Wyatt could weather every storm as long as they were together. And soon they would be united in marriage, their love beginning the next chapter of their lives.

It seemed like only seconds passed before they exchanged vows and Wyatt slid a gold ring on her left hand, his face wreathed with happiness.

"You may now kiss the bride." Pastor Coleman's words triggered a murmur in the congregation as everyone waited for the traditional ending to the wedding ceremony.

Wyatt smiled at Evelyn and whispered "I love you" as he lowered his mouth to hers.

"And I love you," she said in the instant before his lips touched hers.

Everyone was watching, and for the first time in what seemed like forever, that knowledge brought only joy. The time for fear was over.

AUTHOR'S LETTER

Dear Reader,

I hope you've enjoyed your introduction to Mesquite Springs and that you're looking forward to learning more about its residents and meeting some newcomers. Those newcomers' arrival changes the town in ways no one could have predicted — except for me, of course. That's one of the perks of being the author; I get to plan my characters' lives . . . unless they decide otherwise. And, yes, that's happened. In fact, it happened with this book.

When I first envisioned it, Wyatt had no intention of running for mayor. In fact, there was no mayoral race in the story. Wyatt's plan had always been to leave Mesquite Springs, and in the original version, that's what happened at the end. He and Evelyn and Polly headed East. But the more I got to know Wyatt, the more I realized that wasn't the right future for him.

As much as he denied it to himself, he was a born leader, and that meant he'd only be fulfilled if he had people to lead. Why not a whole town? And so the mayoral race came into being.

You know how that ended and that the change of leadership will probably bring changes to Mesquite Springs. What changes? The biggest ones revolve around Dorothy. Like her brother, she yearns for a different life, and the arrival of Brandon Holloway, a young and all too attractive newspaperman, just might give her that change.

While you're waiting for Dorothy and Brandon's book to be released, I invite you to read my earlier books, if you haven't already done so. You'll find information about them on my website, www.amanda cabot.com. I've included information about all of my books there as well as a sign-up form for my newsletter. I've also included links to my Facebook and Twitter accounts as well as my email address.

It's one of my greatest pleasures as an author to receive notes from my readers, so don't be shy.

Blessings,
Amanda

ABOUT THE AUTHOR

Amanda Cabot's dream of selling a book before her thirtieth birthday came true, and she's now the author of more than thirty-five novels as well as eight novellas, four nonfiction books, and what she describes as enough technical articles to cure insomnia in a medium-sized city. Her stories have appeared on the CBA and ECPA bestseller lists, have garnered a starred review from *Publishers Weekly,* and have been nominated for the ACFW Carol, the HOLT Medallion, and the Booksellers Best awards.

A popular speaker, Amanda is a member of ACFW and a charter member of Romance Writers of America. She married her high school sweetheart, who shares her love of travel and who's driven thousands of miles to help her research her books. After years as Easterners, they fulfilled a longtime dream when Amanda retired from her job as Director of Information Technology for a major corporation and now live in the American West.